LINDA
LAROQUE

BIRDIE'S
Nest

Birdie's Nest Copyright © 2013 by Linda LaRoque
ISBN: 978-0-9893792-2-9

Edited By Judy Griffith Gill
Cover Art Diana Carlile
Interior Layout by www.formatting4U.com

First Digital Edition April 2013.

Texas Ranger, Birdie Braxton boards the Brazos Belle to attend a costume party, gets tossed into the Brazos and when she's pulled from the river she's told the year is 1890. A fact she can't accept … until she looks across the river to see Birdie's Nest, her ancestral home, no longer exists.

Tad Lockhart is a content man—a prosperous rancher with a ladylove in Waco. He's not interested in marriage and family, yet … until he pulls an unconscious woman from the Brazos who insists she's a Texas Ranger from the year 2012.

As romance blooms between Tad and Birdie, she struggles to earn enough money to build Birdie's Nest, and Tad strives to mold Birdie into a Victorian lady suitable to be his wife. Can Birdie give up dabbling in police work and other unladylike pursuits yet stay true to herself? When faced with an indiscretion from Tad's past, is Birdie's love strong enough to support her man and be the woman he needs?

THANKS

A special thank you to my husband Larry, my in-house editor, for reading my manuscripts time and again. And I don't even bake pies and cakes for him, as our waistlines say we don't need them. I'd like to recognize my high school friend, Mary Ellen Matthews, for being my beta reader. You were an immense help Mary Ellen and caught things I kept missing. And last but not least, Susan Owens for her clear-cut critiques.

ACKNOWLEDGMENTS

I live in Waco, Texas, and had a wealth of information at my fingertips. I'm sure I missed plenty, but this book wasn't intended to be a historical depiction of the 1890s, however, I did want details to be as accurate as possible. And I do love the research aspect of writing and there will be other books.

I found many places to visit to get a feel for what life was like in the Victorian Era and hope those little touches add flavor to my story. I'd like to list a few. One afternoon I toured "East Terrace," the J. W. Mann house. It was built in the 1870s and added on to at a later date. Surprisingly, the rooms in the house weren't near as large as what I considered a historical home along the Brazos should have. The location of "East Terrace" is very close to where I positioned "Birdie's Nest," though the two houses are not at all similar.

Since my heroine is a Texas Ranger, I toured the Texas Ranger Museum. If you've read about the organization you know their duties, responsibilities and equipment have changed considerably since 1890. The museum holds artifacts from the early years up until today.

The Texas Collection at Baylor University is a favorite place for history buffs, as well as serious researchers, to browse. I wanted to study the large maps, the BIRD'S EYE-VIEWS, of Waco during 1873, 1886, and 1892. They're made available online by AMON CARTER MUSEUM and I spent a great deal of time enlarging and studying them. Unfortunately, the man in charge of the maps wasn't available, so I looked through old telephone books from the late 1800s to the early 1900s. They were a goldmine. Earlier I'd found one reference online to a Waco City Hospital, and the hospital was marked on one of the online maps. So, the phone book gave me proof of the hospital's existence and its location.

BOOKS:

Conger, Roger, N. *A PICTORIAL HISTORY OF WACO, REVISED EDITION*, Copyright 1964 by Texian Press, Waco, Texas, second edition 1998.

Wilkins, Frederick, *THE LAW COMES TO TEXAS, THE TEXAS RANGERS *1870-1901,* The State House Press, Austin, Texas, Copyright 1999.

Knight, Sherri and Pylant, James, Copyright 2011,*Who's Who Among Early Waco's Pimps, Madams, Prostitutes & Shady Ladies*, Jacobus Books, Stephenville, Texas.

ONLINE ARTICLES:

The Texas Rangers: From Horses to Helicopters - http://texasalmanac.com/history/texas-rangers-horses-helicopters

http://wacohistoryproject.org/Moments/geralds.html

http://en.wikipedia.org./William_Cowper_Brann

http://www.ehow.com/info_early-crime-scene-investigation-tools.html

http://www.santoshraut.com/forensichistory.htm

The books and articles listed are only a few of those used.

CHAPTER ONE

June 1, 2012, Waco, Texas

"Why Birdie, where've you been hiding all that... bounty?" Sergeant Ted Weaver, Birdie's co-worker, whipped off his Stetson and laid the hat over his heart. His gaze raked her from head to toe, finally settling on her breasts. Birdie wanted to smack his grinning face. She snorted and covered the bare skin above the red strapless dress with her oversized handbag. It'd taken all the nerve she could garner to exit the ladies restroom in the sleazy garb. Tonight's Victorian costume party dress paled in comparison to her current get-up. Everyone in the unit was counting on her to succeed this afternoon. But tonight her family home was at stake. She couldn't afford to fail at either assignment.

"Watch yourself, Weaver." She slapped her thigh, where her thigh holster held her Ruger, with her free hand. "I can still pierce your ear for you."

His howls of laughter bounced off the walls. At least the other men in the office were courteous enough to bend their heads and try to hide their snickers.

Being a woman in the Texas Rangers wasn't easy. While some tolerated her, others ignored her. If she pulled off this afternoon's assignment, where several male rangers had failed, maybe the stigma of being a woman in their ranks would lose some of its stink.

Captain Smith barreled out of his office, face reddening. "Watch your step, Weaver. I'd be happy to write you up for sexual harassment of a fellow officer."

1

Ted sobered. "Sorry, Birdie. It's just you so look the part."

"That's the idea," said the captain. He walked around Birdie taking in her teased hairdo with numerous colorful feathers woven into little braids. Red and gold rhinestone earrings bounced off her shoulders with each sigh and huff of indignation. The form-fitting scarlet dress barely covered her butt, and her breasts threatened to flop out of the neckline. She'd been so worried, she'd used spray-on body glue to insure what little dignity she had remained unexposed.

"Great job, Sergeant." He glanced down at her red rhinestone stiletto heels. "Can you walk in those things?"

"Yes, though it won't be pretty."

"And you're wearing your Ruger and your Texas Ranger badge?"

She nodded.

His dark gaze pierced hers. "You be careful. Don't take any chances. If the situation turns ugly, get your ass out of there." He handed her the subpoena. She rolled up the paper and slid the document down between her breasts, her eyes daring Ted to comment. He grinned, but kept his mouth shut.

"Don't fret, sir. I don't intend to get shot, or worse."

The captain turned to Ted. "Take Weaver with you for the recovery."

"Yes, sir. We're on it." And Birdie didn't doubt he would be. Ted might be a clown on occasion, but when on the job, she trusted him explicitly.

Forty-five minutes later, Birdie parked the vintage pink Volkswagen bug in the parking lot of Shady Brady's Tavern on the outskirts of Robinson, a suburb of Waco. The establishment sat alone on a farm–to-market road amid tall oak trees. A fork of the Brazos ran behind the ramshackle beer joint, which still sported green asbestos siding and a rusted tin roof. Why Tony Trujillo, one of the most wanted drug kingpins in Texas, liked to hang out in a place like this, she didn't have a clue. Hopefully their sources were right and he'd be here.

She checked her makeup in the rearview mirror. The false eyelashes were still intact and the red lipstick heavy enough to paint ten mouths. She fluffed her hair, filled her mouth with two pieces of bubble gum, and worked the wad into a manageable gob. Grabbing her handbag, she exited the car into the scorching June heat. Acting as if she did so every day, she tripped across the parking lot in her high heels and stepped into the cool interior.

Darkness hampered her vision, and cigarette smoke and stale beer stole her breath. How did people breathe in this foul air? Conversation stopped and chairs scraped as the occupants turned. With all eyes following her progress, she lifted her sunglasses to the top of her head and blew a big bubble. It popped, and she sucked the gum back into her mouth as she twitched her butt up to the bar. The bartender, brawny enough to serve as bouncer, regarded her approach with interest. She slid onto a barstool, put both elbows on the bar and leaned forward. His gaze dropped to her cleavage.

"Hey, sugar, I'm a gift for Tony." She winked. "He here?"

Grinning, he nodded toward the back table.

She blew him a kiss. "Thank ya', darlin'."

With a sexy grin pasted on her face and as much swagger as she could muster in her walk, she sashayed toward Tony's table, her gaze glued to the handsome, well-built man. A cigar hung from the side of his mouth. His blue eyes lit with interest as she approached. Eyes wary, he tilted his lips at the corners.

She stopped beside his chair and let her fingers tiptoe over his shoulders. "Hi, sugar. I'm here to entertain you this evening."

He placed the stogie in the ashtray and slipped his arm around her waist, pulling her closer. "Is that right?"

"Mmm-hmm." She turned her body outward, eased down, and sat on one of his legs, her breasts almost in his face. He reached up to fondle a breast, but she laced her fingers through his. "First, let me give you this." She drew out the subpoena and slapped the document in his hand. "You've been served."

Before he could react, she was up and beating it out of the bar. When she arrived at the bug, she heard his bellow from the tavern door. "I'll get you, bitch!"

The Beetle threw gravel as she sped from the parking lot.

3

* * *

"Ouch, Aunt Patty! That's tight enough."

"Now dear, we want you to be in authentic dress. No self-respecting young lady in the nineteenth century stepped out without wearing her corset." Aunt Patty yanked again, and Birdie grabbed the bedpost to keep from falling back against the petite elderly woman. "There we go. That should do it."

Birdie hoped so. She could hardly breathe.

Aunt Patty raised the mauve satin dress over Birdie's head. She ducked to let the garment slide over, slipping her arms inside the leg-o-mutton sleeves as she did so; the only way she knew they were leg-o-mutton sleeves is her aunt told her so. Aunt Patty had given her a detailed description of the styles in the eighteen nineties. What a shame the older woman couldn't take this journey down the Brazos today. She'd appreciate the ambience a heck of a lot more than Birdie.

While her aunt did up the buttons in the back, Birdie studied her reflection in the mirror. No doubt the dress was a knockout, but she'd rather conduct business in a pants suit, better yet jeans and a T-shirt. The bodice was tight, hugging her breasts, and the neckline dipped to a V revealing a good amount of cleavage. She tugged, trying to pull it higher.

"Leave the bodice alone. You look lovely."

"Isn't it rather scanty to wear during the day?"

"The neckline may be a little low, but not vulgar, and the color is perfect for day wear."

"I thought Victorians were conservative in their dress."

"Though their behavior was conventional, their clothing was quite extravagant."

"Where'd you find this dress, anyway?" No way had it come from Goodwill or a second hand shop.

"One of my Daughters of the American Revolution friends told me about a vintage clothing store downtown. The dress just jumped out at me from the rack. It's perfect. I didn't look at another thing, except for the shoes." She pulled a pair of low-heeled kid leather shoes in the same shade as the dress from a box. "The dress and shoes must have come in together as they're an exact match."

Birdie shivered. This was just all a little too perfect to

be coincidence—Victorian party, the perfect dress and shoes. Staring at her reflection, a sense of déjà vu washed over her. Creepy.

"Aunt, what if I ruin the costume? It needs to be saved, maybe even be in a museum."

She huffed. "Sugar, I know you're a tomboy at heart, but you've always been careful with clothes. I'm not worried."

"Well, I am," Birdie muttered.

"What'd you say, dear?"

"Nothing, just mumbling."

"Well, stop. We don't want folks to think you're talking to yourself. You'll never impress Mr. Samuelson that way. If you can't convince him to build his hotel elsewhere, our home will be sitting in the middle of a resort complex."

If they didn't find the money to pay this year's taxes, the city of Waco might auction her home off on the courthouse steps. Sometimes Birdie wondered if trying to save the old plantation home was worth all the hassle. Every year or so they went through the same upheaval, but when she thought of all the history within her home's walls, she couldn't back down. She'd fight urban sprawl until her dying day.

Losing their home would kill Aunt Patty. Birdie's Nest was the only home she'd ever known. She'd been born here and would die here. The only surviving sibling of James Monroe Braxton, the maiden lady had raised Birdie after Birdie's mother passed away when Birdie was ten years old. The home place had to be saved at all costs, and doing so was up to her.

"Sit down, Birdie, and let me put up your hair."

Birdie angled her butt to perch on the vanity stool in spite of the bustle on the dress. She didn't have a clue why the contraption had been popular. The style certainly didn't make a woman's silhouette more attractive.

She closed her eyes and relaxed as Aunt Patty pulled the brush through the long strands of her hair. She'd had highlights and lowlights added to her dark blonde tresses last week, and it crackled and shone with health at each stroke of the brush. She'd always loved to have her hair brushed.

5

They'd spent hours in front of the antique Birdseye maple vanity over the years.

Her hair was pulled up in the back and formed curls on the top of her head, all held in place with hairpins. Then Aunt Patty placed a large hat, decorated with ribbons and feathers, tilted forward on her head and held in place with three hatpins, each at least twelve inches in length.

Birdie frowned. "Isn't three a little overkill?"

"No dear. We want to make sure it stays in place."

"Or, if Samuelson won't back off, they'll make perfect murder weapons."

Patty giggled, reminding Birdie of a young girl. "Shame on you, young woman." She lifted a brooch from her pocket. "Now, this pin has been passed down from your great-great-great grandmother and will be lovely on this dress."

Birdie took the brooch, a stunning amethyst the size of her thumbnail, surrounded by seed pearls. "It's beautiful. I've never seen it before."

"Yes, I know. I found it buried away in some old things I went through recently. I don't know why it wasn't with the other jewelry passed down over the years." Aunt Patty took the brooch. "Here, let me pin it at the juncture of the V. I'll catch some of the lace and give you a little more coverage."

Feet tucked into the surprisingly comfortable shoes and twirling a frilly parasol, Birdie kissed Aunt Patty and sauntered down the multiple front steps of their home. She stopped beside her silver Ford Mustang convertible. How in the heck would she be able to get in wearing this get-up? Her hat was taller than the roof. She'd have to leave the top down and drive slow to preserve her hair-do.

Birdie sighed. *How on earth did I get myself into this mess? I should have approached Samuelson at his office and turned down his invitation.*

She slid the seat as far back as possible. The width of the bustle allowed her to reach the accelerator and brake. Did she look as ridiculous as she felt? Probably. Thank goodness the boat dock was nearby.

Nineteenth century society folks, here I come!

* * *

6

The Brazos Belle stood at the dock decked out in party streamers of green and maroon to match Samuelson's company logo. A costumed butler took Birdie's invitation and escorted her across the gangplank. "Everyone's aft on the upper deck, miss. Up those stairs. You won't miss the crowd."

"Thank you."

Voices and laughter grew louder as she approached. What a sight. Men and women in period dress graced the deck, milling about in conversation, eating hors d'oeuvres, and drinking wine and cocktails. She lifted a glass of champagne from a passing waiter and made her way to the rail to observe as they cast off. Maybe she could hide out over here for a while.

Watching the ripples of the river glide by soothed her. Though plantation owners had built their homes near the Brazos for economic reasons, she didn't doubt they'd enjoyed the calm breezes blowing in off the water and picnics on its banks. As a child, she'd often played along the grassy area, which no longer belonged to her family but to the public, as did the road that ran alongside the expanse of water.

The boat was almost abreast of Birdie's Nest. Red brick, her home sat on the remaining five acres of family land a hundred yards from the road with a matching brick drive leading to the covered side entrance. Four white columns graced the two stories. A porch ran the entire length of each of the two floors. The carriage house, located at the rear of the estate, had been used for rental property since the nineteen forties. The house looked larger than it actually was. Thank goodness a past ancestor had provided funds for the property's basic upkeep. Otherwise her home would've been sold years ago. What a shame they'd not made arrangements for the taxes and insurance as both ate away at their budget.

Now Samuelson wanted to tear down her family home and use the land for his financial gain. The county had given her sixty days to pay the back taxes. On the first of August the house would go on the auction block and be snatched up for a pittance by Samuelson. The man thought to do her a favor and pay the taxes, if she'd sell Birdie's Nest to him. That wouldn't happen. Somehow she'd raise the money before then, sell some antiques or family jewelry if she had to.

"Miss Braxton!" She turned to find Samuelson bearing down on her. He stopped at her side. His gaze traveled her body, spending too long at the cleavage above the brooch. His perusal turned her stomach. She wanted to deck him. "You are stunning. If I didn't know better I'd think I'd stepped back in time, right into the late nineteenth century. Where did you find such a wonderful costume?"

"My Aunt Patty's friends in the DAR helped her locate it."

"I see." He nodded toward Birdie's Nest, an irritating smile plastered on his face. The man was a salesman through and through. "I couldn't help but notice you admiring the property."

"I'm admiring my home, Mr. Samuelson."

"Yes, of course." He took her elbow. "Come meet some of our investors."

"Couldn't we talk first? I have a few things I want to say." *Like don't count on buying my home.*

"After I make the introductions, we'll talk. They're anxious to meet you,"

She allowed him to escort her to a group of three couples, the men dressed as impeccably as Samuelson in period gray frock coats and striped trousers. The women's costumes must have been tailor-made, as they were more elaborate than Birdie's and complemented their expensive jewelry.

"Miss Birdie Braxton, I'd like you to meet… " Birdie listened with one ear, cataloguing the names away for future reference. She wasn't interested in getting to know them, as she didn't plan to see them again.

"What an unusual name," said the young woman in the red dress. Victorian women wore scarlet during the day? "How'd you come by it?"

"Birdie is a family name."

"How quaint." She turned to her friend and exchanged an amused glance. Birdie wasn't exactly crazy about her name, but she carried the moniker proudly. How dare these rich snobs belittle it?

Discussion turned to the building project. Birdie tuned out their chatter. She nodded and responded when appropriate and started to excuse herself, but froze at the older woman's words.

"Young lady, what a fine thing you're doing selling your property to our corporation so we can build the resort."

All eyes regarded her. She waited for Samuelson to correct the woman. She'd made no commitment. He pretended he hadn't heard and ignored her silent plea. Why, the man was trying to back her into a corner.

"I'm afraid you're mistaken, ma'am. I'm not selling Birdie's Nest and never will. If Mr. Samuelson led you to believe otherwise, he misled you."

"Now, Miss Braxton, we've not had a chance to talk this evening. Don't make a final decision yet. After all, you'll lose your home to back taxes if you don't take my offer. I think you'll change your mind after I tell you how rich you'll become."

"I'm not interested in your money. This is my family home, my heritage you want to tear down. I'll find a way to pay the taxes. You can buy all the land around our five acres and build your resort, but Birdie's Nest will remain in the very center. And, I believe city ordinances are in place that will control what you place within a certain distance of our home. I'm sure you're up on those. If not, I'll have my office direct you to the appropriate agency that can fill you in on the details.

"In case Mr. Samuelson failed to inform you," she added to the nearby investors, "I'm a Texas Ranger. Please don't bother me or my aunt about this again."

Six individuals gaped at her. Red faced, murderous expression on his face, Samuelson stood, hands fisted. He'd try to choke the life from her if they were alone.

She deposited her empty glass on a tray and started for the stairs. Her long skirt swished against her legs as she walked down the steps. She'd rather be below with the help than up there.

For a short while, she stood and observed the paddle wheel turn, lifting and spilling water to propel them through the current. The odor of fish reached her nostrils. Birds dove for bugs, the resulting ripples forming a slowly disintegrating circle. Heat from the sun blazed down, and she was grateful for the parasol.

The craft slowed as the captain turned the boat around

to travel downstream. What had the river been like in the nineteenth century? Probably not as polluted as today. It would be exciting to visit other cities traveling by paddleboat. What a fascinating life that must have been in the old days.

The suspension bridge loomed ahead. People milled about peering over the metal sides and dropping bites of bread to the ducks floating below. A small thundercloud formed over the span, threatening rain, casting a shadow below. She hoped it didn't rain, not until she got home, anyway.

Twirling the parasol, she walked to the middle of the boat, propped her elbows on the rail and stared out at the passing scenery. A warm sensation tingled against her chest. She glanced down and clasped the brooch. It was warm in her hand. Had it absorbed some of the sun's heat? That was odd. The sun drifting down behind the trees in Cameron Park cast mottled rays of light across the rippling water. An eddy formed in the path of the setting sun, swirling deeper, seeming to absorb the shadow of the cloud, the closer it got to the boat. Creepy! Birdie shuddered and straightened.

Just as the boat reached the bridge, a bolt of lightening shot from the cloud hitting the whirlpool. An explosion of light hit Birdie, spraying her with water, just as a footstep sounded behind her. Before she could turn, pain exploded in her head and she sank into the deep.

* * *

June, 1, 1890 Waco, Texas

Thaddeus Lockhart stood under a big oak beside the Brazos and viewed a couple of boys fishing from the bank. As a boy, he'd caught his share of crappie. He'd cleaned them on the grass, and then fried them over his campfire. The hot grease had burned his fingers as he picked the meat from the bones. He sighed. Those carefree days were over. His life now revolved around running the family ranch, caring for his sister and mother.

Today he'd walked over from the Katy depot where he'd supervised the arrival of his new bull from Kansas. The animal hadn't been amenable to being unloaded from the cattle car, and Tad ended up joining in the fracas and getting his suit filthy. Hopefully the bovine brute would use some of his attitude to impregnate a lot of his cows, and next spring the pasture would be loaded with calves.

The river was up from the recent rains, but the mud had settled enough to make the water blue. Always traveling south, the current carried small bits of wood and other debris. Though just a hundred yards wide, he'd hate to drive a herd of cattle across the expanse. Undercurrents could sweep away animals and humans alike. Then there was the occasional water moccasin. He shuddered. Darn snakes! The suspension bridge loomed tall to his right. It had been a godsend to commerce in the area, and the five cents a head to take a herd across was well worth the price.

He stomped out his cheroot and turned to go.

"Help! Mister, help us!"

Tad turned to spot one of the boys up to his neck in the water. He struggled to pull a body to shore. The other boy tried to reach the distance and grab his friend's hand.

"What the hell?"

He bounded down the bank and splashed knee-deep into the water. A woman lay face down, her voluminous skirt, bustle riding on top, floating up around her. He grabbed the boy, tossed him onto the bank, and reached down for the lady. Hands under her arms, he hauled her up and placed her face up on the grassy bank. He dropped to his knees, leaned down, and placed his ear near her mouth. No breath and her lips were blue. If they didn't get help soon she might die, if she wasn't dead already.

"You boys run, get help."

They were off like a shot. He flipped the woman over and yanked on the bodice of her dress sending buttons flying. With his pocketknife, he cut the ties on her corset… *damned torture devices...* and then pressed on her back. *Come on, woman, cough.* When nothing happened, he half stood straddling her body, lifted her at the waist with hands locked, and bounced her several times. Water spewed from her mouth. He breathed a sigh of relief as she hacked and gagged. He eased her down and rolled her to her back.

Her eyes flew open. Beautiful blue eyes stared at him.

11

"Who… are… you?" Her question turned into a cough. She rolled to her side and threw up more water.

"Tad Lockhart, ma'am. Don't talk right now. Help is on the way."

"What…what happened?"

"You'll have to tell us. We just fished you out of the Brazos."

She struggled to sit up, grabbed the base of her head and fell back in a dead faint. He rolled her to the side and lifted the long strands of hair. A lengthy gash across the base of her skull dripped blood onto the grass. Damn, looked like someone tried to kill this woman, and then dumped her into the river. He stood and looked up and down the expanse. He could see nothing suspicious, but most likely the culprit was long gone by now. Would he come back for her when he learned she lived?

He squatted beside her, removed his handkerchief from his pocket and pressed the cloth to the wound. What was taking help so long? Easing the woman onto her back, he brushed long strands of her hair from her face. Half up and half down, hairpins caught in the tangled strands making his efforts seem useless. Her coiffeur resembled a bird's nest. The quickly drying tresses were of varying colors. He'd never seen the like before. Mostly dark blond, some pieces were brown, some white, and darned if red wasn't in there too.

Tad took inventory of her clothes. Good quality, well made, and her skin bore no blemishes or paint. This was a lady, not one of the birds from the Reservation. His gaze drifted to the creamy globes visible above her dress. His body tightened in appreciation. *Lovely!* He grimaced and tamped down his response. Loosening her dress no doubt made the bodice drop. He tugged it higher and tucked the material behind her shoulders to stay in place. No need for the whole town to see her assets. Plus, if they thought he'd taken liberties, they'd be planning his wedding. His mother would be overjoyed. He snorted. Heck, he enjoyed women, but he didn't intend to get leg-shackled for a long time. He hadn't met a women yet who didn't bore him stupid in a short period of time.

* * *

Birdie's head pounded. She opened one eye and groaned as light pierced her brain. Squeezing the lid shut, she took deep gulps of air to calm the roaring in her head. Gradually, she worked her eyes fully open. She lay in an old iron bed, and she'd bet anything the cotton sheets were like some in the linen closet at Birdie's Nest, one hundred percent cotton, starched and ironed. She'd recognize the fresh aroma anywhere. A white metal ware water bowl and pitcher sat on the table beside her bed. The room was large with ten-foot ceilings and a transom above the eight-foot door, much like those of Birdie's Nest. Sounds of activity in the hallway filtered through the opening. Tall windows, with shades drawn, met at the juncture of two walls. So, she was in a corner room. She remembered waking up on the riverbank, a man bending over her. Where on earth had they taken her? She didn't know of any hospitals in the area that resembled this austere place. The atmosphere reminded her of pictures from the early twentieth century.

Her clothes? Where were they? And her gun and badge? She managed to sit up, but the room swam, the pain increased in her head, and her stomach churned. She eased back down and looked around for a call button. There wasn't one. "Hey! Somebody! I want to know what's going on." Shouting hurt and she groaned.

The door opened, and a man came in. Portly and bald, his kindly face oozed concern. A woman followed carrying a clipboard. Birdie gaped. The woman wore a long starched white dress and a cap, resembling a bird in flight, sat perched on her slicked back hair.

"Good morning. I'm Dr. Franks, and this is Nurse Taylor."

The middle-aged woman smiled. Birdie concluded the woman wasn't near as severe as her uniform implied.

Holding a hand to her head, Birdie chuckled. "Is the entire town dressed up in Victorian garb?"

Dr. Franks glanced at his nurse. She shrugged and shook her head. He turned back to Birdie and patted her hand. "It's good to see you're awake. We need to get a few bookkeeping issues out of the way."

"First you need to answer some questions for me. Where are my gun and my ranger identification?" She slapped her left thigh. "It was strapped right here to my leg before I landed in the water."

"They're in good hands. Detective Ethan has them. He'll be in to speak with you later."

Well, that was good to know. A fellow officer of the law would respect her property. She relaxed in the bed.

The doctor nodded. "Since the location of your property is settled, can you give us your name, address, and age?"

Nurse Taylor jotted the information down as Birdie spoke.

"Now then, Miss Braxton, how are you feeling?" The doctor held some round metal thing with a hole in it over each eye, leaned in, and peered at her pupils. She supposed that was what he was doing.

"My head is pounding."

"Yes, that's to be expected. You took a nasty hit on the back of your head." He held a finger up in front of her face. "How many fingers am I holding up?"

She grabbed it to keep it still. "One."

He chuckled. "Uh-huh. Room moving around a little, is it?"

"Yes."

"As I expected, you have a mild concussion. I stitched up the wound on the back of your head. The injury should heal with no problem, but you must lie still and quiet for several days."

Darn. She'd like to go home and let Aunt Patty take care of her. "Do you have a telephone I can borrow to call my aunt? She'll be worried if I'm not home by dark."

"We have one in the office. We'll call her for you." He turned to the nurse. "Please get her something for that headache." She nodded and left the room. The doctor walked to one of the windows, raised the shade and then the window revealing nothing but treetops and sky. A cool breeze accompanied the last rays of the day. The view wasn't one common to Waco, unless they were near Cameron Park.

"What's the name of this hospital?"

"Waco City Hospital. You rest, and I'll be by again this evening."

She closed her eyes and listened to the sounds from the street below. Odd, not one car passed. If she wasn't mistaken, a horse neighed. Where was this place located? She'd never heard of a City Hospital in Waco, but that didn't mean one didn't exist.

The nurse returned with a policeman, his uniform nothing like she'd ever seen. The coat was long sleeved and wool. How on earth had Samuelson talked the entire town into dressing up for his party? Today wasn't even a holiday. Or maybe she was crazy.

Nurse Taylor put her arm behind Birdie's head and eased her up. "Drink this and you'll sleep off that headache."

Birdie peered at the liquid suspiciously. It didn't have a distinct odor other than maybe some type of alcohol. "What is this stuff? Why can't I have a pill like ibuprofen or codeine?"

Her brow furrowed. "I'm afraid we're not familiar with those two medications."

Birdie took a deep breath and exhaled, then took the glass and drank the entire contents. She shuddered, "Blech…that's terrible."

"Yes, but it will help the pain." She motioned the officer forward. "Now Detective Ethan, don't keep her too long. She'll be groggy soon."

Detective Ethan smiled down at her. "Got yourself in a little fix, did you?"

"No, I most certainly did not. Carl Samuelson hit me on the back of the head with something and tossed me over the rail of the Brazos Belle." At least that's what she assumed had taken place. "You need to arrest him for attempted murder."

"Carl Samuelson? I'm not familiar with the name. Where's he from?"

"He's been in Waco about a year, but he's from Chicago. Plans to build a big resort on the Brazos. Thinks he'll buy Birdie's Nest, tear down my historical home, and push away all remains of my heritage." She had to get out of this hospital and find a way to pay their taxes so Samuelson wouldn't have the upper hand. Why had he attacked her? Did he know something she didn't?

"He scratched his beard with his pencil. "Let's back up a minute. What's your name?"

"Birdie Leigh Braxton."

"Are you related to the Braxton's in Hill County?"

"Not that I know of but I guess it's possible."

He jotted something on his note pad. "Where do you live?"

"I live at #7 Brazos River Road."

He frowned. "Here in Waco? I'm not familiar with that address."

"Why, everybody in Waco knows where Birdie's Nest is across the river. A two story red brick home with white Georgian columns and shutters."

He shook his head. "No, ma'am, can't say I've ever seen the place and I know every street and road in this county."

Odd. Most people had at least seen Birdie's Nest from a distance when driving the roads through Cameron Park. Her eyelids grew heavy. She let them drop. "Well, it's an old home, built in 1892 for a then-young Birdie. I'm named after her. Birdie is a ridiculous name, but my family wanted to carry on the tradition."

"I see."

Birdie forced her eyes partially open and studied his expression through half lids. He obviously didn't believe her. "Look detective, don't patronize me. If you don't believe me, just say so."

"Miss Braxton, how could a house built in 1892 be there when it's only 1890?"

CHAPTER TWO

"Good morning, Miss Braxton." Nurse Taylor, chipper voice trilling, waltzed into the room. "How is your head this morning?"

"It's better." Birdie threw the sheet back and eased her legs over the side of the bed. "I need to go to the bathroom." And she wasn't using that bedpan again. Talk about an invasion of privacy.

"You sit right there, young woman. You cannot walk down the hall. I'll bring a wheeled chair." She winked. "You can take a long soak while we're there."

Ah, a soak sounded heavenly. "Can I wash my hair?" Though her hair felt clean, she didn't remember it being washed. Thinking about the muck from the river within the tresses made her head itch. "It must stink something awful."

"Honey, we washed your hair real good before the doctor shaved a small portion where he put in the stitches."

What? Shaved my hair? Her hand flew to the back of her head. She winced at the soreness, but sighed with relief to find the bandaged spot was relatively small, about two inches long.

"You can relax, Miss Braxton, we didn't cut off much. No one will know but you."

It didn't take the nurse long to wheel Birdie to the spacious bathroom. Something could definitely be said about claw foot bathtubs. Even at her five feet, eight inch height, she could sink down in the water up to her chin. She glanced at the old fashioned toilet with the tank near the ceiling. She'd had to pull a chain to flush it. She needed answers. The detective had said something about it being 1890. What kind of joke were they playing on her? Whatever, it wasn't funny and she'd hate to have to arrest them for kidnapping. Since she was a law enforcement officer, the charges against them would be harsh. Wherever she was, the environment was authentic. If the circumstances were different she'd be fascinated and anxious to explore.

An hour later, clean and dressed in a fresh gown, Birdie crawled into the bed and groaned. The bath had sapped her energy and her head pounded. She breathed in the scent of freshly laundered sheets and willed the pain to go away.

Nurse Taylor slipped an arm beneath her head and held a glass to her lips. "Drink this. It's not as much as I gave you last evening, but it will help you rest. You'll feel much better when you wake."

Birdie didn't have the energy to argue. She drank the vile brew and then curled on her side. The nurse adjusted the covers.

She wanted to go to sleep, but Detective Ethan's comment haunted her. Did he say it was 1890? The nurse was almost to the door. "Wait. What year is it?"

Nurse Taylor turned and smiled. If Birdie wasn't mistaken her expression radiated sympathy. "We'll have plenty of time to discuss that later. Sleep now."

At the sound of voices in the hall and Nurse Taylor's orders, her eyes popped open.

"You gentlemen will have to come back after dinner. The doctor will be in to see her after lunch. She's sleeping now."

Gentlemen? Yeah, sleeping.

* * *

Well rested after a relaxing evening at Lucy's home, Tad bounded up the steps of Waco City Hospital to check in on the young woman he'd fished from the Brazos yesterday afternoon. Lucy, his mistress, was quickly becoming too demanding and soon he'd have to move on. He enjoyed visiting the same woman and didn't much go in for frequenting the Reservation, Waco's red light district. He knew the city regulated and checked the women's health so they were disease free most of the time, but there was something to be said for developing a relationship. Someday he'd have to get married. Lord knows his mama nagged him enough about settling down, but he'd not found a woman who could keep his interest for long. Being tied to one for life just didn't sit well.

Carrying a big bouquet of daisies, he strolled down the hall toward the patient's room. Outside the door a policeman and a nurse he'd seen yesterday stood deep in conversation. They looked up as he approached.

"Excuse me. I've come to see how the young lady is doing."

The nurse took the bouquet of flowers. "She's resting and is better today, but she has a concussion." She sniffed the daisies he'd picked up at the florists. "I'll see to it that she gets these."

"My name is Tad, by the way."

She smiled. "I know. You're the young man who came with the ambulance yesterday. Come back after lunch." She nodded to the policeman. "This is Detective Ethan. I expect he has some questions for you too." She turned to leave in search of a vase he suspected.

Questions? What could the man have to ask him? "Detective, I told the policeman who arrived at the river yesterday everything I know."

"Yes, I've read his report, but some things have come up. May we speak in private?"

"Sure. Let's go outside and have a smoke."

They settled on a bench outside in the shade of a live oak. Tad pulled a cheroot from a pocket inside his suit coat while Detective Ethan studied him.

"Do you know the young lady?"

"Nope. Never met her before." He lit his smoke with a match and took a draw of the tobacco. "Did you learn her name, where she's from?"

"Yes, she's Birdie Leigh Braxton. The young lady said she lives across the Brazos in a big red brick house built in 1892."

Tad choked on the smoke he'd swallowed and coughed

to clear his gullet. "She must be out of her head, confused on the date. Plus, there are several big houses over there but none of them red brick."

"Did you know she had a revolver strapped to her thigh?"

His face heated. "How the heck would I know that? Are you accusing me of taking liberties with that young woman?"

The detective chuckled. "Nope, just asking."

"Pleased to hear it, officer." He smirked and released a guffaw. "Not to say in different circumstances I might give it a try, but not while a woman is unconscious."

"Birdie Leigh Braxton. You sure the name doesn't ring a bell."

Ethan remained quiet for a moment, Tad supposed to give him time to think, but he could only shake his head. "I've never heard of her."

"Aren't there some Braxtons on your mother's side of the family?"

"Sounds familiar, but if she's a distant relative…" He shrugged. "Anyway, how would you know?"

"I took the liberty of asking around." He smiled. "Actually, I had my mother do the asking at her weekly ladies' social. She was very discreet, asked the ladies in general if they knew any Braxtons and your mother's name came up."

Thank goodness. His mother wouldn't take kindly to being the topic of social discussion. "I'm headed home this afternoon and will ask Mother if she knows the young woman."

"Let me know what you find out." He reached into his pocket and removed a silver object. "Take a look at this."

Tad took it and ran his thumb over the smooth metal of the silver star, one worn only by Texas Rangers, but this one hadn't been formed from a peso. Stamped across the top of the ring surrounding the star was *Department of Public Safety*. Across the bottom was *Texas Rangers*. Inside the star was *Sergeant*.

"Turn it over."

Engraved on the opposite side was *Birdie Leigh Braxton 9-15-2010*. The date must be an error. Why, 2010 was one hundred twenty-two years into the future. "Where did you get this?"

"It was pinned to Miss Braxton's holster."

20

*   *   *

Nurse Taylor was right. Birdie felt considerably better. Her head still throbbed but not with the nauseating intensity it had before. A grumble from her stomach indicated how much it needed feeding. Rich food odors wafting in from the transom made her mouth water. Thankfully the door swung open and her favorite nurse came in bearing a tray.

She set the food on the bedside table. "I bet you could eat something now, hmm?"

"Something? I could probably eat a horse." She scooted up in bed while Nurse Taylor arranged the pillows behind her back.

"Don't overdo and make yourself sick."

"I won't." She took a spoonful of the thick chicken noodle soup and closed her eyes. "Heavenly." When she was finished, she set the bowl aside and drank some of the cool water.

The door opened and Dr. Franks came in with a clipboard in his hand. He pulled a chair close to the bed and sat. When Nurse Taylor headed out, he halted her. "I'd like for you to stay."

The nurse nodded and moved to stand at the foot of the bed.

"How do you feel today, Miss Braxton?"

"My head still hurts some, but not bad. Why hasn't my aunt arrived to take me home?"

"I'm sorry but we've not been able to locate her." He leaned forward in his chair. "Let me ask you, what day is today?"

"Let's see, I've been here almost a full day. The party aboard the boat was, what, Saturday? So, it is Sunday, right? Or Monday?" Those knockout drinks might have had her sleeping longer than she'd thought.

The doctor and nurse exchanged a glance. "What's wrong? Isn't that right?" She shrugged. "I could be a day or two off."

"It's not the day we're worried about Miss Braxton. It's the date."

"Oh, June second, maybe the third. Why?"

21

He sighed deeply and leaned back against his chair. His gaze probed hers. Birdie turned to see Nurse Taylor wringing her hands.

"What is the year, Miss Braxton?"

Was this guy nuts? "2012, of course."

Sorrowfully, he shook his head. "No. No, my dear, it is not."

She studied his clothes. Her gaze moved to Nurse Taylor's long dress and hairstyle, and the cap on her head. If she wasn't mistaken, they appeared to have stepped right out of a nineteenth century storybook. And that fit right in with the room's furnishings. "Okay, I'll bite. What year is it?"

"It's 1890."

She chuckled. "Yeah, right! You're just going along with this nineteenth century costume party theme, right? But, I have to say you're taking it to the extreme. The party was over last night."

"I assure you, Miss Braxton, Nurse Taylor and I are not part of a costume party." He cleared his throat. "We could not reach your aunt by telephone. The address you gave us doesn't exist. I fear you've suffered some brain anomaly due to the wound to your head or perhaps caused by your near-death experience."

He rose from the chair. "Nurse Taylor will take you outside for a while. Maybe the fresh air will blow the cobwebs from your head."

The nurse scurried for the door. "I'll be right back with a wheeled chair, Miss Braxton."

Dr. Franks patted her hand. "Everything will come back to you in time. If not, there are treatments that will help. We'll move you to a sanatorium and they'll have you back to yourself in no time."

A sanatorium? They used shock treatments and God only knows what other type of primitive means of torture. She hid her hands under the covers to prevent the doctor from seeing her trembling. God, was this Victorian comedy someone's idea of a sick joke?

"We'll put notices in the newspapers and hopefully your aunt will see them and come for you."

"I'm not going to a sanatorium, Dr. Franks. I've read

enough to know what goes on in those places." She couldn't contain a shudder and gripped handfuls of the bottom sheet to still the shakes.

He wrinkled his brow, obviously dismayed by her negative judgment of their methods.

"Well, perhaps we can work out something else for you. Ah, here's your carriage."

Nurse Taylor rolled in the ancient wheelchair, complete with a wicker back, she'd ridden in earlier.

"Enjoy your time outside, Miss Braxton. The water wagon just sprayed down the road so you should be able to enjoy the view without dust blowing in the off the street."

She resisted the urge to roll her eyes and giggled instead. *Water wagon? What on earth was he talking about?* She couldn't remember any dirt streets in Waco. They were laying this nineteenth century business on thick.

A wheelchair ramp occupied half of the wide stairwell. Fearing she'd be tossed or run into the wall, Birdie gripped the armrests as Nurse Taylor wheeled her down the slope, but the nurse was a pro and they were soon zooming through the lobby.

No one else was outside on the lawn. Thank goodness, as Birdie felt ridiculous being wheeled out the door in the ancient contraption. In a gown and robe no less. Nurse Taylor parked her under a large oak tree with her back to the massive trunk. Wrought iron benches were strategically placed for visitors to sit with their loved ones. The white frame building sat alone at the edge of a manicured lawn of Bermuda grass or some other similar variety. It wasn't the St. Augustine she'd grown up with in the yard at Birdie's Nest. One lone road, sure enough it was white caliche, wound in a circle up to the packed clay walkway.

Hair rose on the back of her neck, butterflies fought in her stomach. She struggled to breathe. A carriage sat out front with a horse. A man stood nearby as if waiting for someone. Her gaze returned to the hospital structure. Two stories high, the windows rose tall on each floor, and a wide porch spanned the front exterior. It was lined with rocking chairs. Hanging baskets added color to the white clapboard.

An older lady bustled out the front door and down the

steps. Dressed in dark gray, she unfurled a matching parasol and held it above her head. The man by the carriage pushed away from the bench he leaned against and waited to help her into the buggy. When she was seated in the back, he climbed aboard, clicked the reins and the horse trotted off.

Through the trees, Birdie could see a house here and there, each a great distance from the other. She turned and gazed across the ravine that ran parallel to the road. Buildings rose in the distance, probably two to three miles away so she couldn't make out much, but the black smoke rising from factories was hard to miss. As was the suspension bridge that spanned the Brazos. Her house was missing across the water though a few buildings dotted the green river bank. Her chest muscles tightened and pinpricks dotted her body as adrenaline rushed through her system.

This was too perfect to be an elaborate act. Dr. Franks, Nurse Taylor, and Detective Ethan weren't dressed up in Victorian clothes for her benefit, and this building would make any historian proud. And worst of all, Aunt Patty was missing.

This can't be happening. I'm dreaming and will wake up any minute.

She felt a hand on her shoulder. "Are you all right, Miss Braxton?"

Her chin trembled, but she couldn't seem to still it. She shook her head. "No. I'm ready to go in now."

"A nice nap will make everything appear better. You're not alone. I promise." Nurse Taylor unset the brake on the chair and within a few minutes, was helping Birdie into her bed.

Nap? That's all she'd done. She needed to think, figure out what was going on here, get well and make plans to escape whatever hell she'd found herself in, but her head pounded. She'd close her eyes for a few minutes and try to make sense of her situation. Nurse Taylor removed one of the pillows so she could lie back, and then smoothed the covers and pulled the sheet up over her breasts. "You have a couple of guests." She winked. "Gentlemen callers."

Oh goodie. Probably Carl Samuelson trying to take the heat off himself by attempting to convince her he wasn't the one who'd tossed her overboard. When she felt better, she'd slap him into cuffs. If she couldn't gather enough evidence to keep him in jail, she'd find a way to get it. "Show them in."

Detective Ethan walked in with a tall man dressed in a pinstriped dress suit with a vest. She hid her smirk behind her hand. Darned if his get-up didn't resemble the clothes worn by Billy the Kid and other outlaws of the late nineteen hundreds. She wouldn't have been surprised to see a gun belt strapped to his hip. But no, he was unarmed. Her eyes traveled from his waist, up to his broad shoulders, and settled on his face. She'd seen him before, but where? Time in the sun had lined the skin around his blue eyes and his mouth. No doubt women found his open grin engaging. And though she worked in law-enforcement and enjoyed many pursuits others considered manly, she was a woman and appreciated a fine looking specimen. She smiled back but kept the expression impersonal.

"Miss Braxton, this is Tad Lockhart. He's the man who fished you from the Brazos."

The man fiddled with the hat he held at his waist, smoothing the rim as he turned it round and round. "How are you feeling, ma'am?"

"Much better. Thank you for saving my life. If you hadn't been there, I guess I'd be rotting on the bottom by now."

"Actually, I can't take full credit. Two boys fishing on the bank spotted you. One tried to haul you up, but couldn't. I heard their shouts for help."

Thank God. She had too much living to do to lose her life right now. "Well, thank goodness you were there."

Nurse Taylor came in with a beautiful bouquet of daisies. "These are from Mr. Lockhart. Aren't they lovely?" She set them on the bedside table and then rushed out.

Birdie's heart thumped a little faster. It'd had been awhile since a man bought her flowers. "They are. Thank you, Mr. Lockhart. How'd you know daisies were my favorite flower?"

He flashed a smile, deepening the dimples in his cheeks of his face. Mighty fine-looking face she might add. "They're my mother's favorite also, so I took a chance you'd like them."

"Well, they do brighten up the room. What a shame they'll die in a few days. I wonder if I could get an aspirin to put in the water. It helps keep them fresh."

The two men exchanged confused glances. That's right. This was 1890, or so they wanted her to believe, and aspirin wasn't a household item until 1899 when Bayer supplied powders to physicians. Hmm, amazing that she could remember that little tidbit from high school health class. Actually, with each passing minute, she believed their take on the situation more. How she could be in 1890, she didn't know, but if she were to survive, she had to rethink her theory of a costume party.

Mr. Lockhart coughed. "I understand you've not been able to get in touch with your folks, ma'am. I'll check with my mother. She's related to some Braxtons. Maybe she can locate someone in your family." He grinned. "According to her, she knows everyone within three counties."

"Thank you, but there is no need. I'll be released in a day or two and look forward to getting back to work. Again, thank you for saving my life." She extended her hand. He studied it a minute before grasping it. "If I can repay you in some way, let me know."

"No repayment needed, ma'am. Let me know if I can be of any assistance to you in the future. Just send a message to Tad Lockhart at Lockhart Ranch."

"I'll do that." She released his hand.

Detective Ethan waited until Mr. Lockhart left the room before pulling a chair up to her bed. He sat and removed several items from his pockets. One was her silver star, the other her Ruger.

"Oh, thank God. I'm glad they weren't lost, especially the star."

She reached for them, but the man withdrew them and held up the silver badge. "Where'd you get this, Miss Braxton?"

"It was presented to me by my captain when I became a Texas Ranger. You can see the date on the back, and my name."

"What kind of hoax are you trying to pull off here? Women are not in law enforcement, especially in the Rangers."

"I assure you they are. The first woman was inducted in 1994."

His mouth dropped open and he stuttered, "That's…impossible."

"No it's not." She pointed to the star. "Look at the date. Right there it says September 15, 2010." He merely gaped at her, brow furrowed. Fear welled up in her chest. Her voice choked, she managed to utter, "That's right. I'm from the future and I don't know how in the hell I ended up in what you guys are saying is 1890." Her tirade ended with a sob. "What am I going to do? I'm not going to a sanatorium."

"Now, now, miss, don't get upset. It's not good for you."

"Don't get upset! What would you do if you found yourself in a strange place, occupied by people who dressed like it was the nineteenth century? My house is missing across the river, and I don't know Aunt Patty's whereabouts. People look at me like I've lost my mind. That's what you think, isn't it? That I'm crazy?"

"Well, understandably you're confused. The doctor informed me you aren't exhibiting signs of being mentally deranged or dangerous to yourself or others. We'll get this all straightened out. I assure you in a day or two we'll have all the answers and your mind will be at ease."

She snorted. "I doubt it. My mind will never be at ease." She sniffed and wiped at an errant tear. She didn't intend to let this man think her weak. "Can I have my things back?"

He tucked them in his coat pocket. "I'm afraid not. I'll keep them safe for you. Someone from the Texas Rangers will be here in a few days to talk with you and they'll want to see these and learn how you came by the star and the unusual weapon you were carrying."

"They are mine. You better not lose them."

"Understood."

"Did you clean and oil my Ruger?"

"If you're referring to your revolver, I tried but must admit I couldn't figure out how to take it apart."

She snickered. "It's not a revolver, it's a semi-automatic."

"Yes, well, I did notice it didn't have a cylinder."

"Hand it here and I'll show you how to dismantle it."

He watched closely as she took it apart and put it back together again. He repeated her actions.

"I think I've got the hang of it."

"What about my holster?"

"It's being taken care of at the saddlers. He's getting it dry and oiled to where it'll be good as new. It'd be a shame to let such fine leather dry out and crack."

"Thank you. I'm quite attached to it." Plus it was a gift from a good friend. "When I get out of here and find a job, I'll reimburse you for the cost."

"Just get well, Miss Braxton, and regain your memory. Folks in Waco are a close-knit group. If you don't have family, they'll help you get settled. You might find work as a house keeper or a sales clerk."

She huffed. "Not bloody likely."

He ignored her comment and headed for the door. "I'll see you tomorrow."

"Bring my weapon back with you. I don't want it to rust because it's not been cleaned."

He waved a hand on the way out.

Birdie sighed and settled back against the pillows. She'd not realized how tense she'd held her shoulders until she allowed herself to relax. She rolled her neck and dropped her chin to her chest to stretch the tendon connected to her spine. The stitches at the base of her skull pulled and she grimaced.

How had she landed in such a fix and what was she going to do? Was she truly in 1890? Could she have traveled back in time? Before she accepted that possibility she had to gather more information, put her investigative skills to work so her conclusion would be a well-thought-out one.

* * *

His mother, Olivia Lockhart, listened intently as Tad talked. She enjoyed a good story and his tale of saving Miss Braxton titillated her interest.

"You say she thinks it's the year 2012?" She fanned her face with her napkin. His mother wasn't overly large but her face was often red, and she complained about the heat. "The poor dear. Do you think she's crazy, son?"

"No, ma'am. Her blue eyes are clear as a bell and she talks rationally. If I didn't know it was impossible, I'd believe her." He took another bite of roast beef and swallowed. "She had a gun holster strapped to her leg and a Texas Ranger's star pinned to it."

She paled and the fanning increased in intensity. "You looked under her skirts?"

"No, Mother. The nurse who undressed her found it and turned it over to the detective in charge of the case. He showed it to me."

"Well, thank goodness. All we need is another scandal to tarnish our good name." She shot him a heated look. "If you'd just settle down, you'd --"

"Mother, don't start that again or I'll take my meals in the bunk house."

She sniffed. "Well, I'm just saying, you're not getting any younger."

He laughed. "I'd hardly call thirty-five old."

Her mouth turned down at the corners and she sputtered. "Well, I'm not getting any younger, and I'd like to dandle a grandchild or two on my knee before I die." She fanned her face again. "At the rate I'm going, it may not be that far off."

Tad blew out a breath. "Mother, you are not that old. I've seen you run up and down these stairs like a woman half your age."

She pursed her lips and glared.

"When I find a woman who can keep my interest for more than a day, then I'll marry."

"What about that woman you're keeping time with in town. What if she turns up pregnant and expects you to marry her?"

Thank goodness his sister was visiting with friends tonight. He didn't want her impressionable young ears to be privy to his private affairs, which his mother considered scandalous.

"She'll be sadly disappointed because I'll not marry someone I don't love. Plus, I'm not sure she'd be faithful." As far as pregnancy, Doc Floyd kept him in a supply of condoms. Odd how the Comstock Law allowed a man to have access to them to prevent disease, but wouldn't let him use them to

29

prevent his wife from getting pregnant. Didn't make a lick of sense to him. If he fathered a baby out of wedlock, he'd see the child was well taken care of.

"It's a sinful relationship. God is going to strike you dead one of these days."

"Let's drop the subject, Mother."

"Mark my words, your clandestine affair will come back to haunt you."

He didn't know how secret the relationship was, but if it bit him on the butt, so be it. He was ready to call it quits anyway.

* * *

Birdie's mauve gown had been washed and pressed. Nurse Taylor helped her dress, but didn't pull the strings on the corset near as tight as Aunt Patty had. "We had to find new laces for the corset and buttons for the dress. Mr. Lockhart had to open the back of your garments and cut the ties so you could breath."

"Looks like I'm garnering a large bill here. Who is paying for all this?"

"We have a fund. You can pay us back when you get the money." She finished buttoning Birdie. "There. You look lovely."

Birdie smoothed her hands down the front of the dress. Whoever had cleaned it had done a beautiful job. She straightened the lace in the low V of the dress. "Where's my brooch?"

"You weren't wearing a brooch, dear. What'd it look like?"

"An oval amethyst surrounded by seed pearls. It was a family heirloom."

"Oh no. Maybe it's on the bank of the Brazos. Detective Ethan will take you there today and you can look around." She squeezed Birdie's shoulders. "I hope you find it."

Sitting on the front veranda, Birdie used her toe to set the rocker in motion as she waited. It was a beautiful morning, still pleasant, but by noon it would be over ninety degrees. Nurse Taylor insisted they return by noon so Birdie wouldn't over-tire. Detective Ethan arrived sharply at nine o'clock with a small buggy. He helped her to step up to the one seat. When she'd settled, he joined her and took the reins. A partial cover blocked most of the sun. Anxious to be on their way, Birdie leaned against the leather seat as Ethan clicked the reins and the horse plodded forward.

The road from the hospital turned into Marlborough Street. Birdie studied the houses as they passed. Many were modest homes but a few were larger Victorian types. At Fourth Street they turned left, crossed Barron's Branch, and then right on Washington Avenue. When they reached Thirteenth Street, Detective Ethan steered the horse and carriage left onto Austin Avenue. The sound of the horse's hooves on the packed earth echoed the thumping of Birdie's heart.

The knot in her throat grew as they traversed the dirt streets with Detective Ethan acting as tour guide. He pointed out landmarks; few of the buildings were familiar to her. On Austin Avenue she searched the sky for the Amicable Building, a mocking cloud occupied the part of the sky where the skyscraper should have been visible. They circled the square on their direct route to the suspension bridge finished in 1870.

The detective stopped the buggy at a grassy spot, jumped down and rounded the vehicle. He reached up, gently caught her around the waist and lifted her down. Legs wobbly, Birdie stumbled as they approached the water. He caught her elbow to steady her. "Are you all right, Miss Braxton? We can return another time if you're not up to this."

"No…I need to see now." She stopped several feet from the river and stared out at the flow, its rhythm one she'd seen and enjoyed her entire life. Nothing on either side of the expanse was familiar now. Smoke churned from chimneys on the far bank and farther to the north a herd of cattle grazed. She allowed her eyes to drift to the torn grass where Tad Lockhart had dragged her from the water two days before. There was no sign of her brooch. She struggled to swallow the knot in her throat and coughed. *I will not cry.*

Detective Ethan touched her elbow. "Come along, miss. You don't look too good. Nurse Taylor will take a whip to me if I deliver you back to the hospital in a faint."

Birdie nodded and stumbled along beside him. In the buggy again, she slumped against the seat. The trip back to the hospital passed in a blur. The detective cast worried glances her way and urged the horse into a faster clip.

Back in her room, she stood without moving as Nurse Taylor undressed her and slipped a gown over her head. In bed, she curled on her side and prayed, *"God, please let me wake up from this nightmare."*

CHAPTER THREE

With a copy of *Jane Eyre* in her lap, Birdie sat on one of the iron benches outside Waco City Hospital. A light breeze ruffled the pages, the chirp of birds the only sounds to disrupt the quiet. She'd tried to focus on Jane's story, but her mind wandered to her situation. What was she going to do? She wasn't crazy, she didn't have amnesia, and she hadn't been planted in someone else's body. Somehow she'd plummeted back to 1890, and she had to figure out a way to return to 2012 and Aunt Patty. No doubt, authorities were dragging the Brazos for her body. She hoped they were, but it's possible no one saw her being tossed off the side of the Brazos Belle. Lord, Aunt Patty must be worried sick. Birdie's stomach threatened to choke her, and the leaves on the tree above her head faded in and out. She closed her eyes and inhaled deep to dispel the unsettling sensation before panic caused her to fall apart. *Breathe, Birdie. Distance yourself*

At the sound of hoofbeats and the rattle of wheels on packed earth, she opened her eyes and watched as a carriage approached and stopped out front. It was Detective Ethan with another man sitting beside him. Both men hopped down and talked for a minute. The detective stationed himself beside the buggy while the other gentleman started up the walk. Tall, a stately, middle-aged man dressed in a three-piece suit he, for some reason, reminded her of someone. Maybe it was his odd beard—a mid-length bushy goatee, dark streaked with gray. She suppressed a giggle. Though unusual to her, most likely the style was common in this time period. Suddenly his gaze landed on her. Surprised at his perusal, she straightened her back.

He removed his hat to reveal close-cropped hair and with a serious face, approached her. "Miss Braxton?"

"Yes...sir." It dawned on her where she'd seen him before. A picture of him hung in the Texas Ranger Hall of Fame in Waco. Every day for the past year she'd walked past it on her way to the museum lobby. His distinguished image was hard to ignore. She couldn't believe her eyes—Wilbur Hill King, adjutant general of the state of Texas, the man who'd supervised the Texas Rangers from 1881 to 1891, stood before her. She rose unsteadily to her feet. "General King?"

His dark brows drew together wrinkling his forehead. "We've met before?"

"No sir, but I've seen pictures of you in history books and museums...and...." His startled expression stopped her chatter. "Excuse me for going on so. Would you like to sit down?"

"Yes." He waited for her to sit and joined her. There was something to be said about the manners of men in the nineteenth century, but she'd reserve final judgment until she'd been here a while which she hoped wasn't long. "So, you know my name. Do you know why I'm here today?"

"Of course. You supervise the Texas Rangers in this time period, and you want to know why I'm in possession of a Ranger's star dated 2010."

"Yes, please enlighten me, young woman."

She repeated all she'd told the doctor and the detective.

General King didn't interrupt, but his expression wasn't hard to read. He didn't believe a word she'd said. He turned and motioned Detective Ethan over. He joined them and handed her pistol to King. "Explain this side arm to us."

Birdie leaned forward and took the Ruger. "Be happy to." She pushed the lever to release the magazine and set it in her lap. She then checked to see if the chamber was empty. "This is called a semi-automatic because when it's cocked, a shell slides into the chamber, and it doesn't have to be cocked again. The shooter simply continues to pull the trigger until the magazine is empty. This gun is small, for concealment, and I can carry it in a holster under my skirts. It's not what I'd use if on duty." She chuckled. "Of course, I don't wear dresses while on duty, unless I'm undercover, but when I wear pants, I carry a nine millimeter." She picked up the magazine. "The clip holds seventeen or nineteen rounds, and, in combat situations, I always have several extras already loaded."

Detective Ethan's mouth hung open, but General King's thinned, and his eyes narrowed to slits. "Young woman, women do not wear pants. At least well-bred young ladies don't."

Birdie bristled. "I assure you, General, I am a well-thought-of woman. In my time period, women do wear pants, especially those in law enforcement. And I earned that star you're keeping from me by working as a Waco policeman and then six years as a state trooper. One hundred-fifty men applied for my ranger position, and I got it so that should tell you something about my qualifications." She wasn't about to mention how the men who'd lost out on the job despised her and resented the fact women were allowed in the ranks.

He threw up his hands. "Bah! This is all hogwash. I don't believe a word you're saying." He stood. "Let's go, Ethan."

"Wait. Listen to me. You're going to retire next year and will live out your life on your property in Sulphur Springs. You'll write a well-read history of the Texas Rangers, one sold at the Ranger Hall of Fame in Waco."

He studied her intently so she continued.

"In 1935 the state legislature placed the rangers in with the highway patrol and formed The Department of Public Safety."

"Highway patrol?"

"Yes, you know, to monitor speed limits on highways. Cars in the future can go over one hundred miles per hour, and speed limits are set at seventy-five—up to eighty-five on interstates."

"I'm sorry Miss Braxton, but I can't believe this outrageous tale." He turned to leave.

"Well, believe this, I bet I can outshoot you or at least shoot as well as you can. Find a place and set a time to let me prove it."

He studied her for a moment.

"All right. I'll send word when we've set something up."

Birdie sighed with relief. "Thank you." She slipped the magazine back into the Ruger but didn't throw a round into the chamber. "I assume you're going to let me keep my gun."

"Yes, but don't shoot anyone."

She huffed. "I assure you…"

He chuckled. "I'm keeping the star. If you outshoot me, you can have it."

Birdie turned and strode into the hospital, her spirits higher than they'd been since she'd awakened in this century.

Bored to tears, she harassed the staff trying to find something to do. "I'll even mop floors."

"Miss," exclaimed one of the cleaning staff. "I can't let you do that. Why not sit in the lobby and read?"

Birdie settled in the lounge and had started on page one of *Jane Eyre* again when an attractive middle-aged woman approached the reception desk. Her deep purple dress accented her silver streaked dark hair, and her blue eyes crackled with vitality. A big straw hat with black and purple plumes sat off center on her head. They danced as she marched up to the desk. With her was a young woman, probably her teenage daughter, as they bore a close resemblance. "I'm looking for Miss Braxton's room."

"Yes, ma'am." Pencil in hand, the receptionist asked, "May I have your name?"

"Of course. I'm Mrs. Hamilton Lockhart. My son, Tad, is the one who pulled Miss Braxton from the river. I'm here to take her home with me as she may be a distant relative."

The attendant beamed. "Wonderful. Let me get the doctor, so he can sign the necessary paperwork." She hustled away.

At this news, Birdie rose and approached the older woman. "Ma'am, I'm Birdie Braxton." She held out her hand.

Mrs. Lockhart turned. Sharp eyes studied Birdie from her toes to the loose hair she'd brushed out earlier this morning. Her intelligent study missed nothing, and Birdie waited for her to form a conclusion. She didn't have to wait long. The older woman beamed, took Birdie's hand and covered it with her other one. "Delighted, my dear." She indicated to the pretty young woman at her side. "This is my daughter, Bethany."

"Hello." Bursting with energy and without a shy bone in her body, the girl danced over and slipped an arm around Birdie's waist. "Tad said you don't have a place to stay, so we want you to come home with us."

That's what Mrs. Lockhart had said to the desk clerk, but Birdie wanted to make sure.

"Have you thought this through, ma'am? You don't know me. I could be a murderer or worse."

Mrs. Lockhart patted her hand and before releasing it. "I'm a pretty good judge of character, young woman, and I believe you're harmless. You need a place to stay. We have plenty of room."

"Thank you. I'll be happy to work for my board."

"We'll talk about that later."

Dr. Franks appeared, and Birdie signed the dismissal forms. "You let me know if you start having headaches again, young lady."

"I will. Thank you for my care. Please thank Nurse Taylor for me. I'll pay my bill as soon as I get a job."

He beamed. "I'm sure you will, but there is no rush."

Mrs. Lockhart added. "Let's get your things and be on our way."

She pivoted in front of them. "This is all I have."

"Well, seems we need to stop by the mercantile before we go home."

Thirty minutes later Birdie found herself inside a spacious department store. She could only stare at the bounty of merchandise on shelves, items in wood and glass cabinets, and arrangements of furniture on one side of the large structure. Large ceiling fans stirred the warm air as people bustled around selecting their purchases.

"Come along, dear. This way."

Birdie followed Mrs. Lockhart along the aisle. An hour later, with the counter loaded with what the older woman insisted she needed—two everyday dresses, two church dresses with a pair of summer oxfords to match, underwear, boots, a couple of skirts and three blouses, two dress hats, and a work hat. Birdie even talked the older woman into adding a pair of dungarees to the stack.

Bethany's mouth fell open. "Mother! You won't ever let

me get a pair. Why can she wear them, and I can't?" She stomped a foot. "It's not fair."

Birdie picked the pants up off the pile. "I don't want to cause problems. I'll put them back."

"No, no need." Olivia Lockhart turned to her daughter. One dark brow arched, she studied the girl from head to foot. Under the perusal, Bethany's reddened face paled.

"I'm sorry, Mother. That was childish of me, but I so want a pair."

"Since you had the good grace to apologize, I concede." She shook a finger. "But I better never find you wearing them in mixed company."

Bethany squealed and threw her arms around her mother's neck. "Thank you, thank you." She rushed off and came back to add her selection to their purchases. As the sales clerk rang them up, Bethany moved closer to Birdie and squeezed her waist, her smile conspiratorial and engaging. She'd be shocked and surprised at the fashions in the future. The thought made Birdie chuckle, and she put an arm around the girl and squeezed back.

How Birdie would ever repay the older woman she didn't know, but Birdie would find a way. Loaded down with packages wrapped in brown paper, they approached the carriage. The young ranch hand who'd accompanied the Lockhart women stored them in a compartment in the back and helped them board.

Birdie viewed 1890 Waco with different eyes this trip. Yesterday, she'd hoped to see something familiar; today she drank in all the differences—the wooden sidewalks, a saloon over on Franklin, the train depot, awnings on windows of stores to ward off the heat rays. Her gaze darted from place to place and noted Cooper's Grocery on Mary Street and the Pacific Hotel on Franklin. As they neared the suspension bridge, she observed the toll-keeper's cottage with its picket fence. In her time period, a fee wasn't collected when crossing the bridge. In fact, only foot traffic was allowed across the historic structure.

She focused her attention on the spot Detective Ethan said she'd been fished from the water. Her skin tingled and the hairs on the back of her neck crawled leaving a feeling of intense anxiety. She shuddered. As close as she sat to the other two women, it was impossible to keep her reaction from being noticed.

"Are you cold, dear? We can fetch the blanket we always carry."

"No, I just had an odd sensation wash over me." The desire to step onto the banks of the Brazos was strong. Was the river her way back home? Something had brought her to this time period, but she couldn't imagine what—the eddy in the river, the bolt of lightening, the hit on her head or being near dead from drowning. Maybe God had sent her back for some divine purpose, but no… God didn't need her to carry out his plans. He was all-powerful and could move mountains with a sweep of his hand. Maybe this was all a dream or a coma, and she'd wake up back home in her bed. A horrible thought struck her. Was she dead? Was she in Heaven? It couldn't be Hell because it was too beautiful.

She couldn't breathe. Her gaze rested on the banks of the Brazos. If it was the key, she had to try, didn't she? She tried to resist, but a compelling desire to stop overrode her sense. She nodded toward the bank. "Can we pull over for a moment?"

"Of course." The older woman leaned forward and tapped the man on the shoulder. "Pull over, Hank. We want to get out for a minute."

He stopped the buggy and helped Birdie down. She strode to the river's edge and watched the water ripple by, traveling southeast towards the gulf. With each step, the corset she wore tightened, threatening to choke off air supply. She drew in deep breaths of air, as deep as she could without expanding her abdomen. The desire to go home overwhelmed her, and she bit back a cry. She had to try. She stepped out of her slippers and patted her pocket to make sure her gun was still with her. It wouldn't do to leave a weapon like hers back in this time period.

Birdie didn't really believe in time travel, but she wasn't crazy, and it was impossible for anyone to pull off a stunt like rebuilding a 1890s city to be so real. Yes, movie sets could be made believable, but no way could they have a cast of characters as large as the one she'd seen today. She took a deep breath, lifted her skirts almost to her knees and started toward the water.

"Birdie! Miss Braxton! What are you doing?" Mrs. Lockhart's voice became shriller with each word. "No!"

Footsteps pounded on the grass behind her. Birdie walked farther into the water, stepping up the pace. Just as Hank hit the water, she threw herself forward and using the breaststroke, moved into the current. She drew in a deep breath and dove under. Visibility was poor. She could only see three inches in front of her. Fish veered around her and water grass waved as she passed. Her skirt and petticoat soaked up the river and dirt and drew her slowly down. Her feet touched the bottom. Lungs bursting for air, she bent her knees and shoved upward. Her head broke water.

The current had carried her almost to the bridge and Birdie struggled against its strength to make it to the shore. Hank saw her and shouted. "There she is." He ran along the bank to reach her, came to a screeching halt, twirled a rope over his head and tossed it toward her. She could have made it, but why bother? She grabbed hold, and he pulled her toward the shore.

Soaked, filthy, and still in 1890, she stood and tried to wring some of the water from her dress. The poor garment couldn't take another dunking, and she didn't have an additional nice dress. She sighed and her shoulders slumped. Did her failed attempt mean she was stuck here… forever?

Olivia Lockhart bustled over carrying the blanket, which she wrapped around Birdie's shoulders and rubbed to soak up some of the moisture. She clucked like a mother hen. "What were you thinking, young woman? You could have drowned."

"I had to give it a try... to go back home to my time." She flipped hair out of her face. "Obviously it didn't work."

"Now, now, dear. Everything will be all right. You'll see." She tugged on Birdie's arm. "Come along. We want to get home before dark."

Bethany handed Birdie her slippers. She didn't put them on right away. She'd wait until she dried out some. Bethany sat up front with Hank so her mother wouldn't be squeezed so close to Birdie and get wet. They crossed the bridge, and

Birdie spotted the location where she believed her house stood in the future. Homesickness engulfed her. A large lump formed in her stomach, and she closed her eyes until the sensation passed. What was she going to do? She couldn't throw herself in the Brazos every time she crossed it. They'd lock her up in one of those sanatoriums for sure.

Mrs. Lockhart patted her leg. "After a hot bath and a good meal, things will look better."

Birdie could only nod. Would she? Only time would tell.

CHAPTER FOUR

Birdie woke to the sound of robins and cardinals chirping outside her window. Dawn sunlight cast a ray across the bedroom wallpaper with flowers creeping up a trellis. Her sleep had been fitful. The feather mattress wrapped itself around her, making it difficult to roll over. She had to literally lift her body to turn, which resulted in tangling the long nightgown about her. The breeze through the open window wasn't enough to cool her until after midnight. She supposed her body was too accustomed to air conditioning. Then she'd fallen into a restless sleep. But, the wakeful time lying in the dark allowed her to think, to plan. She had to accept her fate and make the best of it. Somehow, she'd traveled back in time to 1890 and it appeared she was stuck here forever. There was no way the Texas Rangers would allow her to be a part of their regiment in this time, but she'd find a way to use her skills and build a life for herself.

With her decision made, she felt better—could even smile. Heck, she might even dance a jig if she could get out of this bed. She swung her legs toward the side and managed to push herself up into a sitting position.

Finally on her feet, she peeked out the door to make sure the hall was empty before rushing down to the bathroom. She was not about to use the chamber pot beneath the bed. The big claw foot tub was similar to the one at the hospital and soaking last night had been heavenly. She quickly washed her teeth using the brush and tooth powder they'd picked up yesterday. While brushing she held the can up and scanned the label. It read, "Dr. Lyon's Perfect Tooth Powder, An

Elegant Toilet Luxury." Though not her favorite way of cleaning her teeth, it was better than a frayed twig, and worked quite well.

Dressed in a riding skirt and one of her new blouses, she stared at herself in the mirror. What could she do with her hair, and what did the people in this time period think about her up lights and low lights? Her beautician had talked her into adding the red, something new to Birdie and she had to admit, she liked them. With the brush Olivia had purchased for her yesterday, she brushed the long tresses, creating as much order as possible. She could pin it back with the hairpins lying on the glass vanity tray, but it would take practice to create something suitable. They weren't like the bobby pins she was used to. With a shrug, she left her room to head downstairs.

She entered the kitchen to find Olivia and the woman she'd called Maybelle last night, bustling around cooking breakfast. "Can I help?"

Olivia smiled. "My goodness, Birdie, after your exhausting day, I didn't think you'd be up this early." Last night they'd gotten around to dispensing with formal names. Possibly because Bethany refused to call her Miss Braxton, plus it wasn't a moniker Birdie was that familiar with. Now, if someone said Sergeant Braxton, she'd tune in instantly. But that wasn't going to happen, here anyway.

"I'm always up this early, unless I'm sick and Aunt Patty makes me stay in bed." Her heart twisted, but she shook the emotion away. She had to move on.

Olivia patted her arm in sympathy. "I'm sorry, dear. Somehow we'll find your family." She handed Birdie a stack of plates. "You can set the table."

A large family table graced the kitchen. Birdie did as asked, adding the cloth napkins and silverware Olivia lay on the table.

"Maybelle, will you go upstairs and make sure Bethany is up and getting dressed?"

"Yes, ma'am. I'll start making beds while I'm up there."

"Thank you. When you're finished, let's start snapping those black eyes. I'd like to have them for dinner tonight."

Black eye peas—Birdie's mouth watered at the thought.

43

They were hard to come by at home unless you had a garden or could afford to buy them at a produce stand. Usually they were already shelled and bagged, making the price outrageous.

Olivia handed Birdie bowls and platters to place on the table. Soon it was loaded with fried eggs, biscuits, bacon, sausage, and cream gravy. No sooner had they finished than the back door opened, and Tad Lockhart strode in. Dressed in denims, cotton long-sleeved shirt, dusty boots and battered hat, he stopped short at seeing her. He smiled, the expression eliciting a thump for her heart, removed his hat and hung it on a rack by the door.

"Miss Braxton. I'm glad Mother talked you into joining us."

She returned his smile. "It's Birdie. And it's not like I had a number of people vying for a house guest."

His grin deepened the wrinkles around his eyes, his tan highlighting their blueness. Hard to miss, he was a darn good-looking man, his engaging smile definitely woman-killer quality. She didn't intend to become a notch on his gun belt. Oops, he wasn't wearing a belt—worse yet a notch on his bedpost. "Well, folks didn't have much of a chance to get to know you like we did."

She shrugged. "I plan to pay you all back for my room and board and all these clothes your mother bought me."

He held her chair. "I'm sure you will. Now, sit and let's eat. I'm starved."

Birdie sat. She wasn't used to anyone holding her chair. She might get used to this gentlemanly stuff. Olivia smiled down at her plate. Now, what the heck was that about? Before she could ponder the situation further, the swing door from the hallway whooshed open, and Bethany waltzed into the room dressed in her dungarees.

Olivia's eyes narrowed. She opened her mouth to speak but Tad beat her to it. "What in thunderation do you have on, young lady?"

She shot her chin out and sent him a smirk. "They are britches, of course. Mother bought them for me yesterday." She smiled at Birdie. "Birdie got a pair, and I've wanted a pair for ages, but I know I'm not supposed to wear them in mixed company."

His eyes narrowed, as he looked her up and down. "And what do you call me?"

Bethany strode to his end of the table, slid her arms around his neck and placed a kiss on his cheek. "My wonderful brother."

He threw up his hands. "Mother, I hope this doesn't backfire. I'd sure hate to have to run off any of the hands. They're all good workers." He shot his sister a glare. "And I assure you, miss, if I ever catch you prancing around in those in front of any of the men, I'll marry you off to one and see how you like being a ranch hand's wife."

Bethany's eyes rounded in horror. "Mother…"

"He's trying to rile you, honey." Olivia pointed a finger at the girl and used it to emphasize her words. "But you take heed of what he said. If you wear those in front of any man other than your brother, I'll burn them."

"Yes, ma'am."

Tad rubbed his hands together. "Now that's settled, can we eat? I'm starving and we're burning day light."

Olivia lifted the platter of meat and handed it to Birdie. She took one piece of bacon and one of sausage before passing it to Tad. He raked half of what was left onto his plate and passed it along. He studied Birdie as he chewed. "You mentioned a job. Do you have any idea what you might like to do?" He grinned. "I bet Mother could help you find a husband to take care of you." When her mouth dropped open, he laughed out loud.

She snorted. "I don't need a man to take care of me."

"Don't you want to get married, have babies?" Bethany asked.

"Sure, someday when the right man comes along."

"How old are you anyway? Aren't you kind of old not to be married?"

"Bethany!" chided Olivia. "That is rude."

Birdie chuckled. "I don't mind. I'm thirty-three. Not so ancient in my time not to be married. As a matter of fact, many women don't have their first child until they're in their forties."

"Never met the right man, huh?" Tad shoveled the last bite of breakfast in his mouth and chewed while waiting for her answer.

45

"Nope. Oh, there were several I considered marrying, but I just couldn't see spending the rest of my life with them. I'd probably be bored to tears."

Tad nodded as if he understood.

Olivia smiled. "I understand perfectly, dear. My late husband was my one and only love, and there was never a dull moment throughout our marriage." She patted Birdie's hand. "You mentioned your time, Birdie. What year exactly are you referring to?"

"2012."

Olivia coughed into her napkin and Bethany giggled, but Tad remained silent and studied her intently. She remained still under his perusal. "Will you tell us all about it tonight after dinner?"

"Of course."

"Good." He stood and leaned down to kiss his mother on top of the head. "I'll try to be back before dinner." He turned to Bethany. "Remember what I said about those dungarees." Before she could answer, he'd turned and was out the door. It slammed in finality leaving an uncomfortable silence in its wake.

Bethany glanced up at Birdie and then spoke to her mother. "What about Birdie and her britches?"

"She's a grown woman. I don't have control over her like I do you."

Birdie didn't miss the unspoken message. "I'll be circumspect, Olivia."

* * *

Tad leaned back, satisfied. "Great meal, Maybelle, especially the peas." The older woman had cooked for their family for close to thirty years. She'd sneaked him cookies when he'd been a boy. No doubt his parents were aware of the subterfuge and didn't mind. Nothing escaped their notice around the ranch.

She lifted his dessert dish and beamed down at him. "Thank you, Mr. Tad. I do like to see a man eat a healthy meal."

Mr. Tad. She'd called him that from the day she came into their home. "Has Alice gone home?"

46

"Of course she has. She never stays later than four."

Good. He didn't want the young woman who helped Mother and Maybelle with the house to hear tonight's discussion.

Maybelle continued removing dishes. "Y'all want more coffee?"

Tad rose. "No, but thank you. We'll be in the parlor." He stopped. "Maybelle, we can count on you to keep anything you learn about Birdie to yourself, can't we?"

She tucked her chin toward her ample breast and huffed. "Have you ever known me to spout tales about this family?"

He kissed her cheek. "No, never. But, you may hear some real odd things from her, things hard to believe."

She stalked off to the kitchen mumbling under her breath. He caught words like "fool boy" and "outlandish indeed." He grinned and hurried to catch up with the women.

He settled in a wingback chair. Birdie, quite attractive in a blue serge dress with white piping, sat on the sofa beside his mother, Bethany on the floor at her feet. "Whenever you're ready, Birdie."

Her chest rose as she took a deep breath. "Well, I've already told you I'm from the future, from 2012. In my time period, I work as a Texas Ranger." He'd explained to his mother about the Texas star, but not Bethany.

Bethany's eyes rounded and she clapped a hand over her mouth. He expected her to emit a "woo" any minute. She squealed. "Really? A woman ranger?"

"Yes, but now that I'm in 1890 I'll never be able to serve. Wilbur King visited me yesterday morning and wouldn't let me have my star back." She perked up. "But, he promised if I could outshoot him, he'd return it."

Startled, Tad sputtered. "The adjutant general of Texas?"

"Yes. I recognized him from the picture hanging in the Texas Ranger Museum."

Tad would be talking to Detective Ethan as soon as the opportunity arose, to get answers. Of course, with someone having a ranger star, especially a woman, the general would either send someone or come himself to investigate. Due to budget cuts, their numbers had been reduced, so it made sense for King to come himself rather than pull a man from the field.

Mother shook her head. "I can't imagine a woman riding with those roughneck men. Chasing Indians and riffraff of all kinds. It's… it's...." She threw up her hands and shook her head.

"Olivia, the ranger organization in the future is entirely different. Though we work in the field a lot, much of what we do is detective work. Most of my day is spent in an office."

"Well, thank the Lord," Mother muttered as she set her paddle fan in motion.

Tad studied his sister, worried that she'd take Birdie's story to heart and be disappointed when the truth came out. He still didn't believe she was from the future. Breathless with excitement, Bethany asked. "What's it like in the future?"

"We have automobiles that will travel over one hundred miles per hour, we've put men on the moon, and have kitchen appliances that cook food…" She snapped her fingers. "Just like that."

"And the food tastes good?" asked Mother.

Birdie shrugged. "Not when cooked in a microwave, but it does when cooked in a gas or electric oven. You'll see the invention of electric ranges in your lifetime, Olivia." She leaned over and wrapped one of Bethany's curls around her finger, pulled and released. It sprang back into a corkscrew. "Bethany, you'll see electric curling irons and hair dryers."

"You mean you don't have to heat them over a fire?"

"Nope."

Tad watched the women as he listened. Mother was reserving judgment, but he knew she wanted to ask questions. Like him, she couldn't believe in machines flying in the air and certainly not in space. Heck, they'd never get him in one, that's for sure. Everything she said seemed right out of one of those Jules Verne novels he'd read in his youth. They needed some proof. He didn't necessarily believe Birdie was lying on purpose. Evidently she believed every word she said.

"Men on the moon, huh?" He tried but couldn't keep a straight face.

Birdie's eyes narrowed. "I know it sounds ridiculous, but it's true."

"I know you believe every word you're saying, but we can't accept that you actually traveled back in time. Time travel isn't possible. If it was, people would be popping back and forth all the time." *And surely they'd know about it, wouldn't they?*

"How do you know they don't?"

Bethany piped up. "Yeah, Tad."

"I don't, but I think if it happened we'd know at least one person who'd traveled forward or back."

Birdie grinned. "Well, now you do."

"Look Birdie, I don't think you are crazy. I feel you believe what you are saying. But for me to believe you are from the future I'm going to need more than your word and a silver star with 2010 on it."

* * *

Morning found Birdie at a loss of what to do with herself. She'd helped Maybelle wash dishes, one of Birdie's least favorite chores, and now joined Bethany at the barn, located about a mile from the house, to collect a horse to ride.

Tad appeared before she had a chance and gave the wrangler on hand strict orders. "Saddle old Molly. She's as gentle as a baby and don't let Miss Braxton out of your sight. She recently suffered a head wound and a throw might kill her."

"Sure thing, boss." The young cowboy winked at her as Tad stalked off. "Actually, miss, Molly isn't that old, and she's a good ride." He doffed his hat. "I'm Thomas."

"Nice to meet you, Thomas. Call me Birdie.

Bethany led a good-looking chestnut mare, already saddled, from a stall. She stopped beside her. "Molly's a sweetheart, Birdie. I used to ride her all the time until Tad bought Blondie for me."

Blondie? What a modern name for this time period, but the animal did have a beautiful blond mane and tail. "Molly will be fine." To be honest, Birdie wasn't that experienced a rider so gentle was good. Old was good, too, as she wanted to take this relatively new experience slow. They were leading the horses from the barn when Detective Ethan and Mr. King rode into the yard. Both looked comfortable in the saddle. She supposed the buggy they'd arrived at the hospital in was for town transportation only. They dismounted and approached. Tad must have seen them coming up the road as he rode in not far behind them. He sat his horse like a natural, the epitome of what Birdie supposed a real cowboy should look. She snorted. What did she know about them anyway?

Tad dismounted and shook hands with the men. They chatted and glanced in her direction before striding toward her.

"Miss Braxton," called General King.

"General."

"Are you ready to demonstrate your shooting ability?"

All right! She wanted her star back. "I am."

"Good, good. Mr. Lockhart will guide us to a place where we can safely test your skill."

Detective Ethan joined them and handed her a package.

"What's this?"

"Your holster. Picked it up yesterday."

Birdie ripped open the brown paper and fingered the soft leather. "It's as good as new. Thank you, Detective. I'll repay you as soon as I get some money."

"No need, Miss Braxton. It's a get-well gift."

"Why…thank you. That's very sweet of you."

Color rose in his face. "You're welcome."

Tad coughed and covered his smirk. "Are we ready to go?"

Birdie narrowed her eyes and shot him a glare. Impudent man. Detective Ethan's gesture was sincere, and she appreciated having her holster back. And he wasn't sweet on her, was he? She hoped not.

She patted her pocket. "I have my Ruger, but I don't plan to spend all my rounds. I don't think .380s will be invented until around 1908."

General King's mouth twisted as if biting his lip. "Well, I can't say I blame you there."

She couldn't resist a grin. "I will let each one of you fire a round though, as I know you're curious as all get-out."

"Yes, indeed," blurted Ethan.

Tad shrugged. She'd forgotten he'd not seen her Ruger. "Let's get this done. I've got work to do."

Bethany had hung back and watched the exchange, until now. "Can I come along, Tad?"

He studied her a minute. "I guess so, but stay out of the way and be quiet."

They mounted their horses, and Tad led them east, away from the house, barns, and cattle. They rode past fields of maize, feed for their animals she supposed. Barbed wired kept them at bay. Occasionally, an oak tree stood among the crops spreading its shade under its branches. The terrain looked much like the fields in her time, but lacked all the modern additions—paved roads, tractors and other farm implements, and the so-called ranch houses.

Tad turned north and led them toward a creek backed by a tall dirt bluff. Mesquite trees dotted the banks covered with grasses among the sandy soil. They dismounted downstream and tethered their horses where they could graze and drink yet be away from the gunfire.

The men removed rifles from scabbards. Detective Ethan, out of uniform today, wore a gun belt as did General King. Birdie knew it wasn't legal to wear guns openly on the streets of Waco, but many people concealed them in pockets.

Tad lifted his from his saddlebag and strapped it on. He handed Birdie his rifle. "It's loaded. Can you handle one of these?"

Birdie examined the Winchester carbine and looked down the site. "Yes, I think so if I can have a few practice shots. Is this a 76 model?"

Tad's brows rose in question. "Yes. How'd you know?"

"It resembles the ones issued to the Texas Rangers in the 1880s."

"Have you ever fired one?" asked King.

"No, but it doesn't look hard." She glanced across the creek and located a target approximately twenty-five yards away. "I'm aiming for the top paddle of that prickly pear directly ahead." She cocked the rifle, took aim, and fired. Bits of cactus flew. She'd hit it dead on. She engaged the lever to release the spent shell and ready the carbine for her next shot. Her ears rang, and she wished for plugs or headgear.

King stood at her side. "Need any more practice shots?"

"Nope. Let's do this. I want my star back."

"All right young lady. See that empty bird nest on an upper branch in the mesquite tree just to your right?"

She located the target. "Got it." It was farther away, but still within her range of abilities, she hoped. Be just her luck to not be able to hit a barn with this audience. She took aim, took a breath, and fired. The nest exploded, scattering tiny sticks and cast-off feathers. She breathed a sigh of relief.

"Very good, Miss Braxton. Now, see that dead oak above the bank over there? Take off that small branch that's broken."

The rifle was heavy, reminding her she'd recently been sick, but no way would she let on she was feeling the effects. Thank goodness for the hat Olivia had insisted she buy as it protected her vision from the sun. Her blouse, now damp, clung to her back. She drew in several deep breaths and raised the rifle, took aim, and fired. Nothing happened. The branch remained intact. Well darn, she'd missed. Then, suddenly, it dropped.

"Good job, Birdie." Tad patted her on the back. "I bet that was sixty yards."

"Thanks." She glanced at King. "Aren't you going to shoot? I thought this was a contest."

He scratched his chin as he studied her. "Let's see what you can do with that little gun of yours first."

Tad took the Winchester and returned it to its scabbard.

She pulled the Ruger from her pocket. Tad rejoined them and looked down as she clicked the button to release the magazine. "What in tarnation is that?"

"It's a semi-automatic pistol that shoots .380s, a shell that hasn't been developed yet." She removed the bullet from the chamber and dropped it in his hand. He examined it closely before offering it to King.

King shook his head. "Ethan and I've seen it. Odd, ain't it?"

"Sure is."

Birdie continued her instruction for Tad's benefit. "This is the perfect size gun for concealment. People with a license to carry a concealed weapon, undercover officers, or officers who are off duty can easily carry this, and no one will know. You've seen my leg holster. I carry this when I wear dresses. If I'm wearing pants, I conceal it in some other way."

The three men exchanged glances. Evidently they didn't know what to make of what she was saying. She didn't blame them. It was unfamiliar idea for them.

"This magazine holds six shells though you can buy an extended one to carry more. I always carry an extra loaded magazine in my purse when I carry the Ruger." She grinned at King. "When I'm on duty and in uniform, I don't carry a purse as I wear a nine millimeter on my hip, a concealed .38 just above my ankle, and I have a number of other weapons in the trunk of my car."

Tad threw up his hands. "Just show us how this little toy works."

Birdie held up the magazine. "This is loaded with six rounds." She popped it into the butt of the Ruger. "You slide the chamber back to cock it. The Ruger is called a semi-automatic because now I can fire all six rounds without cocking it again."

She turned and found her target—the prickly pear again. "I'm going to aim for the next paddle down on the prickly pear." She fired. The bullet caught the outer edge. Not in the center where she'd aimed, but not too bad. "Who wants to go next?"

"I'm next," barked King. He aimed for the cactus and missed by a hair. "Little gun has a kick to it."

After Ethan and Tad fired, Bethany approached. "Can I shoot it once, Birdie?"

Birdie looked to Tad for approval. He shrugged.

Birdie asked. "Have you been taught about gun safety?"

"Tad taught me how to load the shotgun and his rifle, but I've never fired one."

"Well, today's your lucky day. Firing one is almost as important as knowing how to load one. You need to experience the recoil and be able to recover in case you need to fire again." She placed a hand on Bethany's shoulder and moved her to stand facing forward, then placed the gun in her hand. "Point the gun at what you plan to shoot. Try something closer than the cactus…the base of that tree stump just across the creek. Keep both eyes open when you pull the trigger."

Bethany hit the stump. She squealed and jumped around.

Birdie took the weapon from the girl. "Whoa, watch where you point the gun." She released the magazine, and ejected the sixth shell from the chamber. "You did real well, Bethany."

"Yes, you did, sis. I'm proud of you." The girl beamed.

"Let's head back," said King.

"What? You said we were having a competition so I could get my star back."

"No need to waste good ammo. I can see you know how to handle a weapon. Still doesn't prove to me you're a Texas Ranger."

"But...you promised."

He held up a hand. "Don't get your dander up. I need to discuss a few things first." He turned to Tad. "Can we sit at your kitchen table for a spell?"

"Of course."

Birdie stuffed her Ruger in her pocket and stomped toward Molly. Darn man wasn't a ranger. He was a politician, and the word of a politician wasn't to be trusted.

CHAPTER FIVE

His mother insisted the men stay for lunch. While putting away the horse, Tad delegated his duties to some of the men. He didn't shirk his duties often but wanted to be on hand for what excuse General King would give Birdie about her ranger star. The woman wasn't happy for sure. He'd just finished washing up and sat down when the serving dishes started making the rounds.

Evidently the general and Ethan didn't get many home cooked meals. They heaped their plates. He caught his mother's eye. A smile tilted her lips, and she gave a small shake of her head. If it'd been him, she would've chided him. Of course he was the man of the house and could do what he pleased, but when it came to the table and the kitchen, his mother was boss.

He had to commend Birdie's patience. She didn't interrupt their meal with questions or demands. His mother and Bethany kept the conversation neutral. To give the men credit, they listened politely to his sister's prattle about the upcoming July 4th celebration. Truth be told, he looked forward to it also. They always spent several days in town at the Pacific Hotel, and this year would be no different. Well, except they'd have Birdie with them. He glanced her way. Did she enjoy dancing? Would she take part in the sack races and other games? She didn't appear to be the type to sit in the shade fanning herself.

General King wiped his mouth with his napkin and laid it on the table. "That was a mighty fine meal, Mrs. Lockhart."

His mother beamed. "So glad you enjoyed it." Her face

flushed with pleasure, she pushed her chair back, rose from the table, and lifted her plate. "I hope you saved room for a slice of my pecan pie."

King groaned. "Ma'am, I'm stuffed, but I wouldn't pass up pecan pie. It's my favorite, one my dear late wife fixed for me often."

"Bethany. Help me, please." Mother nodded to indicate the other plates on the table.

"Yes, ma'am." Bethany got up and cleared the table

Birdie stood. "Can I help?"

"That'd be nice, dear. You can pour the coffee."

Tad waited until the door closed. "What do you think about Birdie's story, General?"

He stroked his beard. "Mighty odd, isn't it? She can handle her weapons, but she could have learned that anywhere. It's that little gun of hers that confuses me. Never seen anything like it."

Ethan added. "I've seen a lot of weapons in my time but never heard of .380 shot."

King pulled a gray hair from his beard and dropped it on the floor. It's a good thing Mother was out of the room, as she'd not approve. Not that she'd say anything, but in his head he could see her lips pursing. Tad swallowed a chuckle. "Do you believe her story, that's she's from the future?"

"Nope. Not possible."

Ethan cleared his throat. "I don't know what to think, but she believes it for a fact. I've seen a lot of liars in my day, and she's not one." He shrugged. "Perhaps the knock on the head…?"

King drummed the table with his fingers. "Given any thought to what story you're going to give to folks as to who Birdie is and why she's staying in your home?"

"Mother mentioned she thought there might be some Braxtons on her side of the family. Guess we'll say she's a distant relation who needed a home."

The door swung open and Birdie entered with a tray of coffee cups, Mother on her heels with the coffee pot. From the buffet, Mother poured the coffee while Birdie handed them around. Bethany entered with the pie.

* * *

All right. At last dinner was over and Birdie was alone with the men. Olivia had insisted Bethany help her with the dishes, but she'd told Birdie to stay put. Now was her chance. "Why can't I have my star?"

Before the general could answer, Tad stood. "Let's take this discussion out on the porch where hopefully we'll catch a breeze."

"Fine." Birdie stood and marched toward the front door. Tad offered her a chair, but she crossed her arms and shook her head. "I'd prefer to stand." Standing might give her some advantage.

"Suit yourself." All three men found rocking chairs.

King stretched his long legs out, folded his hands across his belly and eyed her. He cocked an eyebrow. "All right, let's hear it, Miss Braxton."

She took a deep breath to calm her frustration. "I don't understand why I can't have my star back. I worked hard for it." A lump formed in her throat. "If I can't get back to my time, it's all I have left of my previous life."

Ethan squirmed in his seat, decidedly uncomfortable at her situation. If up to him, Birdie bet it'd be in her hand. But, it wasn't up to him. It was up to King.

"My dear, I understand your distress, but it just won't do for you to have a Texas Ranger star. Only men commissioned as rangers by the state of Texas can carry them."

Heat exploded in her face. "First of all, General King, I'm not anyone's dear. I'm a commissioned Texas Ranger. That star belongs to me. It's not my fault I've been tossed back into this archaic time period where women are supposedly delicate and need to be set on a pedestal—called 'my dear.'"

Ethan and Lockhart gaped at her. She sniffed. Guess they were shocked at her tone of voice, but she wasn't backing down. No doubt they didn't believe her story about time travel either, but there was no other explanation for her appearance in 1890.

"I assure you I meant no disrespect, my de... err... Miss Braxton."

"Well, in my time, being addressed as 'my dear' by a man who out ranks her is condescending." She leaned back against the porch rail. "I worked hard for that star. I earned a degree from Texas University in criminal science. I went through the police academy in Austin and spent two years on the force in Waco before becoming a state trooper. The training was rigorous, and I handled it. One hundred-fifty individuals applied for the two ranger jobs open in 2010. I was one of the people chosen. " She stuck her hand out. "Give me my star."

King didn't move a muscle though his eyebrow rose and a muscle twitched in his cheek. "I assure you I have the utmost respect for your situation and understand your distress. I can't say I believe you are from the future, as I don't see time travel as possible. I believe in what I can see and hear. Though I don't believe you are intentionally lying, I do not believe you are a Texas Ranger. You'd never be able to hold up to the hardships my men undergo."

She sputtered, "You don't know that. Test me. Put me in a regiment and see how I handle it."

"My men won't let a woman ride with them." He shook his head. "I can't in good conscience return the star."

Her heart pounded in her chest. *I will not cry, and I will not screech like a weak woman.* She took several deep breaths and turned to Detective Ethan. "I'll be in tomorrow to file a complaint against General King... for theft of my personal property."

The detective choked. He must have swallowed a mouthful of smoke. Tad arched an eyebrow at her. She cocked one back at him. If he thought she was running in for a glass of water, he had another thought coming. He slapped the arm of the chair, stood, and left the porch. He returned a minute later with a glass and pitcher of water. Ethan nodded his thanks and sipped at the beverage. King observed the proceedings with an unruffled smile.

Finding his voice, Ethan croaked out. "Miss Braxton, you can file a complaint, but it won't do any good. When it comes to Texas Ranger business, General King is the law."

* * *

58

Tad had to give it to Birdie. She didn't cry, beg, or try to cajole. Just propped her hands on her hips and asked, "Is that your final answer, General?"

"Yes, Miss Braxton. I'm sorry, but it is. I promise it will be in safe keeping with the Waco Police Department."

She squared her shoulders and muttered, "Fine." Then she swept past them and through the front door. The general jumped when the screen door slammed. The man probably knew today's discussion wouldn't be the end of the debate.

The two men didn't stay long after Birdie's departure. Tad strolled inside to find her pacing in the parlor. At the sight of him, she threw up her hands. "I have got to find something to do. I'm not used to housework. I need to use my mind or do something constructive."

She'd said she had a college education. Would she be able to keep the ranch books for him? He'd much prefer working with the animals than sitting behind the desk doing figures. "How good are you at arithmetic?"

She stopped pacing and waited, hope lightening her expression. "Very good. Why?"

"I could use help with the ranch books. How does a dollar a day with room and board sound?" That's about what he paid his ranch hands, and if she did a good job it'd be worth every penny.

"Why, it sounds perfect. When can I get started?"

Tad was surprised at his sigh of relief. He hadn't realized until this moment how much he dreaded the work. "How about right now? I've already wasted most of the day. I might as well use the remainder of it getting you settled."

"Lead on, sir."

His office lay behind the parlor and was usually closed off. He'd threatened to fire Maybelle if she moved one item in the stacks on his desk while dusting. She did her best to dust around the piles. To keep papers from blowing around the room, he stacked a horseshoe on top of each heap.

Birdie halted just inside the door and took in the scene. He had to admit, it was a mess. He'd not posted entries in the books, paid bills, or filed receipts for a month now. Thank goodness their creditors were accommodating.

She grinned. "You don't much like book work, do you?"

"I hate it."

She lifted a bill off the bottom of one stack, read it, and then waved it in his face. "You haven't paid the grocers in over a month?"

He caught it and placed it back in the stack. "That's why I'm hiring you." He pulled open a drawer and lifted out the checkbook and ledger. "You pay the bills, and I'll sign the checks. Record the amount, date, and payee in the receipt area."

"I know what to do." She lifted one the ink pens from the ink well and studied it a moment before putting it back. "I think if it's okay with you, I'll work in pencil until I get the hang of using a quill pen. I'm used to ballpoints where the ink flows automatically. When the ink runs out you throw it away and buy a new one."

"That is wasteful. These pens do have metal nibs and are much easier to use than the old quills."

She snorted. "Maybe for you."

He remembered how hard it had been for him to learn to use a pen in school. He'd had ink everywhere until he'd gained confidence and skill. "If you want, I could pick up one of the new Waterman pens at the store next time I'm in town."

"No, let's see how I do first. Anyway, on the books I can use pencil for a while but will want to come back later and go over the figures with ink. Of course, the checks have to be in ink."

He watched as Birdie sat and rifled through the desk drawer setting two pencils and a penknife out. She set them aside and started going through one pile, organizing the items to suit her. It appeared she had a plan so he'd leave her to work.

"Mother will know where I am if you need anything."

Without looking up, she called, "Okay, thanks."

By dinnertime, Birdie had Tad's desk organized, had recorded the invoices in their proper column and tomorrow would pay bills. She'd played around with the pen and managed to scratch out a legible scrawl without too many smudges, but her fingers were covered with ink. She glanced down to make sure she'd not ruined her blouse. Whew! Spotless.

Tomorrow, she'd practice a little more before getting down to business. She stretched and, hands linked behind her head, leaned back in the chair. Contentment filled her. She'd found a purpose, a way to earn her keep until she came up with a permanent plan. Unfortunately, it wouldn't be law enforcement, as people in this time period wouldn't accept a woman as a police officer. Hopefully she'd at least be able to use her investigative skills. Her goal required some thought. She closed her eyes. Yes, she'd think of something.

*   *   *

Tad strode into his office and stopped at the sight of Birdie leaned back in his chair. Arms behind her head, the fabric of her blouse stretched taut across her breasts, fine looking breasts he might add. He'd not given them particular notice before but with them pointed almost to the ceiling, they were hard to miss. My, my, she was a tempting sight. His body hardened with appreciation, and he diverted his gaze to the desk. If Birdie caught him eyeing her attributes, she might pull that little gun on him. He chuckled.

Her eyes flew open, and she dropped her arms. "I didn't hear you come in."

He walked around the desk to look over her shoulder. "Caught you taking a nap, didn't I?"

She snorted. "Not hardly. Just closing my eyes for a minute."

He surveyed the neat desk, the piles of invoices in tidy stacks. "You got a lot done this afternoon."

"Yep, have all these invoices recorded and will pay bills in the morning." She flipped the ledger closed and shoved the chair back to stand. She held her hands out to him. "How long does it take this ink to wear off?"

"A couple of days unless you want to strip your skin off with some of Mother's lye soap."

Her blue eyes lit with humor. Pink lips twitched into a smile revealing a beautiful set of white teeth. The ripeness of her kissable lips didn't go unnoticed. He straightened. What was wrong with him? He darn sure wasn't in the market for a woman and if he showed the slightest interest toward Birdie,

Mother would have them married before he could come up with an excuse.

"I think I'll let it wear off on its own." She lifted her arms over her head and twisted from side-to-side. Tad watched, mesmerized. When she noticed the direction of his gaze, her hands dropped to her side like rocks. "I need a walk to stretch my legs. Sitting this long is tiring."

He cleared his throat. "Yes, indeed, I stiffen up like an old man. If you don't mind, I'll join you."

"Sure." She strode to the door and waited for him. "Where to?"

"How about to the stables, so I can check on the horses. By the time we get back it'll be time to freshen up for supper."

Birdie didn't mince along at a slow pace. Her strides were long and fast. He didn't know if she wanted to get their walk over as quickly as possible or what. Should he be offended? He glanced at her to check her expression. Head slightly raised, she appeared to be breathing in the fresh air. Her expression wasn't pained but one of pure enjoyment. Mother would be complaining about the heat. Bethany wouldn't, but she was still a kid in most ways.

"About how far would you say it is from the house to the barns?"

"A mile, give or take. Why do you ask?"

"I usually run five miles three or four times a week to stay in shape. I sure don't want to run up and down this same path all the time. Can you think of somewhere else with pretty level ground where I could run?"

Good Lord-a-mercy! Run to stay in shape? Her figure looked pretty dang good to him. He didn't know any men who had to work to stay in shape. Their jobs kept them that way. "Why on earth would you do something like that?" Heck, he doubted the exercise was good for her womanly parts, but no way in thunder would he say so to her.

"In my line of work, it's required. I can't let a perpetrator outrun me. I may have to tackle him to the ground, overpower him, and cuff him."

"A perpetrator?"

"Yeah, you know—a criminal."

"Oh." Tad just couldn't imagine her doing such a thing. On second thought, he could see it, skirts flying, drawers exposed as she wrestled a big old brute to the ground to cuff. At his loud guffaw, she stopped in her tracks and shot him a steely glare.

"I can see you don't believe I'm capable of overpowering a man."

He struggled to contain his laughter, as he looked her up and down. He finally managed to answer. "It is hard to picture, even with you wearing your riding skirt."

She stuck her chin out and marched ahead. "I guess I'll have to show you sometime."

He hustled to catch up. "Ah now, don't be mad. You have to admit, it's not something I'm used to seeing."

"Uh-huh. By the way, I want to buy a few things. Do you think I could have an advance on my pay?"

"Put whatever you need on our account."

"If I do that, I'll pay you back on payday."

"Good enough."

"You never did give me an answer about another place to run."

He thought about it a minute. "I expect it's about three miles to the road that leads into Waco. Also, the trail we rode with the general and Ethan is about the same distance. I imagine either one of those will work fine. I'll send one of the stable hands with you."

"No need. I can take care of myself."

Dang woman! He knew it would be useless to argue with her. "At least take a weapon with you."

"You can count on it."

CHAPTER SIX

Birdie stood at the counter inside the gunsmith's shop. The name burned into a wooden sign read Joseph Hellman, Owner. Hank waited beside the door. Tad wouldn't let her venture into town alone. It was bring the cowboy along, or she couldn't have the use of a horse. As soon as she had enough money, she'd buy her own ride.

"How may I help you, miss?" The middle-aged man squinted at Birdie over his wire-rimmed spectacles. His leather apron brushed the opposite of the counter as he leaned forward to see what she pointed to.

"I'd like to see that pocket pistol. It's a Colt, isn't it?"

"Yes, indeed, young woman. The latest model, center fire too." He lifted it from the case and handed it to her. His eyebrows rose a notch when she released the chamber and sighted down the barrel. "Know something about firearms, do you?"

"A little." She tested its weight. Not bad. It would be a little heavier loaded. The size was perfect for her holster. "Shoots .38s?"

"Yes. If you want a model that fires .32s, I can order one."

"No, I prefer this caliber." She dry fired it a couple of times. The trigger wasn't too stiff. "If the aim is off, can I bring it back?"

He slapped his hand down on the counter setting his jowls in motion. "My good woman, I assure you I sell the best. If the aim is off, it won't be this gun."

Birdie slapped her hands down beside his. "I assure you,

my good man, if it doesn't shoot true, the fault will not lie with me." What was it with these people, talking down to her all the time?

He lowered his head like a bull and shot her a steely gaze. "Then bring it back, and I'll adjust it until *your* aim is true."

Near the door, Hank was having some type of coughing fit. She walked over and pounded him on the back. "Are you okay?"

He swallowed a chuckle and coughed again. "Yes'm. Just fine."

The fool man was laughing. Guess he'd have a story to tell Tad and the rest of the wranglers. She didn't mind. All she cared about was the gun shooting true. She returned to the counter. "How much for the Colt, Mr. Hellman?"

"Ten dollars with a box of shells included."

Birdie stuck out her hand. "It's a deal then. I'll take it."

He grinned and shook her hand.

"Add three more boxes of bullets."

As he produced the boxes of shells, she loaded the Colt and added it to the pocket of her riding skirt.

He studied her suspiciously. "Planning on robbing the bank?"

"Nope."

"You new to the area, Miss…"

"Birdie Braxton, Mr. Hellman. Yes, I'm new. I'm staying with Olivia Lockhart."

"You the young woman Tad fished from the Brazos? The one with the crack on her head and no memory?"

"That'd be me."

"You need a gun cleaning kit?"

"Yes. Thanks for reminding me."

He added the kit to her purchases and wrapped them in brown paper and tied it with twine. "Got a city ordinance here in Waco. No carrying guns in the city limits. Sure would hate to see you get locked up."

Birdie patted her pocket. "I know. That's why I bought a pocket pistol. No one will know I'm carrying."

He snorted and eyed her pocket. "If they're blind, you mean. That'll be twelve dollars and twenty-five cents."

"Add it to the Lockhart account."

He opened the book and flipped through the pages before jotting down the amount.

A Winchester repeater on the wall caught her eye. She nodded toward it. "How much for the Winchester, Mr. Hellman?" It was a twenty-four inch rifle, a good size for her.

He looked behind him and then turned back to her. "Nineteen-fifty."

"Save it for me, will you? I'll be in next month to purchase it."

His jaw dropped, but he snapped it shut and nodded. "I'll do that Miss Braxton. Have a nice day and be careful."

As they walked out, Birdie turned back. Mr. Hellman stood where they'd left him, hand scratching the bald spot on his head. No doubt about it, she'd made a friend... *not!* She laughed all the way to their horses.

By noon, they were back at the Lockhart ranch. She carried her purchases upstairs to her room to unwrap and put away. For running she'd bought a pair of boys' school shoes. They were sturdy and if kids could run in them, she could too. She folded the new riding skirt and put it in a drawer of the chifferobe and hung the two blouses in the closet side of the large piece of storage furniture. The leather work gloves, she tucked in the other pocket of her skirt.

Over the next two weeks, Birdie's life settled into a routine. Three days a week she donned her dungarees and took her run. On the first day she ran toward the shooting area, she carried a box of shells and practiced with the Colt. Mr. Hellman was correct. The aim was exact. Some days she'd stop by the barn, and, using a low overhead beam, do a number of pull-ups. Some of the wranglers started competing with each other. It lasted a week and when the newness wore off, they quit.

Her job keeping the books didn't occupy enough of her time. At the end of the month Tad had her figure all the wranglers' pay. Accompanied by Hank, she rode into town to the bank for cash, as the men didn't want checks. On payday, she set at a table outside the bunkhouse and doled out their money. She still helped with the dishes, worked with Olivia in the garden, and spent two hours a day tutoring Bethany in math.

After dark, she sat with the family on the front porch and visited, light from the coal oil lamps inside casting a soft glow through the windows and door. It was odd. Her family was close, but not nearly as much as the Lockharts. The ranch was a small community. Each member played a vital role and depended on the other. They worked together, ate together, went to church and socials together. Much of her family's time was spent in front of the television. Of course there were family outings and reunions, but each of them had their own friends. They drifted off to individual activities. Listening to Tad, Olivia, and Bethany as they talked about neighbors, wranglers, and friends was nice.

"Birdie?" Olivia's rocker stopped. "Did you hear me?"

"No, I'm sorry. My mind wandered. What'd you say?"

"Are you looking forward to the July 4th celebration next weekend?"

Bethany stood at the porch rail. She twirled sending her skirt wide. "It'll be so much fun. All sorts of games, a dance, and fireworks! All my friends will be there."

"I'm sure I'll enjoy it. I love fireworks." Actually, she liked to dance too.

"Well, you and Bethany, as unmarried young ladies, will have a box lunch in the bidding to raise money for the church."

"What? I can't cook."

Olivia chuckled. "Don't you worry, dear. Maybelle will pack a nice lunch for both of your girls."

"Olivia, I don't meant to be a spoil sport, but I'm not young, and I really don't want to participate in such an activity." It was degrading in her opinion.

"You're unmarried. It's expected of you." In the moonlight Birdie could see the older woman's eyes twinkle. "Who knows, you might meet a nice man, one interested in marriage."

Her voice a whisper, she muttered, "Heaven forbid."

Tad guffawed. Birdie didn't dare swat him, but she wanted to.

Olivia leaned forward in her rocker. "What'd you say dear?"

"Nothing, just mumbling."

67

The older woman sniffed. "Please don't do that. It's rude."

"Yes, ma'am."

*   *   *

Dressed in a blue gingham dress with short puffed sleeves and a fitted bodice, Birdie sat stiffly beside Tad in the carriage. Thank goodness the garment fit loosely enough she didn't have to wear the dratted corset. It was a pretty dress, but the neckline dipped lower than what was comfortable to her. She resisted pulling it up higher. The large straw hat adorned with blue, yellow, and pink flowers shaded her from the hot July sun. Without it and the frilly parasol, her fair skin would burn to a crisp. Here it was not yet nine o'clock and the temperature was at least 80 degrees, if not hotter.

She still might have enjoyed the drive but for the prettily decorated box on her lap, a reminder of the lunch to come. Why she worried about it, she didn't have a clue. It's not like her fellow rangers would be there. This was an ordinary function for this time period. Yes, she would be considered an old maid, but Tad's admiring gaze this morning told her she wasn't beyond attracting a man.

She cast a glance his way. His three-piece suit fit him nicely, the jacket stretched over his broad shoulders. How men could stand dressing in such hot attire in the summer, she didn't know. They must be used to it. His dark auburn hair curled above his collar, the white felt hat protected his eyes from the glare. The scent of his bay rum aftershave teased her nostrils. Yes, Tad Lockhart was a fine-looking man. She admired that he didn't dip snuff or chew tobacco like so many of the cowboys. Bet tonight he'd have his choice of dance partners. Every single woman in the county would vie for his attention. A stab of jealousy prodded her. Disgusted with herself, she snorted.

He bent closer to her, his smile sending a flutter through her stomach. "Did you say something?"

"No, just coughed." *Liar*.

Her face heated. She hid behind her parasol and tugged at the sleeves on her dress. They were a bit too snug. What she wouldn't give for a pair of cut offs, a tee shirt, and flip-flops. At least she'd avoided the pretty shoes that went with her dress and wore the comfortable school shoes. Not that they'd do her any good. Olivia had outlined expected behavior before they left the house. Standing around with a bunch of silly girls and matronly women did not sound like much fun to Birdie.

A bandstand had been erected on the riverbank. A table covered with a colorful cloth stood in the middle. They'd no sooner stepped down from the carriage than Olivia took Birdie and Bethany by the arm and led them toward the man accepting lunch boxes. He stepped down and led Olivia up the steps.

"Mrs. Lockhart. You're looking lovely as usual."

"Thank you, John." She motioned to Birdie and Bethany. "Come on up, girls. John, you remember my daughter, Bethany."

"Of course, I do. You've grown up, young lady."

Bethany blushed. "Hello, Mr. Samuelson."

Birdie jerked at the name and studied the man intently. He didn't favor the man she knew in her time one bit. That still didn't keep her from being suspicious.

"And this is Miss Birdie Braxton, a distant cousin of mine come to live with us a while. Birdie, John is one of the deacons at our church."

His eyes raked her form briefly, and then he tilted his head. "Miss Braxton, it is indeed a pleasure."

"Likewise, Mr. Samuelson."

"Err, yes. Now, let's get you ladies signed in and your boxes labeled."

Birdie sighed with relief to leave the gazebo. She smiled as Bethany joined her friends. Olivia chatted with a group of matrons and introduced Birdie to her friends, many of them mothers with their daughters in tow. They eyed each other and Birdie suspiciously. Probably saw her as being competition for Tad's attention. Gad, poor man. She didn't envy him having these young women vying for his attention, all with matrimony in mind. As soon as she could politely slip away, she strode toward the riverbank.

Ahead, a group of rowboats were tied up at a dock. Men

stood beneath a tree getting a number pinned to their backs. One waved and hollered, "Hey, Tad. I need a partner." She turned to find Tad strolling toward her.

He shucked out of his jacket. "You mind holding this for me?"

She folded it across her arm. "Not at all."

His friend jogged over with a number and while Tad rolled up his sleeves, pinned it to his back. "I bet you're Miss Braxton." He offered his hand. "I'm James Baker, a friend of Tad's since childhood."

Birdie instantly liked the redheaded freckle faced man. She shook his hand. "Call me Birdie."

He smiled in acceptance and then slapped Tad on the back. "Ready to win this race?"

"Aren't I always?" Tad touched her arm. "The finish line is back up by the bridge. Will you meet me there?"

"Of course."

The men selected a boat, pushed it out a short way before hopping in, and then took position with the other boats in the middle of the river, approximately ten feet apart. They'd be rowing with the current. When they were lined up to suit the starting judge, he held a pistol up and hollered, "On your mark, set!"

The report echoed across the water and the boats shot forward. Birdie ran along the riverbank trying to keep up. Others crowded around her. Cheers and laughter floated amid the crowd, and she found herself jumping up and down, screaming, "Go, Tad, go James! You can do it!"

They were ahead, clearly the winners. Then, they slowed. Oh no, Tad had a cramp in his shoulder. Two young boys rushed past them. The pistol sounded. The race was over, and Tad and James lost.

Gradually the boats pulled ashore. The two boys, probably middle teens were congratulated and received a prize of money. They whooped and slapped each other on the back.

A hand touched her back. She whirled to find Tad grinning down at her. "Disappointed?"

"Of course I am. Y'all were way ahead. What happened?"

He took his jacket and bent down to whisper in her ear.

"We decided it was time to let these youngsters have a turn at winning."

She hissed, "You…you mean you lost on purpose?"

"Yeah."

Well, Birdie didn't know what to think. She glanced back at the two winners. They basked at the attention of the other men, including James and their friends. She smiled up at Tad. "What a nice thing to do."

The two boys rushed over. "Sorry you didn't win, Mr. Lockhart."

He shook each of their hands. "Well, I'm mighty disappointed, but if someone had to beat us, it couldn't have been done by a better pair. Congratulations!"

Yes, the more she got to know Tad Lockhart, the better she liked the man.

"Tad!" An attractive brunette dressed in red calico and ruffles tapped Tad on the arm with her closed parasol. "What happened out there, darling? You never lose."

He turned, impatience marring his handsome face, erasing his expression of joy. She opened the sunshade, held it over her head, and looped her arm through Tad's.

"Lucy, what a surprise to see you here today."

She fluttered her dark lashes. "Why, I'm always here to watch you in the rowing competition." She directed her gaze to Birdie, eyeing her from her feet to the straw hat on her head. With its wide brim to protect her from the sun, it didn't have the style Lucy's creation possessed. Birds, feathers, and flowers adorned the red and white concoction. "Aren't you going to introduce me to your relative?"

"We're only distantly related, Lucy."

"Oh really." She twirled her parasol. "But, Mr. Samuelson said—"

"I know what he said, Lucy, but Miss Braxton's branch of the family is so many times removed…." Tad shrugged, removed the woman's hand from his arm, and extended his hand to Birdie. She took it, and he tugged her closer. "Birdie, I'd like you to meet Mrs. Lucy Jamison. Lucy, Miss Birdie Braxton."

Mrs. Jamison smiled, her red lips almost garish, and nodded. Birdie guessed cosmetics hadn't come very far in this time period. "Delightful to meet you. Will you be staying with the Lockharts long, Miss Braxton?"

"My plans are unsettled at the moment." A tall, thin man started toward them and then stopped. He pulled out a pocket watch and checked the time. He was doing his best to appear uninterested in them, but he wasn't fooling Birdie. Who was he? She nodded in his direction. "Is that your husband, Mrs. Jamison?"

Startled, she turned back, and then around again. Her chortle strained, she quipped, "Heavens no. I'm a widow."

"Oh, I'm so sorry."

"No need, dear. He's been gone five years now. I'm quite used to being on my own." Lucy licked her lips, her smile sly. "But dear Tad here has been so good to help me out, keep me company. Haven't you dear?"

Tad scowled. "Sorry to rush off, but we must be going."

She winked. "I'll save you a dance tonight, Tad."

Tad choked and muttered something like, "You do that."

So, Tad and the widow lady were fooling around. He didn't like the woman's blatant behavior. No doubt she wanted Birdie to know she had a prior claim on Tad. "A pleasure to meet you, Mrs. Jamison. Will I be seeing you again at the Lockhart's?"

Her eyes narrowed and for a minute Birdie thought the woman would slap her. Oops, she'd hit a nerve. Lucy's pinched mouth relaxed into a smile, one that didn't quite reach her eyes. "No, Olivia and I aren't acquainted yet. Maybe one day soon."

As they strolled away from the woman, Birdie couldn't resist. "A girlfriend of yours? One your mother doesn't approve of?"

He growled, "Mrs. Jamison is none of your concern. Please forget this conversation and have a good time."

Tad took her arm and led her to the bandstand. "It looks like they're getting ready to start auctioning off the box lunches. We don't want to miss out, do we?"

"Heaven forbid." She groaned. "Would you shoot me, please?"

CHAPTER SEVEN

"Look at this lovely box, gentlemen." Mr. Samuelson winked at Birdie. "Almost as lovely as this young lady, Miss Birdie Braxton, a distant relative of Mrs. Olivia Lockhart."

Birdie wanted to drop through the grandstand floor and choked on her snort. Young? Was the man blind? She never blushed but darned if her face wasn't heating.

Mr. Samuelson waved it under his nose. "Mmm, smells delicious too. Bet Maybelle fixed this lunch, men. You know you're in for a fine meal as well as Miss Braxton's engaging company."

"I bid two bits, John." A scruffy cowboy with a wad of tobacco in his mouth pushed through the crowd.

Birdie's blush turned to an expression of horror. She quickly hid it with a smile she was sure resembled a grimace.

"One dollar," yelled a portly man in a suit. At least he appeared clean and wasn't chewing tobacco.

"Five dollars," announced someone in the back. Birdie peered over the heads of the crowd to see Dr. Franks pushing his way forward.

Mr. Samuels beamed, thrust out his chest, and rocked back on his heels. "Now that's the spirit, gentlemen."

"I'll make it six dollars." Detective Ethan lifted his hat and grinned at Birdie. Today he wore a three-piece suit rather than his uniform. He resembled many of the other men enjoying the festivities. She grinned back. Now this was more like it. She'd enjoy lunch with the detective.

"Seven dollars." Birdie's gaze jerked to the new bidder—*Tad*. Her heart jumped into her throat. Why, she didn't know. She dined with him every day, but there was something about sharing a meal on a quilt that hinted at intimacy.

"Woo-wee, we've got us a competition going here. Looks like it's your turn Doc."

"I'll leave the bidding to these young bucks, John," said Dr. Franks.

"All right, you gonna up the bid, Ethan?"

"Eight dollars."

"Ten," yelled Tad. The crowd hooted and hollered.

"Fifteen," called the detective. The crowd erupted into shouts and clapping. Birdie could merely gape. Fifteen dollars was a lot of money in 1890. That was half of her monthly salary. Could Ethan afford it? It wasn't her place to question. It was for charity after all.

"All right, Lockhart, what's it going to be? You going to let this man eat Maybelle's fried chicken and enjoy this pretty lady's company?"

All eyes turned on Tad. He studied Birdie and then Ethan. He made a big show of removing his hat and scratching his head as if pondering the subject. "Well, I guess I'll concede if she'll promise me a dance tonight."

Now everyone was looking at Birdie. The big ape. He knew she'd been dreading this event and here he was making her a spectacle. She narrowed her eyes at him and nodded. She'd dance with him but stomp on every one of his toes while at it.

"Congratulations, Detective Ethan. Step up here and collect the lady and her lunch box. Let's have a big hand for this generous donation."

As the crowd clapped, Birdie grabbed the box and stepped down off the stage. After Ethan paid, they collected a quilt from the Lockhart's carriage and found a shady spot on the grassy bank.

Birdie set out the fine meal and while eating, they talked.

"How're you settling in, Birdie?"

"Better than I expected. I'm keeping the ranch books for Tad and tutoring Bethany in ma—arithmetic," she corrected herself, having learned most people didn't use the shortened form of mathematics unless in a university situation. "It's something to do, but it doesn't keep me busy enough. I need something else."

"Do you have any ideas?"

"Not a one." She took a sip of the sweet tea from one of the Mason jars Maybelle had added to their lunch. If Birdie kept drinking the stuff and eating like she'd done today, she'd be as wide as a barn.

"Something will come to you. I'm sure of it."

"I surely hope so. It's bad enough I can't get back home, I've got to be able to use some of my skills to be happy."

"What about marriage and a family? Wouldn't that be enough to keep you content?"

She signed. "Possibly. If love came along. But, in my time women have marriage, family, and a career." Of course, her generation had more conveniences and work around the home didn't take near as much time. She wasn't saying it was better because in truth, she didn't think it was. The old customs were better in many ways. Yes, technology had a lot to offer in educating children, but nothing could replace good old hands on love and teaching.

Ethan looked toward a group of boys carrying baseball equipment to a cleared off flat area across the road from the riverbank. "Looks like the baseball game is about to begin. I'm serving as umpire today."

"Really? A baseball game! I love the sport." She tossed empty containers into the basket and stood. Ethan shook out the quilt and folded it neatly. They stored it and the basket in the back of the carriage and started toward the rowdy boys.

* * *

Tad had deposited his mother at the hotel so she could rest before the dance tonight. He located Bethany with some of her friends sitting on a blanket under a shade tree, chatting. A few boys hung around them, but several matrons not far off appeared to be keeping an eye on the young people. Thank goodness. He didn't want to be babysitting a bunch of giggling girls this afternoon. Where had Birdie gotten off to?

He knew Detective Ethan would watch out for her, but she lived in his home and was his responsibility.

Shouts from the baseball game drew his attention. Whistles, hoots, and boos reverberated off the river. How odd. He'd never heard so much commotion before. He strolled in that direction to see what all the hullabaloo was about. As he drew nearer, a woman's voice rose above the men's. "You'll be eating dust here in a minute, gentleman."

He pushed through the crowd in time to see Birdie bent slightly at the waist holding a bat above her right shoulder. As she rotated the stick, her hips swayed from side to side. Every man and boy over fourteen followed each swing of her rear with their eyes, grins on their mugs. Tad wanted to punch them in the face. Fool woman! What was she thinking? He elbowed the grinning man next to him and shot him a death threat. The man sobered and hit the man next to him and nodded toward Tad.

Tad's ranch hand, Hank, was pitcher. He didn't appear happy about pitching to a woman. "I'll toss it real soft for you, Miss Braxton."

"What for?" She kicked the sawdust bag and then resumed her position. "Throw it just like you have for all the others. I don't need special treatment."

Hank rolled his eyes. "Yes, ma'am." Ethan stood behind the catcher, who'd positioned himself far enough away to not get hit in the head. Evidently he didn't trust Birdie's abilities. Tad didn't either and feared she'd be embarrassed. He wanted to interfere but considered remaining silent the lesser of two evils.

Hank wound up and pitched. Birdie swung and missed.

"Strike one," yelled Ethan.

Snickers rippled through the crowd. He heard one woman mutter, "Shut up, John. It's bad enough she's acting like a man. You have no business enjoying her poor behavior."

"Yeah," added another woman. "Ain't decent the way she's acting." The mumbling in the crowd rose.

He saw Birdie's shoulder's tense and before he knew what he was doing yelled, "Come on, Birdie! You can do better than that."

She turned, found him in the crowd, and shot him a smile. It hit him right in the heart, taking his breath. Their eyes locked, and he couldn't look away. He was a goner for sure. As if struck by lightning, he knew without a doubt this was the woman for him. She would be his. It might take some convincing, especially since she didn't particularly want to get married and with Birdie, he wouldn't have it any other way. He'd bide his time, make her fall in love with him. He was patient and in no hurry to be tied down, but he sure as heck didn't want anyone to step in and claim her. Now that that issue was cleared up in his mind, he winked. Her grin widened. She mouthed, "Thanks."

He nodded, and she turned back to Hank. "Good one, Hank." She took a few practice swings and took position again. Hank threw again. This time Birdie stepped into the swing and hit the ball with a loud crack. It flew. She dropped the bat, lifted her skirts, and ran. The boys on her team yelled.

"Run, Birdie!"

"Keep going."

"It's a homer."

She rounded third and headed for home. Hank ran toward the home plate bent on catching the ball as it was thrown from outfield. Tad held his breath as it looked like Hank would succeed, but as he caught it and turned to touch her, she hit the dirt on her rear end, skirts rucked up around her knees exposing her bloomers, and slid feet first into the home plate.

Her team went crazy—jumping, hooting, and hollering. She stood and dusted off the seat of her dress. Grins stretched the faces of the men. The women sniffed with turned up noses and dragged their husbands away. The single men eyed Birdie with keen interest. Blood rushed to Tad's head, and pounded. *Damn scallywags*. He grabbed a collar in each hand and pulled boys back. "Here now, get out of my way." He shoved through the team members celebrating around her. They inched away, faces alarmed at the anger Tad couldn't hide. Fearing he'd deck 'em for letting her play, a few skedaddled.

What was wrong with him? He'd not minded her playing ball. It was the sliding in and exposing her bloomers that had him in a dither. If they'd been at home and she'd done the same thing, he'd not have been near as agitated. It was the public display.

James grabbed his arm to hold him back. "Ease up, Tad. She wanted to play and she's not hurt."

Tad elbowed James in the side. James uttered "Whoof" and released his hold.

"What about her reputation, man?"

Birdie stood before him, dirt-splotched face rosy with happiness, fists propped on her hips. "What about it?" She shrugged. "How could playing baseball hurt my reputation?"

Teeth clenched, he ground out. "You slid into home plate on your derriere and exposed your bloomers to all and sundry. Ladies do not participate in such rowdy pursuits."

She snorted sounding much like his mother when she announced her disgust. "Well, if I'd been able to wear my dungarees, that wouldn't have been a problem." She shrugged and with a smug grin on her face, and added, "Anyway, women in my time are not fragile flowers to sit back and allow the men to have all the fun. Women participate in all type of sports. They even enter the boxing ring."

It was almost comical to watch James's expression change from humor at Tad's dilemma to shock. If the situation had been different, if it had been any other woman, Tad could have laughed. But it was Birdie. She was staying in his home and under his care, her reputation was his responsibility. After all the stories Birdie had shared about the future, Tad was stunned, but not as bad as James. Not that he believed everything the woman told him. It just was too outrageous to believe. No, he could not see women in a boxing ring. Yes, some women got into fights, even well bred young ladies, but not for sport. He'd seen two women who'd lost control of their tempers and gone at each other screeching and pulling hair like two cats thrown into a potato sack. It'd been so funny he couldn't even remember what the tussle had been about. His father had cuffed him on the ear for laughing and ordered him to help him pull them apart. Dangerous business, in his opinion. He'd gone home with a couple of scratches.

He sure as heck didn't want James hearing more of this conversation. His friend would think Birdie daft, and Tad didn't want that. He put a hand at Birdie's waist and led her away from James's hearing. He didn't have to worry about the others as they remained out of earshot, but watched while pretending disinterest. The few women left in the crowd wore smug expressions, clearly believing Birdie was to be duly chastised. No doubt the single ones were elated by Birdie's misbehavior as it would prevent her from being courted by any eligible males they'd set their caps on. Fool women.

He sighed. "Birdie, I know things are different here, but the women of this community will ostracize you if you don't adapt and follow their code of conduct. You wouldn't want that, now, would you? If you're stuck here, you'll want to marry and have a family." A niggling of regret prodded him at the idea of her marrying and bearing the children of one of the gaping men here today. Not a one of them was worthy of her spirit. Anyway, he had dibs on her. Not that she knew it or would receive the news well if he laid a claim.

Her blue eyes rounded, and her stubborn chin softened somewhat. Then rebellion flashed, turning her eyes a darker shade. "Why do women of this generation have to be so repressed? What if I don't want to change, to be a useless sweet thing who simpers and curtseys at the whims of a man and society?"

Useless? Simpers and curtseys? Is that the way she saw women in this time? "Harrumph! Have you ever seen my mother simper and curtsey?" Not that he hadn't seen many a female flash one of those sly, coy smiles he hated so.

"Well, no."

"Look, I don't mean to make you mad, but what these folks think is important to my mother." Heck, for some reason, it was important to him also. To be honest, he enjoyed her spunk and didn't really see anything wrong with women participating in sports such as baseball, but women had no business wearing dungarees in mixed company. Why, men would be eying their backsides and other parts. No, sir. That's where he'd have to draw the line.

"I understand your desire to take part in more exciting and strenuous activities, but I cannot allow you to do so in public. I have your reputation and that of my family to consider. You're a single woman staying under my roof."

She narrowed her eyes and glared at him through slits. "Did I hear you correctly? *You* can't allow *me*... to..." She waved a hand toward the baseball diamond. "Participate in public sporting activities."

"That's correct. I'm glad you understand."

She poked him in the chest. "Now you listen to me, Tad Lockhart. You're not my boss, you're not my father, and you're sure as heck not my husband." She snorted. "And if you were, none of those relationships would make a difference."

"We'll see about that." He took her arm and started for the carriage. She dug in her heels and wouldn't budge. Men's laughter drew his attention. Tarnation. They were making a scene and folks were enjoying their argument. Through gritted teeth, he growled, "Stop this. You're making a bigger scene. Now come on before I throw you over my shoulder and tote you away like a sack of potatoes."

She shook his hand off her arm. "You and what other ape?"

He'd had enough of this nonsense. He lifted her in his arms and started for the carriage, hoots, hollers, and whistles following in their wake.

"If you know what's good for you, you'll put me down this instant."

Tad didn't even bother with a response, but strode across the grass.

Pain burst in his nose as blood spurted across Birdie's dress and down the front of his suit. Why, the harridan had popped him in the nose.

CHAPTER EIGHT

Tad stopped and roared. "You hit me, woman."

"Oops." Maybe she'd gone a tad too far.

He dropped her and somehow Birdie got her feet under her and landed on them instead of her butt. He drew a handkerchief from his pocket and held it to his nose.

"I told you to put me down!"

"I told you to come on, woman!"

She shook a fist at him. "You are not my boss or my husband." Well, he might sort of be her boss, but they weren't on the ranch. She'd be darned if she'd let him or any other man lead her around by the nose.

He groaned and mumbled something under his breath. Sounded like, "I soon will be."

"What'd you say?" She took the cloth and pinched the bridge of his nose.

"Ow. Be careful. I said, uh …." He shrugged. "I forget."

A man shouted, "Better get a handle on your woman, Tad!"

"Woo-wee, that woman's got a mean right hook!" hollered another.

Titters of laughter and guffaws echoed around them. Birdie couldn't resist a giggle.

Tad stiffened and removed her hand from his nose. "Let's go. We're making an even bigger scene."

True, they were the center of attention. Most of their audience laughed, but a few old biddies had their heads together, plotting, blackballing her she guessed. Not good, she supposed. Why did the people in this era have to be so uptight about a woman enjoying herself? A sense of regret washed over her. She didn't want to be a burden on Olivia. Surely Birdie's behavior wouldn't reflect on the woman who'd been kind enough to take her in. Darn it. She'd better try a little harder to fit in.

"Well, come on then." She took his arm and led him to the Lockhart's carriage. "I'm sorry, Tad. I didn't mean to create a scene, I just wanted to have some fun." She looked down at her new dress, now dirty and splotched with Tad's blood. "I feel so restricted in this time period, like I can't be myself."

He squeezed her arm. "I know, but you must learn to fit in if you're going to be happy and build a life." He helped her into the buggy and joined her on the padded leather seat. He studied her a moment. "Look at you, dirty and bloody like a misbehaving boy guilty of participating in fisticuffs. Why, you've even lost your hat and parasol."

"Well, why don't you add a few more jibes to make me feel even worse?"

With a couple of clicks of Tad's tongue, the horses started forward. He turned them toward Franklin Avenue. "I'm not trying to make you feel bad. Heck, I admit, I admire your spunk, but there's a limit." He chuckled. "It was fun seeing you hit that homer." Mouth drawn into a thin line, he turned to face her. "But, I didn't enjoy seeing every male in the area watching your butt twitch back and forth as you wound up that bat. Nor did I appreciate you exposing your bloomers for every man in the county to see."

Birdie couldn't believe her ears. "My butt was fully covered by layers of clothing, not bare!"

He blushed scarlet. Oops, maybe she'd over pushed her point. "Ladies do not discuss nakedness."

She wanted to weep. "Well, I'm not a lady. In my time women wear bathing suits that show more skin than a danged corset." She waved her hand. "Why, dresses come up to here." She drew a line across her thigh."

His mouth hung open, then snapped shut. Voice low, like someone could hear them over the clomping of the horse, he muttered, "Are you saying you're a loose woman, Birdie?"

"No!" He'd never understand no matter how much she explained. "I'm saying, in the future, things are different.

82

Women wear a lot less clothes. For that matter, so do men. If we were on a picnic in the future, you'd be wearing pants cut off above the knee and a cotton knit shirt with no sleeves."

He shook his head. "The things you say are too outlandish to believe."

"I know, but they're true."

They pulled up in front of the Pacific Hotel and an attendant hurried out to take the reins. Tad jumped down and rounded the carriage to help her alight. Inside, ceiling fans stirred the air. The soft breeze cooled Birdie's heated skin. Guests coming and going eyed her with curiosity. Tad took her arm and hustled her into the elevator. This hotel boasted the first electric elevator in Waco, but many people weren't comfortable riding in it and opted for the stairs.

The elevator operator greeted them as they entered the cage. Tad nodded to the man and gave him their floor number, but his expression was stony when he turned it on her. His nose was swelling and beginning to bruise. Birdie took his hand, squeezed and whispered, "Tad, I'm so sorry. I acted on impulse, but I'm not in the habit of being bossed by anyone except the captain." She reached up to touch his nose.

He jerked his head back and muttered, "Don't touch me. It's sore." He slipped an arm around her waist hugged her close. "Forget about it, Birdie. Just don't do it again."

Her temper flared. "Well, don't try to boss me around and I won't."

"Birdie—"

She snapped her mouth shut just as the elevator stopped.

When they stepped out, Tad stopped a maid in the hall. "Please prepare a bath for Miss Braxton."

"Right away, sir."

She removed her key from her pocket and unlocked the door. Tad waited until she was inside before striding down the corridor to his room. A few minutes later, Birdie opened the door for the maid. She strode in with a long white robe, toiletries, and several towels. "I'm Sophie, miss. I have your bath drawn. If you'll come with me, we'll get you out of this dress and I'll get it laundered for you."

"Oh, thank you." Birdie glanced down at the stains. "I hope the blood will come out."

"It shouldn't be a problem." Birdie followed the maid down the hallway. She laid the towels and bath items on a table then helped Birdie with the buttons down the back of her dress. Birdie slipped into the robe. "Leave the towels in the bathroom and I'll get them later. Pull the bell if you need anything and don't forget to lock the door."

"Thank you, Sophie."

Thirty minutes later, Birdie sat by the open window brushing her hair. With long strokes, she pulled the strands up and away from her scalp. She dropped her head forward and brushed the curly tresses until they hung over her eyes, then flipped them back. When it settled around her shoulders, she ran her fingers through the long strands giving it as much lift as she could. She wanted it to have some curl, but not too much. Why she worried about her looks, she didn't have a clue. According to Tad, her reputation was ruined.

A knock sounded on the door. Birdie rose and opened it. Olivia stood outside, her mouth pinched in a thin line, holding Birdie's hat and parasol. "May I come in, dear?"

"Of course." Dressed in what Birdie assumed was a day dress, Olivia stepped inside and lay the bonnet and umbrella on the bed. Then she moved to sit on the rocker beside the window.

"Where'd you find my things?"

"Detective Ethan had them delivered. I guess he assumed you were sharing a room with Bethany and me. If larger accommodations had been available, it would have been nice for all three of us to be together."

Birdie wasn't disappointed at all. She enjoyed Bethany but after a while the young girl's chatter got on her nerves.

Olivia patted the cushioned chair sitting adjacent to hers. "Come, sit. We need to talk."

Uh-oh. Here it comes. Birdie might spar with Tad, and any other individual who challenged her, her beliefs and behavior, but she didn't have the heart to disappoint Olivia. The woman had been kind to Birdie, inviting her into her home, and was doing her best to help Birdie fit in with society. Whether she believed Birdie was from another era was hard to tell, but she had been patient with her.

With a sigh, Birdie sat. "I'm sorry for my behavior today. It's just so hard for me to give up what I'm used to."

"I understand. Believe it or not, I was young once, too, and fought against the restrictions of society." She shrugged. "Of course, then I married and had children to think about. Though I might want to resist on occasion, I know I can't because others depend on me to be a good example and I wouldn't want my behavior to reflect unfavorably on either Tad or Bethany." She snorted. "Not that Tad is concerned about how *his* conduct reflects on us. I about died when that widow woman approached Tad after the race today… in broad daylight. It's bad enough that he visits her at night on occasion."

"I take it you don't approve of the woman."

"Hardly! I know men have needs, but…" She threw up her hands. "Forgive me. This discussion is inappropriate for your ears." Pushing on the floor with her toes, she set the chair in motion and rocked for a moment. If Olivia knew what all Birdie's ears had heard and her eyes had seen in her years in police work, the older woman would have a heart attack on the spot. "Birdie, the manner in which you behaved today, and the way Tad responded, gave people the impression you're a couple."

"What? Why would they think that?"

"Because he picked you up in his arms and then you hit him. It appeared to be a lover's spat."

Birdie sputtered. "That's ridiculous."

"May be, but that's how it is." Olivia reached over and patted her knee. "Now, just be sure you don't give people more to gossip about tonight. They'll have you engaged and marching down the aisle before breakfast. Not that Tad is a man to be pushed into doing anything he doesn't want to do, but he likes you and would want to preserve your name and standing in the community."

"That will never happen. No one will push me in to getting married." And she'd in no way allow a man to marry her to save her reputation. It would be for love or not at all. Not that she didn't think Tad a handsome man, because she did. When she got married, it'd be to a man who considered her his equal, one who didn't boss her around. She snorted. Tad was as bossy as they come.

"I know you're a good girl and adapting to our ways must be hard. But, you must if you want to be happy here."

"I'll try."

85

* * *

Tad found his gaze returning to Birdie. She was lovely in the mauve dress she'd worn when he fished her from the Brazos. Her hair was lifted on the sides and held up with combs, which allowed curled tendrils to fall down in soft waves. Candlelight caught on the varying colors of her tresses, emphasizing the blue of her eyes.

Bethany caught him staring and grinned. She looked from one to the other and back at him. "How come—"

Guessing the direction of his sister's thoughts, he interrupted. "Birdie, your hair is an unusual color. Did you inherit it from someone in your family?"

"Yeah," added Bethany, "I've been curious too."

"Actually, if I tell you, you'll think I'm terribly wicked so maybe I better keep it a secret."

Bethany's eyes rounded. His mother's stare of horror spoke volumes, but she was speechless.

Tad couldn't believe what she'd implied. "Are you saying your hair color is not natural? That you dye it?"

"Yes." She leaned forward and lowered her voice. "It's common in the future for women to dye their hair, to get perms—a treatment originally called 'permanent waves' to make it curly. Some wear it very short, as short if not shorten than some men."

His mother gasped. "Why would they do that? A woman's hair is her crowning glory."

Tad had to agree. He loved running his figures through a woman's hair. His mind had wandered to Birdie's often enough and had wondered if it was as soft as it looked. Dyed...? He couldn't believe it.

"Yes, I know that's what this generation believes, but many things have changed." She pulled a strand of her hair out and examined it closely. "My natural color is a medium blonde. Every four or five months my hairstylist adds what are called high lights and low lights—high are a lighter color and low are a darker color. They give my hair more texture."

"I like it, Birdie," said Bethany. "Maybe when I get older I can color my hair."

"You'll do no such thing, young lady."

Tad could see Birdie enjoyed shocking them. Heck, he didn't know what to think. Was she a harlot? No, she wasn't. He knew some women colored their hair in the privacy of their own homes and would be horrified if anyone found out. It was something he could see Lucy doing and flaunting. But, Birdie acted as though it was an everyday occurrence, that it wasn't unusual. He peered at her hair closely. It was very pretty, natural looking. Had Birdie really traveled back from a future era? He liked that theory better than putting her in the same category as Lucy. No, they were not the same.

Grin mischievous, Birdie put her arm around Bethany and squeezed. "Maybe we can talk your mother into letting you get an earring in your nose."

Tad couldn't tell who squealed louder—his mother or Bethany. Bethany slapped a hand over her nose and giggled. Birdie laughed out loud and Tad added a guffaw.

"Stop it now! We're causing a scene." Mother's voice demanded obedience but her lips twitched in rebellion. Sure enough, others in the dining room were staring. She leaned forward, closer to Birdie. "You are teasing us, right?"

"Unfortunately, no. It's horrifying to see what some of the younger generation do to their bodies. Piercing their tongues, their belly buttons, and… other areas."

What other areas could she be talking about? He could only think of a few body parts that protruded far enough… no, surely not. His gaze whipped to her.

She smirked. "Of course not."

He blew out a breath. How could someone do that to their body? Better yet, why?

Mother shook her head. "I am flummoxed and can't imagine such a custom. They actually use earrings?"

"Yes. Mostly studs." She held up her fingers about an inch or less apart. "You know … a little post with diamonds, or silver balls."

"Dear, I've thought hard the last few days about some of the things you've told us… and… I have to admit, they sound crazy." She reached across the table and clasped Birdie's hand. "But I know you're not crazy. I just don't know what to believe."

87

"I know the things I've told you are hard to picture in your minds, to deem true. If our situations were reversed, I'd feel the same as you." She pushed food around on her plate with her fork, than laid it down. The utensil clanked against the china. "So much has happened in the last past one-hundred-twenty or so years. Olivia, if you're worried about my hair color being noticed by others, I can go up and put it in a bun and cover it with something."

"You'll do no such thing. If anyone asks, we'll just say something in the river turned it different colors and you're waiting for it to grow off."

Tad snorted. "Then we'll have all the young misses in the area jumping in the Brazos to create the same effect."

His mother shot him a chilling glare.

He swallowed his laugh. "You think they'll believe that story?"

Mother sat up straighter in her chair. "Doesn't matter whether they do or not. I believe it and they'll not question my word." She shook a finger at Birdie. "And you, young woman will leave that beautiful hair alone. I may not understand everything about you and what's at work here—you being with us and all—but I know you're a good person, and I'll not have anyone treating you otherwise."

When Mother spoke, her word wasn't disputed. Usually. He hoped Birdie wouldn't be breaking with tradition.

CHAPTER NINE

Birdie had never seen the Brazos lit so beautifully. Lights strung around the bandstand and along the bridge glowed dimly, their reflection bouncing off the rippling surface of the river. Surely those weren't candles—maybe tiny lanterns. She leaned forward to see more closely. "Are those electric lights?"

"Yes. Aren't they lovely?" Olivia beamed with pride. "Soon they'll have the entire bridge lit up on special occasions."

Wow. Who knew they had electric lights in 1890? It'd be easier to imagine if she was in New York, but this was Texas. Birdie knew the hotel had the electric elevator and some electric light, but never dreamed they'd use them for decorations. Maybe they had Christmas tree lights now too. Obviously, her early Waco history was lacking.

The strains of a waltz wafted toward them on the breeze. Tad pulled the buggy into line behind several others. He jumped out and helped them down before turning the vehicle over to an attendant. Birdie resisted a giggle—just like valet parking in the future.

Olivia and Bethany lifted their skirts, and shook them, smoothing out wrinkles. Birdie glanced down at her own frock and decided she better do the same. Would she ever get used to all the frou-frou?

The older woman announced, "Tad, you escort Birdie. Bethany will walk with me."

Tad winked, eliciting a grin from her. The scoundrel. Did he know how handsome he was? Of course he did. He took her hand and tucked it around his forearm. "Do you like to dance?"

"I love to dance." She lifted the hem of her dress to keep from tripping as they walked down the slope towards the crowd. "It's such a surprise to see the electric lights. I didn't know electricity was widely used in this period."

"It's not. Having it at the grandstand and across the bridge is an extravagance. As you can imagine, we're proud of the bridge and the commerce it brings to Waco. The city council felt electricity on this occasion was justified." He waved toward the dancers. "But as you can see, we still must rely on coal oil."

They were close enough now to see that lanterns hung from poles set up around the plank dance floor. "I don't remember seeing the dance floor earlier."

"A group of men gathered late this afternoon and laid the two by fours. Cameron Lumber provided the boards. After the dance, the floor will be disassembled and returned to the yard. Monday morning the used lumber will be sold at cost."

"That's very nice of him."

"Sure is. Good advertisement too. Events like this bring town folks closer together."

Cohesiveness—that was something, in her opinion, the modern world needed more of. Smaller towns were more community minded. No, that wasn't fair. Larger towns worked hard to do good works with cancer walks and food pantries to name a few.

They stopped at the dance floor. Tad clicked his heels and bowed over her hand. "May I have this dance?"

She smiled and dropped a slight curtsey. Ugh! A curtsey! She was losing her mind for sure. Tad took her in his arms and all humor evaporated. It wasn't often she danced with a man taller than her, and Tad was. Her head fit perfectly just under his chin. The soft aroma of his spicy cologne or hair pomade invaded her senses; the warm skin of his neck tempted her lips. It would be easy to tilt her head just so and place a kiss under his chin. He was a tempting man and exuded sex appeal. Get a grip, Birdie! A man wasn't in her future right now, at least not until her goal was achieved. No need to tempt nature. She eased back a little, but he pulled her closer.

"Relax." His breath rustled the hair above her ear and

she shivered. "Mm, you smell nice." He tugged her closer. If she wasn't mistaken he placed a kiss against her hair.

Her heart thumped in response and she blurted, "You do too."

Tad startled and missed a step. Did the muscles in his arm tense? She thought she heard a soft groan but couldn't tell over the strains of *I'll Take You Home Again, Kathleen.* Her response must have shocked him. Ladies of this time weren't as honest with their thought, but she wasn't about to change to fit in. He was a good dancer, and she relaxed as he led her around the floor, which had been lightly covered with sawdust, so their feet slid easily as they twirled to the haunting ballad.

The song ended and they stepped apart. The audience clapped for the band, and they added their applause as they walked to the side. "They're very good."

"Yes. Our symphony is getting prestigious in the area. A few members travel to San Antonio on occasion to sit in with the orchestra there."

Birdie supposed modern Waco had an orchestra, but her activities ran more toward high school and university athletic activities. Aunt Patty often bemoaned Birdie's lack of interest in the arts. "I'm impressed. Do you often attend?"

"Nah, but mother and Bethany do."

The music, a lively song she didn't know, started up, and Tad took her hand. Before they could enter the group of dancers, Detective Ethan stopped in front of them and tipped his hat. "Evening Birdie, Tad. Birdie, may I have this dance?"

"Of course, Detective."

He glanced at Tad as if to ask permission.

Tad nodded.

Birdie wanted to blurt she didn't need anyone's consent but decided it best to keep her mouth shut.

"Do you think you could call me by my given name? Detective is rather formal."

She chuckled. "I'd be happy to if I knew it."

He grinned. "It's Lloyd."

"Well, Lloyd," She nodded toward the dancers. "I'm not sure I can keep up, but I'll do my best." As they joined the couples, Birdie glanced back over her shoulder. Tad moved into the throng of people visiting on the grass. She'd have enjoyed another dance with him.

Lloyd was a good dancer, the tune lively. She was breathless by the time the music stopped.

"Detective Ethan, Miss Braxton, are you having fun this evening?" Mr. Samuelson stopped before them, all smiles. Birdie wished he had another name. He reminded her too much of Carl Samuelson in her time and just because the modern man was a rat didn't mean this one was.

Birdie smiled as graciously as she could. "Yes, indeed. A wonderful time."

He rocked back on his heels. "Good, good." He clapped Ethan on the shoulder. "I'm pleased to see you got some time off to enjoy the festivities."

Lloyd grinned. "Well, seniority does have its benefits on occasion."

"Might I borrow this young lady for a dance?"

Ethan turned to her. "Birdie?"

"I'd love to, Mr. Samuelson."

Almost a foot shorter than her, the man held her against his barrel chest and stout abdomen, his grip like steel as he pushed her around the room. What he lacked in grace he made up for in enthusiasm. When the music ended, he bowed. "Thank you, my dear."

Before she could answer, another man claimed her, and the music started again. Even Joseph Hellman spun her around the floor and then came to a stop by a stout middle-aged woman she suspected was his wife.

"Mattie, this is the young woman I told you about, Miss Birdie Braxton." He lowered his voice. "You know, the young lady Tad Lockhart fished from the river."

Would she ever be introduced as something other than the woman fished from the Brazos? How about, the new woman in town?

Waving a handkerchief, Mattie fanned her pink cheeks. "Ew-we, this heat!" She pocketed the fabric and gripped Birdie's outstretched hand. "Hello, Miss Braxton. It's a pleasure to meet you."

"The pleasure is mine, Mrs. Hellman."

"Not at all. When Joseph came home and told me about

a young woman buying guns …" She leaned in close. "He thought you really odd." She snorted. "I told him, 'that young woman's got more sense than most women around here.'" She shook her head. "Expecting a man to take care of them… shoot, my man taught me how to handle a gun right after we got married."

"Mr. Hellman did?"

"Yes, indeed."

That was odd. Seemed a contradiction to Birdie.

"I know what you're thinking. Joseph believes few women are smart enough to handle weapons. He figured I was one who was." She winked and chuckled. "He's still thinking on you."

Birdie giggled and then whispered, "Will you keep me posted on his verdict?"

"I will indeed." She tapped her husband on the arm. "Escort Miss Braxton over to Olivia, Joseph."

"All right. I'll bring you back something cold to drink."

"Oh thank you, dear. That'd be lovely." She waved as they walked off, and then shouted, "Come visit me soon."

Birdie would do that. It'd be nice to talk guns with another woman.

Olivia sat with some friends on a quilt just outside the glow of the lanterns. She introduced Birdie. They exchanged pleasantries, and then the women returned to discussing the upcoming church bizarre.

Birdie's gaze traveled around the area. It didn't escape her notice that she was witnessing history. Goosebumps broke out on her arms and she rubbed them away. Sleeping young children lay on blankets with someone watching nearby and visiting. Young people, while not on the dance floor, congregated in groups just past the lanterns' glow. Mothers sitting on folding chairs or quilts kept vigilant watch.

Men and older boys gathered to shoot the breeze. A bottle of whiskey passed between them and gruff laughter carried on the light wind. Occasionally one of them would walk over and mingle with the teens, letting them know they were being watched. Teens? The term wasn't used in this era. When had the term come into being? Whenever, it wasn't commonly used until the 1940s or 1950s she bet. Aunt Patty's mother said she'd been considered a child until she turned eighteen, and then she was instantly an adult.

Tad stood along with his rowing friend James, taking his turn as chaperone, she supposed. As they chatted, Tad's gaze searched and landed on her. She smiled and waved. He nodded, a hint of a smile tilted his lips. James winked and smiled broadly. Birdie laughed which caused Tad to frown at his friend's flirtation. *Humph!* What had soured Tad's disposition? She started to turn her back on the men when a woman approached Tad. It was Mrs. Jamison, the woman she'd met after the rowing race. Mrs. Jamison said something and Tad shook his head. Her reply caused people nearby to glance in their direction. Tad took her arm and led her away from the group. What was that all about?

* * *

"You're causing a scene, Lucy. I told you earlier I'd get by to talk to you."

"I got tired of waiting." Her painted mouthed formed a *moue.* "You've been here all evening when you could have left and come to my house." She reached up and stroked his cheek. "I've missed you, darling."

He grabbed her hand. "Stop it! People are watching."

"So what? You've not cared until lately." She nodded toward the women on the blanket where Birdie sat. "Does your house guest have anything to do with your neglect of me?"

"You know that's not true. We've not been seen in public as a couple. And no, Birdie has nothing to do with us. Before she arrived in Waco, I'd already decided our relationship needed to end. You've become petulant and nagging, qualities I wouldn't tolerate in a wife. Why would I put up with them from you?"

She gasped. "You don't mean it, Tad." Her chin trembled. "I've just been lonely. I can get over it. I promise I'll do better." She grasped at his sleeve. "I love you, and I know you care for me too."

Why had he ever gotten himself involved her? He knew she wanted to marry again, and she wasn't a bad woman. Yes, there had been a man or two before him, but she stayed loyal before moving on—until the man turned to someone else. He'd become bored with her lately.

"Lucy, you're a fine woman, and I do care for you, but I don't love you. It wouldn't be fair for me to monopolize your time when you could be spending it with a man who could love you."

Her eyes narrowed and she spat, "Why can't you love me? I'm not good enough for you, am I?" Her voice rose in volume. "You have to have some fine society lady to dignify your home and I'm just trash. You sure didn't think so while enjoying my company in bed."

"Lower your voice!"

"Why?" she shrieked as she waved a hand at the crowd. Many had turned to stare in their direction. "Afraid all these fine people will learn you've been spending time with me."

"That's enough, Lucy. Don't contact me again. Our friendship is over." He strode toward the dance floor.

Her angry shout followed him. "You'll be sorry, Tad Lockhart!"

He already was.

Tad stopped by James and his friend handed him a bottle of whiskey. He took a swig and enjoyed the fire as it trailed down to his belly.

"Take another," offered James.

"Nope. One is enough."

James motioned over his shoulder to where he and Lucy had talked. "Nasty business, that."

"Should have my head examined for staying in that relationship so long."

"Yep. Guess she wants to get married."

"Not exactly, but she doesn't understand why I want to end things."

"Is it Miss Braxton?"

Tad glanced to where Birdie sat on the blanket. She'd danced a lot earlier and jealousy had gnawed at his insides. "No. I'd made up my mind before she arrived that we needed to go our separate ways. She'd become demanding and frankly, I was bored."

"I know your mother wants you to get married. You about to make her a happy woman?"

"What?" Tad laughed. "What gives you that idea?"

James shrugged. "Oh, I don't know." He nodded toward Birdie. "Thought maybe you'd met someone who could hold your attention for more than a year."

Tad chuckled. "She'd sure do that, wouldn't she? Course, we might come to blows."

His friend threw back his head and guffawed. "Thought you already had." He leaned in close. "How is that nose anyway?"

Tad reached up and gingerly touched it. "A mite sore."

A commotion on the far side of the dance floor drew his gaze. It seemed a group of men were egging someone on, pushing him forward. Tad smiled. Guess they were helping him gather the courage to ask someone to dance. The cowboy finally rolled his shoulders, popped his neck, and strode forward. He cut around the side and stopped in front of Birdie. He bowed and mumbled something. Tad wished he could hear. Birdie nodded and took the outstretched hand. They strolled to the dance floor and were lost in the crowd.

Tad walked over to growl at the boys dancing attendance on his sister. Never hurt to let them know he was on the job, and they were to watch their behavior. They parted as he approached. He scowled for effect and let his gaze roam around the group. "Hey, Bethany, how about a dance with your brother?"

She beamed. "Really?"

"Of course."

She jumped up before he could help her and wrapped her arm through his. She turned to the group. "I'll be back in a minute."

They'd reached the dance floor when a scream of pain bounced back from the water. Tad's heart jumped into his throat. He dropped Bethany's arm. "Go back to Mother."

He ran, fearing Birdie was in trouble. Dancing couples stopped and moved back to the sidelines to reveal the trouble.

Birdie bent over a man lying face down in the sawdust. Knee on his spine, she had both of his arms twisted behind his back, his hands up almost over his head. Howls of pain erupted from the man as he spat out sawdust.

Birdie's voice brooked no argument. "I want an apology, mister."

CHAPTER TEN

"I'm…sor…sorry! Please…you're breaking my arms."

Birdie released his arms and stood. Moaning, the man worked to get his arms down to his side.

Detective Ethan reached Birdie before Tad did. Heart pounding in his chest, Tad watched as Ethan yanked the man up by his belt. A police officer on duty cuffed him.

"Wait a minute." The drunken cowboy groused. "I apologized to the woman."

"Shut up," barked Ethan. "We'll talk to you in a minute."

Tad slipped his arm around Birdie's waist and pulled her to his side. With his free hand, he cupped her face and tilted it up. "Are you all right? Did he hurt you?"

"Of course not. He's soused. I doubt he could have hurt me sober."

The two police officers moved them to the edge of the crowd. The band began a waltz and couples made their way to the dance floor all the time casting glances their way. Intent on the detective and his prisoner, Birdie didn't see them. Tad moved to stand behind her to prevent their scrutiny and returned his attention to the prisoner.

Detective Ethan asked, "What's your name, mister?"

"Jordan, Nathan Jordan."

He turned to Birdie. "What happened here, ma'am?"

"He got fresh."

"Fresh?" The two officers appeared perplexed. Tad was confused too. He'd never heard the expression.

"Yes, you know…" She leaned in and lowered her voice. He grabbed my butt and ground his…err…you know, against me."

Tad lunged for the man. "You son of a—"

Ethan shoved between them. "This is police business, Lockhart. Behave or leave."

Jordan snorted. "It's not like she's a prim and proper lady." He smirked. "Showed her bloomers to anyone willing to look today." He sneered at Tad. "Probably showed you a mite more than that."

Red bloomed before Tad's eyes. He fought his way to Jordan and would have made contact if Birdie hadn't thrown her arms around his chest and pushed him back.

"Stop it, Tad. He's not worth it."

"He's maligning your name."

"I don't care what he's saying, Tad."

"Well, I do." He could just hear the old biddies in town gossiping now. It wasn't fair. Birdie was unusual but she wasn't a loose woman.

She hugged him and patted his back. "Look, I'm new here and different. It will take time for me to adjust and change to fit the mores of this time. Some people won't give me a chance, but others, the ones who are important, will."

He released his pent up breath and enfolded her in his arms. How could a woman with a figure like hers take down that cowboy? Her curves molded to his body, reminding him how well she'd fit against him when they danced, a fit he'd like to explore. He swallowed a guffaw. Lord, he'd probably find himself face down in the dust. Might be worth eating a little dirt.

She stepped back and smiled up at him. "Chill."

Chill? What the heck did that mean?

At his confusion, she added, "It means relax."

"Miss Braxton, do you want to file a complaint?" asked Detective Ethan.

Tad glanced up to see the other officer escorting Jordan toward town.

"No. I think he learned his lesson."

"All right then. We're letting him spend the night in jail and think about his behavior."

"Thank you, Detective."

"No problem, Miss Braxton. Maybe you'll show me that move sometime."

"Be happy to, Lloyd."

"I'll look forward to it." He tipped his hat and walked away. Before he could escort Birdie to his mother, Joseph Hellman's wife descended on them. . He'd always liked her. She didn't mince words, especially with the society ladies she and Mother socialized with.

"Miss Braxton!" the woman chirped as she reached for Birdie's hands. "Why, it was priceless the way you handled that scoundrel. You must show me how you flipped him down."

"I'd be pleased to Mrs. Hellman." She turned to Tad. "Have you met Mr. Lockhart?"

"Of course I have. Go to church with his mama." She reached up and patted his cheek. "We've missed you, young man."

"Mrs. Hellman. It's good to see you."

"Harrumph. We'd see you more often if you'd come to church."

"Ranching keeps a man tied to his homestead, ma'am."

She arched an eyebrow and dropped her chin a notch. Surely she didn't know about Lucy. Shoot fire, the woman knew just about everything.

He coughed and prayed his face wasn't as red as it felt. If so, maybe she'd think his temper was out of sorts because of the drunken cowboy. "I promise to do better, ma'am."

"See that you do and bring Miss Braxton. She'll be like a breath of fresh air to the stuffy crowd around here." She leaned in close to Birdie. "Now, some of the townswomen will look down on you for defending yourself tonight. Don't fret over their opinions. They'll come around in time."

The band around Ted's chest loosened a little. He hoped Mrs. Hellman was right. He so wanted folks to accept, Birdie. Hopefully, she'd tame some of her behavior too. Hitting him in the nose, playing baseball like a boy. Like Ethan, he was curious to learn how she'd gotten Jordan to the ground. A grin tickled his cheek. Durn woman was something else. Whoever married her wouldn't have a dull moment in his life. The thought jolted him like a bolt of lightning and he sobered. *Let's not go there, Tad.* But, he already had. He'd even announced it to Birdie this afternoon as they'd left the ball game. Of course, she'd not heard his words, or if she had, they must not have registered, or he'd have received a wicked tongue-lashing.

"You're sweet to say so, Mrs. Hellman. I'm looking forward to our visit."

"Oh good. Let's make it next Wednesday, say ten o'clock, and stay for lunch."

*　*　*

Olivia insisted they go to church the next morning before heading home. Birdie wore one of the dresses Olivia had bought her. The style required she wear a corset, and she rang for the maid to help her with the ties and buttons up the back. The pale blue pique dress hugged her waist and had an Eton jacket with white rollback lapel and leg-o-mutton sleeves. Not that she knew all the terms but Olivia and the sales clerk had explained them in detail. Supposedly they were the height of fashion. Maybe so, but they were uncomfortably tight; the restriction would drive her nuts. Hopefully church didn't last long, and she could come out of this rig.

She twirled in front of the mirror and grinned. What would her fellow ranger, Ted Weaver say if he could see her now? Probably bust a gut laughing. This outfit was quite a change from the red dress she'd worn on the sting operation. Her heart dropped into her stomach. What were the captain and others thinking about her back at the station? Did they believe she was dead? And Aunt Patty. She had no one to console her. Oh God! She'd lose Birdie's Nest. Where would her aunt live? Tears stung her eyes and she fumbled around in her valise for one of those dang handkerchiefs Olivia insisted she carry at all times. How many more years until they started making tissues?

Birdie dabbed at her eyes and tucked the hanky in the sleeve of her dress. Tears wouldn't help a thing. She had several years until Birdie's Nest was built. Hopefully by then she could come up with a plan, one that would prevent the home from being snatched from Aunt Patty. Would she be able to raise enough money to build such a home? Never. Not unless she devised some kind of scheme to make money. She could marry a rich man. The idea gave her the shudders. No, she'd only marry for love.

Sighing, she plopped a flat straw hat decorated with a blue ribbon, some feathery plume looking thing, and a white paper flower, onto her head. Several long hatpins held the accessory in place. Most of her hair, twisted up on top of her head with a ton of pins, was hidden from view. White kid leather shoes and a frilly parasol completed the outfit. She studied her reflection in the mirror. Who was this woman? She didn't resemble the Birdie Braxton she'd known for the past thirty years. The lady in the mirror was attractive, well dressed, obviously of the upper echelon of society. Birdie had never given much thought to society rankings. Her life revolved around truth, honesty, and the law. Suddenly, everything familiar to her was gone. Along with her life as a ranger, she'd lost her family, her identity, and her heritage. Could she move on, start anew and write a new chapter in her life? Did she have a choice? No, destiny had decided for her.

From past history, Birdie knew Waco had always been a church town. The big frame church with its balcony and domed ceiling would have been impressive even in the future. What a shame the building no longer remained. Typical of the Victorian era, the woodwork was dark, polished to a beautiful sheen. They stood at the entryway for a moment, their eyes adjusting to the darkened interior. Sunlight through stained glass windows cast prisms of colors into the room. Transoms above each one allowed a slight breeze to waft in, as did the open doorway. The chatter of voices echoed through the sanctuary. Tad ushered them forward. Talk diminished considerably as they filed to a pew near the front of the church.

Birdie kept her chin up, a smile pasted on her face. Some of the younger women smiled and nodded in greeting, while several of the matrons nodded to Bethany and Olivia, but ignored Birdie completely. She wouldn't let it upset her, but worried Olivia would be distressed. From Olivia's pinched lips and narrowed eyes, she wasn't happy with her friends' behavior.

As they sat, the chatter started back up, but slowly died down when organ music filled the room and the choir marched into the loft. The pastor stepped behind the podium, raised his hands, and everyone stood.

"Please close your eyes and bow your heads while we go to the Lord in prayer." His prayer was short. Amens reverberated throughout the sanctuary.

"Welcome all. Our house is full today and we're grateful. Let us introduce our guests." He waved to someone at the back of the room. "Let's start with you, John. You and your guest stand up."

When Tad stood, bent to take her elbow, and pulled her to her feet, she almost croaked. "I'd like you to meet our house guest, Miss Birdie Braxton, a distant relative of my mother's from East Texas. I hope everyone will help her feel welcome in our community."

The pastor's smile beamed across the space to her. Its warmth touched her physically. "Yes, indeed, welcome Miss Braxton. I hear you successfully defended your honor last night when that cowboy acted inappropriately."

Gasps and titters could be heard around the sanctuary along with guffaws from some of the men. Okay, hear it comes. I'll be the pariah of Waco and run out of town on a rail.

"I congratulate you." He glanced down at his congregation. "More women in this community need to know how to defend themselves. You'd all do well to take heed of Miss Braxton's example."

A few of the younger women clapped while nodding at her. The mouths of some of the older ladies dropped open and then snapped shut as they rolled their eyes, and dipped their heads to converse with each other. Birdie could just imagine what they were saying.

Wow! The preacher actually paid her a compliment. Most likely the old biddies in the congregation thought him too young to be giving *them* advice and would be bending his ear before the day was over. She suspected him to be in his early thirties. Birdie sat, unable to grasp that he'd actually condoned what she'd done.

Tad put an arm around her shoulder and squeezed. He whispered, "It's all going to work out. You'll see."

Yeah, she'd see when those snooty old women didn't

shoot daggers every time they peered at her. How they were able to huff up like they did in these tight corsets, she didn't know. She couldn't wait to get to the hotel and get out of hers.

When the service was over, several younger couples greeted them. Three of Olivia's friends approached. Mrs. Smith, wife of one of the bankers in town, Birdie had met last night. She'd not been particularly friendly. She nodded to Birdie and grasped Tad's arm. "Lauren and some of her friends are having a lawn party next Saturday evening, Tad. They'd love to have you join them." She simpered. That's the only way Birdie could describe the woman's actions. "You're still considered one of Waco's most eligible bachelors, you know."

Tad covered the woman's hand with one of his. "Now, Mrs. Smith, you know I'm not much into parties."

"Oh, please come."

"Well, let me think about it." He glanced at Birdie. "May I bring a guest?"

Her smile wilted. "A guest?"

"Yes. We do have Miss Braxton living with us, and I'm sure she'd enjoy getting away from the ranch. Bethany also."

Birdie almost choked at the woman's expression. The paper fan she used to combat the heat fluttered like it was motor powered. She took pity on her and said, "Oh, no, Tad. You and Bethany go. I'll keep your mother company." She had no desire to visit where she wasn't welcome.

"You'll do no such thing," said Olivia. "I am plenty capable of entertaining myself. You young people go and have a good time." She patted the woman's hand, expression sweet. "How kind of you and Lauren to include Tad, Bethany and Birdie."

Mouth pinched in a firm line, Lucinda opened her mouth, and took a deep breath. Her smile didn't reach her eyes. "Well, of course, Olivia. We'd be pleased to have them attend."

"We'll let you know, Mrs. Smith." He smiled at the lady before turning away. "Mother, Birdie, do you see Bethany? I want to get home as soon as possible."

Birdie spotted Bethany with a group of her friends. "I'll get her. Y'all go ahead to the carriage and we'll meet you there." She hustled away but turned back to see if the Lockharts escaped the woman's clutches. Birdie had no desire to party with a bunch of young people. She giggled. Bet Tad felt the same way. It didn't take a rocket scientist to know he'd not be attending.

* * *

Birdie rode down Jefferson until she reached Eighth Street. The Hellman's white two-story frame home sat back from the street. Trees and shrubs dotted the yard and blooming roses lined the front porch. A mid-sized home, it was inviting.

Mattie charged through the front door before Birdie ever dismounted. "Ride on around to the back. We've got a barn where your horse can rest while we visit."

An older black man dressed in overalls waited for her. Tipping his weather beaten felt hat, he smiled. "Name's Nehemiah, miss. I'll take care of your horse. Miss Mattie says for you to go in the back door."

She slid off the mare and handed him the reins. "Thank you, Nehemiah. Molly would appreciate a little water, but no food. Tad says she eats too much."

He grinned and noted Molly's rounded body. "Yes, ma'am."

Birdie opened the screen door, stepped into a screened porch with several beds. She'd heard about sleeping porches but never seen one. The coolest ones would have been on the second floor, but the Hellman's home didn't have a balcony. She stepped across the neatly painted gray batten boards and into the kitchen where a woman dressed in gingham stood kneading dough on the counter of a cupboard.

"Hello."

The woman jumped, dropping the wad of dough on the board in the process. A cloud of flour flew up several inches. She slapped her hand to her heart leaving a white handprint on her checked apron and drew in a deep breath. "Laws a-mercy, miss, you startled me."

"I'm sorry, ma'am. I'm Birdie Braxton. I'm here to see Mrs. Hellman."

"She's right excited about your visit." She yelled into the other room. "She's here, Miss Mattie."

"Come on out here, Birdie. Show her the way, Sadie."

Sadie waved a flour-covered hand toward to door on the right side. "Down the hall and to the right. She be in the parlor."

"Thank you, Sadie."

"Yes, miss."

Birdie walked down a long, wide hallway with beautiful polished oak floors and turned right into the parlor. Mattie sat on a stuffed horsehair sofa with needlepoint pillows at each end. She waved to a matching chair beside the sofa. "Have a seat, Birdie. Do you mind if I call you, Birdie?"

"I'd prefer it."

"Good. And please call me Mattie." She handed Birdie a cup filled with hot coffee. "I hope I guessed right, thinking you'd prefer coffee over tea."

"You did. It sounds heavenly right now." She was used to drinking coffee all day long while at the office—a habit she missed.

"Cream or sugar?"

"No, just black."

Mattie handed her a plate with a variety of cookies. "Thin as you are, I suspect you can eat a few of these without worrying about your figure. The teacakes are an old secret family recipe." She leaned in. "But, being's I like you so much, I might share with you."

Birdie choked on a bite and swallowed a gulp of coffee to clear her throat. "Well, I have to admit, Mattie, I'm not much of a cook."

"That'll change. When you marry Tad Lockhart, you'll be in the kitchen whipping up all sorts of goodies for the man." She chuckled. "Happened to me and I expect it will happen to you too."

"Now, Mattie, Tad and I are not getting married. I don't know where you got that idea." Face suffused with color, Birdie prayed no one else thought the same thing.

"Say whatever you want, but I saw him last night. The man's only got eyes for you." She shook her finger. "And I don't think you're immune to him either."

"Please, let's talk about something else. I don't intend to get married. I need to find a way to make a living. I don't want to impose on the Lockharts forever. They've been very kind, but I need to make my own way."

Birdie tried to remain still under the older woman's scrutiny. Mattie studied her for several minutes while munching on a cookie. Birdie busied herself drinking coffee and looked around the room, everywhere except at Mattie.

Finally she spoke. "There's more to this story than you're telling, right?"

"Yes."

"Are you a distant relative of Olivia?"

"No."

"Did you rob a bank, kill someone, or are you running away from a husband?"

"Mattie! No!" Birdie couldn't keep from laughing so hard tears sprang to her eyes. Mattie joined in and soon they were wiping their faces with napkins.

"Okay then. Didn't think so." She leaned in and patted Birdie's hand. "When you get ready to tell me, you will. I won't pressure you." She narrowed her eyes. "And if you ever need me, I'm here."

A sob caught in Birdie's throat, and she croaked. "Thank you, Mattie."

Mattie slapped her on the knee. "You said you needed a way to make money and get out on your own. I think I have an excellent idea on how you can do that."

Birdie couldn't imagine, but she was willing to hear what the older woman had to say. She's certainly not come up with any brilliant ideas on her own.

A smile stretched Mattie's face. "You're going to open a self-defense school for women, and I'm going to be your partner."

CHAPTER ELEVEN

Tad struggled to remain calm. "I still don't think this is a good idea, Birdie."

"But, it is, Tad. I'll be making more money and soon be able to get my own place in town." Dressed in her riding skirt with a bundle of clothes tied behind the saddle, her smile sent his heart skittering. The comment about moving out didn't calm his emotions either.

"Women don't have any business living alone."

He tried to school his features, erase the line he knew furrowed his brow. "We've been over this before. Decent women live with their families." Heck, he knew that wasn't exactly true. Some lived in boarding houses and the schoolteacher had her own house, but Birdie was different. He didn't want her off associating with all and sundry—men in particular. She didn't seem to be a good judge of character if accepting that drunken cowboy's offer for a dance was an example.

She huffed up and Tad anticipated another blow to his nose or his belly, but she just turned her back and checked the girth on Molly. Her riding skills had improved since being with them. It was good to see she was careful. He liked the way she tended to the horse and tack. No worries there. The rifle she'd purchased from Mr. Hellman rested securely in its scabbard, and he suspected her little Colt was hidden somewhere on her person.

He squeezed her shoulder. "Why is it so important to move out of our home? Aren't you happy here?"

She whirled, her eyes wide with surprise. "Of course I

am. I've grown to love your family, but I'm not used to living on charity."

"Charity? You work for every bite of food you eat and the bed you sleep in. We like having you here, Birdie." He liked it a bit too much. Seeing her every morning and evening was becoming the highlight of his day, one he'd miss if she moved. "Why is making money so important to you? Isn't what you make here enough?"

"I don't think I've told you about the home I grew up in, the one on the Brazos River, have I?"

"No, you haven't." He suspected he was about to be exposed to more talk of the future. Why couldn't her memory return with a past he could accept, not more outlandish tales. He cleared his throat to cover his discomfort. "Detective Ethan briefly mentioned it, though."

She took his hand and led him to a bale of hay. "Let's sit a minute and I'll tell you about it." As she described Birdie's Nest, her expression fluctuated between joy and worry. "I must get it built by the end of 1892 and during my lifetime find a way to fund its total upkeep." She chewed her bottom lip. "Or at least develop a plan to keep it intact as long as there is a Braxton to inherit. If I don't, my Aunt Patty will be without a place to live."

Tad wasn't convinced Birdie was from the future, but he could understand her concern for her aunt and her desire to preserve her heritage. Thing was, if she was from the future, she didn't have a legacy, she had to build one. The entire situation was darn confusing to him, but he wouldn't cast shadows on her desires. Maybe in time she'd see things differently.

"Perhaps if you marry, your husband will build you a home on the river."

She snorted. "Not likely. Plus, I'm not in love with anyone, and no one has come calling either."

That was true, but no doubt if she put her mind to it, she'd have suitors galore. She'd have to change her ways though. Men didn't like to think their women didn't need them. She stared outside the barn, eyes on a far target, deep in thought.

"Perhaps if you give up this idea of a self-defense

school and other manly pursuits, they would." Did he want men hanging around, mooning over Birdie? The idea didn't set well with him at all. Not that he intended to court her because he didn't, did he? At the July 4th picnic, he'd been determined to lay claim to her, but that wasn't fair. It'd be a number of years before he took a wife. Being tied down just didn't sit well with him.

"I'll not be something I'm not, Tad, just to find a husband. Especially one I don't want."

He swallowed his grin and breathed a sigh of relief. "You're a nice looking woman, Birdie. Many men in these parts would be honored to have you for a wife."

"Well, they can just be honored with someone else." She sat quietly, picking hay from the bale and tossing it on the ground. "How much do you think it would cost to buy land on the river and build a house like I described?"

"Oh, I expect around ten to twelve thousand dollars." Property along the river was prime and it didn't come cheap.

Her shoulders slumped; her face lost its determined pose. Chewing her bottom lip, she managed to say, "I'll never be able to make that much money…not giving self-defense lesson, anyway."

Tad reached over and rubbed her shoulders. He resisted the urge to allow his fingers to reach up and wrap one of those multi-colored curls around his knuckle, to feel its softness. "It will all work out, Birdie. Now perk up. You're not one to give up easily."

She looked up at him, and he noticed moisture sparkled in her blue eyes. He groaned and pulled her head to his chest. This woman was quickly becoming too important to him. Birdie melted into his embrace, and he breathed in her scent— a scent all her own—soap and water with a hint of lilac. He wrapped both arms around her and patted her back. "Don't cry, now." The desire to take care of her, kiss away her woes, welled up inside him. Bethany often cried on his shoulder and he'd protect her with his life, but this was different. If he could cushion this woman from the world and its hurts, he would. Hell, it was more than that. He wanted this woman— period—not just sexually, but in his life permanently.

She jerked back and wiped at her face. "I'm not crying."

109

She stood up and dusted off the seat of her riding skirt. "You're right. I'll find a way. I'll find a way." She shuddered. "If worse comes to worst, I'll marry some old rich man and get him to build it."

Tad bridled. Over my dead body.

*   *   *

September in Waco in the future could be hot as July and August, but the relief of air-conditioning made the high temperatures bearable. Here in 1890, the heat was downright oppressive and respite was next to impossible to find. Some places had electric fans, but they were few and far between. Plus, the layers of clothing offered little relief. Long skirts, long-sleeved blouses, and petticoats didn't allow air to circulate.

She now had twenty students. They met in a small unoccupied warehouse on Mary Street. Mattie had rented the space because of its large doors and high windows, which could be opened for ventilation. When people gathered to watch, they'd close the doors and relied on the windows for airflow.

Sweat dripped down Birdie's brow as she worked out with her intermediate class.

"Why is this necessary again, Birdie?" The small blonde cocked a hip and continued. "I'm afraid I'm going to look like a man."

"With your figure, Dolly, I don't think you have anything to worry about. Plus, these exercises, if you keep up with them, will keep you from developing flabby arms when you get older." Birdie raised her arm and pointed.

"Flabby arms? Who's going to see those anyway?"

"Your husband."

Dolly blushed scarlet and giggled. "Oh."

The married women laughed and Dolly's group twittered, the sound very similar to the chatter of hens in a chicken coop. Oddly enough, Birdie now knew what the sound was like. She'd been to the hen house with Maybelle to collect eggs on occasion.

"And," said Birdie, "You might want to wear an evening gown with very short sleeves."

Nods and expressions of agreement filtered throughout the ladies.

Birdie held up a hand and they quieted. "The most important thing is you'll surprise your attacker with your strength. If you're ever attacked, which I pray never happens, the person will realize that, though you're a woman, you're not weak and helpless. That little surprise will give you an advantage."

She picked up her bags. "Now, another round of ten lifts each arm." Groans and laughs echoed around the room as they heaved the ten-pound bags to shoulder height. The ladies had started with bricks and had progressed to bags filled with rocks.

After lifting weights, Birdie checked their walking journals.

Julie, a young redhead announced. "It's hard to walk fast wearing a corset and my mama won't let me leave the house without one."

This had been one of Birdie's stiffest hurdles. "I think we need to have a meeting with the mothers of all you single young ladies. Maybe I can express to them how important your exercise is and perhaps convince them of the advantages of being able to breathe during exercises." At their classes, they loosened their corsets giving them a little more freedom.

"Who'll organize a tea for us?"

"Oh, let me, Birdie," said Julie. "Mama will be thrilled to have you visit."

"Wonderful. Do you think Thursday morning be agreeable with your mother?"

"I believe so." Face radiant, she clapped her hands and twirled to face the others. "This will be so much fun." She turned back to Birdie. "But I don't think we should exclude the married ladies."

Birdie smacked her forehead. "What am I thinking? Of course not, everyone is invited. If your mother doesn't mind, we'll all meet, say at 10:00." To Birdie's thinking, it would at least be cooler then. Of course, this was Texas and they might have a cold front blow in. Wouldn't that be wonderful?

"Let's be sure everyone has your address."

"Oh that's not necessary. Mama will send out invitations."

Okay, thought Birdie. Shows how much I know about throwing a tea party in 1890. "Wonderful, but if for some reason your mother isn't up to this, get a message to Mrs. Hellman and she'll let me know."

The following morning, a man on horseback delivered Birdie's invitation to tea from Mrs. Wallace, Julie's mother. Olivia and Bethany received one also. Thrilled to have been included in the outing, Bethany rushed to her room to decide what she'd wear.

On Thursday, Birdie strode up the stairs and studied the new corset lying on her bed. She shuddered at the thought of being tied up in the torture device. Olivia insisted Birdie buy a new one as her old one was out of style. This one was shorter but it appeared the lacing could be pulled even tighter.

Birdie stripped and slipped the Moreno vest over her head. Whoever heard of wearing wool in Texas? Supposedly it kept the contraption from rubbing the skin, and it absorbed moisture. She snorted. Just like wool socks absorbed the sweat in boots and tennis shoes.

She'd just stepped into her petticoats when Olivia tapped on the door. "You ready for me to lace you up?"

"As ready as I'll ever be."

Olivia slipped into the room and picked up the new corset. According to the older woman it was the latest fashion. "All right dear, first let's get you laced into this bust supporter." Birdie guessed it was as close to a bra as she'd get for now. Made of the same fabric as the corset, it had boning on each side.

"Now, I can't wait to see what the corset does for your figure."

"What's wrong with my figure?"

"Not a thing dear, but this will help hide some of those assets." She pursed her lips at Birdie. "You know ladies do not draw attention to their anatomy."

You could've fooled her. What did women go to all this trouble for then? But then, it was the Victorian era and people had funny ideas about their bodies and their sexuality. "You know Birdie, most girls strive to have their waist measurement equal their age. And for the most part, want to marry before they turn twenty-one."

"Since I'm thirty-three, I don't need to be laced as tightly as those girls."

"That's not the way it works at your age. You want to remove as many inches as you can."

Birdie pulled air into her lungs and tried to hold it while Olivia tugged the straps of the corset. Olivia pinched Birdie's underarm.

She jerked her arm up. "Ouch! What was that for?"

"So you'd breathe, my dear." Olivia yanked again. "All right then, I'm finished." She reached for the tape measure on the dresser and ran it around Birdie's waist. "Excellent— twenty-three inches."

Birdie was glad the older woman was happy. Hopefully she wouldn't have to gasp between words when she talked. She slipped the camisole over her head, and then the rose colored dress she'd purchased for the occasion. She didn't realize it was possible to wear so many clothes at one time. Olivia buttoned it up and then stood back. She twirled her finger in the air, and Birdie slowly turned around. The sleeves puffed out from the shoulders, the waist formed a V ending just below the waistline, and the skirt had an A-line shape.

"Perfect, absolutely perfect!" She motioned to the stool before the vanity and Birdie sat down. The woman was in her element. She lifted the matching hat from its box. "Now, let's set it at a slight angle like this." Just like Aunt Patty, Olivia used three hatpins to hold it in place. The memory of that day, when her life had been simple, brought tears to Birdie's eyes. *Please Lord, I pray Aunt Patty is okay.*

Olivia squeezed Birdie's shoulder. "Lovely, my dear. The color is perfect for you and the hat isn't too fussy, is it?"

At least it only had one flower and no plumes. She shook her head and brushed away the tears. No need to upset Olivia. "It's perfect, just the right size."

The older woman beamed. "Wonderful. Now, give me about fifteen minutes, and I'll join you and Bethany downstairs in the parlor. Tad has agreed to drop us off and take care of some business while in town."

Birdie picked up her parasol and little handbag as she exited the room. The small heels on her shoes were quiet against the carpeted treads of the stairs as she descended, the swish of her skirts the only noise. Tad sat in the parlor in a comfortable chair reading a newspaper. He glanced up when she walked in and leapt to his feet.

"Birdie!"

"I'm sorry if I disturbed you. Go back to reading your paper."

He crossed the room and took her hand. "You are lovely."

She wanted to chastise him for foolish flattery, but the heat in his eyes indicated he meant his words. "Well, thank you. It's the clothes. But, I must say, I'm terribly uncomfortable. Not to mention, if I keep spending money on clothes I won't be able to buy the land I want."

Tad led her over to the sofa. "Sit down." He cleared his throat and perched on the other end. "I'd like to talk to you about something." She noticed he still held her hand and moved to pull it back, but he covered it with his other hand.

"Sure, what is it?"

"I'm going to court you, Birdie... until you say you'll marry me."

CHAPTER TWELVE

Her mouth fell open, and then she snapped it shut. She frowned and yanked her hands from beneath his. "No, you're not!"

"Why not?"

"Why would you want to court me? I'm not marriage material, not at all like the ladies you're used to."

He'd tried to talk himself out of being interested in her. In truth, he wasn't looking forward to settling down, but if he waited too long someone else would snatch her up. "Why would I not? You're beautiful." He touched her knee. "By the way, I love this color on you. Plus, I like the fact that you're not slapping my face for putting my hand on your knee."

"So, you think I'm a loose woman." She drew herself up and shot him a steely glare.

He jerked his hand back. "No, not at all, and I meant no disrespect. It's just that I admire you, enjoy being with you, and I don't think you could ever bore me."

She looked down at her dress and the parasol across her lap. "Don't you see, I'm just playing a part here in this time period. This is not me."

"I don't care. I like you just as well in those dungarees I see you wearing when you run in the mornings."

A grin tilted the corner of her mouth. "Really?"

"Yes, really. Now, it does kind of rankle me that you can probably outshoot me."

She chuckled and tapped him on the knee with her umbrella. "It does not. I don't see you as a man needing a weak woman to reinforce his masculinity."

Her comment was just another reason why she interested him. Maybe he'd been born in the wrong era. He might have fit just fine in hers.

"What about love? You don't love me. I admit I admire you, Tad, but I'm not in love with you."

Well shoot, that hurt, but it was honest. He couldn't say he loved her, either.

"As we get to know each other better, hopefully love will come." He winked. "Without a doubt, I'm attracted to you. Have been since the first time I saw you."

"To be honest, I find you attractive too."

His heart leaped. This was going better than he thought. He leaned in closer and slipped a hand behind her head. "Let's see if there is a physical spark between us."

Almost nose-to-nose, they studied each other for a moment. He closed his eyes and breathed in the hint of lilac that blended with her fresh scent. Her lips touched his and sampled. Unprepared for the contact, he jerked back. Those delicious lips twitched and he swooped in to claim them, softly at first. His hunger grew and he explored and deepened the kiss. When her hand clasped the back of his head, he knew the sparks were there, an inferno hiding beneath.

"Ahem…sorry to interrupt, but we must be on our way."

They jerked apart to see his mother and Bethany at the doorway. Bethany's eyes were round in surprise. He could tell his mother wanted to clap in delight, but she restrained herself and cheerfully called, "Come along, children."

* * *

Olivia insisted Birdie sit up front with Tad while she and Bethany sat in the back. No doubt about it, the woman was matchmaking. As they left the yard, she tapped Birdie on the shoulder. "Keep your parasol up, dear. You don't want to get sunburned."

"Yes, ma'am." Birdie flipped it open and positioned it over the hat.

Tad chuckled. Voice low, he leaned toward her. "I can imagine what's going on in Mother's mind right now. She's probably planning the wedding."

She hissed, "Hush! You better set her straight. A kiss does not mean we're courting and it certainly doesn't mean we're getting married."

"I didn't ask you to marry me." He grinned. "I said I intended to court and marry you."

Heat rose in her face. "Thank you for correcting me on your intentions."

He sobered. "I thought you enjoyed our kiss."

"I did. Very much, but it wasn't a commitment." She glanced sideways and added. "It won't be happening again."

Olivia called from the back. "What are you two whispering about up there?"

"Nothing in particular, Mother. Just passing the time."

Tad pulled the buggy up in front of a beautiful Grecian style home and helped them down. "How long before I should be back to pick you up?"

Birdie turned to Olivia. "I'd say an hour and a half would be about right, don't you think, Olivia?"

"Yes, I do." She took Birdie's arm. "Come along, dear." Bethany was left to follow them up the stone walkway.

Julie met them at the door and made the introductions. Mrs. Wallace was a broader version of her daughter and sported the same red hair, toned down with a few strands of gray.

"Olivia, it's so nice to see you again." She turned to Birdie. "Miss Braxton, I'm anxious to hear what you have to share with us today."

"Please, call me Birdie. Thank you for inviting us into your home for this meeting. I know there will be many questions which I hope to answer to everyone's satisfaction."

"Yes, well, refreshments first." She took Olivia's arm and led her to the dining room. Birdie followed.

A long table covered in a white lace cloth bore a variety of sweets and tea sandwiches. Birdie had attended enough social events with Aunt Patty to know how to conduct herself. She'd been told the knowledge would come in handy one day. Who knew it'd be in 1890?

She carried her plate with one finger sandwich, one cookie, and a cup of tea into the parlor. Being careful to not spill anything, she eased into one of the chairs and laid her napkin across her knees. Most of the women knew each other and chatted in small groups. Though they glanced her way and smiled, no one engaged her in idle chitchat. Maybe they weren't comfortable with her yet.

Birdie glanced around for Bethany. She'd found several friends and the girls sat

outside on the patio. French doors opened off the parlor allowing guests to spill outside if necessary.

No sooner had she finished with the snack when a maid appeared. "May I get you something else, miss?"

"No, but thank you."

"Let me take those for you then."

Mrs. Wallace stood. Slowly the chatter died away. "Ladies, I believe it's time for Miss Braxton to speak." She held a hand out and Birdie joined her. "Birdie, I believe if you stand here behind this chair, everyone can see you."

Birdie took her place and looked out at the expectant faces. The girls smiled; their mamas did not. Hopefully, what she had to say would soften the expression on their faces. She nodded to their hostess. "Thank you, Mrs. Wallace, for opening your home to us for the occasion and for the delicious refreshments." Birdie joined the ladies in a round of applause. Mrs. Wallace nodded graciously.

"I understand that image and decorum in dress is very important to you ladies. You want your daughters to remain in good standing in the community and not be shunned for improper behavior or manner of dress." Heads bobbed in agreement. "I know it was hard for some of you to allow your girls to attend my classes, afraid they'd become boyish in behavior. I hope your fears have been put to rest in that department." A few yeses and nods reassured Birdie and she continued. "As you know, the heart is a muscle that pumps blood to the lungs to obtain oxygen and then that blood travels to all parts of the body giving cells fuel. For the heart to operate properly during exercise, the lungs need to be able to fully expand and supply oxygen to cells."

She placed her hands on her abdomen and drew in as deep a breath as she could, and exhaled. "As you see, wearing this corset, I can't fully fill my lungs. If I tried to exercise in this I'd become fatigued quickly, maybe even feel faint. I want your daughters to be strong. To become so, they need exercise. Brisk walking exercises the heart and the lungs as well as toning the legs, abdomen." She patted her butt, or tried to through the many layers of petticoats and skirt. "And other parts of the anatomy." Twitters and laughter rang through the room.

"I'm asking that you allow your daughters to take their brisk walks without wearing a corset. If they need support, bust supporters will help, or I know some of you ladies can create something that would work. And girls, perhaps to appease your mothers you could wear a shirt of some kind, like a smock, that covers your torso."

Julie raised her hand. "But it's so hot out. That's just one more layer to wear."

"Yes, but it will be more comfortable than the corset. And, if you get up early, it will be much cooler."

Mrs. White stood. Birdie had seen her drop Dolly off for class. "I want to know where they can walk safely. It's unseemly for them to walk briskly down the public streets."

"An excellent point, ma'am. I think we need a committee, one that can find a place where the girls can walk without being stared at and are safe. Who would like to chair such a group?"

"I will." Mrs. White raised her hand.

"Excellent. Choose a couple of ladies who'd like to help you." Another thought entered Birdie's mind. "I just want to mention that bicycling is also excellent exercise and is becoming more popular with both men and ladies."

A groan echoed through the room. Birdie bit her cheek to keep from grinning. From their comments, the mamas didn't want to see their daughters on the contraptions.

"I must add, ladies, the bicycling outfits would be perfect for walking." The volume of chatter rose. She held up a hand and the talk gradually ceased. "One last thing before we adjourn. I've explained my reasons behind the change in garments, but these young ladies are your daughters, and you must make the final decision as to what changes you're willing to adopt."

She narrowed her eyes and glanced down at the younger set. "And girls, I ask that you respect your mother's decision."

* * *

119

Tad grinned as Birdie charged from the Wallace home like her tail was on fire. She hopped into the buggy before he could help her up. Mother and Bethany exited at a slower rate, chatting with friends as they walked toward him. "Tough morning?"

"It wasn't bad, but I'm not accustomed to chit-chat, especially in this blasted corset."

"But…but it makes your figure so womanly." Good grief, what was he doing talking about her figure, especially to her. Mother would have his hide.

She shot him an irritated glance. "You wouldn't think so if you had to be rigged up in this torture device."

He couldn't agree more and had never understood why women felt the need to cinch themselves in so. When he touched a woman's waist, he'd much rather feel soft curves than stiff whalebone. "You're right, of course. Fortunately for us men, the fashions aren't terribly uncomfortable."

His mother stopped in front of the buggy, her expression one of surprise as she looked over their new transportation. "Where did you get this?"

"I traded our buggy for the surrey, Mother. We could use the extra room and we'll all be protected from the sun."

"Yes, I can see that." She looked up noting the canopy. "Wise choice, son. I'm glad you selected a plain black one. I don't think I'd want to be seen around town in one with that awful fringe hanging from the top."

"It's called an undercut. We can fold the top back on cool days." He gripped her elbow. "Let's get you in and see how it rides. The suspension is nice and smooth."

A man walked out the front door and called, "Tad, hold up a minute."

Jim Wallace wasn't a large man, but Tad knew his build was athletic. He prided himself on staying fit even though his job kept him in the office most of the day. Today his suit was impeccable as usual and expensive. The man did like to dress in the latest styles. His dark auburn hair, combed to perfection, was beginning to gray. "Hello, Jim. I'm surprised to see you home at this hour."

"I couldn't resist getting home to meet Miss Braxton. I've heard so much about her from Julie the last few weeks.

Jim tipped his hat to Bethany and took Olivia's hand. "It's good to see you again, Olivia. I see that Bethany is growing into a beautiful young lady. She looks more like her mother every day." Bethany blushed and ducked her head. Jim knew how to charm the ladies.

"Hold the flattery, Jim." His mother tapped his arm. "I've known you enough years to be immune to your charm."

"Ah, madam, you wound me."

Mother snorted.

"I'd be happy to introduce you, Jim." Jim released Mother's hand and turned to Birdie, a beaming smile stretching his face. "Jim, this is our guest and distant relative, Miss Birdie Braxton."

Jim nodded and tipped his hat. "It's a pleasure to meet you, young woman. I think you're doing a fine thing by teaching our young ladies how to defend themselves." He wagged a finger. "Just don't put too many ideas in their heads—don't want them starting a baseball team or anything like that." He guffawed and Birdie's face reddened. Tad hid his chuckle. Jim better watch out or he'd end up with a bloody nose.

Birdie raised her chin. "I assure you, Mr. Wallace, that hadn't entered my mind." She tapped her chin and smiled. "But you know, your idea has merit."

"Ah now, you're teasing me, aren't you?"

"Of course, Mr. Wallace. It was a pleasure to meet you."

"We better be going, Jim." Tad shook the man's hand.

He tipped his hat at the ladies, turned, and walked up to the porch.

Tad helped his mother into the back seat and Bethany in beside her. "Birdie, you left in such a hurry some of the ladies didn't get to say goodbye." Mother leaned forward patted Birdie on the shoulder. "You were wonderful dear. I think you won them all over."

"Yes, Birdie," Bethany piped up as she sank into the back seat. "I think Mother is going to let me take a class."

"Not now, Bethany. We'll discuss it later."

Tad flicked the reins and the horse eased out into the street and then into a gentle trot.

"I apologize, Olivia, for rushing out." Birdie's shoulders sagged and he resisted the urge to embrace her. "I'm not comfortable in these unusual clothes and want to get home and change."

"But you look lovely, doesn't she Tad."

"Yes, indeed, Mother. The rose is a very becoming color on her." Birdie shot him a glare and he swallowed his chuckle. He did enjoy teasing this woman. "But, I do understand she's not used to the fashions of this time. Just imagine if you went forward to her time."

"Oh, land o' Goshen! From her descriptions, I'd probably die of embarrassment."

Birdie tossed her head back and laughed. Her delight brought a smile to his face. "Yes, Olivia, I can see you attending a tea in a turquoise sleeveless dress with a bolero jacket trimmed in white." She'd turned in the seat giving him a clear view of her face. Relaxed and animated, she continued. "And you, Bethany, you'd be wearing a sundress with a skirt above your knees. Your shoulders would be bare to show off your beautiful tan."

Bethany giggled, but Mother gasped. "Say it isn't so!"

"It's true. And Bethany would be wearing strappy sandals. If you were older they'd have four inch heels."

"Thank God we're not living in your time," piped Olivia.

He turned to see his mother vigorously fanning herself. "I think it'd be fun, Mother." Tad had no doubt his sister wouldn't have much problem adapting. He'd seen her in those blasted dungarees more than once.

Birdie's radiance dimmed. "Perhaps for a few days, Bethany. And then you'd begin to miss your former way of life and all you hold dear."

She really believes she's from the future. How could it be possible? Yes, strange things did happen in the world, phenomena that were difficult to explain. But time travel? No, he couldn't see it. "I'm sorry, Birdie. I know you must miss your home, your family, and friends."

She nodded. "Yes, especially when no one believes me."

"We need proof, Birdie."

"I know. I've been thinking lately, trying to remember historical events that will take place this year. The only thing that comes to mind is the Massacre at Wounded Knee in late December."

CHAPTER THIRTEEN

Tad's gaze pierced hers. He didn't believe her but that was okay. He would when it happened. "Who was slaughtered? Settlers?"

"No. We, our soldiers, butchered approximately 300 Lakota Sioux—women, men, and children."

Olivia gasped. "But why?"

"The government continued to take their land and the Lakota were forced on to reservations. Bison herds diminished and the people were starving. The U.S. Government failed to keep its promise to provide food, clothing, and housing. Plus, they'd promised to protect reservation lands from further infiltration by settlers and they didn't. Unrest grew."

Tad bristled. "I think you have the story wrong. Our government would not sign a treaty then fail to follow through."

"Are you kidding? They've done it before now. Maybe you haven't heard of those times, but I have. We stole this land from the Native Americans."

He snorted. "We did not. They're still here."

"Yeah, on reservations, starving to death. Some are being transported to other states—away from their homelands. How would you feel if someone came in and tried to take your home and your land?"

"I'd fight to the death."

"Exactly." Olivia and Bethany hadn't interrupted. A sniff came from the back seat. Birdie hadn't meant to make anyone cry. She turned back to Olivia. "I'm sorry if I upset you, but it's the truth."

"Surely the Indians provoked the soldiers in some way." It was hard for Tad to accept his people had been less than honorable. As a child in history class, she'd not wanted to believe it either, but it was true. She may not have all the facts correct but the outcome was the same.

She sighed. "Troops surrounded the compound. Some went in to disarm the Lakota. One blind man refused to give up his rifle. In the struggle, a shot was fired. The army opened fire, the Lakota fired back, and the rest is, well, to me, history.. The Calvary regiment was supported by four Hotchkiss guns and twenty-five of their own men were believed to have died from friendly fire."

"Dear, God, that is terrible," said Olivia. "I pray you're wrong."

Tad sat rigid beside her, his face a mask of anger. "You side with the Indians?"

"I side with what is right."

* * *

Birdie breathed in the fresh November air. She tied Molly to a hitching post within easy reach of the water trough and loosened the girth of the saddle.

Mattie met her at the door of the warehouse. "The new group will be here shortly."

"Sorry I'm late. Had to wait for livestock to cross the bridge."

"Pshaw! We've got plenty of time."

"Actually, Mattie, I think you could teach this class without me."

She flushed scarlet. "No, I don't think so. I'd forget something."

"No, you wouldn't. Think about it. We could possibly have twice as many students."

The class went without a hitch. A few of the students were lazy and would probably drop out after the second class meeting.

In December, the weather turned cold and she and Mattie canceled classes until after the New Year. 1891 was fast approaching and Birdie was no closer to getting her home built. The fact lay heavy on her heart. Her mood matched the bleakness of the winter landscape.

The Lockharts believed in celebrating Christmas to the hilt. On Christmas Eve, Tad and two of the hands erected a huge tree in a corner of the parlor. Olivia sent Tad to the attic for boxes of ornaments—blown glass all the rage and expensive in the future—and small candle holders that clipped to the tree. They sat around the fireplace to stay warm, and while Tad popped corn, the women strung it for a garland.

"Tad, you're eating more corn than you're putting in the bowl for stringing."

He grinned up at his mother. "But, it's good. I'll just pop more."

"We'll be here all night and I'd like to get a little sleep before all the festivities tomorrow," Olivia quipped.

Birdie had to admit it was lovely with the small candles and nothing but coal oil lamps to light the room.

Tad glanced at the tree. "You know, in a few years we'll have a string of electric lights for the tree. Won't that be something?"

Bethany squealed. "Yes, but we'll need two strings because the more lights the better."

"I hate to disappoint you guys, but in some rural areas of Waco, electricity wasn't available until the 1940s and 50s." Birdie shrugged. "Of course, some areas got it much earlier, but I wouldn't count on it for at least ten to twenty years at least."

"Really?" Tad's brow furrowed. "That seems like an awfully long time."

As is often common in Texas, Christmas Day was warm, in the high 70s. Maybelle and Olivia had spent days preparing pies, cakes, and candy for the festivities. It was their custom to invite all the ranch hands and their families for Christmas dinner. Since the weather was nice, tables were set up outside. Birdie couldn't remember having a more memorable day, yet her heart ached for Aunt Patty, and she prayed the older woman was managing somehow. During the singing of carols, she couldn't stop the flow of tears that ran down her face.

Tad appeared at her side, slipped an arm around her

waist, and she dropped her head to his chest. He whispered against her hair. "It's going to be all right, Birdie."

She sniffed, raised her head, and nodded.

On December 29, 1890, Birdie rode into town with Tad and Bethany to do a little shopping. The air was crisp and whipped color into their cheeks as they galloped along the dirt road. When they reached Austin Avenue, Birdie noticed newspaper boys on the street corners hawking papers. One shouted, "Read all about it. Massacre at Wounded Knee."

They stopped in front of the bakery and tied their horses to the hitching post. Tad turned to her and Bethany. "Y'all go inside and get a table. I'll get a paper and join you."

Inside, while drinking coffee and hot chocolate, they hovered around the paper and read the details of the battle. Tad leaned back in his chair, his mouth pinched and face ashen. Birdie reached for his hand and squeezed. "I'm sorry, Tad."

He nodded and tapped the paper. "Here it says only 150 men, women, and children were killed. You said 300."

"You're right. There are conflicting reports, but much of history cites the larger number. Does it matter—150 or 300?"

"No."

"If it helps, Wounded Knee was the last major conflict between the Indians and the whites."

"Maybe a little." He clasped her hand between both of his. She wasn't a small woman, but his hands swallowed hers causing her to feel dainty. It was nice for a change. "You know what this means, don't you?"

She knew, but wondered if he'd admit it, say it out loud.

"We can no longer doubt your story about being from the future."

* * *

Early in February, they were just closing up when Detective Ethan knocked at the door. He touched his hat and nodded. "Ladies. Can I speak to you a moment?"

"Of course, Lloyd. Come in."

He looked at the floor and shuffled his feet. "Doc is the one who asked me to come. I'm not exactly comfortable with the topic."

Birdie was surprised to see a flush rise on his face.

Mattie propped her fists on her hips. "Come on, Detective, spit it out. Are we in violation of some health code or something?"

"All right, but please pardon me for bringing up this unseemly topic." Birdie couldn't imagine what he had to say. "Well, it's like this. Some of the pros…err…ladies down at the Reservation have been roughed up by customers on occasion. Last night one of the girls was attacked in the garden. Guy beat her senseless, cut her face up, and left her in pretty bad shape."

"Will she be okay?"

"Doc says her body will heal, but she'll carry scars forever."

"Was she raped?"

"No."

Bile rose in Birdie's throat. Anger heated her skin. Yes, the ladies on the Reservation lived a dangerous life, but she doubted it was one the majority deliberately chose. More than likely it was chosen for them by circumstances.

"It sounds like a hate crime or revenge of some kind. Or maybe a man unable to have normal sexual relations needing to vent his frustrations on a woman." There were plenty of the types in Birdie's time period.

His face colored at her words. Obviously he wasn't used to discussing such details with women. "That's possible," said Ethan.

"Did she have any idea who it was?"

Ethan shook his head. "She won't talk much either." He cleared his throat. "Anyway, the madams went to Doc to see if he'd talk to you about teaching their girls."

Mattie's mouth dropped open and she sputtered. "You can't be serious. Birdie has no business on that side of town."

"Now Mattie. Those women deserve to be able to protect themselves just like everyone else." Birdie wanted to fit in here, but she couldn't go against her internal code of ethics—protect and serve.

"But if anyone finds out, your reputation will be ruined."

"She's right, Birdie."

"Well, it'll just have to be ruined then. I'll not allow women, regardless of their race, color, or occupations suffer at the hands of abusive men. If I can help them, I will."

Mattie wagged her head from side-to-side. "Young woman, you're too tender hearted for your own good." She turned to Ethan. "I'll go. Birdie just got through telling me earlier I could teach this class so I'll start with the soiled doves."

Status in the community was important to Mattie. Birdie couldn't let her take a chance. "No, I'm going. You have a husband with a business to think about."

Mattie shook her head. "If the ladies in this community find out, they'll pull their daughters out of class. We'll have to close our doors."

Birdie hated to do it as she needed the money, but she couldn't ignore a plea for help. She handed her key to Mattie. "From now on you're the teacher here. I'll disassociate myself so the mother's can't complain."

Mattie's face crumpled. Birdie feared she'd cry, but instead she propped her hands on her hips and protested, "You can't do that. We're partners."

"Ah, Mattie, how about letting me be a silent partner for awhile?"

The detective faced Mattie. "And please, Mrs. Hellman, don't tell anyone about the lessons or the attack."

"You have my word. I won't even tell Mr. Hellman. Not that he's a gossip, but so he won't worry about Birdie." She chuckled. "If we'd had a daughter, he'd want her to be just like you."

Birdie's throat tightened, her voice croaked as she spoke. "I'd be proud to have him for a dad."

Mattie raised herself to her full height and sighed. "I don't like this one bit, but expect I can't change your mind." She gripped Birdie in a tight hug. "You be careful. If you need me, you know where to find me."

They walked outside so Mattie could lock up. Mattie strode off down the street toward her husband's shop.

"I came over in the buggy," said Ethan. "Would you take a ride with me, Birdie, so we can work out the particulars?"

"Yes. Can we tie Molly to follow behind?"

"Sure." Ethan helped her into the buggy and then tended to Molly.

He hopped in and flicked the reins. "I hope you won't regret today's decision."

"Me too. This is so different from what I'm used to. Of course in my time period prostitution isn't legal. Anyone caught soliciting is jailed."

Birdie knew that Waco was the first town in Texas and the second in the United States to legalize the profession. The city fathers had done so in 1889 to better control the businesses. The madams and prostitutes were required to obtain an annual license and the girls had to undergo a physical exam twice a month.

"If the girls are found outside the Reservation, they're arrested for vagrancy," said Ethan.

"That's odd. The city makes money off them and they're tolerated as long as they stay where they belong." If prostitution was legal, why couldn't they move about freely? "Seems like a double standard."

"I expect you're right, but that's the way it is."

They'd reached the river and sat gazing out. Sun glistened off the water as it traveled slowly by.

"Where will we work then?" Birdie couldn't imagine them working outside where anyone passing by could see them.

"Somehow the doc will have to figure out a suitable place on the Reservation. Maybe one of the houses has a basement or a room could be cleared out. If not, the hospital might have an area."

Birdie couldn't imagine how the town folk would respond if they found out.

"But, more importantly, Birdie, I'm hoping you can help me with this case."

Her heart thudded. "Me? Really?"

"Yes, you said you'd been trained in evidence collection. I'm afraid this incident is going to be repeated. I thought you might take a look at the crime scene and be to see some things we missed."

"Has this been cleared with the chief of police?"

He nodded and held up a piece of paper and grinned. "I even talked him into putting you on the payroll."

"You're kidding." She could use every penny.

"On the sly, of course. No one is to know about you working with us. If word gets out there would be uproar." He chuckled. "The chief wants you to be in disguise to protect you as much as possible."

Adrenaline pumped through her veins. "When can we start?"

"How about right now?"

Dr. Franks met them in the lobby and escorted them to his office. "Good to see you looking so well, Miss Braxton. I see life with the Lockharts is treating you well."

"Yes, they've been very gracious. I should soon have enough money to move out on my own though."

He waved at the chairs. "Have a seat." He peered at Birdie over the tops of his glasses. "Has Detective Ethan filled you in on what's going on?"

"Briefly. I want to be honest here, the Texas Rangers don't handle a lot of assault cases."

Ethan spoke up. "But you said—"

"Yes, I am trained to collect evidence and think I can help. I would like to talk to the patient and then visit the area where the crime took place."

Dr. Franks stood. "This way."

"First though, I'd like to know if you still have her clothing."

"I'll ask Nurse Taylor."

"Do you have brown paper I can wrap them in so they won't become cross contaminated?"

"Yes." They followed him up to the second floor to the room at the end of the hall.

The doctor rapped on the door before entering. Nurse Taylor sat by the bed reading a book. "She's been hysterical on occasion so we've watched her around the clock."

Nurse Taylor stood and grasped Birdie's hand. Birdie led her to a corner of the room. "Has she said much?"

"No, just cries and touches her face." She glanced at the bed. "Poor dear. She's in a lot of pain."

Birdie drew a deep breath and forged forward. "Did you happen to keep her clothes?"

"Oh yes. They're right here in the closet."

"Have they been washed?"

"No, I'd planned to take them by the laundry this afternoon."

Birdie squeezed her arm. "The doctor says you have brown paper. Can you wrap them up for me please? I'm going to sit and talk with her a minute."

She approached the bed. Ethan stopped her. "Be careful. She's fragile."

"I understand. What's her name?"

"Lila Sanders."

Birdie pulled the chair close to the bed and took the woman's hand and squeezed gently. She opened her eyes, fear tightening her features. "Who are you?"

"I'm Birdie Braxton. I've been teaching women and girls self-defense tactics." She nodded to the other side of the bed. "Detective Ethan is here too. He wants me to ask you some questions in hopes you'll remember something to help catch this person."

Miss Sanders closed her eyes, shutting them out.

"Please, Lila. If he's not caught he could do it again. Next time he might kill someone."

"I told the detective everything I remember."

"I know, but he thought talking to a woman would be easier. Would you like for him to leave the room?"

She nodded. Ethan handed Birdie a small tablet and a pencil and then left.

"Now, close your eyes and think. Were you able to see him at all?"

"No, it was too dark. All I saw was shadows."

"What did you see in the shadows? Could you tell the shape of his hat? Or was he without one?"

"Yes, he wore a bowler."

"Now, did he say anything to you?"

She covered her mouth with her hand and sobbed, "Called me terrible, vulgar things."

"What about his voice, was it deep or higher pitched?"

"It was deep and scratchy like his throat was raw."

Birdie jotted down a couple of notes in the pad. "Could you tell how tall he was, how strong? Did you struggle with him?"

"How can you ask me those things? Of course I struggled with him. Hit him with everything I had, and he just laughed."

Birdie patted her hand. "I'm not questioning your courageousness. I just need to know if you possibly left marks on him that could be seen by others."

"I screamed and scratched his face, but I don't know how good cause he wore something like a scarf with nose and eyes cut out." She pointed to her cheek just below her right eye. "Tore the mask and made him mad. He slapped me and knocked my head against the wood of the gazebo."

"Oh that's good to know. Let me see your nails." They extended beyond the tips of her fingers about one-fourth of an inch, enough to break the skin. It appeared there might still be tissue, enough to collect. If only they had the means to examine it. "Good, can you guess how tall he was?"

"Not so tall, not much taller than me and I'm five feet, five inches tall."

"Could you tell if he was thin or heavy?"

"He was thick, not fat, but stocky."

"Very good. This will all help." Birdie patted her hand. "What happened after you hit your head?"

Lila shuddered and sobbed. "He started hitting me. In the face, my body, everywhere until I blacked out."

"Were you unconscious when he cut you?"

"Yes. I woke up in that tall grass. I didn't know I'd been cut 'til I tried to get up and my face throbbed. Blood ran down my jaw, wetting my clothes."

Tears rolled down her cheeks, wetting the bandages. What Birdie wouldn't give for a tissue to wipe them away.

"What were you doing outside?"

"It gets so smoky inside to where sometimes I can't breathe. I just wanted some fresh air."

"Did you see anyone else out? Someone who might have seen something?"

"No. It's not uncommon for girls to stroll outside around the gazebo, but last night there was no one."

"You're a brave young woman, Lila. I need you to be brave a little while longer. I need to see your bruises."

Her eyes widened. "You mean you want to look at my naked body?"

"Yes. I promise it won't take but just a moment. Would you like for me to call Nurse Taylor back in?"

"No, let's just get it over with." She squeezed her eyes shut.

Birdie lifted the sheet and raised her gown. The poor girl's body was almost a solid bruise but it was evident the perp had aimed for breasts, belly, and abdomen. Most likely her kidneys were bruised and she had fractured ribs. She pulled the gown down. "Can you roll over for me for just a moment?" Birdie moved to the side of the bed. "Hand me your far hand and let me pull you over."

Lila cried out. Birdie took a quick look, yanked the gown back down and eased her to her back.

"One more question. What did you smell—liquor, tobacco, shaving soap or cologne?"

Gasping from the exertion and pain, she panted, "Oh, lawsy, yes. Expensive shaving soap or cologne. I've never smelled it before but will never forget it to my dying day."

Now that was a clue they could work with. How many men in Waco could afford expensive shave soap?

CHAPTER FOURTEEN

Back in Detective Ethan's buggy, Birdie glanced at the drawing she'd made of the victim's wounds. Miss Sanders would be mighty sore for a good while. Hopefully none of her internal organs were damaged. "Can we go to the crime scene now?"

"Not dressed as you are. I think we better put it off until tomorrow. Come in about the same time the classes start and hopefully Tad won't notice a difference in your routine and start asking questions."

That's all Birdie needed. He'd been quiet since learning about the Wounded Knee situation. She could see his not understanding her take on the situation. His experience with Indians was probably horror stories he'd been told by his grandfathers. Raiding parties attacking and killing settlers. She sighed. Of course, he'd not been out of Waco, and was just a child when the Civil War broke out. In fact, early in Texas's history, several tribes—the Lipan Apaches, the Tonkawas, and the Wacos collaborated with the rangers to defeat the Comanche Nation. The Comanche slowed down progress in Texas and encroached on the other tribe's lands.

Shoot, that might not be the problem at all. The story upset Olivia, and the fact people had starved and been driven off their land might be causing his poor mood. Or, it was possible he still had difficulty accepting the fact she was from the future? She often caught him watching her, as if trying to make up his mind about something. Who knows what he thought. She knew one thing, though. If he found out what she was doing, he'd try to make her quit or kick her out of his house.

"What if Tad finds out?"

"He won't like it, that's a fact. If he suspects something and pressures you, be best to go ahead and tell him." He stopped the buggy by the river and helped her down. "Let me get Molly for you."

Birdie stroked the mare's neck. "Poor girl. I've made you stand around all day. We'll see that you get an extra ration of oats tonight."

She mounted the horse. "I'll see you in the morning."

"Don't worry about clothes. We'll have a uniform for you. Bring something to tie your hair up."

Birdie led Molly into the barn and undid the cinch. Before she could lift the saddle, she was spun around. Alarmed, she raised her arms in defense. Tad eased back from her and slammed a fist into the wooden post.

"Where have you been? I've been worried sick and was about to gather the men to come looking for you."

She bristled. "I didn't realize I had a curfew." She lifted the saddle and carried it to the waiting sawhorse. "Look, I'm sorry I'm late. Some things came up and I got distracted."

"What kind of things?"

"I met some people and visited for a while."

His eyes narrowed. "Was it a man?"

"You are not my brother or my father. And you'd have no right to question me if you were."

He yanked his hat off and raked a hand through his hair. "You're three hours past the time you usually get home. Mother's beside herself with worry, she's been ready to notify the sheriff."

"I am sorry for that, truly." Drat, she hated to make people worry. She'd been inconsiderate and would have to lie about where she'd been. "I'll hurry here, Tad, and get up to the house and apologize." She removed the bit and bridle and quickly stored them away along with the saddle blanket.

Tad grabbed a bucket and filled it with a ration of oats.

"I promised her a little extra."

He cocked an eyebrow. "And you think she'll remember?"

"Of course. Women don't forget things like that."

She swallowed a chuckle as he dropped his head to hide

the twitch of his lips. He hadn't fooled her. "All right. If you say so." He scooped a little more into the pail and hung it where Molly could get to it. While she brushed the mare, making sure to remove any dirt or debris that might have attached itself to her coat, Tad lifted her hooves and used a nail to clean them.

Tad eased an arm around her shoulders as they walked up to the house. She tried to pull away but he squeezed. "Relax. I just want to touch you a minute."

Birdie slipped her arm around his waist and their hips bumped as they walked. "I'm really sorry I worried you. I'm not used to people fussing about my coming and going. My schedule was always so erratic Aunt Patty learned not to panic when I was later than usual."

"Where were you?"

"It's really none of your business."

"True, but it would be nice if you told me anyway."

"Detective Ethan came by the warehouse. We went for a buggy ride down to the river, and ended up going to the police station and talked for a long time."

"Is he courting you? I know he's interested. I need to know if he has a chance."

"No, he's not. We talked about detective work the entire time."

Tad snorted. "Maybe you thought it was all work, but I imagine Ethan thought otherwise. Guess I better start wooing you with a vengeance."

Birdie stopped and whirled to face him. "I told you I don't want to be courted."

"Too bad." He took her by the arm and pulled her behind a tree to protect them from view from the house.

"What are you—"

Before she could finish, his lips were on hers. His arms lifted her off her feet, up against his hard frame, her face even with his. Against his taller body, she made a perfect fit. She struggled for a moment then gave in and twined her arms around his neck. Tad deepened the kiss, grabbed her butt and pulled her hips flush with his. His arousal throbbed against her belly, eliciting a deep moan low in her throat. Breathless and shaking, she drew back and dropped her head to his chest.

"Birdie, sweetheart, I want you something fierce," he whispered against her hair. "But I can wait... for a time." She tilted her head and stared into his blue eyes, searching her brain for a witty remark. None came to mind. He winked and lowered her to the ground. Evidently he'd worked through whatever had been bothering him earlier.

No doubt about it, the man was sexy as all get-out and knew his way around the art of kissing. He was dangerous. Dangerous because she could care deeply for him, and she had a goal to accomplish. If she had to marry, it would be someone with money to build Birdie's Nest. Shame washed over her for her materialistic position, but she had no choice. Her home came before her happiness.

* * *

Dressed in the wool uniform of the Waco Police, Birdie studied the horse Detective Ethan had selected for her. It was warm for February. Probably would get up into the 80s today. Sweat already tickled between her breasts and it wasn't even nine o'clock. Even though it was winter, the sun could get hot some days. Texas was notorious for its unpredictable weather. She scratched her back. What was it about wool and this era? The fabric had always made her itch like the devil. At least she didn't have to wear a coat over the uniform. Regardless, she'd be miserable on warm days. The mare named Brownie appeared gentle enough. She patted the horse's neck and let her smell her hand. Molly munched on a scoop of oats and swished her tail contentedly as they walked by. They mounted and Birdie followed behind. On Washington Street they turned left and on Third Street turned right and crossed a bridge.

"This is Barron's Branch where the Reservation begins," explained Ethan as he waved his arm to designate areas. "Every building along this street on either side of this block is part of the prostitution trade."

There were at least thirty houses—some mere shacks and others large establishments. How could a town of twenty-five thousand bring in enough customers to keep these places going, especially here in the Bible belt? Of course, everyone had vices; many they kept hidden their entire lives. "Every one of them?" she queried his statement.

He scratched his chin. "I expect some are not." He shook his head. "I pity the folks who live here and can't get away from the neighborhood. Though the police are called on occasion, there are rarely problems. The madams don't put up with it for fear they'll get closed down. They administer their own form of punishment."

Birdie rode up beside him as they turned on what would someday become Columbus Avenue. She wondered how many citizens in her time were aware of the area's shady past.

"Let's ride completely around so you'll get a better feel for the layout." His gaze raked her as she sat the horse. He grinned. "Remember, you're a man. Rock back in the saddle a bit."

"Yes, sir." The mustache they'd glued to her upper lip twitched as she talked. She placed her fingers on it to make sure it was still in place. Man, it was going to hurt when she ripped it off.

The houses varied in size and appearance. Many were well kept while others showed signs of neglect—peeling paint and unkempt lawns. Shades covered most of the windows. Likely, the ladies slept days after their long nights of business. It seemed unnaturally quiet. No children played, or shouted or ran around. Inside the square was a large lawn area dotted with trees. Weeds and tall grass grew over much of the space, though a couple of yards sported benches and flowers.

They pulled their horses to a stop at one of the larger houses. From that angle Birdie could see a lone policeman standing guard by an attractive white gazebo nestled within a grove of trees and shrubbery.

The officer nodded to Ethan.

"Jones, take a thirty-minute break."

Jones eyed Birdie. She rocked back on her heels and hitched up her pants as she'd seen men do. She nodded to acknowledge the man. Then she placed her hands on her hips, John Wayne style. She must have passed muster as Jones's attention moved from her to Ethan.

"Yes, sir, Detective."

Birdie followed Ethan around behind the gazebo to an area where tall grass had been flattened. "He must have dragged her over the rail and pulled her into the foliage," Ethan said.

"With all the grass, there's no way we can obtain any footprints." Birdie knelt by the flattened spot. "Has this area been scoured?"

"Men went over it twice."

That may be, but Birdie was better trained to look for minute details. She withdrew a magnifying glass from a pocket and bent to look closely at every blade of grass and underneath it as well. Her first find was a cigarette butt. Using tweezers, she lifted it from the ground, blew off bits of dirt and debris, and then sniffed it to determine how old it might be. "It still has an odor so it's probably not too old. Odd, it doesn't look like one of those roll your own type."

Ethan looked at it closely. "It's not. I bet it's a packaged smoke—Duke of Durham brand."

Birdie didn't know they'd had packaged cigarettes in the 1890s. Of course there was a lot she didn't know about the period. "Did you bring some envelopes?"

He pulled one from his pocket, held it open for her, and she dropped the butt inside. "I don't suppose you have finger printing capabilities yet."

"We've read about it, but only one man in the department has given it a try. Name is James Reed. Spends a lot of time in a little cubicle he's confiscated for his experiments. He's used most of the force as guinea pigs. We walked around for days with ink-stained fingers."

"I'd like to get with him and see if we can develop a system that will work." She knew cellophane tape hadn't been invented yet so coming up with a way to get prints off an object onto paper where they could be studied would be vital.

Birdie continued her search and found only one other thing—a button. Excited to have more evidence, she held it up for Ethan to see. "What do you think it came from?"

"A man's suit coat most likely. From the looks of it, a nice one. It didn't come from one of the department stores. I'd bet it is tailor made." He filed away the two pieces of evidence in his jacket pocket and helped her up. "Here comes Jones. I don't want you talking to him, so you go ahead to the horses. I'll meet you there."

Birdie did her best to execute a manly stride as she headed for the horses. At least she wasn't tottering in high heels on gravel. She was anxious to get back to the station and go over the victim's clothes.

By lunch, she'd collected several fibers from Miss Sanders dress. The garment reminded Birdie of the one she'd worn to serve the subpoena. Red satin, trimmed in black, this one was longer, fuller, and decorated with feathers. Who's to say if the pieces of evidence she found came from the man who'd attacked her, or from one of her customers? One piece was interesting, though—a gray thread, an almost identical match to the color of the button.

CHAPTER FIFTEEN

Birdie stood at the counter of Goldstein-Migel Co. A young clerk rushed over. "May I be of assistance, ma'am?"

"Why yes. I'm shopping for my bedridden aunt. She wants a new cologne for her husband and sent me to collect samples." She pointed at a non-descript bottle behind him. "Can I smell that one?"

"Yes, indeed. It's our newest addition to our exclusive line of imported products. We carry scents designed for both men and women." He leaned in and whispered, "We don't handle those cheap brands, if you know what I mean."

"Indeed, I do." He tilted the bottle, removed the lid, and dabbed a bit on one of the business cards lying on a glass tray. After waving it in the air for a moment, he handed it to Birdie. "It is Penhaligon's English Fern, just in from England—a hint of clove, lavender, and fern—earthy."

Birdie waved the card under her nose, testing its strength. It was clean and refreshing, not over powering. "Nice. I like this very much. Will you write the name on the back of the card so I won't get them confused?"

He wrote the name and then tapped the card with his pencil. "I added my name so when you come back you can ask for me."

She fluttered her lashes and smiled like a giddy schoolgirl. Gad, she hated this flirtatious stuff. "Of course. I'll be sure to do that." She slipped the sample into a clean envelope in her bag to help preserve the smell until Miss Sanders could smell it.

"Now, let me show you one other new item." He set

141

another plain bottle on the counter but this one had a gold lid. "This one is also from London. Some find it a bit sweet, but it still has that tart, clean scent." He slid another card forward and wrote on it before adding a dab of the cologne.

Birdie took a whiff and jerked back. "A bit sweet for my tastes but my aunt may like it." The card found its way into another envelope. "I thank you so much for your time. I'll see what Aunt thinks and get back to you." She turned and walked toward the exit, the heels of her shoes loud against the wooden floors.

She entered the hospital in her regular clothes. Nothing wrong with visiting a patient and no one had to know who she was. Lila, still as a statue, sat in a chair by the window. The breeze ruffled tufts of her hair around her face. Birdie tapped on the door. Lila jerked and turned toward her. A smile that didn't reach her eyes angled the corners of her mouth.

"Hello, Birdie. Come in."

Birdie pulled the other chair across the room and sat down facing the woman. She pulled one envelope from her bag, sniffed the contents to make sure the scent was still strong, and then handed it to Lila. Eyes locked on the sample, she took a deep breath, and then took it from Birdie's hand. She lifted it to her nose, took a tentative sniff, and then smelled it again.

Lila's gaze connected with Birdie's, and then she shook her head. "No, this isn't it." She handed the sample back to Birdie.

They repeated the same process with the second sample with the same results. "These are light. His was heavy, woodsier."

Birdie leaned over and patted the woman's hands. "Don't worry. We'll keep looking. I'll be back about the same time tomorrow with a couple more samples. We will catch this man, Lila."

The girl brushed a tear from her face. "I'm going home tonight. Doc says I'm well enough, and Miss Josie says I can stay until my scars heal." Lila's eyes dropped to her lap. "She'll put me to cleaning or helping in the kitchen until then."

"Well then, how about if I meet you around the same

time tomorrow afternoon in the gazebo?" Birdie got up and headed for the door. She stopped and turned back. "Don't mention anything to anybody, even Miss Josie, about the cologne or the scratch you put on the man's face. For all we know, he could be a regular customer at the house."

Lila's eyes rounded with fear. Bottom lip caught in her teeth, she nodded.

Darn it. To visit the Reservation, Birdie would have to wear that darn wool suit.

* * *

Tad strode into the warehouse where Birdie was teaching class. The day was warm so the bay doors were open to allow for a breeze. At the sight of him, all the ladies stopped what they were doing. Mattie turned around and fisted her hands on her hips. "We do not allow men in here." From the tone of her voice, she'd dealt with unwanted visitors before.

"Sorry, Mattie. I just stopped by to talk to Birdie."

She shaded her eyes against the sunlight behind him. "Is that you, Tad Lockhart?"

He yanked his hat off his head. "Yes, ma'am. I came to see Birdie." He looked around, his eyes searching the darkened corners of the large space. "Isn't she here?"

"Well, uh, no. She had some errands to run today, so I took over the class."

That's odd. She was totally dedicated to teaching these women self-defense. Why would she turn it over to Mattie? "Is that so? Did she say where she was going?"

"No, I'm sorry, she didn't."

Darn. He'd wanted a chance to take her for a ride along the river and had brought the surrey. His attempts at courting were failing. "I have some business to tend to at the bank. I'll stop back by in a while. Aren't classes over soon?"

"Yes, in thirty minutes, but I'm not sure if Birdie planned to come back by here before heading home."

Outside, he slammed his hat on his head and got into the buggy. What kind of errands could she have? He stopped by the bank and made a deposit. A niggling in his brain drove him to drive by the jail. No, he wasn't jealous, just curious to see if Birdie was spending time with the detective. Tad had no claims on her, but if she favored the man, Tad intended to step up his suit. He wasn't about to let Birdie get away from him.

In the rear of the jail building, Tad saw Detective Ethan and another officer ride into the stable. He pulled the surrey to a halt, threw on the brake, and hopped down. The two walked out of the building, heads together in some discussion. When they noticed him, both stopped mid-stride, and gaped. Ethan quickly recovered. Now, what was that all about? "Ethan, you got a minute?"

"Sure do." He spoke to the policeman. "You go on in and start writing up a report, Jenkins. I'll be in shortly."

Jenkins mumbled something like, "On it, sir." Then he shuffled toward the main building at a leisurely gait.

Something was sure odd about the fellow. Tad had never seen a man walk quite like that before. He hitched his pants up and kept going. Danged if his hips didn't sway. He chuckled and shook his head. "Is he a new recruit?"

"Yep, took him out in the field today." He scratched his chin. "I know he's rather peculiar, but he's smart as a whip. Just what we need with the case we're trying to solve right now."

"What's going on?"

"Haven't you read the papers?"

"No, not in the last week. I've been too busy and by the time I get a chance to take a look, Ma has already wrapped food in it to take to someone."

"Some mad man is attacking the doves over on the Reservation, cutting them up pretty bad." He lifted a hand to his face and made an X across each cheek. He shuddered. "The one from last night was also cut across her breasts and down her belly."

Tad knew crime occurred in the Reservation area, but it usually involved men getting drunk and fighting. Occasionally someone was killed, but nothing like what Ethan described as the madams ran a tight operation and kept their girls in line. Each of the bigger houses had their own security guards—more like well-armed ruffians—to make sure patrons behaved. If they didn't, they were tossed out, some taking a beating first. "Are they still alive?"

"Oh yes, but they'll be scarred for life and have to find another way to make a living. Poor souls, their bodies battered black and blue and then disfigured for life."

Tad's stomach roiled. Who could do such a thing? Prostitution was a terrible way to live, but most of those women didn't choose their profession. They were forced into it. "Sounds like someone is on a vendetta. You think he's trying to close the Reservation down?"

"If so, he's going about it the wrong way." Ethan's mouth thinned. "We're going to get him, Lockhart. We've got some good evidence, but need to do more investigative work yet." He grinned. "That's where my partner comes in. He's well trained in evidence collection. And by golly, he found something at each scene that we'd overlooked."

"That's what Birdie said about her training in the Texas Rangers, isn't it?"

Ethan hesitated. "I believe you're right."

"Have you happened to see her today?"

"No, why do you ask?"

"I know that you took her for a ride down by the river last week. Thought you might be making it a habit to go by her school." Tad watched the man for his reaction. "Are you courting her, Ethan?"

Color suffused Ethan's face. He coughed. "Now, I admit I'm interested, but look Lockhart, she's not interested in me."

Tad rocked back on his heels. "Good, because I don't want any competition."

"I can't speak for the rest of the male population of Waco, but you have nothing to fear from me." He offered his hand. "I wish you luck."

Tad couldn't resist a grin as he grasped the detective's hand. "Thank you, I'll probably need it.

* * *

Birdie quickly changed clothes and watched until Tad drove off in the surrey. *Wonder what he was doing coming over to talk to Detective Ethan.* Surely he didn't suspect what she was up to. If so, he wouldn't be a happy man. Women of this era didn't involve themselves in police work, especially gruesome crimes like they were dealing with. This last woman, younger than Lila, was hysterical. Doctor Franks had to keep her sedated. No wonder. Seems the cuts on the face wasn't enough this time. He cut her across the breasts with another line down to her belly. Being cut like she'd been would be enough to send a woman, or a man for that matter, over the edge.

Crosses. Suddenly it dawned on her. Those weren't X's on Lila's cheeks they were crosses. He'd made sure on the second victim they didn't mistake the cuts for anything else. He was proclaiming that the women on the Reservation were sinners and should carry a mark of their shame, sort of like a scarlet letter. Pervert. Why couldn't he wage his war in the open? Get a petition to have the city close the place down?

They'd found an additional cigarette butt at the crime scene, and on her clothes Birdie found another gray fiber and a bit of hair not belonging to the prostitute. Ethan had watched Birdie's techniques closely and learned fast. Not to say detectives in this era didn't know how to collect evidence, as they did, but she'd taught him a few tricks used by modern science. Today he'd found a small piece of wadded up paper less than an inch square. It had been stepped on and bore a lot of dirt, but a small portion of print was visible. Hopefully it would give them another lead.

Evidently this woman had fought back. Her knuckles were bruised, her nails broken and bloody. Their man, the perpetrator, surely wore multiple scratches. Birdie was anxious to talk to the girl and hear what she had to offer.

Lloyd held Molly for her while she mounted. "What did Tad want?"

"He wanted to know if I was courting you."

She rolled her eyes, a habit Aunt Patty hated. "What'd you tell him?"

He cocked his head. "That I was interested, but you weren't."

Why couldn't she be attracted to him? He was such a nice man. "I'm sorry, Lloyd."

"Don't be. We don't always have control over where our hearts lead us."

She smiled. "You sound like a poet."

"Good grief!" He glanced around. "Don't let anyone hear you say something like that. I'll be the laughing stock of the department." With a slap to Molly's flank, he hollered, "See you tomorrow."

Birdie kept Molly at a steady trot. She could see Tad ahead. Occasionally someone would greet him and he'd wave. She stayed a safe distance behind and watched as he started across the suspension bridge. The toll keeper's cottage sat empty. The county had bought the bridge and sold it to the city in 1889. Her interest piqued when he turned onto the road on the far side that ran parallel to the river, the one where her home would stand in the future. She eased Molly into a gallop and rode up beside Tad.

"Where are you headed?"

He glanced her way, and then pulled the surrey to the side of the road and stopped. "If you'd been where you were supposed to be, you'd know."

"Humph. Well, I can't stay at your beck and call. I have things to do."

"Do you have time to take a ride with me down River Street?"

How could she refuse the boyish grin stretching his face? Plus, she wanted to see the land where Birdie's Nest had been—would be—built. Time travel made for odd tenses. "Will your mother be worried if we're late?"

"I told her where we'd be. She'll hold supper for us."

He set the brake while she dismounted and tied Molly to the back of the buggy. He held her arm as she stepped aboard and settled into the seat. She could get used to all this gentlemanly stuff. Women had it made back in the day. Wait, she'd open her own doors if she didn't have to wear this corset. At least the one she wore today laced up the front and wasn't near as tight as when Olivia fastened her up.

The surrey rocked gently when Tad climbed aboard. He was dressed in a suit today. "What are you doing all dressed up?"

"Had business at the bank." He winked. "Then, I planned to go courtin'."

"What kept you from it?"

"My girl was absent from her place of business."

Uh-oh. He'd gone by the school. "What time were you there?"

"About thirty minutes before closing time. Looks like Mattie can handle the class without you."

"Yes, she's very good and the girls like her." He still hadn't set the horse in motion. "Are we going to sit here, or go for a ride?" Actually a light breeze blew in from the water and it was growing chilly.

"And by the way, I'm not your girl."

"Oh yes you are, sweetheart." His heated expression warmed her insides and she wanted to give in to her attraction for him, but she had a goal.

His gaze landed on her mouth. He cocked his head and peered closer. Was he going to kiss her?

"What's that on your lip?" With a finger, he tried to wipe it off. "It feels like glue."

CHAPTER SIXTEEN

Yikes! Birdie turned her head and peeled the little tab of glue off her upper lip. She wiped it on her dress and would be sure to clean it up later. She turned back to Tad and let her tongue feel for any residue. "Mm, sugar from that bun I had with my lunch." *Lord, forgive me for lying.*

Tad's attention followed her actions. She squirmed under his perusal. Mischief gleamed in those blue eyes of his. "Sugar, huh?" He put his arm around her shoulders and brought her face closer to his. "I love sugar."

Birdie melted under his gaze, the warmth of his voice washing over her like hot icing oozing over a cake.

"I long for the taste of your lips. Meet me half way, love." His eyelids lowered, his breath touched her mouth drawing her closer as if his inhaled breath drew her in.

Unable to resist the draw, she closed her eyes and touched her lips to his. She slipped her arms around his waist and reveled in the masculine strength of the muscles in his back. He groaned into her mouth and pulled her closer, her breasts flattening against his chest, as he took possession of her mouth, tasting and molding her lips to his liking. And oh, she liked. She opened for him and he explored, twining his tongue with hers and inviting her to taste him.

It would be so easy to lose herself in this man, forget her goal, but she couldn't. She had to save her home. She broke the kiss and tried to smile, but the expression wobbled on her face and she choked out, "I thought we were going to take a drive."

He caressed her cheek as his thumb caught a tear and wiped it away. His blue eyes dark with concern and longing made her wish things would be different. "What is it sweetheart? Why are you crying?"

She caught his hand and kissed the palm. "I can't fall in love with you, Tad, no matter how much I want to. I've got to buy land and build a house."

The furrows in his forehead eased somewhat. He kissed her lightly and then nuzzled her ear. "Come on before we cause a scene out here and set tongues wagging."

She couldn't resist a wet snort. "You don't think they are already?"

"No, I've not heard anything, and believe me, Mother would have boxed my ears if I was anything other than circumspect."

"You mean she wouldn't be offended by that kiss out here on a public road?"

He winked. "If she saw it she would."

Birdie laughed and turned her attention to the river and the land that followed its path. She grabbed Tad's forearm. "Can we stop up ahead?"

"Sure." He pulled the buggy onto the grass by a For Sale sign. "Is this far enough?"

Breathless, she gasped, "Yes." After he set the brake she jumped down from the surrey and strode past the sign into the grassy field.

Before she could get far he was beside her and tucked her arm through his. "So, this is the place, huh?"

Her heart in her throat, she nodded and looked around.

"It is beautiful," he allowed. She smiled and nodded again. He looked thoughtful. "I bet it gets a wonderful breeze off the river." Then, his brow furrowed. "Did your home ever flood due to rising water?"

She managed a squeak. "Yes…several times in its earlier days. But over time, the river was rerouted and Birdie's Nest wasn't as close to the water."

"That's not good."

"No, it's not, but this time I'll build it farther back so rising water won't be a worry."

He chuckled. "Pretty sure of yourself, aren't you?"

"I have to be. Don't you see, if I don't, no telling where Aunt Patty will end up living."

They walked back to the buggy and Birdie noted the real estate agent's name and the amount of acreage available. Thirty acres, exactly what they started out with before selling off some of the land. She wanted to jump for joy. Maybe her plan would work out after all. She tapped the sign. "I'm going to stop by the office tomorrow and see how much they're asking for this property."

"Do you think you have enough saved?"

"I don't know. I have close to a thousand dollars, but I hate to spend it all."

"Maybe the owner will let you make payments."

That would be perfect. She had three jobs now and was doing pretty well financially. Though she didn't work much at the school, she was working with the ladies from the Reservation. Detective Ethan insisted she wear a long cloak with a hood. They worked in the basement of one of the houses. "I'll ask them tomorrow."

If she could stop spending money on clothes, it would help. The cool weather required that she buy a warm cloak and now she needed a couple of warmer dresses. There was no end to expenses. Plus, she wanted to buy her own horse. She'd given up on the idea of moving out. When moving was mentioned, Olivia insisted there was no need as Birdie had a home with them.

Tad took her arm and looked up at the sky. "We better get home. It will turn colder here soon."

Once they were in the buggy, Tad reached back and lifted a blanket from the back seat. "Wrap up in this if you get cold."

"Thank you."

"You're welcome." He released the brake and turned the surrey around in the road. When they were on the road leading out of town, he took her arm and tugged. "Scoot over here closer and keep me warm."

It was chilly so she inched nearer and threw one end of the blanket over his shoulders and twined her arm with his. "Warmer now?"

He winked. "Yes, indeed."

Her heart thumped in appreciation. This man tempted her like no one ever had before. Oh, she'd had relationships, but none held the charismatic lure he did. "What am I going to do with you, Tad Lockhart?"

"Well, sweetheart, you could take my courting seriously. Why don't we take a picnic lunch out to one of my favorite spots on the ranch this Saturday if the weather is nice?"

She would like to see more of his property, what all ranching involved. "All right, on one condition."

He cocked an eyebrow. "And what would that be?"

"You help me pick out a mare Friday afternoon. It's time I bought my own horse."

"You have a deal."

*   *   *

Birdie couldn't believe her luck. The agent told her the land she wanted was being sold for $600.00. "Would you like to ride out to see it?"

"I saw it yesterday and it's beautiful…perfect…just what I want. Now, we are talking about the parcel where your sign was posted, aren't we?" Be her luck to buy some land and it wasn't the property she wanted.

"Yes, miss, right on the Brazos River, approximately one mile north of the suspension bridge. Thirty prime acres." He pulled out a surveyor's map so large it covered most of the counter. "Here let me show you the exact location."

Sure enough, they were talking about the same place. Six hundred dollars? Birdie couldn't believe her good fortune. Maybe land didn't cost as much as she thought in this era, but she'd expected to pay a lot more.

"I'd like to buy it and will pay cash."

His bushy eyebrows rose in surprise. "Without even seeing it? Young woman, you need to go out and walk every inch of the land before you buy the property."

Maybe he was right. "All right, I'll do that, but will you let me pay down on it so no one else can buy it?"

"Sure thing. How much will your deposit be?" He lifted a receipt book from underneath the counter and started filling in the form.

"One hundred dollars."

"That'll be fine." With his pen, he tapped the map. "See, it's written right here. This is parcel ten. Thirty acres is written right there. I'll put the details on your receipt."

When he'd taken her name and she'd signed the receipt, he gave her a carbon copy. She tucked it into the pocket of her riding skirt. She'd done it; she'd actually bought the land that was her heritage. Joy filled her and she resisted the urge to dance a jig. Instead, she grabbed the land agent's hand and shook it eagerly. "Thank you, sir, for being so helpful. I'll be in tomorrow to pay the remainder and pick up the deed."

"I'll have everything ready."

In her excitement, she slammed the door too hard and the glass rattled. She looked back at the realtor and mouthed sorry.

She mounted Molly, and spread her wool cloak back across the horse's withers. It was perfect for the cold days and it resisted moisture. Anxious to get home and tell Tad about her good fortune, she prodded the mare into a trot. "Let's go home, girl."

* * *

Tad looked up from brushing down his horse just in time to see Birdie leap from Molly and come running into the barn. She flew at him, grabbing him around the neck. He landed on his back in the hay with Birdie sprawled on top of him. Before she could move, he caught her around the waist, held her close, and captured her lips in a kiss.

She jerked back, rolled off him, and sat up in the hay. Cheeks flushed from the cold, her eyes sparkled like a child's on Christmas morning.

He winked. "Well, darlin', this is a nice surprise. Miss me that much?"

"No, you oaf! I've got good news."

"Well, let's hear it."

"I bought the land." She grabbed his hand and squeezed. "The seller only wanted six hundred dollars. Can you believe it?"

He sat up. "Well, no. That's an outrageous deal. Who's the seller?"

Frown lines wrinkled her forehead. "I don't know. He didn't say and I didn't ask." She pulled the receipt from her pocket and handed it to him. "Does it look legit? I didn't get gypped, did I?" She scooted closer and looked over his shoulder.

He studied the document. "Looks legal to me and this land agent has a good reputation." He handed the paper back to her. "I don't think you have anything to worry about. It's possible the agent bought it outright from someone down on their luck."

She plopped back down on her back in the hay. "Whew! Scared me there for a minute. I didn't question the transaction until you were surprised about the price."

With her arms thrown up behind her head, Tad couldn't help but enjoy the view where her cloak gaped open. What would she do if he reached for her waist and smoothed a hand up her rib cage to cup a breast? Probably put him a death grip like she had that cowboy at the dance. He picked up a piece of straw and twirled it in his fingers. "I'm glad you got the land. You're one step closer to seeing your home built." He leaned back in the hay and propped his head in his hand so he could watch Birdie's reactions.

Her face glowed with happiness. "Thank you, Tad. You and your family have helped make it possible, you know. You took me in and gave me a job. I can't imagine how frightening it would have been without your family's support."

With the straw, he outlined her lips. She giggled and swatted his hand away. "Stop it. That tickles."

"Hmm, just thinking, with your good news and all, maybe we should celebrate with another kiss."

She arched a brow and grinned. "Well, I guess I could bear another." With her forefinger, she tapped her rosy cheek. "A small one right here."

Before she could resist, he leaned over, grabbed her waist, and pulled her closer. His noise an inch from hers, he asked, "Like this?" He moved to kiss her cheek, and then allowed his lips to trail down to her jaw before rising to her mouth. "And this?"

Her pulse rate increased and matched the tempo of his. "That's not my cheek."

"Oh, but darlin', these lips are such a temptation." He nibbled at each corner before claiming her mouth and kissing her in earnest. When she didn't push him away, he deepened the kiss and explored the inner recesses of her mouth. Sweet, her taste was sweet like cinnamon rolls. Had she visited the bakery again for lunch? Her arms circled his neck and held him close, her curves crushed against his hard chest. His body craved hers, he wanted to touch every inch of her, learn the texture of her skin. He cupped a breast, amazed at the softness. Thank God she wasn't wearing a corset. His thumb brushed across her nipple and she gasped. He couldn't stifle the groan that rose up from his chest. "Birdie, I want you so. Why won't you marry me?"

"Oh, Tad, you don't love me. A marriage can't work without love."

"If this isn't love, I don't know what is. I've never wanted anyone like I do you. Honey, I think about you almost every minute of the day." He was happiest when in her company.

"But I don't love you, at least I don't think what I feel is love. Yes, I want you, I enjoy being with you, and I respect you." She stroked his cheek. "But, I'm not sure it's enough."

"How will you know unless you try, unless you give us a chance?"

"But, I've got to concentrate on building my home. Surely you understand that."

"Of course I do." He stood up and offered her a hand. "And I promise I'll do everything I can to help you get it done in time, even if it means picking up a hammer and pounding nails."

Her eyes rounded in surprise. "You'd do that for me?"

How could she doubt that he'd help? He was crazy about the woman. Birdie was nothing like anyone he'd ever known or was likely to meet in the future. She'd never bore him. Yes, she had a little bit of a wild streak. Well, maybe not wild, but she did things different, but in time she'd accept the restrictions of this society and fit right in.

"I'd do anything for you, sweetheart."

He watched as she chewed on her lip trying to make up her mind. "I'll give you an answer tomorrow.

CHAPTER SEVENTEEN

Birdie sat across from Detective Ethan in his office. "None of our men on duty have seen a thing. He must know we're out there hiding in the bushes."

There had to be a way to trick him. What was it? "Call them off for a few days, maybe a week, and let him think we've given up. What we need to do is dress up a couple of police officers in women's clothes as bait."

He guffawed and pounded the desk. "I don't know how the heck I'll get volunteers for this duty."

"You're the boss. You assign your best men to do the job. I'd be willing to dress up like one of the girls."

"Lord, help us. If Tad found out he'd murder you and me both."

"He won't find out. Plus, we're not married. He doesn't tell me what I can and can't do."

He shook his head, brow furrowed. "If folks found out, Birdie, they'd ostracize you."

She shrugged. "So be it. My goal is to catch this weirdo, not make friends."

"I don't care. This is where I draw the line." Ethan opened his desk drawer and lifted a bundle of envelopes out and placed them in front of them. With a pair of tweezers, he removed the items and placed them on a white sheet of paper. "Let's review what we have here."

Two envelopes had similar gray fibers. Birdie had examined them closely under a microscope and concluded they came from the same garment and were wool. At the scene where Lila was attacked, they'd found the matching gray button, and a cigarette butt from boxed cigarettes. At the second scene, they'd found another cigarette butt and on the woman's clothes, a tuft of hair. "Wouldn't you say this hair is auburn, Lloyd?"

He pulled a magnifying glass from his desk drawer and peered closely. "I believe you're right, but I believe I see one gray strand so our culprit most likely is middle-aged."

"I agree," said Birdie. She removed the small square of folded paper. With tweezers she carefully laid it flat against the paper and using the magnifying glass, tried to read the small print at the edge. It didn't make sense to her at all. "Does this print mean anything to you?"

Ethan studied it closely. "It's possible it's part of a receipt, but I can't be sure. We'll have to recover the rest of it to make that determination."

A receipt? Would they have to canvass stores and get a copy of each of their receipts for comparison? She sighed. There were a lot of stores in Waco.

"I've collected several more cologne samples and none were familiar to Lila. I think I'm going to recruit Mattie to help me out." They needed more help to scour the expensive tailors and haberdashers in town. "I believe you'd be the best person to visit the local tailors and ask about the button. Since you're official, maybe they'll talk to you and keep the information under wraps."

He nodded. "Yes, I'll do that. So, our plan of action is to pull our men from the Reservation for, say a week. I'll see if I can find some men to dress up for the next step of our plan." He rubbed his chin. "We'll plan to put the plot in motion the middle of the month."

*   *   *

Birdie, head bent against the wind and to hide her identity, walked past the gazebo to where she had her police loaner horse tied to the hitching post. She chuckled at the ridiculousness of her situation—living in 1890, skulking around incognito. *What's so odd, Birdie? You did the same thing when undercover.* She'd just finished her self-defense class with the ladies of the night.

If she thought some of the young girls resisted exercise, they were nothing compared to the doves on the Reservation. Birdie complained to the madam on duty at the last session about their lack of enthusiasm. Evidently she'd met with the other house owners and tattled. There was less griping today and a little more effort exhibited. One more class and she'd be through with the group. She'd taught them basic defensive skills. What they did with it was entirely up to them.

She tightened the girth on Brownie, and patted her neck before mounting. Some years younger than Molly, she had more spirit but Birdie had learned to control the horse. In just thirty minutes she'd be meeting Tad in front of the Pacific Hotel for a light meal before heading out to his friend's ranch. Her stomach rumbled with hunger as her heart thumped with a need of another kind. How was she going to answer Tad's question of last night? She could only pray the answer would strike her suddenly.

A groom waited for her at the police stables. He took Brownie's reins and handed her Molly's. "Thank you for having her ready."

He doffed his cap. "Happy to help, miss."

Molly butted her with her head. "Are you happy to see me, girl? I'll make sure you get some extra feed tonight." She stepped up into the saddle and headed for the hotel. She leaned forward and patted the gentle animal's neck again. "I guess you've heard the talk around the stable… that I'm going to buy a horse. Now, don't be hurt. That doesn't mean I don't like you. I just don't want to overwork you." Molly tossed her head. "Guess that means you understand." She turned Molly toward Franklin Avenue and Fourth Street.

Tad stood outside the hotel talking with a gentleman. When she rode up, he bid the man good-bye and came to help her from the horse. Like she needed help but there was this gentlemanly thing in this era. He flipped the reins around the hitching post beside his mount Chester and took Birdie's elbow. "Ready to eat?"

"Yes, but you're so dressed up and here I am in a work dress."

"You look just fine, sweetheart." A grin stretching his face, he leaned in closer and spoke softly. "You want me to kiss you right here and show you how wonderful I think you look?"

"No, I do not."

"Shucks. Let's go eat then." Arm around her shoulders, he ushered her into the hotel and toward the dining room.

Five hours later, Birdie was the proud owner of a bay mare named Strawberry. She patted the horse's neck as they rode toward home, Molly following Tad on a lead rope. "She's a beauty, isn't she, Tad?"

"Yes, she's a fine animal. Strawberry is the mount I would have chosen for you."

Birdie wouldn't have been able to make a good choice if it not for Tad. He'd inspected every horse the man brought out for them to look at, picked three, and told her to select the one she preferred. Strawberry was the friendliest of the three. She'd nibbled on Birdie's pocket looking for sugar and nudged her with her nose to get an extra pat and scratch.

The man wanted sixty dollars for Strawberry, but Tad talked him down to fifty—an amazing price when you considered how much the animal would have cost in Birdie's time. Of course, she wasn't making near what she did as a ranger, either. Now she had to watch her money closely, to make sure she could achieve her goal.

She knew she had a giddy smile on her face and that Tad had difficulty not laughing at her. Well, maybe not laugh, but he glanced at her often and appeared to be enjoying her happiness. With the acquisition of thirty acres and a horse, she'd become a property owner. Had she turned a corner and accepted the fact she was here forever? Yes, she supposed so. She'd been here seven months. It was time to make the most of her situation and build a life in the nineteenth century. Well, she'd been doing that, but in the deep recesses of her heart, she'd clung to the hope that she'd make it back home. For some reason, unknown to her, she'd been thrust into this time period for a purpose. It was her responsibility to follow her destiny.

It was late, almost ten o'clock, when they rode into the barn. An hour later, all three horses were groomed and contentedly munching on eats in their stalls. Clouds covered the moon as she and Tad headed for the house. An icy wind whipped up dust around them. They pulled their hats down on their foreheads and tilted their heads into the wind. Tad's strong arm held her close to his body to protect her as much as possible.

They entered through the back screened in porch, a glow from the kitchen lighting their way. An oil lamp, wick turned down low, sat on the counter. The aroma of ham and cornbread filled the room, still warm on the large cast iron range. Tad removed his hat, hung it on the hat rack, and raked a hand through his hair. "Are you hungry?"

"No. Are you?" She was too excited to eat and didn't know how she'd be able to sleep tonight. Fortunately tomorrow was Saturday and she'd probably stay on the ranch and get to know Strawberry.

He removed her hat and tossed it toward the hat rack. It barely caught on one of the knobs. "Oh yeah, I'm ravenous for you, love." His large hands whipped the heavy cloak from her shoulders and it joined their hats. He stood before her, his blue eyes dark with passion, and something more. Could it be longing? Did he care more for her than he let on? Birdie's heart thumped with hope. Was it because she cared more for him than she'd revealed—even to herself? Her breath caught in her throat at the suggestion—her mind realizing the truth. She was in love with him.

Tad wrapped his arms around her and lifted her to meet his kiss. She grabbed the back of his head and answered his demand to deepen the kiss. He explored her mouth and their tongues twined becoming familiar with the taste of each other. When he allowed her feet to touch the floor again, he gazed into her eyes as if reading her mind as his hands moved from her waist up to cup her breasts and stroke their pebbled peaks. "Tad," she moaned and pressed closer enjoying his hardness against her belly.

Breath ragged, he dropped his forehead to hers, and ground out, "Sweetheart, you promised me an answer tonight. Will you marry me?"

Birdie had to take a leap of faith and pray Tad was part of her destiny in this time period. If not, why had he fished her from the river, and why was she here in his home with his family? Her body craved his touch almost more than she wanted to see Birdie's Nest rebuilt. Thank goodness she didn't have to choose between the two. She believed Tad when he said he'd help her. He wasn't rich, but just knowing he supported her was enough. Plus, she loved him.

* * *

Tad waited impatiently for Birdie to come down to breakfast. Twice Maybelle tried to set breakfast on the table and he'd asked her to wait until Birdie and Bethany arrived.

Mouth pinched into a frown line, Mother asked, "What's wrong with you, son? You're usually in a hurry to get out to the stables to work."

"It's Saturday. I may not work today."

Maybelle gaped at him and his mother laid a hand over her heart. "Are you ill?" She shoved up from her chair, rounded the table, and slapped her palm against his forehead. "You don't feel feverish."

"I am not sick. I just want us all to eat together this morning. Is that so odd?"

She returned to her seat and studied him. She was suspicious for sure. "Well, I expect not."

Bethany stomped into the room and plopped down in her chair. "I don't see why we can't eat a little later on Saturday mornings."

Tad hid his grin. "We do, an hour later than we do during the week."

"Why can't it be two hours? I need the rest."

"You get plenty of rest, young lady. I'll not have you grow up to be lazy like some of the girls you hang around with." Mother shook a finger at her. "No man wants a wife who sleeps in when chores are to be done."

"But—"

"Good morning!"

Tad glanced up to see Birdie standing in the doorway, her smile shy. No doubt she wondered if he'd shared the news with his family.

His huge grin drew a quirked eyebrow from his mother, but he couldn't contain his happiness. She couldn't hide the questions in her gaze, but for once, she didn't say anything.

He pushed back from the table and strode to meet Birdie. "Good morning, my love." Unable to resist the glow of her smile and her rosy lips, he caught her to him and kissed her, oblivious to the gasps echoing around the room.

When he drew back, Birdie touched his cheek. "Good morning, Tad." She nodded to the women and flashed them her beautiful smile.

Arm around her waist, he pulled her close to his side. "I have an announcement to make. Birdie has agreed to be my wife."

CHAPTER EIGHTEEN

Squealing with joy, three women converged on Birdie. Mother caught her in a fierce hug. "My dear, we're so happy to have you become a permanent member of this family." She turned on Tad, caught him around the waist and sobbed against his chest.

He patted her back, suddenly concerned. "Mother, what's wrong? I thought you'd be thrilled."

She pulled back and caught his face with both hands. "I'm delighted, young man…so pleased with your choice and that you finally decided to settle down." She caught Birdie's hand. "From the very beginning I knew you two were made for each other." She glanced at Maybelle. The older woman wiped tears from her cheeks with her apron. "Isn't that so, Maybelle?"

Maybelle sniffed. "Yes, indeed, it is."

Tad hugged the older woman. "Hey, now, no tears, Maybelle. This is a joyous occasion."

"I know, but I still see you as a little boy stealing cookies when you thought I wasn't looking."

He'd had a wonderful childhood. If one of his parents weren't available to doctor a scrape or cut, Maybelle was. He kissed her cheek. "Hopefully one of these days we'll have a houseful of kids for you to bake for."

"That'd be mighty fine."

Lordy, he hoped Birdie wanted kids. They'd not discussed a family last night but they had plenty of time.

"Birdie, can I be a bridesmaid?" asked Bethany.

"Of course you can. I intended to ask you and I hope Mattie will be my Matron of Honor."

"Ooh," squealed Bethany. "What colors will you have? I hope you won't pick yellow as it makes me look sallow."

Birdie tweaked Bethany's nose. "I promise no yellow."

Mother clapped her hands. "We have so much planning to do. I can have a wedding planned in two weeks time."

"We'd like to wait a little longer than that, Mother." He glanced at Birdie. "Say a month or two?"

Birdie nodded. "Yes, I think March would be perfect. And Olivia, we thought it'd be nice to have a small service here on the ranch."

"Not get married in the church? Why the whole community will be disappointed if they don't get to attend." Mother sighed and shook her head. "Of course, the choice is yours, but I'm afraid we'll hurt feelings if we keep the guest list too small."

"Well, my feelings are going to be hurt if I have to throw this breakfast out and start over again," announced Maybelle. "Sit down and discuss plans over breakfast."

They all obeyed and she set platters loaded with food on the table. Mother jumped up, ran to the cabinet, and retrieved another plate and silverware. She laid it out beside Bethany. "Maybelle, you join us. You're as much a part of this family as everyone else and we need your help."

"Oh no, ma'am, I couldn't do that."

"Yes, you can." Tad stood and held her chair until she sat down.

Bethany jumped up and returned with an additional place setting and set them before Maybelle.

She sniffed and brushed away a tear. "I'm honored to be included."

Mother smiled at Maybelle and if she'd been within reach would have patted her hand. "We need you, Maybelle." She picked up the platter of eggs and started it around the table. "Now, we'll not discuss wedding plans until we're through eating."

Three hours later, Birdie sat atop Strawberry. Tad handed her the picnic basket to hold while he mounted his horse, a bay gelding, a different animal from the one he usually rode. "What's your horse's name?"

He took the reins and patted the animal's neck. "This is

Brodie. I've had him since he was a colt. He's smart as a whip, aren't you boy?" The animal whinnied and tossed his head. Tad grinned. "See I told you so."

Birdie couldn't resist a laugh. "He doesn't have an ego, either, does he?"

Tad grinned. "Maybe a little one."

They rode east and found the spot where they'd picnicked once before—back before their relationship had turned serious. Birdie couldn't believe she was getting married, but she loved Tad and wanted a life with him. And children. She wanted them too. It'd be nice to postpone them for a short while, but in this day and time, with no birth control, women had no control over when they became pregnant.

Tad spread the quilt in an area vacant of cattle and settled the basket of food at one corner. He took her hand and led her to the center of the quilt. "Your expression is serious. What are you thinking about?"

She sat cross-legged on the blanket and he settled beside her. "About children and the lack of birth control in this era."

"Don't you want children?"

"Of course I do, but I would like to space them three or four years apart."

"How would you do that in your time?"

"Well, there are birth control pills, but I'd probably use a diaphragm." She sighed. "I suppose the Comstock Law makes it next to impossible to obtain condoms."

Reddening, he cleared his throat before speaking. "Yes, doctors usually give them only to unmarried men who frequent certain establishments—for health reasons, you understand."

"Of course. I've never understood the reasoning behind that practice. They will protect men against disease but allow women to die because their bodies can't tolerate another pregnancy." She picked at a loose thread on the hem of her riding skirt. "You know they aren't one hundred percent effective, don't you? For generations, couples have had children even when using prophylactics." Birdie stretched out on the quilt. Propped on her side, she took his arm and pulled him down beside her. "Don't worry, if we have a baby every year, so be it."

"But I don't want you to be pregnant all the time. It can't be healthy for you." He twirled a strand of her hair that had escaped her ponytail. "I'll work out something."

"What do you mean?"

"I'll find a way to get condoms."

"Not at the expense of going to jail, I hope." She slid into his arms and tilted her face up to his face. "One kiss before lunch."

He arched a brow. "Just one?"

His wicked smile was almost as arousing as the feel of his lips, the taste of his mouth and the heat of his length molded to hers. Her body hummed with a hunger of its own and Tad's kisses left her seeking more. She needed closer, wanted to touch his skin. Before she could unbutton his shirt, he'd yanked hers out of her skirt and shoved it up to her neck. She giggled. "Are you trying to choke me?"

He rolled to his back, a deep chuckle bursting from his chest. "No, sweetheart, just wanted to touch the beautiful breasts that have fascinated me since I first saw them."

She propped up on an elbow and pinched his side. "What are you talking about? When have you seen my breasts?"

"Uh, well, the day I pulled you from the river, your dress slipped down and exposed your assets a little."

She swatted him on the belly. "You dirty old man!"

"Hey, I didn't sit there and stare, but promptly pulled your gown up so no one else would see your beautiful flesh."

Birdie snorted. "Yeah, I bet."

"I promise. My mama raised me to be a gentleman."

Swallowing the smile that threatened to break out on her face, she quirked an eyebrow. "If you say so."

He turned back to face her. "I want you something fierce, Birdie. Are you sure we can wait until March to get married? That's a month and a half away."

She coughed. "Well, in my time, it's not uncommon for couples to anticipate the wedding night."

He grinned. "It's not totally unheard of in this time either, but sweetheart, our first time will not be on the ground surrounded by cattle munching on grass."

"Tad, I think you should know, I'm not a virgin. There haven't been a lot of men in my life, but a few."

The hands she loved so much cupped her face. "It doesn't matter...as long as I'm the last."

* * *

They conceded and allowed Olivia to reserve the church for the second Saturday in March. The woman had made an appointment with a dressmaker to have a gown made. Today was Birdie's first visit. After viewing a number of fashion dolls and magazines, they'd agreed on a design. The dress was simple—a scooped off-the-shoulder neckline inset with lace, with abbreviated leg-o-mutton sleeves and a form fitting bodice that ended in a v just below her waist. The skirt flared slightly from the hips and back, while hanging almost straight in the front. She'd wear a waist length veil with a crown of flowers.

"But, it's all so plain, Birdie. Can't we add a flounce here?" Olivia pointed to the sleeves and then to the dropped bodice seam. "And one here?"

"I'd feel ridiculous in something with flounces."

The dressmaker interceded. "Mrs. Lockhart, Miss Braxton has chosen a dress perfect for her height and figure. She'll set tongues wagging and other brides will be copying her dress before the season is over."

Olivia chewed her lip. "You really think so?"

"I know so. This dress speaks of elegance. I'm overjoyed to be the one to make it as it will bring me lots of business." She patted Birdie's hand. "Now, stop back by at the same time in a week so I can make further adjustments."

Oh goodie. Birdie hated standing still and being poked and prodded, but to be beautiful for Tad, she'd do it. She grinned. Wonder how he's doing at the tailor's?

* * *

Tad stepped from the tailor's shop, grateful to be free to return to the ranch and get to work. He wondered how Birdie was managing with his mother and the dressmaker. He grinned at the idea of Birdie getting trussed up in a bunch of frou-frou. His smile wilted. He hoped they didn't talk her into something she'd be uncomfortable wearing. Birdie was a beautiful woman, but ruffles and flounces didn't suit her.

He approached the surrey outside the dressmaker's. Chester whinnied a greeting. Hank looked up, strode toward him, and handed him a letter. "Some kid delivered this. Said I was to give it to you and tell you it was urgent."

Urgent? If something had happened at the ranch, one of the hands would have ridden in to fetch him. He ripped it open and read the familiar script. His first instinct was to wad it up and toss it into one of the trashcans along the street, but the word "son" caught his eye.

Tad,

I know you don't want to hear from me, but I have no choice. I've recently delivered your son. If you don't come take him, I'll put him in one of the orphanages. I can't raise him. The choice is yours.

Lucy

A child? His child? If true, why hadn't she told him sooner, asked for help? He would have provided for both her and the child. An orphanage? No way in hell would a child of his be given away—not while he lived and breathed. His heart thundered in his chest. Could it be true? If so, what would Birdie say? Would she refuse to marry him knowing his relationship with a woman like Lucy had produced a child?

He stuffed the letter into his jacket pocket and mounted Chester. "Thanks, Hank. Tell the women I have business in town and will be home by dinner." The first thing he had to do was find out if Lucy was telling the truth. And how would he know if the child was his? The timing was right. He'd last been with Lucy on June first, the date he'd pulled Birdie from the Brazos.

Lucy's home appeared neglected, not the neat little place he'd visited last year. He rode around to the back and put Chester in the lean to—hiding as he'd always done when he'd visited the woman. Only now, shame nagged his conscience. He strode to the back door and knocked. An elderly woman opened the door and invited him in. "I assume you're Mr. Lockhart."

"Yes, ma'am, I am. Where are Lucy and the baby?"

"They're upstairs." She smirked. "I expect you know the way."

His heart thundered with each step he took. When he reached the top, he tapped on Lucy's bedroom door. "Lucy. It's Tad."

"Come in." She lay in bed, a pale comparison to the woman she'd once been. Her beautiful black hair was dull, matted, and in disarray, her skin a sickly color.

"Are you ill?"

She laughed, the sound bitter and unforgiving. "What do you think? Giving birth is hard, but not that hard." She sighed, deflated, her body sagged against the pillows. "Yes, I'm dying. Doc says a cancer of some sort on my lung."

Guilt and shame washed over him. She'd been a friend. He shouldn't have cut her out of his life completely, could have checked on her occasionally. "I'm sorry, Lucy. I wanted to end our relationship, but I'd never wish you ill."

She coughed and gasped for breath. He lifted a glass of water on the bedside table and held her head as she drank. "Thank you."

"Can I do anything for you, Lucy, to make you more comfortable?"

"No, not unless you want to put me out of my misery."

Kill her? No way could he take a human life unless in self-defense or protecting another. She moaned and clasped her chest. A skeletal hand waved at the medicine bottle by the bed. "Add several drops to a glass of water."

He held the glass for her. She drank it all and shuddered. "Vile stuff but it does help the pain for a short while." She closed her eyes for a few minutes, and then opened them. "I intended to make you pay for deserting me, Tad, by keeping your child from you. You'd see him around town and know he was yours but not have access to him. I knew I was pregnant at the July fourth celebration. I would've told you that night if you'd come to see me."

Tad dropped into the chair beside the bed, his head cradled in his hands. "I would have helped you if I'd known. You should have sent me a message."

"Yeah, I should've and you shouldn't have tossed me aside so."

"We never had an understanding. You know that, Lucy. Our relationship was strictly business."

She pounded on the wall behind her bed. A moment later a young woman came into the room holding a baby. Tad stood to meet her. She handed him the bundle and he stared down into the blue eyes of his son. His little mouth smacked as he sucked on two fingers. Through tears he examined the baby's fingers and toes and rubbed the soft down on his head.

Voice gruff, he choked out, "He's beautiful, Lucy." Tad didn't question if the baby was his. There were no identifying features but the tug on his heart was all he needed. This was his son.

Her smile transformed her features, reminding Tad of the beauty she'd once been. "Yes, he is. His name is Nathan."

"It's a good name."

"This is Sarah. She's been his wet nurse since his birth a month ago. Her own child died shortly after birth." She closed her eyes. "Go. Take him, and go. Please. I can't bear losing him and the sooner you're gone, the better."

"I'll love him always, Lucy. I promise you he'll have a good life."

"I know."

CHAPTER NINETEEN

Early in March, Birdie picked up a bunch of men's cologne samples from Detective Ethan and carried them to the gazebo on the Reservation. Lila met with her first and smelled each of the business cards. She kept returning to one. Finally, she waved it at Birdie. "This is it. I'm sure of it." She started to turn it over.

"Don't look at the name on the back. I want to make sure no one else knows which one you selected."

"I understand. I'll send Rose out. She's still pretty shook up. Don't know how much help she'll be."

"Maybe she'll garner some courage by watching you. You've been a big help, Lila. I hope we catch this man and can lock him away."

Lila stopped in mid-smile, putting her hands to her cheeks. The wounds must pull when she smiled. "I hope so too." She ran into the house without looking back.

Birdie waited for Rose, and had about given up when she stepped from the dwelling. With her head completely covered, she wrapped her arms in the cloak and pulled it tighter around her. When she stepped into the gazebo, she never looked up at Birdie but kept her head bowed.

"Here, let's sit down." On the bench that ran around the small pergola, Rose sat three feet away from Birdie.

"Rose, I'm going to hand you a card. Smell the cologne on it but don't turn it over and look at the name." Birdie laid the first card out on the seat between them. Rose unwound her right arm from the cloak, lifted the paper and smelled, and then laid it back down in the same place. "If you think one is it, wait until you've smelled them all before coming back to it."

Rose nodded and proceeded to the next sample. When she'd finished, she lifted two of them again. Finally she lifted one up and held it toward Birdie. "This one."

"Are you sure? One hundred percent positive?"

"Yes."

They had a winner. It was the same fragrance Lila had selected. "Thank you, Rose. You've been a big help. Do you think you might be up to answering a few questions for me now?"

"I'll try."

Over the next thirty minutes, Rose reiterated what Lila had told her—the vulgar words the man used, the mask he'd worn, clawing at his face, knocking his hat off and pulling his hair.

"Good." Rose peeked up at her so Birdie smiled. "You did real well, Rose. We even found a piece of the man's hair you'd yanked from his head. It will help us identify him."

"What'll the police do to him if they catch him? Nobody cares about us Reservation girls."

"He'll be tried and go to prison, I hope for a long time. Your profession shouldn't have anything to do with his sentence. Guilty is guilty." Birdie stood and looked at the sky. It was beginning to look like rain so she'd better head home. "You let me and the police worry about this man. Take care of yourself and remember, there are people who can see beyond scars."

* * *

On the ride back to the station, Birdie pondered the change in Tad's behavior. She knew something was bothering him and for three nights in a row he'd ridden into town. Surely he wasn't seeing that Lucy woman? If so, there wouldn't be a wedding. She wouldn't marry a man who broke his wedding vows before he said them. No, it had to be something else. Tonight she'd find out what. If he rode out, she'd be on his tail.

After dismounting in the stable at the station, she hurried into Detective Ethan's office. "We have a match."

He looked up, eyes sharp. "Shut the door."

She closed it behind her and sat in the chair facing Lloyd's desk. "I can't believe it. Finally." She took all the envelopes from her bag and laid them out in a row. With her index finger, she tapped the one to the far left. "It's this fragrance from France—Fougere Royal 1882 by Houbigant."

Ethan removed the card and smelled. "Ugh, kind of sweet, isn't it?"

"Yes, and it has a sweet price too. Do you remember where this one came from?"

"I sure do. It's a small, exclusive men's shop, only been open a year or so. Their shirts cost as much as my suits. I'll be speaking with the proprietor first thing in the morning."

"Can I go with you?"

"I don't know. You don't look very manly in that uniform."

"Would it help if I wore an overcoat over the police outfit?"

He worked his mouth into a variety of contortions while thinking. She'd noticed him doing that before. "On one condition. You take notes and don't say a word."

* * *

Tad walked from the jewelry store where he'd just picked up Birdie's ring. She'd insisted on a plain gold band, but he'd had it engraved inside. He'd almost bought a band for himself but decided he'd rather wear his father's wedding band instead.

He had to make a decision about Nathan soon. It hurt to leave him each night after visiting him. As he rocked him to sleep, he talked, and sometimes received a coo in response. Nathan seemed to hang on his every word. The boy stared up at him with the same eyes he looked at when he shaved in the mornings. Oh, God, he had to tell Birdie. It wasn't right to keep her in the dark. She had a right to know before they married. If she left him, it would break his heart, but he couldn't give up his son.

Stuffing the small box in his pocket, he turned and plowed into Detective Ethan and the young officer he'd seen with Ethan once before. "Oops! Sorry, I wasn't looking where I was going."

"No problem, Lockhart. Sorry we can't take time to chat. Jenkins and I are investigating a case."

Tad glanced at Jenkins. But for the mustache, the young man's face was as pretty as a girl's. He wore a long overcoat with his uniform. An odd character for sure, since it wasn't cold enough today to warrant that. "Well, don't let me keep you."

"Be sure to see I get an invitation to the wedding." Ethan waved as they strode off down the street.

"I'll see to it." Tad scratched his chin as he watched them enter Simmons Clothier for Men, a new fancy place for men to buy suits and whatnot. Not as tall as Ethan, Jenkins had a delicate build, almost fragile. Jenkins's hips swayed just like— Tad gaped. Those hips swung like those of a particular woman he enjoyed watching. He snapped his mouth shut before he made a spectacle of himself and shook his head. No, it couldn't be. Birdie was a little wild, but she wouldn't dress up like a man and parade around town. Dadgummit! Yes, she would. But by golly, today would be the last time. He'd put a stop to her outrageous behavior.

He started for the clothiers, but pulled himself up short. *Calm down, Tad. You don't want to barge in and make a scene.* Yes, he did but he wouldn't. It wouldn't do to jeopardize Ethan's case—Ethan and Birdie's case. Now he knew who Ethan's investigator was. Birdie probably loved every minute of helping out. He should have known something was up with her getting home later in the evenings.

Tad ducked behind a storefront and waited. Thirty minutes later Ethan and Birdie left the shop, walked past him, and mounted their horses. Darned if Birdie wasn't riding a different horse. Guess she didn't want Molly or Strawberry to be seen around town with someone else on her. She and Ethan had planned this charade to a T and were thick as thieves.

He couldn't believe Birdie would go behind his back and do something she knew he disapproved of. When they passed, he left his secluded spot and mounted Chester to follow them to the station. He hung back until they'd stabled their horses, then tied Chester up to one of the hitching posts.

Inside the building he marched to Ethan's office, rapped on the door, and walked in without an invitation.

Ethan shoved back from his desk. "What do you think you're doing barging in unin—" His eyes widened when he recognized Tad, but he kept a poker face. "As you can see, Jenkins and I are in the middle of an important consultation." Jenkins didn't turn around and acknowledge him but buried his head in a notebook. "Come back in an hour and I can see you then."

"I want to see you now. And I'd like to get to know Jenkins a little better. He reminds me of someone, especially the way his hips sway, even under that heavy coat he wore today."

"That's insulting, Lockhart." He rounded the desk and took Tad's arm trying to usher him from the room.

Tad stood his ground. If it came to a shoving match, he was out to win. "How dare you expose Birdie to the criminal elements that frequent this place?" He yanked Birdie's hat off. Her pinned up hair broke loose in places and tumbled to her shoulders. "Where are the clothes you wore into town this morning?"

She grabbed her hat from his hands and shoved the loose strands up under the felted brim. "You have no right to barge in here and question my actions."

"I most certainly do. In less than a month we'll be married. Can you imagine what the people in this town would have to say about you if they knew you were dressing up in men's clothes and parading about town?"

She stuck her chin out. "I really don't care." He resisted the urge to shake some sense into her.

"Well, I do. Your behavior reflects on me and my mother."

Her shoulders sagged. "It's not like anyone could recognize me. I've been careful and am rarely out of Lloyd's sight."

He shot Detective Ethan a glare and spit out, "I just bet you're not."

"Now see here, Lockhart, our relationship has been strictly business. Birdie's been a big help in collecting evidence and gathering information from the attacks on the Reservation ladies."

Tad's face heated and he could almost feel steam pouring from his ears. He ground out, "She's been over on Two Street? Please! Tell me she hasn't been mixing with the prostitutes."

Birdie stood. She poked Tad in the chest with her index finger. "I'm not a child and you are not my husband yet. I'll not have you or anyone else telling me what I can and cannot do."

"What were you thinking, Ethan?"

His expression mulish, the detective muttered. "That she might could teach us something."

"So, you've come to the conclusion she's really from the future and was a Texas Ranger?"

"*Is* a Texas Ranger, Tad Lockhart." Birdie strode to the door. "Excuse me, gentlemen. I'll go change clothes while you discuss me like I'm not here."

"Yes, I do believe she's from the future," Ethan said. "Don't you?"

Tad released a pent up breath. "Yeah, I do, especially after the Massacre at Wounded Knee. She'd told us it would take place on December 29th, and it did." He dropped into the chair Birdie had vacated. "It's hard to believe, but with that little gun of hers, the massacre, and a few other things she's told me, I've come to accept it."

"I know one thing," said Ethan. "She's not like women of this era and though she'll try, she'll never fit into the mold of what we consider womanly behavior. If you try to keep her on a short leash, you're going to lose her."

CHAPTER TWENTY

Birdie argued with Tad all the way home. He insisted she at least quit going to the Reservation.

"Why? No one knows who I am. I'm Jenkins, the skinny cop." Well, that wasn't exactly true. Lila and Rose knew who she was but they'd never tell.

"Don't you realize how worried I'll be for your safety, not to mention your reputation?"

She glanced his direction. "Why is my reputation so important?" He appeared as miserable as she felt.

"It's important because I couldn't stand to see you unhappy. You may think you don't need other people, but we all do, including you. I couldn't stand it if folks shunned you, and you'd feel terrible."

"I don't know if I can withstand the confines of nineteenth century society. I can't play ball, I can't ride with the Rangers, and you don't want me working with the police department, doing what I've been trained and love to do."

He yanked his hat off and ran his hands through his hair. "If anyone finds out, you'll be ruined in this town. Remember, your actions have an effect on Mother also." He slapped his hat against his leg and situated it back on his head. "I can handle the gossip, the whispers. Of course, I may have to beat the stuffing out of a man or two, but it's the women who are most vindictive."

Tad had that right. Women in the twenty-first century were the same way. Of course, society's rules had changed, but if a group of women got it in for you, they'd make your life hell. That's one reason she didn't want to work in a largely female environment—too much sniping and other petty nonsense. Birdie didn't want to bring gossip down on Olivia's head or on Bethany's, either. But, Olivia had mellowed somewhat since she learned the truth about Birdie—that she really had traveled back in time. Plus, Olivia was a pretty tough lady. Not many people would have the nerve to defy her and turn their nose up at Birdie. She sighed. Still, didn't want to put the older woman—soon to be her mother-in-law—in a position where she had to defend her.

"Tad, I understand your concerns, but please, let me finish out this case. We're so close to solving it, and I'll give up my job until the department might need me again."

He pulled Chester to a halt. "Your job? Do you mean to say you're getting paid?"

Strawberry passed them by so she turned her and brought the mare up alongside the gelding. "Yes, I am and quite nicely I might add. More than you pay me to keep your books."

She pulled Strawberry closer to Chester and reached for Tad's hand. "I promise I'll be careful and no one will recognize me."

He brought her hand to his lips and kissed her knuckles. "Birdie, I believe it would kill me if that crazy man hurt you."

The pained expression on his face weakened her resolve, but she couldn't give in. He'd never said the words, "I love you," but his actions betrayed his feelings. She hoped he'd say them one day soon. "I'm not going to get hurt."

"How can you know that?"

She withdrew her hand, took a deep breath, and exhaled. What could she tell him? In her life this was her job and dangers were part of the territory. "Tad, this is what I've been trained to do. Give me a little credit for knowing how to take care of myself."

He groaned. "Do you know how hard this is for me? I realize you're from the future." He shook his head. "I sure as heck don't know how it happened, but I believe you were a Texas Ranger in your time and that you're well trained, but you're a woman. Putting yourself in danger and participating in police matters is just not done in this time. Consider how I feel."

"Are you saying you'd be embarrassed or ashamed of me if someone found out?"

"No, never! But folks could make life mighty uncomfortable for you." He cocked a brow and grinned. "In doing so, they'd make me mad as all-get-out. I'd sic Mama on the women, but I might end up busting a few noses of the men."

"Tad Lockhart, you'll do no such thing. Lloyd would end up having to put you in jail."

"I have an evil temper sometimes, was known to be a scrapper when growing up. Just ask James."

She cocked a brow at him. "Are you proud of your fighting?"

"No, but I guarantee, no one will hurt me or mine and not feel some pain in return."

"Tad, believe in me. I can handle whatever they dish out. This case will be over soon. Afterwards, I'll only help with evidence." Lloyd needed her right now. They were so close to finding the man cutting up the women. She reached up and caressed his cheek. "Please be patient and give me to until this guy is locked up."

He sighed and leaned over and kissed her. "All right, Birdie."

"Thank you, Tad."

She turned Strawberry around and they rode along in quiet for a while. The sun was setting behind them, casting their shadows on the dirt road before them. Fields of winter wheat grew on either side of the road. Cows or steers, whatever the difference, munched on grass. Life was so different and yet, she couldn't say she didn't like the differences. The air smelled cleaner, except for the odor of manure, even in town and life was slower, more laid back. It didn't do much good to get in a hurry because the speed you got somewhere depended on how fast a horse you owned.

Just ahead the ranch, cast in a yellow glow, came into view. Birdie drew a deep breath, let it trickle out, then asked, "Tad, where have you been going the last few nights?" His head jerked toward her. His lips parted. His jaw tightened, but he said nothing.

"Surely," she said, "you didn't think your evening trips

179

would go unnoticed, especially when you used to spend that time with me."

"It's… it's something I need to deal with. I promise, though, I'll tell you soon." He didn't appear defensive, which was a good sign, so she let the subject drop. For the moment.

* * *

Tad sat in the parlor of Mrs. Mayberry's home. Sarah, whose child died shortly after birth, and Nathan had moved back in with her mother after he put Lucy in the hospital for better care. Hopefully, Dr. Franks could control her pain until she passed. The creak of the rocking chair sang a comforting tune as he gazed down at his son. His heart swelled with love and concern. He couldn't give this baby up, yet he feared Birdie wouldn't marry him when she found out. What woman would want to raise her husband's child from an illicit relationship?

He couldn't keep Nathan's existence from her any longer. She had to be told, as did Mama and Bethany. A child needed his family. He prayed Birdie would understand and stick by him. Tonight. He'd tell her tonight. God, he loved her. Shocked at the revelation, because he'd never consciously admitted his feelings before, not even to himself, he lifted Nathan, one hand under his butt and the other around his head, he met the baby's gaze. "I love you, little man, but I love Birdie too."

The baby cooed at Tad and he gasped to keep his heart from bursting with joy. A woman to love, one who he was sure loved him, and this precious child, as well. How many gifts could a man like him deserve? Tears clouded his vision. He had to get a grip on his emotions. He couldn't go around crying every time he thought of Birdie, or heard this little tadpole coo. A chuckle erupted from him. "You are my little tadpole," he said, and Nathan's eyes widened. Tad leaned down, kissed his forehead, and cradled him within the crook of his arm.

A knock sounded on the front door. Sarah walked past the doorway of the parlor on her way to answer it. "Hello. Can I help you?"

"Yes. Is Tad Lockhart here?"

Tad instantly recognized Birdie's voice. She'd followed him. He froze for a moment, then relaxed. It was time. "Bring her in, Sarah."

Birdie stood in the entryway to the parlor, eyes wide, staring at the baby in his arms.

"This," he said, his voice husky as he rose to his feet, "is my son. Nathan."

She moved closer and looked down at Nathan. A fleeting expression of longing crossed her face before she lifted shocked yes to him. Her bottom lip trembled. She tried to still it by pinching her lips together, which made her effort to smile a grimace. Oh, God, he'd hurt her so much, and hated himself for it, but he couldn't regret this child.

"Birdie, sweetheart, I'd planned to tell you. I just found out about him last week and— I've been in shock. I've racked my brains, trying to figure out when would be the best time, the best way to tell you. Please, forgive me."

Voice choked, she asked, "Forgive you? For what? For waiting until our wedding is two weeks away? Tell me, Tad, did you intend to marry me and then tell me about your love-child?"

Her body shook. He wasn't sure if it was anger or despair, but it didn't matter. He'd caused her pain and could do nothing to make it better. "Forgive me for not telling you sooner—immediately. For allowing you to find out this way. I wouldn't have waited until after the wedding." His voice broke. He cleared his throat. "Surely you know me better than that, Birdie."

With Nathan tucked in his arms, he stood. "I'll take him to his wet-nurse. Please, stay and talk with me." He passed through the door that opened to the dining room from the parlor. Sarah sat in one of the chairs but stood when he entered. Her smile was forced. No doubt she'd heard every word. She gently took Nathan and raised him to her shoulder. Tad took a deep steadying breath and clasped the doorknob to the sitting room, noticing how his hand shook. Would Birdie still be there?

She hadn't moved an inch. He started toward her, but she stopped him with a raised hand. "Don't come any closer. I don't trust myself to be near you right now."

"Will you… will you sit down then? Please?"

"No, we don't have that much to say to each other. Why does your son have a wet-nurse? Where is his mother?"

"Lucy is in Waco City Hospital dying of a cancer on her lung."

Birdie closed her eyes for a moment, and then popped them open. A tear leaked down one cheek. "I'm very sorry to hear that."

"I can't give him up, Birdie. He's my child and I love him." His heart ached in his chest. Now, seeing it from her point of view, he realized he couldn't possibly hope she'd marry him. After all he'd said about her needing to lead a more circumspect life, here he was, looking as if he expected her to forgive his own scandalous behavior, producing a child born to his former mistress? "I'm sorry… about not telling you. About… the wedding, but he's my blood and I have to keep him. I couldn't let him go to an orphanage."

Her face a mask of pain, she wiped at tears. "Of course you have to keep him. I wouldn't respect you if you didn't." Her hand shook as she covered her mouth to stifle her sobs. "But… but I have to give this some…serious thought." She took a deep breath and managed to get her emotions under control. "I'll let you know if we'll be having a wedding or not."

Before he could say more, she turned and opened the door. Back rigid, she stopped for a moment, "Goodbye, Tad," then left the house.

* * *

Birdie's legs felt like lead weights as she climbed into the surrey with Hank's help. "Will you take me to the Hellman's home?" Struggling to keep her voice steady, she rattled off the address. What took ten minutes seemed like a day. Hank cast worried glances her way, but she dared not speak for fear of falling apart.

In front of the Hellman's house, Hank helped her down. "I'll not be returning to the ranch, Hank. Thank you for bringing me in."

"Any time, Birdie. Happy to help. I'll wait right here until you're inside."

She started toward the house, and then stopped. "Hank, I'd appreciate it if you didn't tell anyone where we went tonight."

"No problem, ma'am. If anyone asks I'll say you had a meeting at the church."

"I appreciate it. And tell Tad I'm not sure when or if I'll return to the ranch."

"Yes, ma'am, I will."

Joseph had the front door open when she stepped on the porch. "Birdie, what are you doing out this late?"

She turned and waved to Hank and then turned back to Joseph. Voice hoarse, she choked out, "Can I spend the night?"

He slipped an arm around her shoulder and drew her inside before closing the door. Mattie came through the swinging door from the kitchen and stopped in her tracks, mouth open. "Birdie." She must have recognized the pain on her face, as she approached her with arms open. Birdie threw herself into the older woman's embrace. Mattie patted her back and led Birdie to the sofa. "Joseph, will you be a dear and make us a pot of tea?"

"Be happy to." He disappeared through the swinging door.

Mattie took Birdie's hands. "Now, tell me what's going on. Did you and Tad have a fight?"

Birdie shook her head. "It's much more than that." She proceeded to tell Mattie the entire story.

Mattie poured tea as she listened. She handed Birdie a cup and she sipped between tirades. Mattie didn't interrupt, but when Birdie finished, Mattie closed her eyes and murmured, "A baby. Joseph and I have longed for one for years."

Shame washed over Birdie. Here this sweet couple would give anything for a child and she, Birdie Braxton, was devastated because Tad had fathered one. No, that wasn't the issue; it was the fact he'd kept it from her. He should've told her the minute he found out.

"I'm so sorry, Mattie. I must sound childish."

"No, dear. You have reason to be upset with Tad. But, let me ask, do you resent the baby?"

"Oh, no. He's innocent in this situation. Truth be told, I don't know what I'm so hurt about." She chewed her bottom lip. "Maybe the fact that he's not my child. Jealousy."

"But that's exactly the point, Birdie. He can be."

"Can be what?"

"Your child, dear, if you but accept him into your life. And into your heart."

* * *

In the Hellman's guest room, Birdie quickly stripped and washed before slipping into the nightgown Mattie had loaned her. The feather mattress gave with her weight as she lay down and it conformed to her body like a welcoming embrace. Alone, where no one could see her, she curled on her side allowed the tears to fall freely, dampening her pillow. Before her eyes, the scene of Tad rocking his baby replayed in her mind. He seemed so content and proud. Love radiated from his eyes as he looked down at the child. In the few minutes she'd stood there before him, many emotions crossed his face; one was deep regret and sorrow. The image brought fresh tears to her eyes and she sobbed into the pillow. She wanted it to be their child he held and adored. She pounded the pillow with a fist. Life could be so unfair.

Though he hadn't said it, Birdie knew he loved her, else he'd never have asked her to marry him. He'd had to make a choice between her and the baby and that grieved him. He hurt because one joy had taken another from him—her.

She couldn't love a man who didn't claim his child. As much as it hurt, he'd made the right decision. The man who'd tried so hard to control her behavior for her reputation's sake would now be dealing with fallout from his affair with Lucy. She didn't doubt his ability to handle it. And Lucy? In the hospital dying. She couldn't fault Tad for taking care of her. He was the type of man who'd do the right thing.

Tad had said, "I can't give him up." Did that mean he planned to bring the infant home? She knew in many cases during the Victorian era men, or women for that matter, would hide their indiscretions. Yet, others gave the child to relatives to care for, or brought a baby—"born on the wrong side of the blanket"—home to be raised by their wives. She could imagine how much resentment the latter caused, but people had rarely divorced then. She shook her head. "Then" was actually "now" and she and Tad weren't married.

Birdie couldn't imagine herself accepting such an arrangement, but then she'd not lived it either. Until tonight. Still, Tad's relationship with Lucy had occurred before Birdie came on the scene, at a time when he didn't know her, let alone owe her any fealty.

What was she going to do? She didn't think she resented the baby. He truly was an innocent victim. She resented Tad not telling her right away, not giving her time to adjust. Could she forgive him and get past his failure to inform her?

* * *

Tad had plenty of time to think as he rode home. He couldn't feel any worse if his mother was riding with him chastising him about his relationship with Lucy. Mother had warned him, but he'd never dreamed Lucy would get pregnant. He regretted his relationship with the woman, but not the child. Never the child.

Why hadn't he told Birdie about Nathan right away? She knew about Lucy. He should've trusted her enough to be candid. Why couldn't she love him enough to accept Nathan? Love? He was a fool. He'd never told her he loved her. Surely she knew by his actions, but women needed to hear the words. She'd said she couldn't respect him if he denied his own son. Did her phrasing mean she no longer loved him? His head hurt. His stomach hurt. His heart hurt. What was he going to do?

He rode into to the barn, surprised to see Hank waiting for him. "What are you doing still up?" Tad dismounted and led Brodie to his stall, and breathed a sigh of relief to see Strawberry put away for the night.

"I need to give you a message." Hank's flat tone told him nothing.

"I'm listening."

"I took Birdie in to town tonight in the surrey. Knew you've have a fit if she went in alone at night."

185

"I appreciate you looking out for her."

Hank coughed. "She didn't come back with me. Had me leave her at the Hellman's house."

Tad froze in raising his saddle, but recovered and lifted it off Brodie and onto the side of his stall. "Thanks for letting me know."

"Sure thing." Hank remained as expressionless as a wooden Indian "Good night."

"Good night." Tad wiped Brodie down and then grabbed a brush. With slow, deliberate strokes, trying to even out his churning emotions, he curried the animal. When he finished, he gave the horse a ration of oats and fresh water. He turned out the lantern and closed the barn doors making sure the latch fell into place. The small kitchen light appeared a million miles away. He lifted one foot in front of the other and started the loneliest journey he'd ever made.

CHAPTER TWENTY-ONE

Tad didn't sleep. He rose early and made his way downstairs to put on a pot of coffee before heading outside to watch the sunrise. Maybelle made her way down the path from her cabin and stopped beside him. She eyed him with suspicion. "What's wrong, Mr. Tad?"

He cleared his throat. "I'll be in shortly and tell both you and Mother. Can you hold off breakfast for a short while?"

"Yes, I surely can."

He suspected his mother was up and in the kitchen, so he waited long enough for Maybelle to relay the news. When he entered, both women sat at the table with a coffee at hand. One waited for him. He sat down and took a healthy slug, enjoying the heat as it traveled down to his stomach. If only it could warm his heart.

His mother covered his free hand with hers and squeezed. "What's going on, son?"

"Birdie spent the night at the Hellman's."

"Why, that's nice. Birdie's lucky to have Mattie as a friend."

"She might not be coming back here. There may not be a wedding."

"Why? Did you do something, Tad? Is that why?"

"I guess you could say that, only more like what I didn't do." He rose at the sound of a horse approaching the back of the house. It was Joseph Hellman. Tad walked out to join him and offered his hand. "Joseph."

He grasped Tad's hand. "Tad." He cleared his throat. "I'm real sorry about the situation between you and Birdie."

"I—"

Joseph held up a hand. "I don't know any of the particulars. Left the two women alone to discuss it. Just know that Birdie cried a lot last night. Mattie sent me here to pick up a few clothes and Birdie's horse."

Pain lanced through Tad's heart. He rubbed at the spot trying to ease the ache and nodded to Joseph. "Come in the house and have a cup of coffee while Mother gathers the items."

"Sounds good. The wind is nippy this morning."

When they entered, Maybelle had another cup on the table and set about refilling everyone's cup. Joseph removed his hat. "Morning, ladies."

"Joseph, what's got you out so early this morning?"

His brow furrowed, he jerked his head to Tad. *Not up to me*, his manner said.

"Have a seat, Joseph. I told them Birdie spent the night at your house."

"Yes, ma'am. That's right. Mattie sent me over this morning to get a few of Birdie's things, enough to last a couple of days."

His mother's face tightened, her lips forming a stern line. She scooted her chair back and stood. "It won't take but a few minutes to gather the items. I'll be right back."

"No rush, ma'am."

"Joseph, do you mind riding down to the barn to pick up Birdie's horse? Just tell one of the men what you need."

"Don't mind at all." He studied his coffee for a minute. "I expect this whole situation will blow over in a few days, Tad."

"I expect so." Lord he surely hoped so. He couldn't imagine his life without Birdie any more than he could envision it without a small, blue-eyed baby boy whom he loved. The only thing keeping him sane at the moment was the thought of Nathan, the sure knowledge that, no matter what, strangers would not raise his son.

As soon as Joseph left, Bethany came down the stairs. "What's all the activity around here this morning?"

Tad sighed and ushered her to a chair. "I might as well tell all three of you at one time."

"Tell us what?"

Tad cleared his throat. "Bethany, you don't know this, but last year I was seeing a woman in town. Mother knew and didn't approve. You see, she's not the kind of woman I'd bring home to meet my family."

Bethany's mouth formed a silent O.

"I stopped seeing her about the time Birdie arrived, but what I didn't know was that she was pregnant with my child."

Olivia groaned and covered her trembling mouth. Maybelle grabbed her hand.

"I found out two weeks ago because Lucy sent an urgent message for me to come to see her, said she'd had my son and couldn't take care of him. If I didn't take him, he'd go to an orphanage. You can imagine my reaction."

"An orphanage!" shrieked Olivia. "Over my dead body."

"Lucy is very ill. She's dying of lung cancer. I had her admitted to the hospital for proper care."

Olivia shook her head. "Sad. I've heard it's very painful. It's good she's getting good care."

"I'm sorry for bringing this scandal down on our family. I hope it won't cause your friends and others in town look down on you."

"You have Birdie to think about, son. You can't expect her to raise another woman's child. We can find a family, someone close so we can keep an eye on him, to take him in as their own."

"No, Mother. He and his wet nurse and are coming to live with me. If you don't want him here, I'll find a house in town until I can build another."

"Is this the problem standing between you and Birdie? Does she resent the child, refuse to raise it?"

"No, Mother. The problem is that I didn't tell her when I found out, that she had to discover it on her own. She'd noticed I'd been leaving in the evenings and followed me last night."

He dropped his head into his hands and massaged his temples. "I'm sorry to say but it looks like we won't be having a wedding."

* * *

Birdie walked with Mattie outside in her garden. Not much was in bloom but the fresh air cleared her head. Earlier she'd been to see Strawberry. Nehemiah had settled her in a stall and she'd nickered a greeting as Birdie entered. That had been yesterday morning. She'd been here a full day and Tad hadn't come to see her. Had he just given up on her? His lack of response unsettled her. Maybe he didn't love her as much as he'd claimed. A hard lump formed in her stomach, and she drew in a deep breath of air to ease the discomfort. And what did she expect—to see him groveling for her forgiveness? Surely she wasn't the type that wanted to see him suffer. Well, she was certainly suffering right now. On the other hand, what did he expect from her—to have that forgiveness simply for the asking? His lie of omission hurt, hurt her deep inside where her soul lived. Why hadn't he trusted her with the truth?

They sat down on a wooden bench. Birdie turned her face up to let the sun's rays warm it. If only it could warm her heart. Indecision ate at her. Her life was a mess and she didn't know how to fix it.

"Do you love Tad, Birdie?"

"Yes, yes I do."

"You've said you don't resent the child. Why then can't you forgive Tad?"

"Because he didn't tell me as soon as he found out! We're engaged, for gosh sake. He should have told me."

"Hmm, I suppose you haven't deceived him about one thing or another since you've been here, right?"

Birdie remembered her time at the Reservation, the days she'd been dressed up as Detective Jenkins and stayed late pretending she was teaching classes. He'd been angry and upset, but he'd not turned her away. He'd understood. He'd… forgiven her.

"Oh, God, Mattie, I've been acting like a fool, acting as if his fathering little Nathan was a betrayal of me, and it's not. My pique over his not telling me right up front is a betrayal of what I feel for him. I have to go back to the ranch."

Having made up her mind, Birdie insisted she leave right away. She packed the valise Olivia had sent with her clothes while Nehemiah saddled Strawberry. As she walked through the kitchen Sadie muttered, "Bout time you got your head on straight, Miss Birdie."

Birdie giggled, but Mattie rolled her eyes. "You can roll them eyes at me all you want, but you knows I'm telling the truth, Miss Mattie."

Birdie couldn't resist kissing the smooth black cheek. "Thank you, Sadie."

"Pleased to help. Now, you get yourself home where you belongs."

It was about quitting time when Birdie rode past the house and toward the barn. One of the cowboys let out a piercing whistle. Standing at the corral, Tad's head came up and he glanced her way.

With slow deliberate ease, he mounted Brodie and turned the horse in her direction. He didn't nudge his horse into a gallop so Birdie kept Strawberry moving at a walk. The darn man wasn't going to make this easy for her.

They stopped about three yards apart. Tad tipped his hat. "Birdie."

"Tad."

"You coming home or just passing by?"

"I'm coming home."

He merely nodded and turned Brodie. "Let's get these horses in the barn."

At the barn, the cowboys scattered, leaving them alone. Butterflies raced through her stomach and she drew several deep breaths to calm herself. They dismounted and she and Strawberry followed Tad as he walked Brodie in to the barn. Tad stood by Brodie's stall, arms crossed, waiting. No smile, nothing. So, that's the way he planned to handle it—force her to make the first move. Well, we'll see about that.

With a smile as big as Texas, she propped a hand on her hip, tossed her head and challenged him, "Well, did you miss me, cowboy?"

One step and he was on her. One hand fisted in her hair, sending her hat flying, and the other caught her around the waist and yanked her body flush with his. Face less than an inch from hers, he growled. "Dammit, don't ever do that to me again."

She screeched, "You? What about me?" She knocked his hat off and grabbed handfuls of his hair. "You didn't come see me, or try to make things right."

"Sweetheart, I'd said all I could. Do you forgive me?"

"Why should I? You've never even said you love me."

His eyes rounded in shock. "Haven't I told you in a thousand ways?"

"Maybe, but I need to hear the words on occasion. And yes, I forgive you. Mattie reminded me I'd kept a thing or two from you also. Maybe not this important, but...."

His grin wicked, he muttered, "Yes, there is that." He closed the inch between them and took her mouth. His kiss sent a longing to her core and she wrapped her legs around his waist. Off balance, he fell back into an empty stall, landing on his back in the straw. Unwilling to break their kiss, they rolled until Tad lay on top, between her legs. He rocked against her, the friction in that sensitive place about to send her over the edge. She pulled his shirt from his jeans and ran her hand across the muscled plains of his chest and back. He grabbed her ankles and ran his hand up her legs and under her pantaloons. She caught his groan in her mouth as the flesh of her buttocks quivered against his touch. "Oh, God, Birdie, you're so soft."

From outside, they could hear the men gathering. Hank yelled, "Hey Thomas, is that Miss Olivia walking this way?"

"Yep, sure is. Bet she saw Miss Birdie ride in and come to check on her."

"Did you hear me, Thomas?"

Tad groaned and yelled, "Hell, yes he did, along with half of Texas. Thanks for the warning." Guffaws and titters arose outside.

Birdie blushed scarlet, but Tad jumped up, pulled her with him and started stuffing his shirt in his pants. He knocked the straw off Birdie's clothes and picked it out of her hair. She ran her hands through the long tresses, trying to restore a modicum of order. Tad grabbed his hat off the ground a plopped it on his head, and then took Birdie by the shoulders.

"And for the record and for always, I love you with a passion I never expected to feel, Birdie. I'm so glad you came home."

192

Hank whistled Dixie as he made his way into the barn. "How about I be putting Strawberry away for you, Miss Birdie?"

"Thank you, Hank. I'd like that."

Arms around each other they walked to meet Olivia.

* * *

Birdie rode Strawberry into town. Olivia had been shocked when she and Tad brought Nathan home, and she searched Birdie's eyes for the truth of her feelings. Though caring for a child would take more of her time than she'd hoped to give right now, she couldn't give up on her dream to build Birdie's Nest. There was no other alternative. The child needed a mother. She'd just have to work longer hours and it wasn't like she wouldn't have help. She was content with her decision.

A smile teased her mouth as she remembered her morning with Nathan. The little cutie. He'd gazed up at her with those beautiful eyes just like his daddy's, trust radiating from them. He cooed, the sound awakening an emotion new to her. Could she love him already? Her throat clogged and she struggled to keep her chin from quivering. "I'm your mama now, Nathan. No one will hurt you when I'm around, or your daddy, or your granny." She bent down and placed a kiss on his forehead, and then cradled him in her arms as one foot set the rocking chair in motion.

Later that day, she tied the mare to the hitching post outside Waco City Hospital. Inside she asked to visit Lucy Jamison and was directed to the last room at the end of the hall. She tapped on the door.

"Come in." The woman's invitation ended with a coughing spasm.

Birdie hurried into the room and poured her a glass of water. Before Lucy took the liquid, she spent a minute or so gasping for breath. She nodded her thanks and took a couple of sips before handing the glass back.

Lucy was a wasted vessel of the woman she'd once been. Her dark hair no longer shone with health, her skin had a sickly pallor. Birdie's heart ached for her. Her beauty was gone, but being unable to breathe had to be a frightening experience, one she hoped never to go through. And giving up her baby had to be contributing to her quick decline.

"May I sit down?" Lucy nodded and Birdie drew the chair closer to the bed. "Do you have everything you need? I know Tad is paying for your care, but is there anything I can get for you?"

"No. They are taking good care of me here." She closed her eyes. "Why did you come?"

A lump formed in Birdie's throat making it hard to speak. She didn't want to break down and cry in front of this poor woman. She was here to reassure her, make her passing easier. "I wanted you to know that Tad and I have decided Nathan will live with us. We'll raise him as our child." Birdie reached for the hand lying atop the covers and squeezed. "I promise you, I'll love him as if I'd given birth to him."

Fat tears rolled down Lucy's cheeks. She opened her eyes and stared at Birdie. Lips trembling, she asked, "Why would you do that? Aren't you afraid of what folks will say?"

Birdie swiped at the tears that overflowed her bottom lashes. "Because, he is innocent in all this, and he's Tad's son. He already loves him, and I can assure you, between Olivia, Tad, and myself, we will handle the gossip and whatever folks dish out. We won't allow anyone to hurt your child."

Lucy's body shook with sobs. Birdie jumped up and patted her shoulder. "Hush now, you can't do that. You'll start coughing again." Not good at comforting, Birdie panicked. She took Lucy's hand and stroked it as she talked. "Breathe slowly now. That's it. In and out."

When Lucy stopped shaking, Birdie sat down again. "Have you talked to a preacher or priest to set your house in order?"

"Why should I?" Her dark eyes closed, blocking Birdie and her comments out. "People like me don't deserve forgiveness."

"That's bull. Everyone deserves absolution. Anyway, you've not done anything that bad, have you?"

Lucy eyes popped open. Her brow wrinkled in confusion.

"Have you killed anyone, been cruel to children, beat your mother?"

"Of course not."

"Okay, there you go. Even murderers deserve forgiveness. How about on my way out I tell the receptionist you'd like to see someone."

"All right. I grew up Catholic so I'd like to see a priest." Her lips tilted into a smile. "Thank you, Miss Braxton."

"Please, call me Birdie." Maybe she could give this woman a little something more—an unusual story to distract her from her situation. "Now, I want you to close your eyes, and I'll tell you an unbelievable story, but you have to promise not to share it with anyone else."

"I promise."

"Do you remember the day Tad pulled me from the Brazos River?"

Lucy nodded.

"Someone had hit me on the head and tossed me off a riverboat into the water. It's a wonder I survived. But the odd thing here is the year was 2012 and…."

* * *

Birdie stopped by the Self Defense School, which sported a brand new sign, to visit with Mattie a moment between classes.

"Hey, Mattie, the sign looks great."

"Doesn't it, though. That sign maker over on Eight Street made it for a great price."

"You are keeping tabs and making sure part comes out of my share of the profits?"

"Of course I am, dear. You don't think I'd cheat myself, do you? Mattie hugged her. "How are the wedding plans coming along?"

"Good, I guess. Olivia is taking care of everything." Thank goodness, as Birdie never enjoyed planning parties and such. Aunt Patty had insisted she learn, but Birdie did as little entertaining as possible. She guessed one day she'd be required to entertain guests for Tad, but right now she'd rather be at the police station. "How are fittings going for your Matron of Honor dress?"

Mattie patted her belly. "As long as I don't gain another ounce, I'm good."

Birdie eyed the older woman. "You're looking good, Mattie." She'd lost probably twenty pounds and her new clothes showed off a fine figure.

Mattie preened. "Joseph seems to think so too." She blushed and giggled like a schoolgirl. "You'd think we were newlyweds."

Birdie laughed, delighted the woman appeared so happy. "That's wonderful." She thought for a few minutes. "I wonder what I'll look like after as many years of marriage as you've had."

"As active as you are, I'm sure you'll look very much like you do now."

"I better start back on my exercise schedule soon. I've been so busy I've neglected to jog and go through my training routine."

Even though no one was in the big open area, Mattie lowered her voice. "Have y'all determined who's been cutting up the doves?"

"I'm hoping Detective Ethan will have a list of possible suspects today." Glancing at the watch hanging around her neck, a gift from Tad, she muttered, "I better get a move on. See you again soon."

It didn't take her five minutes after leaving the warehouse to reach the police station. Lloyd stood when he saw her come in and waved her toward his office.

"Do you have some names?"

He grinned. "Sure do and you're not going to believe who's on the list."

"Well, let me see it." Her heart thundered with excitement and anticipation. They were near to catching the culprit.

He removed a slip of paper from his desk drawer and scribbled three names on it before turning it around for her to see.

Birdie stared at the list—John Samuelson, a deacon at the Lockhart's church, Jim Wallace, Julie Wallace's father, and Ted Bankston, a name unfamiliar to Birdie. No, it couldn't be Julie's father and she hated to believe John Samuelson would do such a hideous thing. Again she wondered if John was an ancestor of Carl's—the unscrupulous rat.

Lloyd nodded. "A pretty high profile list. We'll have to be very careful how we conduct ourselves in this or there will be repercussions."

"How long does it usually take to get search warrants?"

"Less than a day. We should be able to start searching first thing in the morning."

CHAPTER TWENTY-TWO

Mrs. Wallace's maid answered the door. Her eyes widened at the sight of Detective Ethan, Birdie, dressed as Officer Jenkins, and the three officers waiting on the street behind them. One man drove the small 4-wheel carriage to carry any evidence they collected while another went around the house to watch the rear exit.

"Yes, sir. May I help you?"

"I'm Detective Ethan." He handed her a card. "I'm here on official police business and need to speak to Mr. and Mrs. Wallace. Are they in?"

She glanced at the card and then up at Ethan. "Let me check. I'll be right back." Flustered, hesitant to leave the entry open, and with a smile resembling a grimace, she closed the door. They could see her through the glass insets as she bustled down the hall.

Ethan glanced at Birdie. "I don't think we're welcome."

"I expect not. Can't say I blame them. It's not everyday the police show up on your doorstep in this neighborhood."

Out of breath, the maid returned and opened the door and gasped out, "Mrs. Wallace will see you in the parlor."

They waited while she closed the door and then followed her into the room where Birdie had taken tea with the society woman and the other mothers of her students.

Perched on the sofa like a queen holding court, Mrs. Wallace nodded to them. Her gaze probed Birdie's features and uniform. Lordy, Birdie hoped she didn't recognize her. The older woman lost interest and turned her attention to Ethan. "Would you gentlemen care to have a seat while you tell me what your visit is about?" She smiled, dropping her chin slightly in a nod. "I expect you're collecting money for the policeman's ball or some such event."

"No, ma'am. We're here with a search warrant." He removed the document from his breast pocket, strode forward and handed her the paper.

Mrs. Wallace opened the document and started to read. With each word her face deepened in hue, from a slight pink to almost purple. For a moment Birdie feared she'd have a heart attack. This must be what they call apoplexy.

"This is preposterous!" She stood and waved the search warrant at Ethan. "I'll have your job for this, detective."

"Yes, ma'am." He walked to the door and called the other officers in. They avoided looking at the irate woman as she threw verbal insults at them. Ethan turned to Birdie and the others. "We'll work in teams of two. You know what we're looking for. Be thorough, but don't leave Mrs. Wallace's home in a mess."

"Yes, sir."

They started upstairs. Birdie went through the chifferobe in the Wallace's bedroom. A gray wool suit hung far to the back. She lifted it to her nose and sniffed. No stale cigarette smoke odor. That was a good sign. She examined the buttons to see if one had been replaced recently. The fabric was close enough to their clues, so they bagged the garment to inspect more closely at the station. Before closing the wardrobe door, she went through every pocket—suit coat, vest, and trousers. Either Jim Wallace kept his wardrobe neat or his wife did it for him.

The front door banged open. She heard Mr. Wallace's roar. "What in thunderation is going on here, Rachel?"

"You will lower your voice in my home, Jim." She must have pulled him into the parlor and closed the door. A few minutes later he bounded up the stairs.

"Ethan, this is preposterous. Take your thugs and get out of my house now."

"Sorry, Mr. Wallace. You can either submit to our search peacefully or we'll do it the hard way. We're trying to keep it quiet so no one will know what's going on. You raise a ruckus and the neighbors will be peeking out their windows. Plus, I'll have to arrest you."

She heard paper rattle as Wallace sputtered, "How can you begin to think I committed crimes like those described in the warrant?"

"We have several pieces of evidence found at the scene that could incriminate you. Truthfully, I don't think you hurt those women, but every possible suspect must be scrutinized carefully."

Forceful footsteps descended the stairs but they were measured and controlled.

Birdie studied the shaving items below the mirror on the chifferobe. A bottle of Fougere Royal sat on top of a scarf with embroidered edges. Beside it lay a comb and brush. She took the cologne, ensured the cap was on tight, and placed it in a separate bag. It'd be a shame to spill some of the expensive stuff, not as bad as having to wear it on your person, though.

She rifled through the drawers of the chest looking for a knife. Most men of this era wore or carried one—if not in their boot, then in their pocket. But Jim Wallace wasn't a boot wearing man. They'd have to question Wallace.

She and the other policeman moved on to the other bedrooms, but came out empty handed. Ethan and his helper exited the attic, shutting the door behind them. They carried a couple of large bags.

He nodded to the three policemen. "I want you to go out the back door and search the stable and any other outbuildings on the property."

Downstairs Birdie and Ethan joined the Wallaces in the parlor and Ethan closed the door behind them. Mouth in a grim line, Mr. Wallace sat on the sofa with his arm around his distraught wife. Birdie had to give her credit. She was obviously upset but not weeping and wailing like some women do.

Ethan waved at a chair. "May we sit down? I'd like to ask you a few questions."

Jim nodded. Birdie sat in a chair opposite Ethan's and watched the body language of the suspect. "Do you own a knife, Mr. Wallace?"

"Of course I do." He reached into his pocket and pulled out a knife measuring probably four inches, folded, and tossed it to Ethan.

The detective opened it and tested the edge on the blade. "Not very sharp. What do you use it for?"

"Cleaning and trimming my nails, cleaning the dirt off my shoes…" He shrugged. "Stuff like that."

"You don't have any other knives—a hunting knife or something bigger than this?" He tossed the blade to Birdie. She caught it and placed it in a separate bag.

"I have a penknife at the bank but rarely use it anymore." He shook his head. "No hunting knives. Never developed a taste for the activity."

Ethan stood. "All right then. That's all for now. We'll take very good care of the items we've taken from your home." He started for the door and then turned back. "By the way, do you happen to smoke cigarettes?"

"No. I do enjoy a good cigar on occasion."

"I'm sorry to have upset your day. If your neighbors ask questions about us taking so many bags out of your house, feel free to tell them you offered to donate clothes for the needy, a special project instigated by the department this year. We won't contradict you."

* * *

Ted Bankston's palatial, corner lot home sat atop a berm comprised of two five-foot thick, back-filled cement walls where steps leading up to the sidewalk provided access to the high porch. The lawn was groomed to perfection. It might be winter, but the shrubs around the building gave it a distinguishing air, as did the white Grecian columns across the front. Birdie gazed across the property as they stood on the front porch and waited for someone to open the door. A large gazebo graced the sprawling yard on the left side of the house and from what she could tell, the home boasted a stable as well as a barn.

The door opened. On the threshold stood an extremely attractive middle-aged man. "Yes, officers. May I help you?"

"May we come in, Mr. Bankston?"

"I can't imagine whatever for, but please do." He stood back and after he shut the door crossed the shiny wood floors to what appeared to be the men's parlor. "Have a seat." He sat in a wingback chair near the fireplace.

"Thank you, but first, I have this for you." Ethan handed Bankston the search warrant and then sat in a chair beside Birdie.

The older man read for a moment before in eyebrows rose in disbelief. "Do I need a lawyer?"

"I don't believe so, but in truth, that's for you to say. The warrant says we are to go through everything in your home and outbuildings looking for evidence which might incriminate you."

Bankston's outer demeanor appeared calm, but fury burned inside him. His eyes narrowed and he pinched his mouth closed. Taking a deep breath, he exhaled and then barked, "Well, get on with it then. If anything is damaged the Waco Police Department will be held responsible."

"Understood, Mr. Bankston. Now, a few questions first. Do you smoke cigarettes?"

"On occasion, yes."

"A specific brand?"

"As a matter of fact, yes. Duke of Durham."

"Do you own any knives?"

"Of course I do. I have an entire collection." He stood, crossed the room and unlocked a mahogany cabinet. "I have to keep this locked because my niece and nephew are rather precocious, and their mother doesn't keep them in line." He stepped back out of their way so they could get a good look.

Probably more than a dozen knives lay in velvet pockets designed for their exact size. "They are—" Hearing her own voice, Birdie shut up, then cleared her throat and added in a rasp—"beautiful"

"My good man, do you need a touch of brandy to ease your throat?"

Ethan covered for her. "My partner lost his voice with the flu last week and is just now getting it back."

"Nasty, stuff, that flu."

"Where did you acquire your collection, Mr. Braxton?"

"They were passed down to me by my grandfather. He collected them while serving in Her Majesty's Navy." He rocked back on his heels. "We're rather proud of them in the family."

Birdie lifted one from its velvet bed and ran the blade down her finger. Blood welled on the skin. "Watch it!" Bankston said. "They're extremely sharp." She hadn't felt the blade slice into her. The cut now began to sting. Mr. Bankston rushed to a teacart by his desk and grabbed a napkin, which he handed her. She wrapped it tightly around her finger until the bleeding stopped.

"Sir, is your collection intact?" Ethan inquired. "Are any pieces missing?"

He made a cursory check and then shook his head. "All are accounted for."

"Well, then, we'll be making our way through your home. Any items we take will be returned to you in due time—if you're not guilty."

They left with a bottle of the expensive cologne, a suit coat, and little else.

* * *

John Samuelson lived on Seventeenth and Washington in a beautiful brick home similar to Frank Lloyd Wright's Prairie Style. Birdie liked it immediately, especially the stained glass window in the front door. When Samuelson opened the door, his gaze moved from Ethan to Birdie and then to the three officers at the street.

"What's going on here, Detective Ethan?"

"May we come in? We need to speak with you."

"No you may not. I'm busy right now and about to leave for a church meeting." He tried to shut the door but Lloyd's foot kept it open. He shoved his way in. "Now see here. This is a violation of my rights. I demand an explanation."

"You'll get one, John, as soon as you cool down and sit down. You don't want what I have to say aired on your front porch for your neighbors to see and hear."

Samuelson peered left and right, and then nodded to the men at the curb. "Bring those men in also. I don't want people seeing them stopped in front of my house. No telling what kind of lies they'd make up." He plopped his stocky frame down on the sofa.

Ethan gestured to two of the officers to come in, the

other remained in the buggy to protect the evidence previously collected. "Where is Mrs. Samuelson, sir?"

"She's already at the church, no doubt wondering where I am." He made to rise but Ethan placed a hand at his chest and eased the man back down.

"Hold on, John. This is a warrant to search every room in your home and all your out buildings."

Color rose in the older man's face. Shaking a fist, he yelled, "Over my dead body!" Like a raging bull he jumped from the sofa and lunged at Ethan. His efforts were to no avail. Ethan popped him in the chin, stunning him. Before he landed on the sofa again, the two officers had him cuffed and on his way to the buggy.

Before they left the Samuelson home, they'd run across the smoking gun—a receipt with one corner torn off. The following day, Samuelson was arraigned. He entered a plea of not guilty and the court set a trial date of August 1, 1891.

CHAPTER TWENTY-THREE

Birdie, a vision in white, appeared in the narthex on Joseph Hellman's arm. Bethany and Maggie blocked Tad's view somewhat, but what he could see of his bride stole his breath. Radiant in her simple, off the shoulder gown with a slimmer skirt than was fashionable, she glowed. The veil trailed past her shoulders and framed her hair and face. How had he gotten so lucky? She could have married anyone, but chose him. His throat clogged and moisture blurred his vision.

James poked him and whispered, "Close your mouth, you're drooling." Tad chuckled. The comment was just what he needed to distract his emotions and ease the tension.

Tad knew he was grinning like an idiot, but he couldn't help it. He tried to catch her eye, but she stood chewing her bottom lip, glancing quickly, nervously, around the room. He hoped she wasn't looking for an escape route. No doubt she'd rather face a gang of cattle rustlers than stand before this large crowd in her wedding finery. If it'd been up to her, they'd have had a small, at-home wedding but she'd conceded to make Mother happy. At last her gaze lifted to him. He winked. She beamed, her features relaxing.

The music began, and Bethany started down the aisle, then Mrs. Hellman, several paces behind. Shock hit him as he studied his sister in the rose colored dress, one designed for a woman, not a child. She'd grown up while he'd been preoccupied with Birdie and the ranch. Dang, it wouldn't be many years until he'd be giving her away to some man. His tie threatened to choke him, and he tugged at his collar. Panic gripped him. He didn't know anyone worthy of his sister. *Relax, Tad. She may look like a woman, but she's still a girl.*

205

The organist pounded a chord, and the congregation rose to watch Birdie make her way down the aisle.

Unable to wait, he walked forward and took her hand drawing her to his side. When they reached the altar, he leaned down and kissed her lightly on the lips.

The reverend cleared his throat to hide his laughter. "Now's not time for the kiss, son. That comes later in the ceremony."

The congregation roared with laughter. A guffaw ripped from Tad's mouth as he hugged Birdie. Her face reddened, but she chuckled.

The preacher looked down at them. "Are we ready to begin?"

* * *

Birdie, glad of Tad's arms holding her close as they waltzed around the room, snuggled closer to him. Her past life seemed millions of years away. She missed it horribly, but she loved Tad and would be content to live forever in this fairy tale past. Obviously she was here for a purpose, exactly what, she didn't yet know. Most likely it had something to do with her home or it could be she was here to be a mother to Nathan.

Olivia had outdone herself in overseeing the decoration of the ballroom at the Pacific Hotel. As they twirled, the many mirrors on the walls reflected the twinkling of the glass teardrops in the gas chandelier and the multitude of candles placed on every surface. She had to hand it to her new mother-in-law. She'd given them a wedding to remember their entire lives. A photographer had taken their pictures immediately after the ceremony. The picture would add to the memory and beauty of this day.

Tad whispered in her ear. "I'm ready to call it a night, love. How about you?"

"Yes! I'm ready to get out of these shoes and into something more comfortable."

He arched a brow. "I'm more interested in getting you out of this dress, lovely as it is, and the contraption underneath." His lips touched her ear sending a shiver through her body. "I want to see what lies beneath, touch every inch of you and make you mine."

"Is that so?"

"Yes, ma'am, it is."

She stopped in the middle of the dance floor and took his hand. "Let's go say goodnight to your mother."

Olivia smiled as they approached. "I can see you two are ready to leave this crowd."

Birdie took both of Olivia's hands. "Thank you for all you've done. The wedding was beautiful, more than I'd ever hoped for."

"It was my pleasure, dear." She cradled Birdie's face in her hands. "I'm so proud to have you as part of our family, as my daughter."

Birdie's voice cracked with emotion. "I couldn't be happier, Olivia. I'm proud to be a Lockhart." She slid an arm around Tad's waist. "You did a good job raising this man."

"All right, you two. Enough of this emotional stuff." Tad kissed his mother's cheek. "Good night. We'll see you at breakfast."

* * *

They could hear Nathan's wails as they stepped off the elevator on their floor. Tad had booked a suite of rooms, two bedrooms with a sitting room between, so that Nathan and Sarah could be with them.

"Oh boy, we better see what's happening or people will be complaining to management."

"I don't think there are many other people on this floor." They stopped in front of their room. Tad removed the key from his pocket, the small piece of brass so different from the key cards of her time, and unlocked the door. "At last, Mrs. Lockhart, you are mine. When we cross this threshold, our life together begins." He kissed her, his lips a mere whisper against hers. "I promise I'll do all in my power to keep you happy."

Before she could reply, Tad lifted her off her feet and carried her across the threshold of their suite.

"You don't have to do this. This is a hotel room, not our home."

"Well, you're going to get carried across the threshold again then when we get home."

This man was too good to be true, so different from modern men, or at least the ones she knew. Yes, they loved their spouses, but they didn't treat wives like princesses. She'd have to work on that. She didn't want Tad to mollycoddle her. She didn't think he would. He respected her independence and wouldn't try to hold her back—in most things. An image of him discovering "Detective Jenkins" made her smile. He'd get used to her behavior in time.

Tad took her hand. "Do you mind if we go in to see Nathan for a while?"

"Not at all." His wails had turned into whimpers, suggesting Sarah had picked him up. Maybe this new environment bothered him. He'd been moved twice already. It was hard to know what took place in a baby's mind, but she wouldn't discount the notion.

Tad knocked on Sarah's door before turning the handle. Sarah looked frazzled as she walked Nathan up and down the room.

Brow furrowed, she said, "I don't know what's wrong with him. He's eaten and been burped. It's too soon for him to be teething."

Tad's large hand stroked Nathan's head. "What's wrong, little man?" He reached for the baby. "Come to Daddy for awhile." Tad lifted him to his shoulder and rubbed his back as he walked. He sang softly, the words Birdie didn't recognize.

Sarah's wearied expression changed into a smile. "You're a natural, sir."

Birdie had to agree. Within a few minutes, Nathan had quieted and his eyes drifted closed. Birdie stood behind Tad and stroked the baby's head. The dark hair felt soft and downy. She wondered if it would darken when he grew up. "He's a precious baby, Tad." She leaned in and kissed his forehead.

"Thank you Birdie…for everything. Not many women would have accepted Nathan into their homes." He turned around to face her. "It would have killed me to give you up, but I couldn't give my child away."

"I know." She caressed his jaw, enjoying the warmth of

his skin and the subtle scent of his shaving soap. "I couldn't have loved you if you had, Tad."

* * *

Tad loosened the row of buttons on the back of Birdie's dress, and pushed it down her shoulders to her waist. His hands shook as he caressed her soft skin. "You are beautiful, Birdie." He placed a kiss on the nape of her neck, her shiver fueling his love and desire for this woman. Her breasts filled his hands as he explored the curves under her chemise. With his palm he circled her nipples feeling them pebble in response. Her head dropped back against his shoulder as he pushed her dress down over her belly and hips.

She stepped out of her dress, turned and tossed it across a chair. His most erotic dreams paled at the sight of the vision before him. Silk stockings covered her long, beautiful legs, the corset pushed her breasts higher, like an offering of ripe fruit. She epitomized perfection. He stepped forward and allowed a finger to trail from the pulse point at her neck, down to between the bountiful globes and then across each one. "Turn around and let me unhook this thing."

Five minutes later, they stood thigh-to-thigh, belly-to-belly, nothing between them but Birdie's chemise and his drawers, which were growing tighter by the minute. He reached for the pins in her hair and it flowed around her shoulders. Over time, the different colored strands had grown out, leaving it a honey blonde with hints of red—a perfect complement to her creamy complexion and blue eyes.

She ran her hand through the tresses, giving it a semblance of control.

If he didn't do something to slow himself down, he'd disgrace himself. Voice hoarse, he asked, "Where's your vanity set? Let me brush it out for you."

He stood behind her while she sat on the stool before the dressing table. There was something sensual about brushing a woman's hair, especially when she wore next to nothing, and he could see her reflection in the mirror. The strands glistened with life as he pulled the brush through the long mass. His eyes were drawn to her beautiful skin as it glowed through the thin material of her chemise, the rosy crests of her nipples protruding.

She closed her eyes, and smiled. "Mmm, that feels so good. Will you brush my hair every night?"

"Every night I can." He laid the brush aside and stroked her shoulders. "Will you always be this open with me with your body?"

"Yes, I promise."

He stepped back, and removed a small box from his jacket lying across a chair. He handed it to Birdie.

Forehead furrowed, she asked, "What is this?"

"Just a little something to show my love."

She stood and pulled his head down for a kiss. "Thank you, but it's not necessary, you know."

"I know, but it gives me pleasure. Open it." He'd spent a lot of time in the jewelry stores when he had some free minutes in town. The gift had to be perfect. He hoped he'd gotten it right.

She opened the box and gasped. "Oh my, God. Tad, where did you find it?"

"At one of the jewelry stores in town."

She lifted it from the box, turned it over and studied it carefully. "This is my brooch…the one I lost in the river. Do you think it's possible someone found my brooch and sold it to a jeweler?"

"No, Birdie. Yours is lost." He picked it up and turned it over. "Look, here is the jeweler's mark on the back. It's too new to be the one you had on." Had she ever described her missing brooch to him? No, she hadn't. "Plus, I didn't know what yours looked like."

She perused it again, turning and examining it from every angle. "You're right…on both counts." Her eyes rounded. She tapped the pin. "I'm almost positive this is the same pin I wore, only now its new, but was old in the future." She shivered. "Talk about a déjà vu moment."

"If you don't like it, I can take it back."

"Don't like it?" She threw her arms around his neck and squeezed. "I love it! It's part of our future history to be passed down for generations to come."

Tad liked the sound of that. Perhaps Nathan could give

it to his wife someday, or perhaps their first daughter could inherit it, keeping it purely in Birdie's line. He took her hand. "Come, let's go to bed."

Birdie sat on the bed, rolling a stocking down her leg. While Tad turned down the lamps she admired his body—his broad shoulders, taut abs and buttocks. His body rivaled a male model's on the cover of a romance novel, but hard work sculpted Tad's, not weights and machines in a gym. Her skin tingled at the anticipation of his touch. Her throat clogged with emotion, she swallowed the urge to cry. At long last they'd be one. Tad was a beautiful gift to her heart. She'd never imagined she'd love a man like she loved Tad. She ached to touch him and learn the texture and taste of his skin. The long drawers could not hide his desire behind the buttoned front and she longed for him to strip them off.

"Here, let me do that." She lay back and held her leg up for him. His eyes watched hers as he slowly rolled the stocking down, stroking her leg with his long fingers as he did so. Her flesh jumped at each tender touch. When he tossed the stocking aside, he kissed the sensitive spot behind her knee before moving to the other leg. By the time he'd finished with her opposite leg, she was shaking with need. She sat up, grabbed the waist of his drawers and pulled him toward her.

"You're teasing me, Tad."

He grinned. "You don't like it?" He stretched out over her, holding his weight off her with his hands and knees.

Like it? She loved it. She slapped his chest. "You know I do, but that's enough. I want more—to feel you against me."

"Ah, sweetheart, I love you so." He touched his lips to hers, nipped and sampled until she threw her arms around his neck and opened her mouth to him. Their tongues twined and explored. Oh, the man could kiss. He didn't smother her with his lips, but coaxed hers to do his will and want more.

They broke apart, gasping for air. "I'm glad you're a greedy woman, sweetheart, because I'm a greedy man, and I'll never get enough of you."

"Thank God for that." She sat up and slipped the chemise over her head, wiggled out of her lacy drawers and tossed both garments to the end of the bed.

Tad straddled her and looked his fill. "You are beautiful, Birdie."

"So are you, Tad." She ran her hands up his chest loving the twitching of his muscles at her touch. He ran his hands down her sides, stopping to fondle and kiss each breast before moving to her hips. His lips teased her navel and his tongue trailed across and around the indention.

She squirmed beneath him. "Tad, enough." She reached up, unbuttoned his underwear and pushed it down to his knees. Using his feet, he shoved it off onto the floor. He settled between her thighs. "I don't want to rush you, sweetheart."

"You're not, I promise." She pulled his head down and captured his lips. As he slid inside her, she wrapped her legs around his hips and pulled him deeper.

"Birdie, love, too fast. I want to make it last."

"No, *now!*" she gasped. "It can last… next time." They moved together, straining to get closer until pleasure built inside Birdie and exploded. "Tad, I love you!" Her legs tightened around him as her body quivered in rush after rush of pleasure.

He dropped his head to her shoulder and groaned, "Oh, God," as his body jerked in completion. She closed her eyes, and lazily stroked his back while their breathing returned to normal.

He rolled to his back, taking her with him. She sighed with contentment as his hands smoothed up and down her spine and shoulders. She raised her head, laced her fingers together and propped her chin on top of them. Their gazes met and she smiled. "I don't think we'll ever have problems in the bedroom." One arm wrapped around her waist, his other hand moved to hold her head as he rolled her to her back and settled between her legs.

"Thank you, God." He nuzzled her neck. "How lucky can a man get?"

She giggled, draped her legs around his waist and squeezed. "I'd say pretty darn lucky."

* * *

Birdie slapped Tad's hands away from her breasts as he pretended to help tie her corset. "Stop it. We'll never get to church on time."

He bent and nuzzled her neck, his breath tickled her flesh as he whispered, "We don't have to attend services this morning. I'm sure everyone would understand." He turned her to face him. "Let's stay in. I want to spend the day with you."

She curled her arms around his neck and sighed deeply. "Me, too, Tad, but this is the morning we introduce Nathan to the community." His body stiffened. She knew all too well his apprehension and fear that their neighbors wouldn't accept his child, would label him a bastard. All Birdie could say is they'd better never call him names or shun him in her presence. Dressing her up in fancy clothes might make folks think her a lady, but hurt her new family and the gloves would come off.

Arms on her shoulders, he held her from him. "You are right, my love." He placed a kiss on her forehead. "We'll have all afternoon to ourselves." Olivia and Bethany would be taking the baby and his nurse home after church to give Tad and Birdie some time alone.

Birdie, with Nathan in her arms, and Tad followed Olivia and Bethany down the aisle to their family pew. Gasps and titters of conversation followed them, but Birdie ignored them and smiled at the baby's soft coos. Tad stepped aside to let Sarah and then Birdie file in before joining them on the maroon colored cushioned seats. Bethany remained standing, her arms crossed over her small bosom, her eyes shooting daggers. Birdie stifled a chuckle. No doubt about it, Nathan's aunt would be a fierce protector.

Olivia tugged on her daughter's skirt and hissed, "Sit down, child. You'll make things worse." Bethany flashed one last glare, twisted around, and flopped onto the pew.

Birdie noticed Tad's shoulder's shake and she pinched his underarm. "Don't encourage her."

He placed his arm around her shoulders and leaned in to whisper in her ear. "My little sister is becoming as feisty as her sister-in-law."

Nathan chose that moment to fuss. Tad lifted him from Birdie's arms and placed him on his shoulder. He softly patted his back. Soon they were rewarded with a healthy burp. Birdie grinned as the people behind them chuckled. Maybe this wouldn't be as difficult as they believed.

The organ boomed to life, with *Praise God from Whom All Blessings Flow*. The pastor stood and raised his hands for everyone to stand and sing. Voices, rising to reach the rafters, set goose bumps alive on Birdies arms. This hymn always touched her heart. Her Aunt Patty would be proud to see her standing in church today. Birdie hadn't attended regularly during her adulthood—not intentionally, but because her work hours often made it impossible.

"What a beautiful day it is. Welcome all and especially to our newest family, Tad and Birdie Lockhart and their child Nathan. We'll be christening Nathan here in a few moments and I hope you'll be praying for this young fella whose natural mother is dying of lung cancer. What a blessing that he's been welcomed by the Lockharts."

Murmurings of sympathy, "poor little tyke", and others of disapproval, "who is his father?" flashed around the room. Birdie had no doubt, by suppertime the disgruntled folks would ferret out every juicy detail. She hoped they'd leave Lucy alone. She didn't need the negative attention.

Pastor Thomas waved them forward. Tad carried Nathan and with a hand at her back, directed Birdie to the rail. Olivia and Bethany took up position, one on each side of them. Thomas took Nathan from Tad. The baby studied the person now holding him and for a second, Birdie feared he would howl in discontent, but he blinked and tried to eat his fist. "Tad and Birdie, how is this child named?"

Tad's arm tightened around her waist. "He is Nathan Thaddeus Lockhart."

CHAPTER TWENTY-FOUR

Some racket in the hallway outside their room disturbed Tad's sleep. He snuggled Birdie closer enjoying her warmth and scent. He'd almost dozed when pounding jolted him again. Someone was knocking on the sitting room door. Had something happened at home? Now on his feet, he grabbed his robe from the bedside chair and stumbled in the dark through the parlor to the door. "Who is it?"

"It's Hank, Tad. Have a message for you."

Tad threw the door open and Hank handed him an envelope.

"Your mother wanted me to wait until you'd read the note."

A stone weight settled in his belly. Oh, Lord, what had happened? Please let Nathan be all right. "Sure, come on in." Tad found the switch on the lamp and a soft glow infused the room. He sat in the stuffed chair by the dainty table and read the missive. It was from Dr. Franks at Waco City Hospital. Lucy had passed away earlier this morning. He inserted the paper back in the envelope and slapped it against his knee. "I assume you know what's in the message."

"Yes. Your mother filled me in before I left. She had me bring the surrey and my horse."

Tad nodded. Yes, she'd want to make sure Hank came prepared. Sitting here wouldn't get anything done. "Hank, will you go downstairs and ask the kitchen to send up breakfast and coffee for three?"

"Yes, sir, boss."

Birdie appeared in the bedroom doorway, her sheer

gown revealing her luscious assets. She shoved her hair up and away from her face. "What's going on?"

He wanted nothing more than to take his wife back to bed and avoid the responsibilities he faced—laying Lucy to rest, but he'd made a promise and he didn't break them. "Lucy passed away this morning."

"Oh no!" She moved forward and sat in his lap. With her arms curled around his neck, she laid her head atop his. "I'm so sorry, Tad. You cared about her at one time, and losing a friend is never easy." Her hands soothed his neck and shoulders and he lowered his head to give her better access.

He groaned. "If you keep that up I'll fall asleep in this chair." Yes, he'd cared about her. Though they'd entered the relationship with no strings, no promises, he couldn't help feeling guilty. She'd been at a disadvantage. Though he didn't believe she needed his money, he saw now that he'd salved his conscience by buying her gifts and paying many of her bills. After finding her in such dire conditions last month, it was evident she'd needed more than she'd let on.

He patted Birdie's hip. "Better run put on a robe. Hank is ordering breakfast for us and he'll be back any moment."

An hour later, fed and dressed, Tad helped Birdie into the surrey. Hank mounted his horse. "Tell Mother we'll be there around noon or shortly after." Hank touched his hat and spurred his mount up Franklin toward home.

Dr. Franks waited for them when they arrived at the hospital. Birdie stood close to his side, her arm around his waist, as they viewed the body. Her presence was a comfort, one he'd not realized he needed until this moment. The doctor had called the funeral home and two men with a stretcher waited in the hall to take possession of Lucy's remains.

Since death didn't occur on a schedule, Tad supposed funeral homes kept odd hours. The director was expecting them when they arrived and they soon had Lucy's graveside service planned and set for the following morning at First Street Cemetery. They visited the parsonage and Reverend Thomas agreed to conduct the ceremony. Their last stop was the florists. He selected red and white roses with carnations for a casket spray. Lucy would have enjoyed the vibrant colors.

Only a handful of people, other than family, attended. Most were curiosity seekers though Nathan and Birdie both were pleased to see Detective Ethan and the Hellmans. Nathan howled through the entire service. The weather was beautiful—sunny and warm, but he seemed to sense the somberness of the occasion and didn't like it. He finally settled into contentedness when they were on the road home.

Poor little tyke. He'd been ripped from his mother's arms, first by her declining health and then her impending death. Though they'd brought him home and tried to restore stability in his life, he felt the undercurrents of change. In time he would feel secure.

Sarah passed Nathan up to Birdie. She cuddled him on her lap. He watched the horse's tail swish back and forth. Throat clogged with love, Tad smiled at his son and cupped his downy head with his palm. Nathan turned toward Tad, his big blue eyes filled with innocence and wonder. *I promise you, little man, I'll keep you safe.*

* * *

Birdie lay curled on her side in the feather bed, her head propped up on one hand as she gazed down at her son. Nathan kicked and cooed. He'd recently discovered his toes and spent time carefully examining them. Birdie reached over and tickled one of his feet. His chuckle was delightful. She smacked her lips and brought the appendage to her mouth. "Yum, yum, delicious! Nathan's toes are yummy!" He squealed and reached for a handful of her hair.

"Hey, you two, what's going on in here?" Tad strode through the door and sat down on the bed at Nathan's feet. Nathan swung his arms and kicked his feet anxious for Tad to pick him up. He lifted the baby over his head. "Hey, pint-sized man, you trying to steal my woman? That requires a little torture from daddy." Tad made blowing noises with his lips against Nathan's bare belly. It was a game they played often and Nathan loved every minute.

Birdie giggled at their antics while she quickly dressed. Maybelle would have breakfast ready and Birdie needed to get to town as John Samuelson's trial began today and she didn't want to miss getting a seat in the courtroom. She didn't expect the trial to last very long. The evidence against the man was cut and dried. Of course, the defense attorney could come up with some surprise and likely false, exculpatory information, but she couldn't imagine what.

When she entered the dining room, Nathan sat in his high chair stuffing scrambled eggs in his mouth with his hands. Very little made it to his stomach. Though he was still breast-fed, Nathan, at only five months, loved table food, and the family enjoyed having him join them at breakfast. "Sorry I'm late." She bent to kiss Nathan's head and straightened him in the chair. He'd only been sitting up a couple of weeks and needed more strength in his back. "We spent too long playing this morning."

"Never be sorry for playing with your child, dear," said Olivia. "We could hear all the noise and I assure you I enjoyed it almost as much as you."

Bethany sat up a little straighter. "Yes, and today is my turn to baby sit. We're going to sit under the big oak beside the house and play on a quilt before he has to take his morning nap."

Maybelle smiled at Bethany's enthusiasm and Olivia nodded her approval. Birdie wondered how long Bethany would remain committed to entertaining her nephew. Hopefully until she married and had a family of her own. Not having brothers or sisters, Birdie had missed out on the joys of nieces and nephews. Now she'd have a second chance. "You're a wonderful aunt, Bethany. He loves you dearly."

The young woman beamed. "The feeling is mutual."

"Yes, he's one lucky child to be surrounded with so much love." Too bad the community hadn't accepted him as readily. It was their loss.

Today was August 1, 1891. She'd been here two months over a year and had a year and a half left in which to build Birdie's Nest. Sometime today she needed to see the architect she'd hired to draw the plans from the crude drawings she'd made. Not that she had the money to start building, but hopefully soon she'd have enough to at least clear the land and start the foundation.

Birdie wore a light gray riding habit with a white blouse and green and maroon striped tie. While standing, she appeared to be wearing a nice suit, but the full divided skirt allowed her to ride astride. Her matching hat held a few green and maroon blooms for accent. Oh, what she'd give to be able to wear a pantsuit with plenty of Lycra.

She lifted the amethyst brooch from the box on the chest and held it up to the lapel of her jacket. The stone sparkled, catching the green and maroon of her hat. Should she wear it today? She'd never so much as pinned it on because every time she brought it out, the hairs on the back of her neck stood on end. Why, she didn't know for sure but suspected she was afraid to wear it. Could it have had something to do with her time travel? She shivered and set it back in its box. As beautiful as it was, she couldn't take a chance. Her life was here now. If Tad asked why she never wore it, she'd tell him the truth about her apprehension.

Tad met her in the barn with Strawberry saddled, Birdie's Winchester in the scabbard and an extra pistol in the saddlebag. Her Colt was strapped to her thigh but Tad insisted she carry an extra revolver and ammo. "You be careful now."

"I always am." She twined her arms around his neck and kissed him. He walked her around behind Strawberry and allowed his hands to roam from her waist up to cup her breasts.

"Is it my imagination, or are you filling out up here?" He unbuttoned her jacket and continued his study.

"Stop that. You're wrinkling my clothes."

He grinned. "Come on, love, answer me."

"Well, I have noticed my bodices are tighter."

"Have you been sick in the mornings?"

"No, thank God."

"Do you think we might be having a baby, love?" His expression of hope left a fluttery sensation in her stomach. She thought back trying to remember the date of her last menstrual cycle. It was the first week in May. She didn't worry about it, as she'd never been regular. But, she'd never missed three months either.

"I'd not really thought about it until now, but yeah, we might."

He lifted her off her feet and twirled her around. The horses stomped and whinnied in distress.

"Stop it. You're upsetting the horses. Anyway, we don't know for sure."

He set her on the ground and lifted her chin. "If you have time, check in with Doctor Floyd. He's on Twelfth Street and Austin." He pulled her close again. "Maybe you should let me take you to town in the surrey."

She pushed him away. "Now, you listen here, mister. If I'm pregnant, I'll take precautions, but having a baby doesn't mean I'm sick or disabled in anyway. You can't hold me in a gilded cage, Tad. I'm an energetic woman and I'll not be treated like an invalid."

He took Strawberry's bridle and led her from the barn. "Hmm, well, we'll see, madam." He tweaked her nose. "If you're not home by seven tonight, I'll send out the posse."

She snorted as she mounted her horse. "You do that." As she reached the road leading to town, she looked back. He stood there grinning like a jackass and waved.

* * *

Birdie nodded to Detective Ethan as he testified on the witness stand. Jonathon Douglas, the district attorney, led him through every piece of evidence—the wool fibers, the hair, the torn edge of the receipt—which had been the smoking gun—they'd found in Samuelson's suit pocket. Added to that was the Fougere Royal cologne. Mr. Douglas called several other officers to the stand and also the shop owner who carried the expensive cologne. Defense attorney Tyler Johnson attempted to trip up the witnesses on cross-examination, but was unsuccessful. It was one o'clock when he finished badgering the shop owner. The DA still hadn't called the two victims in the case. Birdie glanced around the room and didn't see them. She assumed they were being held in a private room.

Judge Tyler pounded the gavel on the sound block. "Mr. Douglas and Mr. Johnson, I suggest we postpone calling the two victims until first thing in the morning. Is that agreeable?"

"Yes, your honor."

"Fine by me."

"Good. Then court is adjourned until eight thirty in the morning."

Detective Ethan walked her out of the courthouse. "Do you have time for lunch?"

"Sure, as long as it's a short one. I have several other stops to make today before heading home. Tad has threatened to come looking for me if I'm not home by seven."

"I can't blame him in the least."

After a quick lunch at a café on the square, the detective walked her to the livery stable to pick up Strawberry. An hour later she left Dr. Floyd's office in a state of shock. She was pregnant. Her baby would be born sometime in the middle of February, a little more than a year since Nathan's birth. The doctor assured her all was as it should be, though what they knew about a woman's health in the nineteenth century she didn't have a clue. But, she did know being active helped with labor and delivery and she'd always been the picture of health. She breathed a sigh of satisfaction. She couldn't wait to share the news with Tad.

In her state of distraction, she almost forgot to stop by the architect's office. Mr. Teague had her plans ready. They spent an hour going over them. She asked for several changes. Yes, they were different from her original home but would allow for modernization to be much easier. They left space in the ceilings for air conditioner ducts, space in the walls for insulation, added three small bathrooms and a larger one by the master suite, and she insisted it be wired for electricity even though it might be several years before it would be available to them.

Mr. Teague shook his head. "Whatever you say, Mrs. Lockhart, but the expense is adding up."

"I understand. And if the money is not there to add the bathroom fixtures and indoor running water, the space and plumbing will be there for later."

"Do you know when you'll have the funds to begin?"

"I have enough for clearing the land and beginning the foundation. Will that be satisfactory?"

"Yes, that will get us started."

She stood and shook his hand. "Thank you, Mr. Teague. I'm so pleased with the plans. You've done an excellent job."

He beamed. "My pleasure, ma'am. I'll have a copy of the adjusted plans next week if you want to stop by."

* * *

Tad found excuses to stay close to the barn after lunch in case Birdie came home early. His attention wandered to the road from town more than it should have. Suddenly, there she was, flying down the road. She pulled Strawberry to a stop just outside the barn. Before he could help her down, she'd swung herself from the saddle and threw herself into his arms.

"Congratulations, my love. You're going to be a papa again!"

He caught her to his chest. "Birdie, you're sure?"

"Well, Dr. Floyd said so. How much surer can I get?"

Words escaped him. He tried to talk but a roaring in his ears drowned out his words. The ground was suspiciously moving around him.

"Hey, don't you faint on me, mister." She pulled Strawberry close and propped him up against her.

"Me…faint? Never." But his knees threatened to buckle and he grabbed the saddle horn to steady himself.

"Take some deep breaths. You'll feel better in a minute."

He was already feeling better. "I did not almost faint." With his free hand, he cupped her face. "Are you pleased, Birdie?"

She turned her face into his palm and pressed a kiss there. "I'm ecstatic, husband."

CHAPTER TWENTY-FIVE

Tad insisted she learn to handle the surrey and until she did he'd be driving her into town. She'd humor him and then do what she wanted. He slid in beside her at the courthouse. Fortunately they'd arrived early enough to get a good seat. Detective Ethan nodded as they settled in their seats.

The DA stood. "Your honor, I'd like to offer into evidence several items, all of which were found in Mr. Samuelson's home."

"Proceed, Mr. Douglas."

The DA raised each item as he set them on the table. "This is a bottle of cologne, a package of Duke of Durham cigarettes, a knife with blood evidence on it, a gray wool suit with a button missing and a receipt from an exclusive men's shop in town." He allowed the jurors to get a good look before he laid them down.

"Now, I wish to introduce items found at the crime scene and show you their relationship to the articles presented earlier."

He carefully opened the bags they'd taken such care in keeping contamination free. With a pair of tweezers he lifted the cigarette butt out and carried it to where the jurors could see the connection. When he came to the small scrap of paper they'd found, he held it to the corner of the receipt found in Samuelson's suit pocket. Jurors leaned forward to get a close look. "I think you can all see the two pieces are a perfect match." Some nodded in agreement, others didn't alter their expressions of reservation. He put each item back in its bag.

"Now, your honor, I'd like to call Lila Sanders to the witness stand."

A bailiff opened the door and Lila, wearing a hooded cloak, walked haltingly through the group of gaping people in the courtroom. One man said quite clearly, "Whore," with an ugly sneer on his face. Lila stopped midway along the aisle, as if frozen in indecision.

Another male voice barked out, "Slut!" in a threatening tone. "You got what you deserved."

Birdie's heart jumped into her throat. *No, don't back out now, Lila.*

Judge Tyler hit the sound box once and the *crack!* resounded around the room. Lila appeared to take a steading breath and continued forward.

The judge turned to the bailiff, standing to his side. "Did you see who made those remarks?"

"Yes, sir."

"Escort them from the courtroom immediately." The bailiff dragged a resisting man from a bench and hustled him toward the door. The other fella, face flaming, stood on his own and walked out.

The judge peered over his glasses at those present. "You will keep your remarks to yourself. This is my courtroom and when I say no talking, I'll enforce my mandate to the letter. If you want to get kicked out of here, just open your mouth."

Lila entered the witness box and was sworn in. The judge studied her intently. "Miss Sanders, I apologize for the uncouth behavior of those two men." She turned to him and nodded. "Now, I need you to do two things for me—speak a little louder, and please lower your hood. It's important that the jurors be able to see you when you testify."

She lowered the hood. The scars on her cheeks had healed but left large, ugly welts. Muscle had been damaged on one side, making her mouth slant downward. Big tears rolled down her face and Birdie could see by the movement of her shoulders she struggled not to sob out loud. Women in the courtroom gasped and at the sound of the gavel striking again, covered their mouths to stifle their cries. The men shook their heads or looked away.

Birdie glanced at John Samuelson to watch his reaction. He didn't look up, just doodled on a pad of paper.

"All right then," said Judge Tyler. "You may begin, Mr. Douglas."

He approached the witness box and stood to the side so as not to block anyone's view, but at his close presence, Lila sat a little straighter. "Miss Sanders, will you relate the events as they occurred on the night of February 3, 1891." She told how she was grabbed from behind, beaten and then while unconscious, slashed across her face.

"Were you able to see the man's face?"

"No, sir. He wore a mask."

"What do you remember most about him?"

"His height, that he wore a bowler hat and the smelly cologne he wore."

Mr. Douglas produced a bottle and using one of the cards provided by the store, touched it to the opened bottle. He waved it in the air before handing it to Lila. "Is this the scent?"

She held it to her nose, shuddered and quickly thrust it away. "Yes!"

The sample was passed to the judge. He took a whiff. "Nasty stuff." Samuelson's ears reddened at the judge's remark. Judge Tyler t turned to Lila. "Are you positive this is the right cologne?"

Lily raised her chin. "Yes, sir. One hundred percent sure."

Judge Tyler nodded and then waved for the DA to continue.

"I might add, judge, the bottle here came from John Samuelson's home."

"Get on with it, Douglas."

"Did he say anything to you, Miss Sanders?"

"Yes. He called me a bitch, whore and a child of Satan."

"Were you conscience when he cut your face?"

"No, sir. He hit me all over my body and face. My head hit something and when I woke up he was gone. It was then I realized my face was bleeding bad." Lila visibly trembled. Birdie wanted to do something to ease her distress but stayed seated.

Mr. Douglas patted her hand. "You've done very well, Miss Sanders. Thank you for being brave enough to face the courtroom and bear witness against the accused."

Judge Tyler cleared his throat. "Mr. Johnson, would you like to question the witness?"

The pompous man rose and tugged on his vest as he

strutted forward. "Yes, indeed I would, judge." He leaned on the witness box. "Now, Miss Sanders, why should we believe anything you say?"

For a minute Birdie thought Lila would crumble. But her expression hardened and she glared at him. "Look at my face, Mr. Johnson. Do you think this is makeup I'm wearing? Do you think I'd expose myself to the ridicule of the community for a lie?"

"Well now, how do we know it wasn't a purchaser of your… unseemly commodities who did this to you and you're just trying to blame it on this good man?"

"If I'd been treated like this in the house, Madam would've seen to it that he didn't rough up another one of her girls. She takes care of her own."

"Are you saying he'd have been murdered?"

"No, I'm just saying he wouldn't be able to frequent our neighborhood again…if you know what I mean."

Face pale, he said, "No more questions, your honor." He walked back to his table, looked at Samuelson for a moment and then at his notes before sitting down.

The DA rose. "The defense calls Miss Rose Means to the stand."

After escorting Lila out of the courtroom, the bailiff returned with Rose. Her body shook so, he took her elbow to help her make the short walk down the aisle. Mr. Douglas met her and patted her hand reassuringly as he led her to the witness box. The bailiff swore her in.

"Now, Miss Means, would you describe the events of February 17, 1891?"

Rose raised her head so all could see her scars. Fortunately they weren't as bad as Lila's as muscle and nerves hadn't been severed. She spoke clearly as if supported by an unseen force. Pride in the girl swelled Birdie's heart.

The DA turned to the jury. "You can see her facial scars, but Miss Means has other scars, ones you can not see." He turned back to Rose. "I hate to ask, but the jury needs to know. Please describe the hidden scars."

Rose took a deep breath. "He cut me across the top of my breasts and down to my pelvis." With her hand she mimicked the direction the knife had taken.

One of the ladies in the courtroom fell into the aisle in a dead faint. Doctor Franks rushed forward with smelling salts. A few minutes later her husband and the doctor helped her from the room.

"Carry on, Mr. Douglas," ordered the judge.

"Your honor, with your permission, we're going to conduct a smelling experiment to further solidify the importance of the fragrance in this case against Mr. Samuelson."

Mr. Johnson rose. "I object, your honor."

"On what grounds, counselor?"

"The district attorney is resorting to theatrics."

"Overruled, counselor. You may proceed, Mr. Douglas."

Mr. Douglas moved a folding screen to separate the table he'd moved perpendicular to the judge's bench and the witness stand. He lined up bottles of all the colognes they'd presented to the two ladies before they found the Fougere Royal. "I'd like for one of the ladies in the courtroom to come up and help." He gazed around the room. "Do I have a volunteer?" Several hands went up. "You ma'am, at the very back with the green hat."

She stood and walked forward. "Thank you, Mrs...? "

"Hoover, Lydia Hoover."

"Mrs. Hoover, do you know Mr. Samuelson?"

"Yes. Mr. Hoover and I attend the same church as the Samuelsons. Is that a problem?"

"No, not at all. Are you related to anyone on the police department?"

"No, sir."

"What does Mr. Hoover do for a living?"

"He's a journalist." She nodded toward a gentleman on the second row. He raised a hand in greeting.

"One last question. Have you ever met me before?"

"Not that I recall."

"So, it's safe to say you and I have not collaborated on this experiment prior to today."

Her jaw dropped, her expression indignant. "Of course not!"

"Fine then." He took her elbow and led her to the table.

"If you'll change these bottles into a different order and then one at a time, dab a little sample of each on one of these cards. Use this pencil to number each one. Don't open another bottle until the witness has had a chance to smell the first one. Do you understand?"

"Yes, I do."

"Good. Let's get started then."

Mrs. Hoover rearranged the five bottles and then dabbed a small amount on the first sample. Mr. Douglas took it, waved it in the air, rounded the screen and handed it to Miss Means. She smelled the card and shook her head. The cycle continued with negative results until they came to number four.

"This is the one."

"Are you positive, Miss Means? There is another sample."

She waved the card. "No doubts. This is it."

He returned to Mrs. Hoover. "Would you please tell the court the name of the fragrance?"

She picked up the bottle, read the name and giggled. "I don't think I can pronounce it, but it is from France."

"I realize it's hard to pronounce." He raised his voice. "Anyone in here speak French?"

Birdie glanced around the room. When no one raised his or her hand, she raised hers. "I speak a little."

"Excellent!" Mr. Douglas walked back to where Birdie sat with Tad and offered his hand.

"Please stand and give us your name please, ma'am."

She rose and took the bottle. "Mrs. Birdie Lockhart. The fragrance is Fougere Royal 1882 by Houbigant."

Douglas took the bottle. "Thank you, ma'am." He approached the bench. "Your honor, the prosecution rests."

"Mr. Johnson, do you have any questions for Miss Means?" He watched as John Samuelson wrote something on his notepad and shoved it over for Johnson to read.

"No sir. No questions for Miss Means, but I do have a question for the prosecution."

"Go ahead."

"Mr. Douglas, why hasn't the other officer who searched Mr. Samuelson's home been called to the witness stand?" He glanced down at the pad. "Let's see. His name is Detective Jenkins."

CHAPTER TWENTY-SIX

Birdie sat rigid with apprehension. Of course, she could dress up as Detective Jenkins again and testify, but it would be hard to control her voice. She cast a quick glance at Tad. His stiff shoulders and mutinous expression said no way would she be testifying. Detective Haney glanced back at her. She dipped her head. If necessary, she'd get up there. Tad would be furious but she figured it'd be one time in many to come in their marriage.

Mr. Douglas stood. "My understanding is that Detective Jenkins was on loan from a city back east. He signed all the necessary documents pertaining to his part in the investigation and returned home."

Johnson, hands stuffed in his pants pockets, rocked back on his heels. "Isn't that rather unusual? Shouldn't he have stayed or at least returned for the trial?"

"No, as a matter of fact, it's pretty standard procedure. He worked under the direct supervision of Detective Ethan the entire time."

The counselor snorted. "I disagree. Your honor, I move we postpone the remainder of the trial until Detective Jenkins can be present to testify."

Birdie held her breath while Judge Tyler flipped through a folder. He slapped it closed. "Is Detective Ethan in the courtroom?"

Ethan stood. "Here, your honor."

Judge Tyler steepled his hands and peered over his glasses. "How long would it take to get Detective Jenkins back to Waco, Detective?"

"Actually, sir, his train isn't due to leave until tomorrow. He's spent the last few months helping us with other matters."

Birdie glanced over to see the Chief of Police lower his forehead to his hand. He wasn't a happy man, and Ethan would probably get a sever tongue lashing—if he didn't get fired.

"Can you have him here in a couple of hours?"

"Yes, you honor."

"We'll adjourn for lunch and reconvene at two o'clock. Mr. Johnson, after questioning Detective Jenkins, be ready to state your case for Mr. Samuelson."

He tapped the sound box. "Court adjourned."

Oh, boy. I may be in a heck of a mess. "I know, I know, don't say it," she murmured to her husband, "but I have to testify. We can't let Samuelson get away."

Hand at her elbow, Tad helped her rise. "I could throttle you, Birdie. What if your disguise fails, someone recognizes you? It'll not only further taint your reputation, but it could cause the DA to lose the case. I hope to goodness Detective Jenkins isn't going to haunt us for years." He narrowed his eyes. "He is retiring, isn't he?"

"I don't know. We'll see."

He growled, "Birrr-dee."

"Whenever they need my detective training, I am going to work, Tad. The money will help build Birdie's Nest."

"You can't give up on building your house, even though you have a home now at the ranch?" Startled, she glanced up at his face to see that he was serious.

"No. I cannot. Aunt Patty wouldn't exist, or at least not as I knew her." How dare he even suggest giving up her goal? "I can't believe you'd suggest giving up, Tad."

They were outside on the lawn of the courthouse. Thank goodness it wasn't Monday, market day, and the square wasn't filled with people selling their wares. Birdie struggled to hide her disappointment, more like her hurt, at Tad's suggestion she give up Birdie's Nest. She shook off his hand and quickened her step to reach the buggy.

"Birdie, slow down." He caught her arm. "Look, sweetheart, I'm sorry. I had to ask, to be sure how important it was to you." He hugged her close and rubbed her back.

"We'll get Birdie's Nest built in time and it will be our home. I promise."

Birdie tried to believe him, but why had he brought it up? Was it because he didn't want her working with Detective Ethan? Or did he want her to give up teaching self-defense? She supposed because she was pregnant he expected her to sit around and do nothing. He'd soon learn otherwise.

They grabbed a quick lunch at a small café on the square and rushed to the police station for Birdie's disguise.

She was dressed and putting up her hair when Ethan knocked and entered the room with a wig. "Birdie, you better wear this as you can't wear a hat in the courtroom."

Birdie took the ratty looking hairpiece. Tiny pieces of lint were stuck in amongst the strands of dark. "Goodness, it's in terrible shape. Folks will think I have head lice. I need a comb." When it was lint free, she plopped it on her head. Ethan adjusted it to fit just right. She looked at Tad, but he merely shook his head and pursed his lips. Her mustache was glued on. She shrugged into the long coat and, with her hat in hand, she and Ethan left the room. Tad would follow along later as he couldn't be seen entering the courtroom with them, especially since she wouldn't be sitting by his side.

People turned and stared as she followed Detective Ethan into the courtroom. Amid the inquisitive murmurs, she put as much masculinity in her walk as she knew how. A few giggled and guffaws told her she wasn't doing that great a job. She must look ridiculous.

Judge Tyler entered the courtroom. After sitting down he lifted the gavel and hit the sound box sharply. "Court is now in session. Mr. Johnson, you may call your first witness."

Mr. Johnson rose and strutted back and forth in front of the witness box like a banty rooster, his thumbs in the pockets of his vest, as he called his first witness. "The defense calls Detective Jenkins."

Birdie rose and made her way to the witness box. Tension left her body stiff and robotic in her movements and she tripped but caught herself against the rail. The defense attorney watched her approach, doing his best to keep from chuckling at her stumble. The bailiff swore her in and Johnson approached.

"State your name for us, sir."

She cleared her throat. "Detective Jonathon Jenkins of Chicago, sir." She hacked for a minute and her speech came out in a croak. "Beg pardon 'bout my…my speech and walk. Had a di…disease in childhood. Affected both."

Most of the people in the courtroom glanced at their hands. Even Johnson looked contrite for his earlier laugh. "No pardon needed, Detective."

Birdie glanced at Ethan to see him holding his head. Tad's grin stretched across his face. Sweating in the wool uniform, she struggled to keep from laughing.

"Now, I understand you were called in specifically from Chicago to help with this case."

"Yes…that is correc…t."

He turned to the jury and waved a hand. "Can you explain to us why the Waco Police Department would need outside help? Are they unskilled, inept?"

Birdie's neck burned. No doubt her ears were red too. She resisted the impulse to cover them with her hands to cool them. "No, sir. They are…are a top-notch force. In Chi…cago we've developed some new pro…procedures and I'm on loan to introduce them to the officers here."

"Like what?"

"Evidence   collection…and   skills   like   fiber com…comparison." Her mustache tickled and she placed her fingers over her mouth to make sure it hadn't come loose. It flipped out some on the side facing the jury. Dang, the glue must be getting old and too thick. She applied pressure hoping it would stick and stay. "Why…in the near future, sir, crimes will be solved using fin…ger prints."

"Harrumph. Pure speculation, I'm sure." He turned his back and walked back to his table. "No further questions, your honor."

"Mr. Douglas, would you like to question Detective Jenkins?"

"No, your honor. I believe Mr. Johnson has covered all of my concerns." He smiled and nodded at Birdie. "Detective, I'd like to be on the list to receive additional information on the finger printing procedures as it's developed."

Birdie grinned, loosening her mustache again. She

sobered and pressed her fist against her mouth and coughed. "It will be my…my pleasure to keep you informed."

Mr. Johnson stood. "Your honor, this chit-chat is uncalled for. May we proceed?"

"I find it most interesting, counselor. It is wise to stay informed on the latest in criminal investigation." Judge Tyler nodded to Detective Jenkins. "Thank you for coming in and when you send Mr. Douglas information, please include me."

"Be honored, judge."

"You may step down."

Birdie rose and deliberately eased herself down from the witness box. She stood a moment as if gaining her balance and returned to her seat by Ethan. Every eye in the courtroom followed her as she made her way.

"Now then, Mr. Johnson, are you ready to proceed?"

"Yes, sir, your honor. My next witness is Mrs. John Samuelson."

All eyes were on the attractive middle-aged woman as she entered the courtroom and marched up the aisle. The fabric of her high-necked navy blue dress swished with each step she took. Her only adornment, a large cameo brooch at her throat, emphasized the white strands highlighting her dark hair. Mr. Johnson took her arm and led her to the witness stand as if she were royalty. The bailiff swore her in. After the "so help me God" she glared at the prosecutor and bit out, "I do."

"Now then, Mrs. Samuelson," He walked to stand behind John. "Is this your husband?"

"Yes, sir, it is."

"And how many years have you been married?"

"It will be thirty-five years in September."

He nodded. "So, I assume you know Mr. Samuelson pretty well by now."

"Indeed I do." She let her gaze pan the jurors before looking out at the audience. "My husband would never do the atrocious things he's accused of." She shook her finger at Mr. Douglas. "You've got the wrong man, sir."

"Ma'am, do you remember your husband going out on February 5th and February 17th of this years?"

"No, sir, I do not. Those were both nights we had church socials. We attended together and were home by nine o'clock that evening. We retired at ten o'clock as is our usual habit."

"I understand you and Mr. Samuelson have been members of the same church for many years. Please tell us what roles your husband fills in the church."

Mrs. Samuelson sat up straighter, lifted her chin and smiled. "He's been a deacon, on the financial committee, the building committee, and on occasions when the church was without a pastor, he gave the Sunday sermon." Her bosom swelled with pride as she took a deep breath. "And he did very well. Several members commented that he might have missed his calling."

"Would you describe your husband's character, Mrs. Samuelson?"

The woman spent a good fifteen minutes extolling her husband's virtues and ended with, "My husband couldn't have possibly committed this crime." No doubt she believed every word she'd said. In her mind, John Samuelson was a saint. Birdie supposed that's how it should be in a marriage. Evidently her husband had been good to her and she thought he could do no wrong.

"Thank you, Mrs. Samuelson. I have no further questions."

Judge Tyler arched a bushy eyebrow at the prosecutor. "Cross-examination Mr. Douglas?"

The prosecutor rose. "Yes, your honor." He glanced at his notes before walking to the witness box. "Mrs. Samuelson, I think Mr. Johnson covered just about everything but I have just a few more questions for you."

Chin in the air, she nodded.

Mr. Douglas smiled and stepped to the table holding all the evidence. He lifted the bottle of cologne for the jury and Mrs. Samuelson to see. "Is this the cologne your husband wears, ma'am?"

"Yes."

For just a minute, Douglas stood thinking, his gaze moving between the two Samuelsons. "Ma'am, we've heard about your husband's standing in the church and community, all very commendable, I might add. But, you didn't mention children. Do you have children, ma'am."

234

The smile on Mrs. Samuelson's face wilted. "No, sir. Unfortunately we were not blessed with children."

Mr. Douglas's head bobbed with sympathy. He cleared his throat. "I'd like to review a few things Mr. Johnson went over with you. First, you testified that on both afore-mentioned dates, you and Mr. Samuelson attended a church social, returned home by nine o'clock and went to bed at ten o'clock. Is that correct?"

"Yes, it is."

"Thank you, ma'am. You've been very cooperative. That's all, your honor."

She stood to rise. Mr. Douglas whirled. "One more question, ma'am." She returned to her seat. "Do you and Mr. Samuelson share a bedroom?"

A collective gasp rippled through the room. Mr. Johnson lunged to his feet and yelled, "I object, your honor. That question is highly improper."

Mr. Samuelson appeared ready to commit murder. He tried to shove past his lawyer and get to the prosecutor. A bailiff caught him by the collar of his coat and jerked him down into his chair. Judge Tyler struck the sounding block repeatedly until the room quieted. "Mr. Samuelson, you'll remain seated or I'll have you tied to your chair."

He turned to Mrs. Samuelson. "You will answer the question, ma'am, and I remind you, you are under oath."

Mrs. Samuelson's gaze darted from Mr. Douglas to her husband. Red faced, John glared at his wife. His rage made Birdie wonder if the man was abusive. The courtroom waited, silent, as if holding its breath.

"I will repeat the question, ma'am. Do you—"

Her brow furrowed. "No, sir. We do not." The woman's gaze never left her husband's. She exhibited no fear. Perhaps for the first time she considered the possibility he might be guilty.

"Is his room next to yours or down the hall?"

Voice clear, it resounded in the room. "Down the hall."

"Then how could you possibly know if your husband left his room in the middle of the night?" Mr. Douglas waved a hand. "Never mind, ma'am. No further questions, your honor."

Mr. Johnson called several character witnesses who sang Samuelson's praises, each saying pretty much what the other said. Birdie wondered if the jury considered the repetition monotonous. The last gentleman had to be urged several times to speak up.

"Would you like to cross-examine the witness, Mr. Douglas?" asked Judge Tyler.

As he had answered concerning each of the other character witnesses, he said, "No, your honor."

"Mr. Johnson. Do you plan to call anyone else?"

"No, your honor. The defense rests."

"We'll break for ten minutes and hear closing arguments."

Few people left though some stood and stretched. Birdie joined them. The wooden pews weren't the most comfortable of seats.

Judge Tyler returned to the bench. Those in the hallway rushed back in before the bailiff closed the doors.

"Mr. Douglas, are you ready for closing arguments?"

"Yes, your honor." He strode to stand several feet from the jury box. Voice clear and controlled, he reviewed the evidence and how each piece was tied to the items found in John Samuelson's home. He again described the wounds each woman suffered and emphasized their religious connotation. "Gentlemen of the jury, with the evidence presented and the horrific crime perpetrated against these two women, you must find Mr. Samuelson guilty of aggravated assault."

Mr. Johnson's closing arguments revolved around Mr. Samuelson's reputation. He waved toward the table where John sat. "Gentlemen, look at this pillar of Waco society. Does he resemble a religious zealot, someone who would commit the crime of which he's accused?" He pounded the rail of the jury box. "No, he does not. I beg you, do not convict this innocent man."

Judge Tyler removed his pocket watch to check the time. He peered over his glasses at the jury. "Folks, it's about supper time but I don't want to release you to discuss the case. So, I want a verdict before you go home tonight. We'll bring supper in for you."

The bailiff ushered the jurors into a side room for deliberation.

The judge stood and addressed the audience. "You folks go get something to eat and if you want to hear the verdict, check back."

Two hours later they had a verdict.

Mr. Samuelson joked with Mr. Johnson while they waited for the jury to enter.

Lila and Rose were ushered into the courtroom and sat beside Mr. Douglas.

After the jury was seated, Judge Tyler asked, "Mr. Foreman, do you have a verdict?"

"Yes, sir, we do."

"Well, let's hear it."

The tall elderly man cleared his throat. "We the jury find John Samuelson guilty on both counts of aggravated assault with a deadly weapon.

CHAPTER TWENTY-SEVEN

Tad shouldered his way, through the crowd in the courtroom, to the exit in time to see Birdie, Ethan by her side, striding across the lawn on their way to the police station. That columnist, Mr. Hoover and his wife hurried after them. At the journalist's call, Birdie and Ethan stopped. *No, Birdie, no. Don't talk to them.* But, Birdie and Ethan waited for them. She was taking a chance talking to the reporter. Ethan must know that. Why didn't he hustle Birdie away? He probably didn't want to cause any more speculation about Detective Jenkins. Tad hesitated at the bottom of the steps. If he ran over and interrupted, they might be even more suspicious. Best to hang back and let the situation play out.

Dang, Birdie's mustache was dangling from her upper lip again. Mrs. Hoover pointed and said something. Before Birdie could respond, the woman reached up and jerked the brush off. Mrs. Hoover's mouth gaped as she studied the object in her fingers. Before either of the Hoovers could speak, Birdie snatched the mustache from the shocked woman, waved goodbye and strode quickly away. Ethan said something to the couple, and then turned to follow Birdie.

Tad called, "Mr. Hoover. Hold up a moment." The couple turned and waited for him. Tad held out his hand. "Tad Lockhart, Mr. Hoover. I wanted to let you know how much I admire your work. You've done a fine job covering this case."

"Thank you. I appreciate your words." The man shook Tad's hand but his gaze returned to Birdie. "Did you see that? Detective Jenkins is a woman."

Tad allowed his gaze to follow Mr. Hoover's. "That

238

can't be. I've seen him several times over the past six months while he's been working here. He may be small in stature, but his childhood condition may have something to do with his size."

"But, his mustache was glued on."

Brow furrowed, Mrs. Hoover added, "I held it for a second, but then Detective Jenkins yanked it from my hand."

Mr. Hoover put his arm around her shoulders. "This is my wife, Mr. Lockhart."

Tad tipped his hat. "It's very nice to meet you, ma'am. May I say you did an excellent job with the DA's cologne experiment?"

"Thank you, Mr. Lockhart." She chewed her lip and glanced at the retreating figures of Birdie and Ethan. "I know what I saw."

Tad hustled to think. He snapped his fingers. "Maybe he can't grow a mustache, but wanted to be in style. They seem to be all the rage these days."

She thought for a minute. "You may be right." But, she didn't appear convinced. She looked around. "Where is your lovely wife?"

"She rested this afternoon." He leaned closer and lowered his voice. "She's in a delicate condition."

Her mouth formed an O. "Oh my, how exciting. Congratulations."

"Thank you. We're very happy but please, don't tell anyone. Birdie will have my hide for telling."

"We'll keep it quiet, Mr. Lockhart." He turned to his wife and arched a brow. "Won't we dear."

She flushed. "Yes. Of course."

Tad tipped his hat. "I better run pick up Birdie so we can get home. He glanced back to see them staring toward the corner where Birdie and Detective Ethan turned to reach the police station.

Hoping to throw them off, he jumped into the surrey and headed toward the hotel. He drove round the block and came up to the police station at its rear entry—just in time to see Birdie walk out of Ethan's office and run right into the Hoovers. They must have hotfooted it over here.

Mrs. Hoover, expression bewildered, called to Birdie.

239

"Mrs. Lockhart, what a surprise to see you here. Why," she glanced at her husband. "Mr. Lockhart said you were resting." She touched Birdie's arm, leaned close and whispered, "Congratulations, by the way."

* * *

Birdie took Tad's hand as he helped her into the surrey. "What were you thinking to tell her about the baby? Now it will be all over town."

He sighed. "Birdie, she asked where you were and I had to tell her something. I was trying to distract her from your mustache. Anyway, would that be so bad?" He stepped up, sat beside her and took the reins.

"Yes. People in this century will expect me to sit around and twiddle my toes. I can't do that. I'm an active person."

"You don't know that, sweetheart. Maybe you'll set a new trend. Anyway, Mrs. Hoover said she wouldn't tell anyone."

Birdie shot Tad a look. "It will be all over town by tomorrow."

He smiled and shrugged. "I didn't really have a choice. After telling me about your mustache coming off and then asking where you were, I didn't have time to come up with anything better." He leaned over and kissed her cheek. "After all, you know I'm quite delighted."

"Yes, you'll be quite the cock of the walk around here for fathering two babies in such a short period of time."

Birdie chuckled at his shocked expression. He sputtered, "You don't really think that, do you?"

"No, I'm teasing." She scooted closer to and looped her arm through the crook of his. "How I can tease about anything right now, I don't know."

He switched the reins to his other hand, put his arm around her waist and squeezed. "It's going to be all right, sweetheart. No one's going to figure out you're Detective Jenkins."

She snuggled against him enjoying his male scent combined with his spicy aftershave. "What did you tell them about the mustache fiasco?" She could only imagine what the woman thought.

"I said you might be one of those men who can't grow facial hair, yet wanted to be in style." He coughed into his hand. The scoundrel, he was trying to hide his laugh. "I also mentioned your childhood illness—that it might have been the cause, which I must say was very clever of you."

"Fortunately the idea just popped into my head." With the odd looks she was receiving from the jurors and the others in the courtroom, she'd had to come up with something. "Do you think Mrs. Hoover bought your excuse?"

"I don't know. She started looking around and asked where you were. When I told her our news and that you were resting, she seemed to forget the mustache and offered congratulations."

"I can't imagine what she thought, seeing me at the police station. I'm glad we were able to escape before they could start asking questions." She wished she could say the same for Detective Ethan. The pair had caught him in the hallway. Hopefully he'd been able to come up with a good story. "I guess we better tell the family about the baby tonight. I'd hate for them to hear the news from someone else."

"Do you mind getting pregnant so early in our marriage?"

"In some ways. I wish Nathan was a little older, but we'll manage." She slipped her arm around his waist and laid her head against his shoulder. His arm moved up to wrap around her shoulders. He slid his large, calloused hand up and down her arm, a motion that caused delicious goose bumps to break out on her skin. "No, I don't mind, Tad. At my age, if I'm going to have children, it needs to be now." Birth defects occurred in this era, but she didn't know if they were as common as they were in the future. Somehow she didn't think so. She touched her flat belly and imagined being big with their child. She glanced at Tad. "Will you still want to make love to me when my belly is swollen?"

* * *

Three days later Detective Ethan dropped by shortly after breakfast. Birdie met him on the porch. "Would you like a cup of coffee?"

241

"Sure would."

"Let's sit out here on the porch. It's cooler." Sometimes they actually caught a slight breeze. "Have a seat and I'll be right back."

She returned with the pot and two cups. After pouring their servings, she placed the pot on the porch to prevent scorching the table. The last couple of mornings' coffee hadn't settled real well on her stomach, so she merely sipped rather than drank.

Lloyd placed his hat on his knee and then glanced toward the barns. "Tad around?"

"Yes. I imagine he saw you ride in and will be up in a minute."

His mouth turned up in a grin. "He's not still jealous, is he?"

Birdie chuckled. "No, he just likes to stay informed." And it'd be easier on her if she didn't have to retell the news.

"Good, good." He took a large swallow of coffee. "Yeowee! That's hot." He blew on it and took a sip. "What's he say about you doing anymore work for the police department?"

"He doesn't want me to, of course, but I told him if you all needed me, I'd be there."

His face sobered. "Now, Birdie. We don't want to cause problems between you and Tad. Plus, the chief is against it altogether. I guess you saw him in the courtroom when they insisted you testify."

She tried not to laugh, but the memory was funny. "Did he give you a tongue lashing?"

"Nothing any worse than what he's given me before."

Tad rode up and tied his horse to the hitching rail. Birdie shook her head in wonder, amazed again she really lived in this, to her, historical period. How long before she completely accepted "the past" and forgot where she'd come from?

"Hey, Lloyd, what brought you out today?" Tad stepped up on the porch, pulled a rocker closer and sat, his long legs stretched out in front. "You're not here for Birdie, are you?"

"No, I'm not. Thought I'd bring you the news from town."

Birdie topped off her cup of coffee and handed it to Tad.

"Thank you, hon. You sure you don't want it? I can go get another cup."

"No, I had plenty earlier." She seemed to remember caffeine should be avoided during pregnancy.

Tad removed his hat and tossed it onto the porch sending dust flying. His hair held a crease where the hatband had flattened it. With his free hand, he scrubbed at his head lifting the slicked down strands for air circulation. She smiled at the gesture she'd grown used to seeing each evening when he came in from working.

"Have they announced Samuelson's sentence yet?"

"No, that's not why I'm here." He removed a newspaper from his inside jacket pocket. How did the man keep from smothering in the wool coat? "I thought you'd want to see this right away. Fresh off the printer this morning."

Birdie reached for it and moved to sit on Tad's lap so they could read it together. "What page?"

Ethan finished off his coffee and set the cup on the small table. "Turn to page two. The article is in the right hand column."

Tad squeezed her waist. "Read it aloud, Birdie."

Birdie skimmed the heading and glanced between the two men before sharing with them. Ethan sighed deeply, his mouth pursed in a frown.

She took a deep breath and read. "*Could Detective Jenkins be a Woman?*"

CHAPTER TWENTY-EIGHT

"*I find it shockingly strange that Detective Jenkins can't keep his moustache on his face. From the detective's small stature and smooth complexion, you'd think his baby face that of a woman. Or his lack of facial hair and his body frame also be a result of that 'childhood' illness he alluded to on the witness stand?*

"*Both my wife and I were surprised to see a certain woman with the initials of B. L. at the police station in the company of Detective Ethan. On his way to greet them was the lady's husband, T. L. Of course this is speculation on my part, but could B. L. have posed as Detective Jenkins and if so, why?*

"*If you can shed any light on this situation, please contact me at the news office.*"

Robert Fuller

Birdie folded the paper, stood up and placed it on the table. "I'm sorry, Tad."

Tad was livid. He lurched from the rocker, bounded down the few steps and stalked up and down in front of the porch holding his head and swearing. Olivia came to the screen door. "What on earth is going on out here, Tad? We can hear you roaring all the way to the back of the house."

He stopped and took a deep breath. "Sorry, Mother, just letting off a little steam." He cast his gaze toward Ethan, eyes narrowed. For a minute Birdie was afraid he'd let some off by pummeling the detective. She glanced at Ethan. He sat ramrod straight, his body ready for the attack if it came. The two men would be evenly matched. Though Tad was taller, Ethan had more brawn. It wouldn't take Tad long to cool off. He was quick to anger but quick to let it go.

"Well, hold it down, please, or you're going to wake Nathan." She stuck her head out the door. Her earlier frown grew into a smile. "Hello, Detective Ethan. It's been a while since we've seen you. Will you stay to dinner?"

He finished his coffee and stood. "No, ma'am, but thank you. I have to get back."

"Come back again when you can stay longer."

"I'll do that, ma'am."

Olivia turned and went back in the house. Birdie walked down the steps with Ethan and joined Tad by his horse.

"I'm sorry as heck about this, Tad. You too, Birdie. I never dreamed Detective Jenkins would have to appear in court."

"It's not your doing, Lloyd." Birdie took Tad's arm and squeezed close to his side. "Tad, love, it's really not Ethan's fault. It was that darn old glue. I'd have escaped notice if it hadn't been for that moustache coming loose."

A muscle in Tad's jaw jerked. He bit out. "I know that but it doesn't make the news any less disturbing. Next they'll be printing your name in the paper. It won't take people long to realize who B. L. is."

"They can speculate all they want, but they'll never be sure," said Lloyd. "How do you want to handle this?"

"I'd just as soon admit to being Jenkins and get it over with. It's not like my participation can have any impact on the case."

"You'll do no such thing." Tad looked to Ethan for support. "Don't you agree?"

"For now, yes. We just continue as if nothing is out of the ordinary."

* * *

Birdie rode by the construction site on her way to meet Mattie at the warehouse they called their studio. She snickered. Studio indeed. Maybe in time they'd have some money to put into it and spruce it up.

She was surprised to see so much activity going on at

Birdie's Nest. Men were everywhere doing one job or another. A man hollered, waved his hat and headed her way. It was Mr. Teague, the architect. Stunned at the amount of work they'd done, she dismounted and let Strawberry drag the reins and munch on the grass as she walked toward the man. Fortunately, they'd leveled the ground for the drive and she didn't have to worry about where she put her feet in the overgrown vegetation.

He whipped off his hat. "Hello, Mrs. Lockhart." He wave toward all the construction. "What do you think?"

"I'm amazed." She couldn't believe how much they'd gotten done. The cellar looked almost finished and they'd started some framing. Where had the money come from? "Mr. Teague. I don't have enough money for this. Surely you didn't buy this on credit."

"No, ma'am. Your husband came by the office earlier in the week. He'd opened an account at the bank for me to draw funds from as needed."

Birdie's chin quivered and she cleared her throat to keep from crying. Darned hormones. Mr. Teague didn't seem to notice. He continued to update her on the work they'd done. "I've put in an order for the brick, but you might want to go by the brickyard in the next day or two and decide on the color."

She threw her arms around the astounded man's neck, almost knocking him to the ground. "Thank you, thank you, Mr. Teague. I surely will."

Mr. Teague patted her on the back. "Now, now, ma'am, don't be thanking me. Thank that husband of yours."

She pulled back and wiped at the tears on her face. "You can bet I will."

"Good, good." He pulled a paper from his suit coat pocket and handed it to her. "This is a list of some things you'll need to decide on soon so I can order in supplies."

Birdie glanced at the sheet, the writing covering almost the entire page listed items from wood for paneling and floors, to wall paper choices. She hugged it to her heart. At last, it was really happening. They were building Birdie's Nest. "I'll see to it, Mr. Teague."

She sang all the way to the warehouse. When she

arrived, she found Mattie sitting at the desk. Unable to contain herself, she rushed the woman from behind and hugged her around the neck.

"What on earth, child?"

Birdie removed her arms, scooted paper out of the way and sat on the desk. "They're actually building Birdie's Nest. You need to ride by and take a look."

"Where'd you get the money?"

"Tad. He's paying for it." Birdie teared up again. She swiped at the moisture on her cheeks. "Isn't he a sweetheart?"

"Well, he sure is, but why the tears?"

"I'm so happy, Mattie." She grabbed one of the older woman's hands and squeezed. "We're also going to have a baby."

"A baby?" Mattie's face lit and then she broke into tears. "I'm so happy for you."

Birdie had never seen the older woman cry, even when she was overcome with joy. "Mattie, are you all right?"

She sniffed and smiled through her tears. "I think Joseph and I are going to become parents too." She dropped her head to her hands. "I'd given up on ever having a child. I've been making excuses for my symptoms for weeks."

"Oh, my goodness!" Birdie pulled Mattie from her chair and danced her around the room. Suddenly the room swayed a bit and Birdie held a hand to her head. "Whoa, we better sit down."

Mattie shoved her into the chair and took Birdie's perch on the desktop.

"Mattie, how old are you and Joseph?"

"I'm thirty-eight. Joseph is almost fifty."

Birdie nodded. Lots of women in this day and time had babies up into their forties. Mattie's should be fine. When they'd first met, Birdie believed Mattie to be middle-aged. Since she'd lost weight and toned up, she looked younger and healthier. "Well, you need to get to the doctor for a checkup right now."

"No, not until I'm much farther along."

"Now, today or tomorrow. Believe me, early medical care is very important for the child's health as well as yours."

Face radiant with happiness, Mattie conceded. "I will. Promise."

It suddenly registered with Birdie that Mattie should have been in the middle of a class. Her mood sank like a sack of rocks in the Brazos. "Where are your students?"

"No one showed today. Can't imagine why."

"Really? Didn't you see the newspaper article about Detective Jenkins?"

"Yeah, I did but didn't think it would have that much affect on the school."

"I'm sorry, Mattie. I never dreamed it would hurt the school and you."

"Don't worry about it. The situation will soon blow over and things will go back to normal." Mattie shrugged. "If not, we'll have other things to occupy our minds."

Birdie was just now learning about motherhood. She wasn't sure she could just stay home and be a wife and mother. Not that she wasn't excited. She was, though she was a little frightened too. Not about giving birth, but the responsibility involved. Nathan was darn good training. Oh, how she loved the little bugger. He was so sweet. At least she had Olivia, Bethany, and Sarah to help out.

They waited until the next class was due to arrive. When no one showed, they tacked a sign to the door that read, CLOSED UNTIL FURTHER NOTICE.

* * *

Tad chased after Nathan as he crawled across the parlor rug. He was fast and squealed like a greased pig when he knew Tad was after him. Laughing, Tad scooped him up and tossed him over his head. Birdie came in the room wearing a pretty blue suit dress with a frilly white blouse. She grinned and quipped, "Better be careful or you'll be wearing his breakfast."

Oh, yeah. He settled the boy on his hip and looked at his knees. They seemed to be relatively bare of dirt. His job was to keep him clean before they left for church. The more active Nathan became, the harder it was. He approached his wife and fingered the lace on the throat of her blouse. "Why don't you ever wear your brooch? It would look nice with this dress."

She bit her lower lip and leaned close. "I'm sorry, Tad,

248

but after thinking back, I'm afraid it had something to do with my time travel and that if I put it on I'll disappear."

Disappear? Fear welled in his stomach. Could it be? "Well, let's get rid of the thing."

"No. For some reason I know we're supposed to have the brooch." She shrugged. "I guess that reason will become clear at some time during our life."

He wrapped an arm around her shoulders and squeezed. "Don't worry, sweetheart. Put it up somewhere safe in case Bethany decides to try it on or heaven forbid, our baby, if it's a girl."

She laughed. "Little boys try on jewelry too, love."

"Egad! That cinches it. Maybe we should have Mr. Smith put in his vault at the bank."

"Not a bad idea, at all. I'll see to it next time I'm in town."

Tad leaned close and placed a kiss on her lips. "Brooch or not, you are lovely this morning, love."

"Thank you. May I say you are especially handsome, quite the rake with Nathan on your hip."

"Hmm, yes, ma'am, you may. If I'd known women were so attracted to babies, I'd have borrowed one a few years ago to aid my pursuit of the fairer sex." He leaned in and placed a kiss on her lips.

She snorted. "Only women interested in marriage would be drawn to a man holding a child, Tad."

"Well, rats." He grinned. "There's only one woman I'm interested in attracting." He wiggled his eyebrows and lowered his voice. "The one who kept me awake making love half the night."

"Are we ready to go?" Olivia entered the room with Bethany on her heels.

"Yes we are, Mother." He walked to open the front door. "Your carriage awaits, madams and mam'selle."

Bethany giggled as Tad handed her up into the surrey. "You're so much more fun since you got married, Tad. Not nearly as stuffy."

"A happy marriage does that to a man, child," Birdie said, sounding much like his mother.

Tad glanced at Birdie and winked. "And I am one happy

man." After he'd handed Nathan in to Sarah, Birdie poked him in the rear with her parasol. He jumped and shot her a mock scowl. She'd have to stay on her toes or he'd be paying her back. To keep him from squeezing a handful of her butt, she turned sideways for him to help her in. He leaned close. "Spoil sport."

Olivia and Bethany led the way down the aisle at church. Birdie held Nathan, struggling to keep him from snatching feathers off her hat as Tad, hand at her waist, guided her along after his mother and sister.

Sarah saw her dilemma and whispered, "Let me take him, ma'am." Birdie handed him over. Before Sarah could move down the aisle, Nathan howled and lunged from Sarah's grasp. Birdie caught him, pulled a feather from her hat and handed it to him.

Several women around them chuckled and when Birdie looked up, they nodded in greeting. Even Mrs. Smith, the banker's wife who'd been so snooty a year ago, smiled and dipped her head. Well, will wonders never cease? Maybe the women in town didn't take note of the initials in the article, didn't put two and two together or just didn't care. Hmm, interesting.

Mr. Smith pulled his wife back around and whispered, much too loudly, "Turn around. Ignore that woman." He sniffed as if there were a bad odor in the church. "Dressing up in men's clothes, indeed." He glanced back and hissed at Birdie. "Hussy."

His wife gasped and pinched his arm. "Shush! People are staring."

Birdie stiffened and quickly glanced to see if Tad had heard. She relaxed. Tad was engaged in conversation with the man across the aisle. She scanned those in the congregation. Several men stared at her with contempt. She lifted her chin and glared at them until they lowered their gaze. Oh, boy. Finally the women were easing up on her. Now the men were against her. They probably thought she'd have their wives and daughters wearing pants. She snorted.

Tad looked at her, furrowed his brow and mouthed *what?* She smiled and shook her head. Nathan dropped the wet feather and lunged for Tad. He cuddled him close and the baby laid his head on his shoulder and yawned. Tad gently rubbed his back and soon Nathan was asleep.

When the service was over, Birdie ignored the rude stares of a couple of the men, Mr. Smith included. Just outside, Tad handed Nathan to Sarah and stalked after Mr. Smith. "Raymond Smith, I want to talk to you."

The man stopped and turned. "What do you want, Tad?"

He shrugged out of his coat and tossed it to Birdie. "You called my wife a name in the church."

Birdie grabbed Tad's arm. "It's not really important, Tad. Come on. Let it go."

"No, sweetheart. Move back out of the way. This is my fight."

Mr. Smith puffed out his chest. "Yes, sir. I did. You need to keep a firmer hand on the woman."

His wife tugged on his arm. "Apologize to Mrs. Lockhart and let's go."

He shook her hand off. "I'll do no such thing. She's a disgrace to womanhood."

Tad's jaw was rigid as he spoke through his teeth. "No man shows disrespect to my wife. I want an apology."

Mr. Smith shrugged out of his jacket. "Well, you're not getting it from me."

The man turned around and grinned. Before he could move, Tad landed a blow to his chin. He went down like a felled tree and didn't get up. Tad made eye contact with the men in the crowd that had gathered. "No man calls my wife names or is disrespectful to her." He nodded to Mrs. Smith. "Remind your husband that I expect Birdie to receive an apology from him by tomorrow or we'll be having another talk."

CHAPTER TWENTY-NINE

"Tad, that wasn't necessary. I'm not some little woman who needs protecting."

"Don't nag at me about it, Birdie. You are my wife. I'll not allow any man to talk to you or any woman in my family in that manner."

Olivia tapped him on the shoulder with her parasol. "Never thought I'd see the day when I'd be glad to see you fighting, but that man deserved it. I'm proud of you, son."

Birdie shook her head. What could she say? She suspected many men in modern time would have done the same thing. It was a first for her. She'd never dated that much and there had been few opportunities for insults. Of course, on the job, men she had to arrest talked ugly to her but since she couldn't knock them out, she ignored them. When another Ranger worked with her, he might step on the guy's hand or something and tell him to shut up. If a man insulted her on the street today, she'd probably deck him. Well, not now that she was pregnant. She wouldn't take a chance on hurting the baby. It felt rather nice to have her husband standing up for her though. Warmth blossomed in her stomach and eased up to her chest. She scooted closer and wrapped her arm around his. He smiled down at her.

As they neared the suspension bridge, she turned around on the seat. "Do you all mind stopping by the house to see how much they've gotten done?"

"Not at all, dear. I must admit I've been curious."

For the first time Birdie wondered if her plan to move once the house was built bothered her mother-in-law. She'd not thought of the older woman's feelings, just her own. "Olivia, do you mind us moving into town?"

"No, dear. Every woman needs to have her own home." She patted Birdie's shoulder. "We'll miss having you at the ranch, but expect we'll all be visiting back and forth."

"That's true. Now you'll have a place to stay in town for social activities." It would be good for Bethany to be able to attend more socials with Tad close by to supervise her activities. She grinned. No doubt he'll love that, but in truth, he'd have done the same if they were still in the country.

Tad stopped the buggy and helped them down. Sarah stayed with a sleeping Nathan. Birdie talked as she walked them through the house and described where bedrooms would be located on the second floor.

Olivia was amazed. "You're going to have *four* bathrooms?"

"Yes, one downstairs, two upstairs by the bedrooms and a large one with both a tub and a shower connected to the master suite."

"My goodness. That sounds mighty extravagant." Olivia turned to Tad. "Are sure you can afford all this?" Her eyes narrowed. "You're not selling land, are you?"

"Mother, you know I'd never do that. Building this house will not take away from the ranch, plus, Birdie has contributed all the money she's made from her self-defense school and from working with Detective Ethan."

"Forgive me, son. I should have known you'd never do anything to endanger our means of livelihood." She slipped an arm around Birdie's waist. "I hope I didn't insult you with my questions."

"Of course not. You're the matriarch. It's your job to keep up with things."

Olivia beamed at the title. "Well…I never considered myself such, as Tad's the boss."

"Birdie's right, Mother. We couldn't function without you."

Bethany blurted, "Yeah, he's the boss of me, that's for sure. Mama always takes his side when it's about me."

"He *is* the man of the house and has your best interests at heart, dear."

"Yes, but I'll soon be seventeen years old. I think I

253

deserve to be allowed a little more freedom. I don't need an escort everywhere I go."

"We'll talk about it later." Olivia patted her daughter's cheek. "Now, let's get back to the surrey and go home. We forgot our parasols and will be as brown as field hands if we stay out here much longer."

Bethany walked ahead with her mother while Birdie and Tad followed a little way back. Olivia's earlier comment worried her. "Tad, you're not strapping your budget to build this house are you? I mean…you know I want it, but I don't want to take away from your family's security."

"No, sweetheart, the ranch is fine financially. Now, we may not be able to furnish the house right away."

"That's not a problem. We can make do with very little—use crates for seating and put mattresses on the floor to sleep on."

"Whoa! I draw the line at sleeping on the floor. I think we can afford a bed and some chairs. For that matter, I bet there's furniture in the attic we can use until we can afford to buy."

Two days later, Birdie rode out and found the construction site deserted. *Where on earth is everyone?* From atop Strawberry Birdie could see no work had been done since the previous week.

Fifteen minutes later she dismounted in front of Mr. Teague's office and tied the mare's reins to the hitching post. The bell above the door jangled as she entered, and the delicious smell of aromatic pipe tobacco welcomed her.

"I'll be right there." Mr. Teague called from his inner office. Birdie heard papers rustle and then a light tapping. She assumed he was emptying his pipe. Footsteps sounded against the wooden floor as Mr. Teague entered the outer office. When he saw Birdie, he stopped. "Ah, Mrs. Lockhart, I assume you're here about no one being on the work site." He stepped aside to allow her to enter and motioned toward a chair. "Have a seat." Rather than sit, he leaned against his desk, arms folded across his chest. "I'd planned to ride out this afternoon and update you on the situation."

"And what is the situation?" Birdie knew, but she had to hear it from him.

He cleared his throat. "The men refuse to work on your house because of…of the Detective Jenkins situation."

*   *   *

"Birdie, the men will forget, or they'll need the work in a few days, a week or two at the most. Then they'll be back on the job."

In Detective Ethan's office, Birdie faced him across his desk. "You really think so?"

"Yes, I do. Those men have families to feed and winter is coming. They may not like working for you, but they'll do it."

And idea struck her. Would they purposely do a lousy job? She opened her mouth to ask, but he held up a hand. "Those men have a reputation to uphold. They won't do something to sever their chances of more work."

She allowed her shoulders to relax. "Is there anything I can do around here?" She reached for some of the paperwork on his desk. His hand stilled hers and she sat back. "So, it's like that?"

"Until things die down, yes."

Birdie stood. "All right. Come out for dinner on your day off. I'm sure Olivia would enjoy your company as much as Tad and I."

He pushed back from the desk, stood and walked to hold the door for her. "I'll do it. Wouldn't want to miss one of those fine meals."

"Are you busy this coming Saturday?"

"Sure not."

"All right. We'll see you then." Birdie strode from the building to where Strawberry was tethered in the front of the building. No need for her to hide any longer since her cover was blown. Disguises. If only the people of this century could've seen her when she served the subpoena. She couldn't restrain a giggle. The men would have had a heart attack, the women the vapors. Her giggle burst into a loud guffaw and people passing by looked at her oddly. No, what am I thinking? Men didn't have heart attacks these days—they have apoplexy. She mounted her horse and the mare plodded toward Mattie's house, Birdie grinning the entire way. The town would have something to add to her earlier misbehavior. She could hear them now. *That Birdie Lockhart is peculiar.*

Nehemiah met her at the back drive and took Strawberry's reins. He ran an appreciative hand down the mare's neck. "It be good to see this fine looking animal again, Mrs. Lockhart."

Birdie stroked the horse's forelock. "She's a sweetheart too, Nehemiah. Gentle and smart."

"I can see that by looking at her eyes. Now, you go on in and visit with Ms. Mattie. I 'spect she'll be happy to see you."

He turned his attention to Strawberry. Birdie smiled at the sound of his gentle voice fading as she walked away. "Come on, pretty girl. I's gonna make you comfortable."

Birdie tapped on the back door. She didn't want to startle Sadie again and have her throw flour all over the kitchen. She called out. "Sadie, it's me, Birdie Lockhart."

Sadie opened the door. "Come in this house, sweet lady. Ms. Mattie will be mighty happy to see you." The colored lady narrowed her eyes at Birdie. "Now, don't you be paying any mind to what the mens in this town are sayin' about your costume." She chuckled. "Why the womens are right proud of you."

Birdie grabbed the woman in a big hug. Sadie hugged her back. "You a mighty fine woman and don't be forgettin' it." In the next breathe, she yelled, "Ms. Mattie, you gots a celebrity out here come to visit."

"A celebrity? Who on earth?" Mattie appeared in the kitchen door. "Birdie! Come in here. I have so much to tell you." She glared at Sadie. "You didn't tell her, did you?"

Sadie rose up to her considerable height and propped her hands on her ample hips. "Ms. Mattie, you know I don't gossip 'bout this family."

"Sorry, Sadie. Will you fix us a pot of tea and lay out some of those delicious tea cakes you made yesterday?"

Furrow lines appeared in Sadie's forehead. "For both of you? I remember Ms. Birdie preferring coffee."

Mattie winked. "Yes, tea for us both."

Sadie beamed. "Be happy to."

Mattie pulled Birdie into the front parlor. "Sit, sit."

"What's going on, Mattie?" Mattie sat down beside her.

"I did like you said and went to see the Doctor—Dr. Floyd." Her chin quivered.

Oh, Lordy I hope everything is all right. "You're healthy aren't you?"

"Oh yes, healthy as a horse." She leaned closer. "He said I'm almost five months along. Our baby should arrive in late December or early January." Mattie burst into tears and threw her arms around Birdie. "I'm just so happy."

Birdie patted her friend's back and let her cry. Sadie appeared with the tea tray, large grin stretching her face as she set the refreshments on the table. "She's been that way since she got the news. 'Spec she's about the happiest person in the world…except for Mr. Hellman, that is. You should see him, Miss Birdie." She sniffed and wiped at a tear in the corner of her eye. "He's 'bout to bust his vest, so proud he is. Course, I guess Mr. Lockhart is pleased hisself."

"Yes, indeed he is, Sadie."

"Now you'll have two babies. You a mighty fine woman to be a mama to that child." She shook her head. "Nothing like a house full of babies." She left the room mumbling. "About time this house had some little darlins'."

Mattie pulled back. "Isn't she a mess? Don't know what I'd do without her."

"She is indeed and you're lucky she'll be with you."

"Now, let's eat and you tell me what brings you here today." Mattie set about pouring tea. It wasn't Birdie's favorite beverage but it didn't upset her stomach as coffee did. She picked up one of Sadie's teacakes and took a bite letting the crumbs drop into her tea.

"Mmm, these are delicious. I believe they're better than the ones my Aunt Patty makes." At the thought of her aunt not being around at the birth of her child, tears welled in her eyes. She missed the woman so much.

Mattie set her teacup on the table and put an arm around Birdie's shoulders and squeezed.

"Did you hear that the construction crew quit because of me pretending to be Detective Jenkins?"

"No, you don't mean it."

"Yeah, I do." Her cup and saucer rattled as she talked. "I'm afraid we won't be able to get the house built in time and I don't know how that will affect my future and Aunt Pattie's past."

257

CHAPTER THIRTY

Birdie continued her trips to the construction site, each day hoping workers would be busy at work. The lack of progress week after week depressed her and with no job, she struggled to stay busy. She enjoyed taking care of Nathan and helping around the house, but she needed more, something to occupy her mind.

Today, in late October, she'd dressed in a suit rather than a riding skirt and blouse, as she would visit the bank—the bank owned by Raymond Smith. After the incident at church a couple of months before, she and Tad had discussed changing banks, but Mr. Smith did apologize. It was obvious he'd not been happy about doing so. Most likely his wife had pushed him. The businessman had ridden out the Monday following the insulting episode. Since he'd made the effort, they decided to stay with his bank.

The ranch hands would expect to be paid this afternoon so she'd withdraw the cash. Tad didn't like her going alone, but she had her revolver and her Winchester under the seat of the surrey. If Tad sent a guard along, they'd draw attention. First she planned to visit the store to buy a few clothes to accommodate her pregnancy. Fastening her skirt this morning had been difficult. It had been altered twice already. Sarah enjoyed sewing, so Birdie gave in to her plea to help, but she needed to be doing it herself. Ha, like she knew how to sew. Olivia or Sarah would teach her. Birdie doubted she'd prove to be a good pupil but she'd try.

Birdie pulled her cape around her against the cool wind. Tad said this winter would be colder than the last. Today she'd also purchase a warm coat. She flicked the reins and the horses broke into a slow walk. Tad had insisted she learn to drive the surrey. She wasn't a quick study but had eventually gotten the hang of maneuvering the horses. On occasion, she rode Strawberry, but not often and not to town. She moved her left hand down and caressed her expanding belly. The baby kicked, reaffirming its existence. Birdie's heart warmed and she patted the protruding appendage. "Mama knows you're there sweet thing. I'm going to take good care of you."

They turned from River Road onto Bridge Street to cross the suspension bridge. The narrowness and the slight movement of the wooden planks under the horse's iron shoes made her nervous, and she remained tense until she turned left on Second Street to maneuver around the square before turning right to continue up Austin Avenue. She had to admit, the clip clop of the horse's hooves, on the hard packed earth, combined with those of the other horses was rather soothing. Folks called greetings to people they knew, but it was nothing like the blare of horns in the future. It was odd not to see the red lights and the city offices where the courthouse now stood. Sometime in the future it would burn and a new courthouse would be built on Washington Avenue.

She pulled the horses to a stop in front of Goldstein & Migel Co. She remembered to set the brake before she left the carriage. Once she'd forgotten and the horses ended up on the boardwalk. Several men were kind enough to back them up for her. Evidently they didn't know of her notorious stint as Detective Jenkins.

Inside a matronly woman outfitted Birdie with four dresses, sleepwear, a petticoat and a navy blue coat that fit across her increasing waistline. The sales lady shook her head and sighed. "It's not the prettiest thing, but it will keep you and your baby warm. Now, what about a corset for support?"

"No, ma'am, I'm not wearing a corset and cut off my baby's oxygen supply. He needs it to grow healthy." She'd also stopped wearing her leg holster, fearing it could reduce circulation in her leg and cause a blood clot or something. She didn't know a lot about those things but did know her legs were swelling and that something too tight wasn't good. Now she stored her revolver in a dress pocket and would transfer it to her coat pocket when outside.

"Well, we have some that are very light weight and support your lower abdomen and back."

"I appreciate your concern, but I'm determined. Now, how about some comfortable shoes to wear to church?"

Birdie walked from the department store wearing the long coat and loaded down with paper wrapped packages. She stopped by the surrey and stored her purchases under the front seat. Before crossing the street to the bank, she waited for the mule drawn trolley to pass.

Town was crowded today. Maybe folks were getting an early start on their Christmas shopping. Located on the corner with four curved steps leading to the beautiful carved wooden door, Birdie entered and stepped into the shorter of the two lines. The light color granite floor accented the black marble squares reaching half way up the wall. Above the marble, mahogany paneling reached to the ten-foot tin ceiling. They didn't construct many businesses with such extravagant materials in the future. As she waited in line, the door to Mr. Smith's office opened and he ushered his wife and daughter, Lauren, out. He looked up, saw Birdie and nodded.

Something or someone in line caught Mr. Smith's attention. He urged the two women toward the door. As they reached the exit, a man, dusty from travel, in dungarees, a well-worn black hat and a long coat entered and bumped into Lauren, separating her from her parents.

Mr. Smith bristled. "Watch where you're going, mister." He reached for his daughter but the man stepped between them.

The man tipped his hat to Lauren. "Beg your pardon, miss." Before she could respond he spun her about, grabbed her around the neck and pointed a revolver at her head.

Mrs. Smith screamed.

Lauren sobbed, "Please…let me go." She clawed at his arm. "I…can't…breath."

"Shut up and be still. Then I'll ease up a bit." She dropped her hands to her sides and her struggles stopped. The crook must have let her have a bit more air.

Birdie eased her hand into her coat pocket and touched the cold steel of the Colt. *Come on, Lauren. Go limp. If you'd taken self-defense classes you'd know that.*

But, she hadn't.

Mr. Smith took a step toward his daughter, but the robber waved the gun. "Get back or I'll start shooting." He gestured to Lucinda. "Lady, get over there in the corner."

"Please…let my daughter—"

"Shut up! Get moving."

Mr. Smith gently pushed his wife. "Go on, dear." Hand covering her mouth, she stifled her sobs and walked to the corner at the far end of the teller's cage.

He waved at the line of people gaping at him. "All of you. Get right over there." He yelled at someone at the banker's window. "Get to it Sam, and let's get out of here."

Birdie peered around people to see the man with a gun pointed at the teller. He threw a bag on the counter. "Hurry up, man. Empty both tills." He gestured at the second teller. "Get out here with the others. Make it fast." The teller almost ran to do his bidding. The one emptying the cash drawers seemed to be relatively calm.

The door opened, a man dressed in a three-piece suit entered with his hat pulled down to hide his eyes, and flipped the open sign to closed. He pointed his gun at Mr. Smith. "Escort me to the back and open the vault." The vault was clearly visible through the bars so depositors could see how safe their money was. The brass six-foot wide, one-foot deep circular door with its round wheel crank looked like it belonged on a ship.

Mr. Smith's gaze moved from the vault to his customers cowering in groups. "I'll do no such thing."

The man didn't bat an eye. He aimed at an older bank customer and shot him in the chest. As the report shattered the quiet, screams echoed throughout the room. They watched in horror as the gunned down man hit the wall and slowly slid to the floor leaving a blood-streaked path. Several men rushed to help, but he was obviously dead. The women, weeping in fright, huddled together in a corner with the men surrounding them as the gun smoke slowly dissipated.

Mr. Smith's face was chalk white. "All right, mister, I get the message." With a gun in his back, Raymond started walking to the vault located behind the teller's cage.

Birdie quickly assessed the situation, separated herself

from the others and dropped to the floor. "Everybody get down." They hesitated for a second, and then fell to the floor. The fancy dressed robber was the one to fear. The other two were merely his puppets. She'd have to put them out of commission before tackling the headman. And it would have to be fast because he'd be back in here at the first gunshot. It was days like this that made people wish Waco didn't have a law against wearing a gun in town. Of course, some carried pocket pistols. Hopefully someone other than herself was carrying.

The man stopped, studied her a minute and then scowled. "Smart thinking lady. I'd sure hate to have to shoot any more of these nice folks." He shoved Mr. Smith in the back and they continued toward the vault.

Sam, the robber at the teller's window, busily stuffed money into a bag. The outlaw at the door kept checking outside to see if anyone had heard the shot and was coming to the rescue. Birdie made up her mind, drew her revolver and shot him first. Her bullet caught him in the right shoulder, disabling his gun arm. He dropped his pistol and howled, "I'm shot, Gabe! Help me. Oh, God, it hurts." He released Lauren to use his left hand to staunch the bleeding. She ran to her mother.

Gabe was already homing in on Birdie. She fell to her left side and fired. A bullet caught him in the chest and he dropped. She rushed to Gabe, took his pistol and shoved it over to the men. One grabbed it and checked the chamber. A young cowboy sprinted from the huddle and rushed to pick up the gun by the door. Before he could get all the way back, a shot rang out from the teller's cage and caught him in the leg. He scrambled to get his feet to working. Mrs. Smith and a man, crouched low, ran to grab his arms and pulled him to safety.

Birdie scooted closer to the huddle but kept herself five feet from the others. The two men with guns moved to either side of her.

"All right you yahoos," shouted the boss in the fancy duds, "I'm coming out with your banker in front of me. If you don't want him or another one of you shot, you'll toss your weapons into the middle of the floor—one at a time."

Birdie whispered. "Either one of those guns shoot

.38s?" The cowboy nodded, released the chamber, reached over and poured six shells into her hand. She breathed a sigh of relief and filled her revolver with ammo.

When she nodded, the middle-aged gentleman tossed his gun. It clanked against the granite floor. Before the cowboy's pistol left his hand, the other man was scooting forward to retrieve his and hustled back. Then he tossed his gun again. Three clangs.

"Now!" shouted the boss. "We're coming out. Anyone make a move and I'll shoot the banker and then you."

The outlaw by the door had been watching the proceedings. He hollered, "Hey, boss, it's—" Before he could finish, the teller in the cage threw a glass paperweight and it caught the wounded robber square on the forehead. He went out like a light. The teller tossed Birdie a grin before he ducked out of sight.

Mr. Smith appeared first. Red-faced, he looked ready to blow at any moment. Evidently the man wasn't used to being ordered about or his having his business disrupted. He carried a large sack of money. His gaze caught hers. She covered her heart with her left hand, sagged, and then looked up and slightly tilted her head. *Come on now, Mr. Smith, let's see some good theatrics.*" He nodded in response.

The boss glanced at the two pistols in the middle of the floor. His jaw tightened. "You think I'm stupid, can't count?" He waved his gun. "Guess I'll just have to start shooting until I find it."

Suddenly Mr. Smith groaned, dropped the sack of money and clutched his chest. "Help…help me…." He fell back against the wall and pulled at his collar. "My heart…can't breath." He moaned and fell to the floor.

His wife screamed, "Raymond, Oh God, somebody please help him."

The boss waved the gun, "Sit down woman, before I—"

Birdie fired off three rounds, each hitting him square in the chest. At the same time the door was kicked open and police and sheriff's deputies, guns drawn, filled the room. The sheriff also toted a double barrel shotgun. He glanced around the room, took a quick inventory and then issued orders for those hurt to be transported to the hospital.

The two men flanking Birdie helped her to her feet. Mrs. Smith rushed over and gripped Birdie's shoulders. "Are you all right, dear? You're not hurt anywhere, are you?" Birdie's ears rang from the shots. She could barely make out Lucinda's words. The pungent smell of gunpowder hung in the air and on her clothes, stealing her breath.

Birdie shook her head and placed both hands protectively on her baby. *My God. I didn't think once about my child, just flew headlong into this situation like it was only my life at stake. What was I thinking? What kind of mother am I going to be?*

"No, not the baby. Please tell me you're not cramping or anything like that." Lucinda turned and hollered, "Raymond, Raymond, get over here and help me take care of Mrs. Lockhart. Her child may be in danger."

The roar in her head grew and her vision dimmed. The last thing she remembered was Mrs. Smith trying to hold her up.

CHAPTER THIRTY-ONE

Birdie tried to sit up. "I am not going to the hospital."

Lucinda placed a hand on her chest and pushed Birdie back down. "Yes, you are dear. We insist."

"I just fainted."

"I know, but you need to get checked out to make sure you and the baby are fine. Raymond sent someone after Tad. So he'll be there soon."

Birdie let her head drop. "Oh, God, he'll never let me leave the house again."

The older woman patted her hand. "Now, don't be thinking like that. He's going to be so grateful you're not hurt, he'll forget all about your actions at the bank. Which I might say makes you a heroine." She sniffed and wiped at a tear. "No telling what would have happened to our sweet daughter or Raymond if you hadn't been so smart and skilled."

The ambulance started up and Birdie began giggling hysterically. "If I'm not in labor a ride in this thing will sure bring it on."

Lucinda grinned. "It is a mite rough." She yelled to the driver. "Slow this thing down. We've got an expecting mother back here." Birdie was seeing a different side to Mrs. Smith today. She had more spunk and courage than Birdie realized.

"Yes, ma'am. Sorry about the bumpy ride."

He slowed down and Birdie couldn't tell which was worse, hitting the bumps and ruts slowly or fast. This ride was uncalled for. Someone could have driven her home in the surrey if they were worried. Of course, getting checked out with Dr. Floyd was the smart thing to do. "Thank you, Lucinda for taking care of me."

"It's my pleasure, dear. After all you've done for us, it's the least we can do."

Birdie refrained from saying, "Whatever."

When they reached the hospital, two attendants met them and opened the door. Birdie sat up. "Okay, let me out of here. I can walk."

"Here we are, Mrs. Lockhart. Your carriage awaits." Nurse Taylor stood to the side with the antiquated wheeled chair she'd used during her first stay here.

"I really don't need it, Nurse Taylor. I can walk just fine."

"You let the doctor make that decision after he examines you."

"Oh, all right." Birdie felt ridiculous being made over so. She'd just had too much excitement this afternoon. That combined with her pregnancy and she'd fainted. No big deal.

Nurse Taylor took Birdie's arm and eased her into the chair. "Doctor Floyd will be here shortly. We called him as soon as we got Mrs. Smith's call from the bank." She turned to Lucinda. "Would you like to wait with her until her husband arrives?"

"Yes, indeed."

"Don't you need to be with Lauren? She's had a frightening experience today."

"She'll be fine with her father. I rather think she's enjoying the attention and the activity at the bank."

Imagine that. Birdie wouldn't have thought the girl gutsy enough. She pictured Lauren boo-hooing and wanting her daddy's constant attention. Lucinda followed them inside and up to the second floor to the corner room she'd occupied on her first visit.

Birdie stood and moved to sit on the bed. Nurse Taylor started unbuttoning her coat and slipped it off Birdie's shoulders. "Can you stand for me and let us get you out of your clothes and into a gown?"

"I don't need to get into a gown. If you want me to lie down, I'll just take my shoes off and stretch out."

"The doctor will want to examine you and it would be easier for him if you had on something else."

"Oh, all right." Birdie unbuttoned her suit jacket and

slipped out of it, the blouse and the skirt. Lucinda hung them up in the closet.

Nurse Taylor handed Birdie the gown. "You can leave your camisole and drawers on but step out of that petticoat." Birdie had never thought she'd admit wearing crotchless drawers could be a blessing. She'd always hated OB exams, stripping and wearing those gowns you couldn't keep on your shoulders.

As Birdie did so, the nurse turned down the cover. Birdie crawled onto the bed and pulled the cover up to her chin. She closed her eyes and sighed. "Guess if I have to be here I might as well rest my eyes a minute."

Lucinda patted her shoulder. "You do that, dear." She fiddled with the covers. Birdie peeked through her lashes to see the older woman folding the sheet back over the top of the blanket, just as Aunt Patty always made the bed. A lump rose in Birdie's throat making swallowing difficult. She squeezed her eyes to staunch the tears forming and pretended to doze.

* * *

Tad's heart thundered in his chest. What had Birdie been thinking to put herself and their baby in danger? He pushed Brodie harder.

"Slow down, Tad," yelled Ethan from behind. "I told you she was all right. You're going to ruin that beautiful animal of yours."

Tad sat up straight and slowed the animal. Crazy with worry, he'd been leaning over Brodie's neck to urge him to go faster. He gave the horse a friendly pat. "Sorry, fella. That woman's gonna be the death of me. Guess that doesn't mean you have to die also."

Detective Ethan rode up along side. "She is fine, Tad. Don't you think I'd tell you if it was otherwise?"

"Yeah, guess so, but why did they take her to the hospital?"

"Because, even though she wasn't hurt, the Smiths felt she should be checked out just to make sure the baby is doing okay."

Voice choked, he asked, "She's not having any pain, is she?"

"No, Tad. I wouldn't keep something like that from you. She fainted, was only out for a minute, but she didn't fall and hit her head or anything like that."

Tad nodded and they continued to town in silence. When they reached Fourth Street, Tad waved at Ethan and turned right. The detective would go pick up the surrey at the bank and bring it to the hospital. Surely they would let him take Birdie home.

Mrs. Smith was sitting at Birdie's bedside when the nurse escorted him into the room. The older woman raised her fingers to her lips before he blurted out his wife's name. She lay on her right side facing them. Lips slightly open as she breathed, her features were relaxed as she slept. Tad breathed a sigh of relief. Surely if she were in pain, her face would show it.

Mrs. Smith stood and beckoned him to follow her outside. She pulled the door closed to not disturb Birdie. "She and the baby are both fine, Mr. Lockhart. Dr. Floyd just left and confirmed they are both in no danger."

"Did he say why she fainted?"

"He said probably the excitement, the tension. You know she saved all our lives." The woman teared up. "One of the men had our girl, Lauren, around the neck and a gun at her head."

She plopped one hand on a hip and pointed a finger at him with the other. "You mark my word, the men in this town will be singing a different tune about your wife from here on out. She killed two of the robbers and wounded the third. Plus, she saved the citizens' money." Face pinched, she shook her head. "Such a shame one of our bank's customers was killed by the leader of their gang."

Overcome with relief, Tad hugged the older woman. "Thank you for taking such good care of Birdie, Mrs. Smith. I can't tell you how grateful I am."

"Call me Lucinda." She blushed but her smile was radiant. "Think nothing of it. Why it was the least I could do. She is a brave woman and I'm sorry we misjudged her in the past. But, that won't happen again." Looks like Birdie had made a lifelong friend. No doubt she'd now have many more.

She took his arm and led him to the door. "You get on in there with your wife. I'll leave you to help her get dressed."

"Yes, ma'am. I expect Mr. Smith will want his supper soon too. Detective Ethan will be here in a minute with the surrey. I'm sure he'd be glad to take you home."

"No need. I'll telephone the bank from the lobby and Raymond will either come or send someone." She patted his arm one more time, then turned and walked down the hall toward the stairs.

When he re-entered the room, Birdie was sitting on the side of the bed, stretching. Her face lit with joy and she stood and held her arms out to him. He enfolded her in his and with his face pressed against her hair, breathed deeply—lavender and Birdie. Her lips touched his neck sending a shiver through his frame. "Birdie, Birdie, how could you scare me so, put yourself and our baby at risk?"

"I know. It was foolish, but instinct took over." She shrugged. "I didn't think and I'm sorry. When that man's arm circled Lauren's neck, I couldn't ignore her need…and then, the head honcho came in and shot that poor older man." She pushed back and gazed up into his eyes. "Don't you see? I had to do something."

Heat suffused his face. He gripped her upper arms. "Why couldn't you sit tight and let someone else take care of it?" He wanted to shake some sense into her, but when she gripped his forearms to steady herself, his temper cooled.

"Who, Tad? There wasn't a soul in there with a gun but me." Tears gathered in her eyes. It was evident she was sincere, but dammit… "Can you forgive me?"

"Honey, of course I can forgive you, but don't expect me to forget." His heart threated to choke him as he struggled to speak. "I couldn't bear it if something happened to you."

She laid her head on his chest. "I understand."

"And I don't imagine Mother, Maybelle, and Bethany will either. They're all three fit to be tied. Wanted to come with me but I wouldn't let them." It was a good thing she couldn't see his grin. He doubted the women in his family would let Birdie out of their sight until this baby arrived. Arrived, heck, probably until the baby was six months old. "Let's get you dressed and home"

* * *

269

Tad chuckled as he watched the two horses pull the surrey out of the circular drive in front of the house and down the road towards town. It was Birdie's first trip since the bank episode. For two weeks after the robbery attempt, town folks and country folks alike found an excuse to stop by and have a cup of coffee. Some brought baked goods, others tiny clothes for the baby. They had so much food, to keep it from wasting Mother sent much of it down to the bunkhouse. The men declared Birdie needed to prevent a holdup once a week. They'd never eaten so well.

Birdie and Bethany waved from the surrey. Bethany was driving. Since the bank robbery, the women had made a pact that Birdie wouldn't leave the house without one of them. Today Bethany swore she needed fabric to make a new dress. No doubt next trip Mother and Sarah would need more fabric for the baby's layette. Their love and concern for his wife warmed him inside. He was a lucky man.

His father had spent hours on the range and in the fields building this ranch up, making it prosperous, to leave to him. It was now his turn. He had one son already and if the coming child was also a boy, he wanted to have something to leave to him. He knew Birdie wanted a girl. That'd be fine with him too. When she married, he'd like to give the couple some land if they needed it.

Man, he was spending money, in his mind, he didn't have. He better get busy and earn some more. Roscoe, the bull delivered by train the day Birdie arrived, had proven to be reliable when it came to performing his duties. And the offspring were healthy, strong animals. The ranch could earn a goodly sum by renting Roscoe out for breeding purposes. After he replaced the funds spent on Birdie's Nest, he might branch out into breeding and raising horses.

He never dreamed he could be so content. For a man who hadn't wanted to be leg-shackled, marriage suited him. There wasn't a boring minute in his day, either. He'd never been happier—a wife he dearly loved, a son, another child on the way and a means to support them. What more could a man ask for? Nothing. Well, there was the matter of getting Birdie's house built on time.

CHAPTER THIRTY-TWO

Bethany turned the Surrey onto River Road. There was no chance of Birdie getting bored on the trip as her sister-in-law talked the entire trip. "I don't understand why you insist on coming out here, Birdie. It's not likely anything else has been done. The women in this town have more sense than the men. It's going to take a long time for the men of Waco to forget the detective episode, and they're probably embarrassed it took a woman to stop those bank robbers."

Birdie grinned at the young woman's tirade. Sitting straight on the cushioned seat, Bethany shot her chin up a notch, and then reached over and patted Birdie's leg. "I just don't want you to be hurt anymore."

"That's sweet of you, but I'm okay." Okay heck. Somehow she had to get this house built and she had just a year. Birdie sent up a little prayer. *Lord, please let the crew be working on my house.* They rounded a small curve and the site loomed in distance. Was that activity she saw? She leaned forward in the seat to better see. The site crawled with workers, more than had been on site before. She reached over and gripped Bethany's leg. "Look, they're working on my house."

"Well, I'll be. They sure are." Bethany loosened Birdie's grip on her thigh. "Ease up, you're going to leave a bruise."

Birdie jerked her hand back. "Sorry, I just can't believe it. Look at all those people." Her heart swelled and thumped wildly in her chest. She controlled her breathing in an attempt to slow it down. She didn't want to get over excited and have another fainting spell. Wouldn't her Ranger co-worker, Sergeant Ted Weaver, get a kick out of knowing she'd fainted under duress. No, he wouldn't, either. There was more to the man than met the eye.

Bethany grinned at her. "I love seeing your face so lit up."

Birdie didn't realize the happiness showed on her face. Of course it did. How could she be so elated and it not? *Thank you, Lord!* Maybe there would be a chance to meet the deadline after all. For Aunt Patty's sake, she hoped so.

She held onto to the arm of the bench-seat and pushed her feet against the floorboard to bounce as little as possible as they rolled over the ruts in the road. Bethany planned to get them as close to the site as she could.

Mr. Teague, face split in a happy grin, waited for them. He rushed over to help Birdie down while Bethany set the brake. "I'm so glad you stopped by today, Mrs. Lockhart."

"I can't believe it. There are more men here today than you had several months ago."

"Yes, indeed. Two days after the attempted bank robbery, my foreman stopped in to say the crew would be on the job the following day. That afternoon men started showing up and saying they'd work for half pay for one week to show their appreciation." He yanked his hat off and smoothed what little hair he had on his head before plopping it back on again. "A few even volunteered to work for free."

Birdie feared she'd burst into tears. Those darn hormones. She covered her mouth with her hand to hold back the sobs. Bethany handed her a handkerchief as her arm slipped around Birdie's waist. She dabbed at her eyes and finally squeaked out, "I don't know what to say."

"No need to say anything. The men can all see how you feel."

Birdie glanced up to see every man on the site staring at her. She waved the handkerchief in the air and yelled, "Thank you!" They roared with laughter and waved their hats, and then went back to work.

Mr. Teague offered his arm. "You want to look around a bit?"

"You bet."

An hour or so later, they piled back into the surrey and headed to town. Bethany pulled the surrey into line with the other carriages and horses lined up in front of Goldstein-Migel's.

Inside, in the fabric department, a clerk rushed forward to help them. The young woman beamed. "Mrs. Lockhart, Miss Lockhart, how can I help you today?"

Bethany scanned the stacks of fabric. "I'd like to see a lightweight wool in red. Something festive but not too hot in case we have a warm Christmas."

"I've just the thing for you. Come this way." She led them to bolts lined up against the wall and pulled out a beautiful piece of fabric. She carried it to a table and spread it out so they could examine it closely. "It's very finely woven, but feel, it's light as air."

Birdie ran her hand over the soft wool. She didn't know much about material, but she could recognize its quality "This is lovely, Bethany and would be perfect with your coloring."

Smiling, Bethany's eyes lit with appreciation. "You really think so?"

"I know so. You should buy it, unless you see something you like better."

"No, this is the one. Looking longer will just confuse me." She and the sales clerk put their heads together to discuss how much she'd need.

Birdie wandered over to the infants' department. She couldn't think of a thing the baby needed as the neighbors, along with the women at the ranch, had made so many items. But, she enjoyed looking over the displays. A frilly pink bonnet caught her eye. *Oh yes, dear Tad, you and I are having a girl.* She carried it over to domestics and paid for it. They put it in a box so it would keep its shape and wrapped it in brown paper.

They left the store and approached the buggy. Once seated, Birdie turned to Bethany. "Would you mind if we stopped by Mr. Hellman's gun shop? I want to see how Mattie is doing."

Bethany's face lit. "You think I could get that gun Tad promised me?"

"Well, we could at least look and see what would suit you."

The bell above the door rang as they walked inside. Though the day was relatively warm outside, the shop was toasty and Birdie enjoyed the warmth.

"Hello, ladies. Birdie, it's good to see you out and about." He rounded the counter and took her arm. "Do you need to sit down?"

"No. I'm fine." She arched a brow at him. "Are you mollycoddling Mattie and driving her nuts?"

He guffawed. "Probably. She's always fussing at me to leave her alone."

"Sounds like she's doing well then."

"She is, indeed." His expression turned serious. "The doctor says she's probably going to deliver in a couple of months." He raked his hand over his face. "I have to admit I'm scared to death."

"Now, Joseph, worrying about things you can do nothing about will only cause you both more stress." He signed and nodded. "Do you have a pistol that would be suitable for Bethany? Not a pocket pistol. Something to learn and shoot targets with."

"Sure, let's look over here." He moved behind the counter and lifted a couple of revolvers. "Either one of these would be good. Not as fine as your Colt but a good beginners gun." He laid them on the counter and nodded to Bethany. "Pick them up and see which one feels right in your hand."

Bethany spent several minutes testing the feel and grip. She handed one to Birdie. "This is the one I think I want. What do you think, Birdie?"

Birdie studied the pistol carefully even though she'd already compared the two revolvers and purchased one. Joseph was holding it for her until closer to Christmas. "It's a good choice, Bethany."

Eyes rounded with hope, she grasped Birdie's hand. "Can I get it then?"

"Not today. We need to talk to your mother and brother first."

"You know, I am seventeen now."

"Hey now, don't put me on the spot. I don't want them to be upset with me." They'd already agreed to the purchase but Birdie wanted the gun to be a surprise for her.

"Oh, all right." She brightened and flashed a big smile. "Thank you for letting me look, Mr. Hellman."

"Anytime, young lady. When you do get that pistol, you've got the best teacher around. Which reminds me. Mattie said girls have been coming by the house wanting to know when self-defense classes will begin again."

With both teachers pregnant, it'd be a good while. Maybe they needed to train some of their past students to take over as instructors. "Do you have a hammer I can borrow? Also a small can of paint."

"Sure do." He went into the back and returned with the items. "Here are some extra nails in case you need them."

An hour later Birdie and Bethany had repainted the sign and nailed it to the side of the building. It read, "Classes will resume the first week in May 1892."

A week before Christmas, Mattie went into labor and delivered nine-pound Joseph junior. The Hellmans were ecstatic. Holding the tiny baby, so much smaller than Nathan had been when they got him, Birdie realized her baby would be similar in size as Joseph. Fearing she'd drop him, she passed him back to Mattie. "He's so tiny, Mattie."

She chuckled. "After you've held him awhile, his size isn't so noticeable. I was afraid at first, but it didn't take but a day or two for me to become comfortable picking him up."

Birdie gazed at Tad as he stood over the cradle. He didn't look any more assured than she did. But, mothers and fathers did it every day, so they'd be no different. As if to reassure her, their baby stretched. She rubbed the hard, taut skin and felt something protruding—a foot or elbow.

"Not much longer for you, Birdie. Does Dr. Floyd still think you're due in the middle of February?"

"Yes, but as I'm sure he told you, first babies don't always present themselves on time. He had your date pretty close though, didn't he?"

Mattie nodded. "It was a good thing too, as I was ready to pop."

* * *

The first Sunday in January, shortly after dinner, someone knocked on their front door. Tad answered it and ushered Detective Ethan into the parlor where they were all gathered. "Look who's here."

Birdie hadn't seen him since right after the robbery. "Hello, Lloyd. What's brought you out here on this cold day?"

Tad raised a hand. "Don't even think about it, Ethan. Birdie has her hands full right now."

Ethan laughed. "No detective work. I just need to talk to Birdie a minute."

Olivia stood and headed for the kitchen. "I'll put on a fresh pot of coffee." She winked at the detective. "I bet you can eat a slice of my pecan pie, can't you?"

"Ma'am, I'd be a fool to say no. I'd love a slice if it's no trouble."

"No trouble at all. We enjoy a pot of coffee in the afternoons, though Bethany and Birdie have taken to drinking tea or cocoa." She motioned to Bethany. "Come help me, dear."

Birdie sighed. Coffee still didn't settle well on her stomach. She'd have a big cup as soon as the baby was born. "Take your coat off, Lloyd, and have a seat. What's on your mind?"

He handed her a small package. She opened it to find her Texas Ranger Star. "Oh, my gosh!" She held it up for Tad to see. "Look! It's mine? I got it back?"

"Yes, ma'am. After hearing about your bravery during the attempted bank robbery, General King decided you should have it back. On one condition."

Her heart sank. What hoop did she have to jump through? "And what is that?"

"You're not show it to anyone except the trusted members of your family."

*　*　*

Tad caressed his wife's abdomen, hoping the child inside could feel the love in his touch, before helping her into the surrey. For January, the weather was nice, probably in the fifties, but just in case, he came prepared for a cold front to

276

blow in. Today would be Birdie's last trip into town until after the baby was born. She'd insisted she had to see the construction site one more time before being confined to the house. This was the first time he'd seen it since before Christmas and was amazed at how much work the crew had been able to get done with the additional workers. Mr. Teague had assured them Birdie's Nest would be finished by next Christmas, meeting the deadline Birdie considered to be so important—late in 1892.

He kept the horses trotting at a steady pace trying not to bounce Birdie too much. The springs on the vehicle gave a smooth ride, but some of the ruts in the road jolted the passengers.

The air was crisp this morning. Birdie wore her new coat and he'd tucked a wool blanket around her legs and feet. Additional blankets were in the back in case it turned colder.

When they pulled into the site, Birdie caught his arm. "I don't want to get down, just look."

"Good, because I'd worry about you trying to get around out there. It'd be too easy to fall." He set the brake. She smiled and nodded. He scooted closer and put an arm around her shoulder. She nestled into the warmth of his body and allowed her gaze to roam over the house noting each bit of progress since her last visit.

She turned, laid her head on his shoulder and sighed, her breath warm against his neck. "It's going to be beautiful, isn't it?"

"Yes, sweetheart. Almost as beautiful as you."

She chuckled and swatted him on the chest. "Oh, you masher, you!" Her gloved hand cupped his cheek. Nose pink from the cold, her blue eyes sparkled as she smiled up at him. "Thank you, husband, for making it possible."

CHAPTER THIRTY-THREE

Birdie rocked Nathan in the nursery. He'd fought his nap for thirty minutes so she hoped a story would help him fall asleep. Finally, on the third reading, she was rewarded with a yawn. She continued, "Mary had a little lamb..." His little eyes sagged with sleep, and then popped open, as the motion of the rocker and the tone of her voice lulled him. Two minutes later she rose from the rocker and placed him in the crib Tad had found in the attic. He'd cleaned and oiled it until the beautiful old wood glowed. The bars appeared to be too far apart to be safe, so Tad had someone in town carve duplicates and insert them between the existing ones. You couldn't tell they'd been added, and Birdie breathed easier about Nathan's safety.

It was time for her to put her feet up. They'd been swelling the last couple of weeks and her shoes were uncomfortable. She quietly closed the door and then walked across the hall to the master bedroom. Birdie kicked off her shoes, lay down on the bed and pulled a quilt over her. Ah, it felt so good to get off her feet. How did women who didn't have help in their homes manage to do all their chores when pregnant? Of course, all women knew they were the stronger sex. Just try to convince a man of that, though.

Birdie woke with a backache. Darn, she never had back problems. The swelling in her feet had gone down so she stepped into her shoes and peeked in on Nathan before walking downstairs. The pain in her back continued, so when she reached the bottom, she leaned forward, back, and to each side trying to ease the kinks out.

She entered the kitchen to find Maybelle and Olivia shaping rolls for supper. "Can I help you with anything?" She rubbed at a particularly achy spot on her back. The two women exchanged glances.

"You feel all right?" Olivia wiped her hands and came around behind Birdie. "Show me where it hurts."

"It's just a little backache." She pointed to the general region of the pain.

Olivia's hands covered Birdie's belly. It's a good thing she wasn't modest because when it came to her and this baby the two other women in the house weren't shy about touching her body. "Any contractions, dear?"

"No, just this niggling little backache. I think I'll stroll down to the barn and see Tad for a minute."

Olivia's brow furrowed, the look she gave Birdie one of command. "You know, the pain could be the onset of labor. If it gets any worse you come straight back to the house. For that matter, take your pistol and fire a shot so someone can come help you."

"Yes, ma'am. I will." She slipped into her coat, wrapped a scarf around her head and felt for her revolver in the pocket.

Birdie sucked in deep lungs full of the fresh air. The day was clear, not a cloud in sight. It felt good to stretch her legs and the exercise seemed to be helping her aches. She was halfway there when a pain started in her back and worked its way around her belly. *Hmm, guess that's what a contraction feels like.* It wasn't so bad. She continued on her way. Walking was good during labor, made the process move along faster, or so she'd heard.

Another pain had her doubling over. More intense, this one lasted longer. A gush of warm water escaped from her body wetting her underclothes and petticoat. Well, rats! Should she go back? *Stupid question, Birdie.* She turned around and started back to the house, stopping every so often to deal with the pain.

She opened the back door.

"You back so soon…oh dear, child. Lets get you upstairs." Olivia took one arm, Maybelle the other. Olivia yelled up the stairs. She never yelled. "Bethany, ring the bell. Birdie's in labor."

* * *

The peal of the ranch bell rang out above the noise in the cattle pen and the barn. Tad froze, his heart stopped for a moment, and then he broke into a run. He was halfway to the house when Hank rode up, and extended an arm. Tad grabbed hold and Hank pulled him up onto the back of his horse. He drew the animal to a halt by the back door. Tad slid to the ground and rushed for the door. Hank kicked his horse into a run. As previously arranged, at the sound of that bell, Hank was to go for Dr. Floyd. Dang, he needed to have one of those telephones installed.

Tad took the stairs two at a time and slid to a stop just inside the master bedroom. Mother had stripped Birdie and was helping her into a gown. "Birdie, you all right?"

"I'm fine." Her smile turned into a grimace as she held her belly.

Mother directed Birdie over to the chair. "Sit down now and let us get the bed ready."

He quickly sat down and eased Birdie down on his lap. He rubbed her belly. "I'm sorry it has to be so painful, sweetheart."

She slipped her arm around his neck and kissed his forehead. "I can handle it, love."

"Hank has gone for Dr. Floyd. He'll be here as soon as possible."

"According to your mother, we probably have plenty of time." She clutched her belly and groaned. Tad felt her muscles tighten as the contraction gripped her. "Oh, God, Olivia, they're getting stronger."

"Things are moving faster than normal. Tad, help her into bed."

"Yes, ma'am." Birdie stood and with an arm around her waist, Tad walked her to the bed. She eased down and scooted to the center of the mattress before lying back against the pillows. He drew the covers up to her waist before sitting on the side. "What can I do sweetheart?"

"Just be here and hold my hand when a contraction hits."

"I'm not going anywhere."

Eight hours later, Dr. Floyd delivered their baby. The infant immediately voiced its displeasure at this cold new environment. "Congratulations, you have a healthy baby girl." He spent several minutes examining their daughter and then returned his attention to her. "Both of you are doing well. No complications, so more babies in your future shouldn't be a problem."

Tad wasn't sure he wanted to see Birdie go through so much pain again. They had a boy and a girl. He could be content.

Dr. Floyd cleaned his equipment and packed up his supplies. "I best be going. Have another lady about to deliver any day now. Just give me a yell if you need anything." He nodded at Olivia and Maybelle. "It appears I'm leaving you in good hands, so goodnight."

Tad walked the doctor to the front door. "Thank you, Doctor. Hopefully by the next child we'll have telephone service out here."

"Don't count on it. The phone company is just now getting poles up across the river." He waved as he jogged down the front steps.

Upstairs, he sat on the side of the bed facing Birdie. She smiled. "I told you we'd have a girl."

"Yes, ma'am, you did." The baby continued to scream as Mother bathed and wrapped her in a warm blanket. "Do you have a name picked out for her?"

Birdie lifted her hand to his cheek, her blue eyes gleamed and a tear leaked from the corner of one. "I'd like to name her Patricia Leigh and call her Patty."

Tad had difficulty speaking around the lump in his throat. He wished there was some way her aunt could join them. "It's a beautiful name and fitting. In honor of your Aunt Patty?"

She nodded.

With tears in her eyes, Mother kissed the baby's forehand and then laid Patty in Birdie's arms. "Here's your beautiful daughter, Birdie. You hold her for a few minutes and then let Tad take over so we can get you cleaned up."

Tad stretched out beside Birdie on the bed and slipped an arm behind her head. She unwrapped the infant and checked fingers and toes. "She's perfect."

"Yes, she is." Birdie wrapped the blanket back around

281

their daughter. He leaned forward and ran a finger down the baby's soft cheek. She turned toward the appendage with her mouth open. Birdie chuckled. "Let her suck on your finger. She's hungry but that might satisfy her for a minute." He did as she suggested, amazed at the strength of the child's grasp as she held onto his thumb.

Warmth spread through him, and he felt the embarrassing need to cry. It was the same sensation he'd felt when he'd first held Nathan—pride and instant love he supposed. But there was also joy in this situation. The joy of loving Birdie and the gifts she'd given him, her love and acceptance of Nathan and now this precious baby girl.

He coughed to remove the knot in his throat. "She's beautiful, Birdie, almost as beautiful as her mother."

Birdie's palm cupped his cheek. "She is, isn't she?" She pulled his head down to hers and kissed him, her lips soft and lingering in her exploration. "I love you."

"I love you, Birdie. I never dreamed I could be so happy in marriage and though I regret what you went through, time traveling and all, I'm grateful I was the one to pull you from the Brazos that day. Because otherwise I wouldn't have you."

"All right you two let me take her while you get up, Tad." Mother lifted the baby from Birdie's arms and placed her in his.

"I'm going down to show Bethany and Sarah."

"Be careful going down those stairs."

"Yes, Mother." Poor Birdie. Mama would probably try to take over, but he bet Birdie could handle the situation.

Bethany was asleep on the sofa but Sarah jumped up and rushed over for a look. She looked at him with questions in her eyes.

"A girl, Sarah. Her name is Patty."

"Oh, for Birdie's aunt. I know Birdie is thrilled. You watch. She'll have that little pink bonnet on her as soon as she's up and around." She stroked the soft downy hair. "Oh, she's sweet and I can't imagine two more deserving parents. Congratulations, Mr. Tad."

"Thank you, Sarah."

Thirty minutes or so later, Mother called from upstairs. "She's ready, Tad."

It was a good thing as Patty's fussing had increased in volume. He couldn't resist a grin. She'd suck on his finger a minute and then cry. This little one wouldn't be easy to pacify.

He took the stairs slowly. His mother waited at the bedroom door and ushered him in. Tad placed the wailing baby in Birdie's arms. He sat down on the edge of the bed and watched as his daughter nursed greedily. "She was hungry."

"Yes, indeed she was."

Mother and Maybelle, smiles on their faces and arms loaded with linens and basins, slipped from the room.

They watched their daughter until her little fists relaxed and she allowed the nipple to pop from her mouth. Birdie lifted Patty to her shoulder and patted gently. After several minutes they were rewarded with a small burp.

Birdie handed the baby to him. "Lay her in the cradle. In a minute we'll know if she burped enough or not."

Tad placed Patty in the heirloom cradle that had been in their family since his father's time. Though she was wrapped in a blanket, he pulled a knitted blanket up to her chest. He straightened, but before he could leave the baby's side, her little hands came out and she was sucking a fist. "She acts like she's still hungry."

"Let's give her a minute and see if she fusses."

Well, she was a woman so obviously she knew more than Tad. He returned to the bed, kicked off his shoes, stretched out leaning against the headboard and cuddled her close. "Don't you need to get some sleep?"

She yawned. "Mmm-hmm, but I want to make sure Patty is going to stay down for a little while."

The baby started fussing and within minutes had worked up to a full scream. "Wow, she's got a set of lungs." Tad lifted his daughter from the cradle and placed her in Birdie's arms.

"Yes she does, Daddy." Birdie grinned. "Welcome to our world for probably the next six months."

CHAPTER THIRTY-FOUR

January 1920, Waco, Texas

Birdie sat behind her desk in the office. She held a family picture taken in front of Birdie's Nest when the children were young. Bethany's husband had taken the photo with a Brownie Camera after a family picnic down by the river. Nathan, the oldest stood with his arm around Patty's shoulders. The twins, Julie and Jason sat on the grass at their feet. Birdie and Tad were behind the two oldest children, each with a hand on their shoulders. All five of them wore big smiles. With a finger, Birdie touched each of the faces so beloved by her and Tad. Her gaze returned to Tad, the man who was her all. Now, in their sixties, their love was as strong as it had been thirty years ago.

The years had flown by so fast. With the children to keep her busy, she'd had very little time to devote to police work. Occasionally Ethan would come by and ask her opinion about something, but he came less and less as the years passed. He'd married Lauren Smith and they now had five children. Lucinda was ecstatic to have grandchildren and doted on them. Not that Birdie and Tad were any different. They had seven grandchildren and five nieces and nephews.

In 1917, when Germany resumed the use of submarine warfare and sank seven U.S. merchant ships, President Wilson called for war on Germany and on April 6, 1917 Congress declared war and the U.S. joined the other Allied countries in the Great War. In 1918, the United States began sending 10,000 troops a day to France. Both of their sons were drafted. With both of their boys, as well as Patty's son, overseas, the family spent much of their time in the evenings listening to the radio for any news coming from the front. Those were terrible times. Due to new technology—wireless communication, armored cars and tanks, aircraft and chemical warfare the casualty rate was high. Tad carried his worry silently, but it aged him considerably. The day their boys came home safe and sound, the sparkle returned to his eyes.

After the Armistice Treaty in 1918, the country faced the Spanish flu, an illness of pandemic proportions. It was first identified in troops at Camp Funston, Kansas in March of 1918. By October it had spread worldwide and affected one-third of the world's population, the casualty rate higher than that of the war. Several in the family contracted the disease, but by the grace of God, no one died.

The front door opened and closed. "Mother." Nathan called from the entryway.

"In the office." Birdie smiled. She'd not seen her eldest son in several weeks. She stood as he entered the room and gave him a big hug. "It's about time you came to see us. Your father will be here shortly."

"I'm not sure I can stay that long."

"You can't stay for supper?"

"No, I better get home to Angela and the kids. With the baby close to arriving, she tires easily."

"I understand. Tell her hello for us and to bring the children by when she needs time to herself."

"I will. She'll like that."

"Come on, let's take a seat over here on the sofa."

As was his habit, he sat close to her with an arm behind her—so much like his father. He'd always been protective and the bond between them was close. She reached up and patted his cheek. With his hair dark like Lucy's, his blue eyes were startling against his tanned complexion. Though his coloring was different from the other children, he'd always been the first born in her heart and number one son. Not that she loved the other children any less, because she didn't. But Nathan appeared to need her more.

When he decided to go into law, she and Tad decided he should inherit Birdie's Nest and Jason would take over the ranch. At twenty-six, Jason was already an integral part of running the large operation. The girls, Patty and Julie were both married and each had been given a tract of land. Fortunately, all their children lived near in and around Waco so they were able to get together often.

Nathan patted her shoulder. "It's done, Mother, just as you stipulated."

Thank you, Lord. Now the future of Birdie's Nest was secure and wouldn't be razed to build condominiums or some resort.

Tears stung her eyes and she dropped her head to his shoulder. She spoke around the lump in her throat. "Thank you, son. I can't tell you how much that eases my mind."

"I think I do, Mother." He chuckled. "After all, you told me often enough as soon as I was old enough to understand."

She swiped at the tears on her cheeks. "You're right, but I couldn't let you forget. They didn't mind the stipulations we placed on the bequest?"

"Nope. The members of the legal department were pleased with the arrangement." He took a document from his inside coat pocket. "Here is your copy. The University has several copies and will serve the paperwork to Patty Braxton on July 15, 2012."

"But, the title is in my name."

"True, but your document supersedes any will left after the date your bequest was signed—June 1, 1920. A court would have extreme difficulty trying to over turn it."

Birdie exhaled a sigh of relief. "And they have the note for Aunt Patty, the brooch and my silver star and will deliver them to her?"

"Yes, ma'am. I think you've thought of everything, but Mother, I'm curious as to how our ancestors are going to be named Braxton."

"I can't remember for sure but a Braxton inherits somehow. It will work out, Nathan, don't worry."

* * *

July 15, 2012

Patty's heart thumped in alarm as the doorbell sounded. Was it someone with word about Birdie? She hurried to see who had stopped by. It could be Captain Smith and Sergeant Weaver. The two Rangers checked on her often. She knew they were doing all they could to find Birdie, but dragging of the Brazos had stopped. Divers believed she'd moved south and her body might never be found. Thank goodness she'd baked a fresh batch of teacakes. Those two men enjoyed them so.

She opened the door to see two men, both dressed in fancy suits and one carried an attaché case. "Yes, may I help you, gentlemen?"

"Ms. Patricia Braxton?" He held out a card and she opened the screen door to take it. The first thing she noticed was the embossed Baylor University symbol and then his name—Jonathan Sanders, Legal Department.

"Yes, I'm Patricia Braxton."

"I'm Jonathan Sanders and this is my co-worker, Lane Price. May we come in and talk with you about a legal matter?"

"Well I can't imagine about what, but yes, come in." She stepped back and the two men entered, closed the door behind them and stood in the entry hall waiting for her directions. "Come into the parlor and have a seat. Could I get you a cup of coffee?"

"No, ma'am, but thank you."

They sat on the sofa and she sat in one of the chairs facing them. "Now, what's this all about?"

Mr. Sanders laid his briefcase on his knees, opened it and withdrew a large manila envelope before closing and locking the case. "From what I understand, you have no idea about the legal documents I'm going to show you today, so, if you'd like to call someone to be here with you for advice, please feel free to do so.

What on earth were they talking about? Were they here to take Birdie's Nest before August first? "Yes, I believe I will. If you'll excuse me, I'll be right back.""

She telephoned Captain Smith and briefly explained her situation. "We'll be right there, Patricia." She hung up the phone and brewed a pot of coffee. She stacked five cups on a silver tray and a china plate filled with teacakes. When the coffee was finished she poured it into the silver coffee pot, added containers of cream and sugar and carried it into the parlor.

When she entered the sitting room, Mr. Price jumped up and

287

rushed to take it from her. "Thank you, young man." She cleared a space off on the coffee table. "Set it right here." The doorbell chimed. "That will be Captain Smith and Sergeant Weaver."

She let them in and made the introductions. The two Baylor officials stood and shook hands with the two officers. Captain Smith asked, "May we see your business cards and a drivers licenses?" Both were quick to present their identification. He nodded. "Looks like everything is on the up and up, Ms. Braxton. Let's hear what they have to say." He added. "Let's all take a seat."

Mr. Sanders took a long paper from the envelope. "This is the original deed to Birdie's Nest, issued in December 1892." He handed it to Patricia. She flipped through the pages and gasped at what was on the last page. The signature at the bottom was Birdie Leigh Braxton Lockhart.

"I can't believe it. It's signed by Birdie. I'd know her handwriting anywhere." She handed the papers to the captain. "But... Lockhart?" She shook her head. "I don't understand."

When they'd all perused the deed, Mr. Sanderson handed her another document. "This is a bequest document saying that on August 1, 2012 Baylor University will inherit this home. To do so, they must fulfill the following stipulations. Pay the back taxes and undertake to preserve the building and grounds in current condition for the enjoyment of the town of Waco or Baylor University, whichever Baylor decides. Any living relatives of Birdie Leigh Braxton Lockhart will be allowed to live in the carriage house for free until death and be able to bring his/her favorite items from the main house." He handed the record to Patricia.

Patty could only stare at the words. Again, there was Birdie's signature. How could this be? She handed the document over to the two rangers. Both looked it over and then sat deep in thought. Captain Smith leaned forward and handed the paper over. Mr. Price took it and placed it with the growing stack on the table.

The captain poured himself a cup of coffee. He sipped quietly for several minutes. "The date on these documents is June 1, 1920. Rather odd, isn't it?"

"It's quite common for people to bequest their property to Universities years before their expected death," said Mr.

Sanders. "However, this is the earliest one we've ever handled."

Ted filled several cups with coffee and offered them to Sanders and Price. They both accepted the hot brew, but Sanders was quick to move the papers to a safer spot. "Thank you."

"Aunt Patty, would you like coffee?"

She smiled. The young man had started calling her Aunt Patty when he'd visited with Birdie. Both Rangers had visited on occasion since her disappearance. It was just a month and a half, but felt like years. "Yes, thank you."

He lifted the plate of teacakes and held it forward. "Cookie anyone?"

Patty smiled as all four men took one. No one could resist her teacakes.

Captain Smith frowned at Ted. "How is it that you call Ms. Braxton Aunt Patty, Ted?"

The younger man grinned. "I've been eating her teacakes for a long time. I've earned the right."

Captain Smith snorted. "You've been over here mooching, huh?"

"Actually, Captain, he's been a blessing to have around since Birdie disappeared."

A shocked Sanders and Price traded glances. "Disappeared?" asked Price.

"Yes," said Smith. His eyes narrowed as he studied the reaction of the two men. "She was one of our best Texas Rangers. She disappeared on June 1st of this year."

Price stammered, "I can assure…you…we knew nothing about a disappearance." He tapped the papers. "This has to be a different Birdie." He glanced around at them all. "Right?"

"I don't know what to think." Patty rubbed her temples in confusion.

Sanders sat his cup down. "I suggest you contact your lawyer, Ms. Braxton. We know the arrangement is legal, but you need to be reassured. You will not be tossed out of your home and your taxes will be paid. This house will probably become a museum of sorts for Baylor University." Price handed the documents to her. "These are your copies. We have a different set. We also have some personal items to give you when you vacate the main property and sign the documents signifying that you're conceding to Mrs. Lockhart's wishes."

Two days later, Ted and several of his friends helped her move into the carriage house. When she was settled, she opened the envelope Mr. Sanders had handed her that morning, after she'd signed the papers. It had taken all of her will power to wait until she was moved. "Okay, Ted, I'm opening it." She patted the sofa cushion beside her.

She carefully opened the package and poured the items into her hand—Birdie's silver star and the amethyst brooch. "My God, Birdie had these on her when she disappeared. I don't understand what's going on here."

Ted patted her shoulder. "I don't understand it either, but let's take a look at that letter before we jump to conclusions."

Patty carefully unfolded the fine stationary.

June 1, 1920,

Dear Aunt Patty,

No, you're not crazy. It took me a while to figure out I wasn't. Something strange happened on the Brazos Belle. The locket warmed, there was some lightening and then someone hit me on the head and tossed me overboard. Thaddeus Lockhart pulled me from the water. The year was 1890. It took me a long time to believe I had traveled back in time, but when I accepted the fact, my main goal was to get Birdie's Nest built by the end of 1892.

The brooch was lost in the river. On our wedding day, Tad gave me one that I believe is the same—it was just new in 1891. I've never worn it because I feared it had something to do with my time travel. I didn't want to take a chance of being separated from my new family.

Please give my star to Captain Smith or Ted Weaver. They'll know what to do with it.

Love to you always,
Birdie

290

EPILOGUE

July 22, 1920

Birdie sat beside Tad in the glider on the front veranda. A cooling breeze blew in from the Brazos and the hand fan she waved back and forth in her hand helped. They needed to get ceiling fans installed out here. She pulled the gauzy dress away from her legs. At least the clothes in 1920 were more bearable and nylons hadn't become a required accessory yet.

Tad slipped his arm around her shoulders and leaned in to kiss her cheek. "Happy, sweetheart?"

"Yeah, I am. How about you?"

"I couldn't be happier. The kids are all settled and happy, you've gotten the future of Birdie's Nest settled." He nipped her ear and whispered. "I think we should take a trip. Fly somewhere on one of those new-fangled air planes."

She giggled. "You're a brave man. I'm not sure I want to risk my life."

He sat up straight and looked out across the lawn. "Do you recognize the car stopped out front?"

Birdie stood and walked across the width of the porch, shaded her eyes with her hand and tried to get a better look. It was a Ford Model T. "No, I don't." A woman got out of the back seat. She turned and said something to the driver before turning and walking across the lawn to the house. The dress she wore was slightly shorter than the one Birdie had on, and she wore a large straw sunhat, one most women wouldn't wear away from their back garden. Curious, Birdie left the porch and walked across the lawn to meet her. Something about her hair…the way she walked… Could it be?

"Aunt Patty?" Birdie yelled as she broke into a run. "Aunt Patty!"

Birdie caught Aunt Patty to her in a hug, and held on tight, afraid if she let her go she'd disappear. She sobbed, "I can't believe it! You're here, you're really here!" She struggled to stop crying.

"Turn me loose, young lady, so I can look at you." They stood arm's distance apart. Except for a few additional worry lines on her face, Aunt Patty appeared as she had the day Birdie disappeared. "My God, Birdie, you're almost as old as me."

Birdie giggled and choked out, "Well, it has been thirty years."

"Maybe for you. It's been a month and a half for me." She shook her head and touched Birdie's face, wiping away the moisture. "No tears, now." Her aunt ran her fingers over her face, touched her hair and looked her up and down. "I can't believe it. Thirty years." She smiled and shook her head. "You are still beautiful."

"Why don't you ladies come in out of the sun?" Tad had joined them and slipped an arm around each of their shoulders. He steered them toward the porch. "Sarah is bringing a pitcher of sweet tea."

"Aunt Patty, this is my husband, Tad."

She looked up at him. "You found a good-looking one, didn't you, dear? Tall too."

"Yes, ma'am, I did. Tad, as you know this is my Aunt Patty."

"It's wonderful to meet you at last. Birdie has missed you every day she's been here." He dropped a kiss on her forehead. "Are you happy, sweetheart?"

"Ecstatic."

Tad pulled chairs closer together so they could visit. Sarah poured tea and passed glasses around.

"Aunt Patty, this is Sarah. She was Nathan's—you'll meet him later—wet nurse until he was weaned. She married one of the wranglers at the ranch and decided to stay with us."

"Hello, Miss Braxton. I feel as if I know you. Birdie talked about you so much."

"Well, I hope it was good. And you call me Aunt Patty, just like everyone else."

292

"Yes, ma'am."

"Sarah, will you call all of the kids and tell them we need them tomorrow? Don't tell them why... just say we need to discuss something with them. Oh, and include Bethany and her family." Birdie picked up a plate of teacakes and passed it around.

Aunt Patty took a bite and her face lit up. "These are very good. I'll have to compare recipes with your cook."

"Actually, I made these."

"No!"

"Yes. I swore I wouldn't be doing all that womanly stuff but somewhere along the way, I picked it up. I actually enjoy cooking on occasion."

"She's quite good, especially with desserts. Makes a mean pecan pie, just like my mother's." Birdie had learned shortly before Olivia's health started to decline in 1909.

"Well, will wonders never cease!" Aunt Patty reached over and patted Birdie's leg. "I'm proud of you." She sniffed and wiped at the corners of her eyes. "I've gotten so maudlin in my old age." She coughed to clear her throat. "I can't tell you how horrifying it was to think you'd drowned in the river."

Birdie stifled a snort. "More like Samuelson tried to murder me. And of course, I can imagine how distraught you were. I'm sorry for the pain you had to suffer. Now that I look back on it all, I'd probably still have time-traveled anyway, but he hit me in the head and tossed me over, right into that eddy."

"Harrumph, he didn't get off Scott free, young lady. The police and your Ranger friends bugged him for weeks. Because of the suspicion, his financial investors backed out of the building deal."

"Ha-ha, served him right. I'm glad. Do Captain Smith and Ted Weaver know what happened to me?"

"Yes, indeed. Saw them both several times after the Baylor lawyer came to call. And both rangers will know what's happened to me now that I've disappeared." She winked. "That Ted checked on me often. I really think he was after my teacakes, but I did enjoy having him around."

Tad reached for another teacake. "Ladies, I'm enjoying the conversation, but let's get to the meat of the situation here. Tell us how your time travel occurred, Aunt Patty."

"Birdie, you know those beautiful yellow roses you love so?" Birdie glanced across the lawn to the rose garden in the center. A variety of colors were planted around a recycling water fountain. Yellow "Sulphur" roses surrounded the assortment. Fortunately, through hybridization they now had a much more pleasing aroma.

"Yes, I remember."

"This morning, wearing the brooch, I went out to the garden and cut the prettiest bloom I could find. Then, I grabbed my handbag and my hat and walked to the suspension bridge." She patted her hip. "Oh, and I was afraid to leave your letter behind so stuck it in my pocket. Standing in the center I looked down, day-dreaming about the many times we'd walked the bridge and enjoyed the spring weather, when I saw an eddy flowing toward the bridge with the current, getting deeper the closer it got. It was odd—frightening." She shivered. "As I tried to think up a few fitting words to say in your memory, this dang brooch became alive... it got warm and vibrated. I accidently dropped the rose into the eddy at the same time as a bolt of lightening shot from the sky. It knocked me to the ground. I thought I was dead."

She drew in a deep breath. "Until that old Model T sounded 'ah-ooo-gah' and the screech of the brakes halted the contraption not two feet from my body."

"Good grief, you could have been killed!"

"Scared me, I tell you." She placed her hands over her heart. "Thought for a minute there I'd had a heart attack. The driver of the Model T helped me up and fussed over me. Of course, I was confused. I knew you'd said you'd time-traveled, Birdie, but had no idea that I would. It wasn't until I was on my feet and looking around that I realized what had happened." Her expression turned dreamy. "There in the distance sat Birdie's Nest looking like a regal lady, with no wide boulevard running parallel with the river, no apartment complexes down the road and no Cameron Park."

She tried to smile but her chin trembled and sobs shook her frame. "I knew at that moment... I'd come home... to my Birdie."

Birdie stood and folded her arms around the woman who'd raised her. Choked up, she begged, "Please don't cry,

Aunt Patty." She sniffed and pulled one of the darned handkerchiefs she'd finally gotten used to from a pocket and blew her nose.

Tad stood beside Birdie with one arm around her, the other on the older woman's shoulder. "Birdie's right. This is a happy time—one to celebrate."

"Aunt Patty, Tad and my family have been my life these past thirty years. Only one thing could have made me happier—to have you here with us.

"Welcome home, Aunt Patty!"

LINDA'S BIO

Linda LaRoque is a Texas girl, but the first time she got on a horse, it tossed her in the road dislocating her right shoulder. Forty years passed before she got on another, but it was older, slower, and she was wiser. Plus, her students looked on and it was important to save face.

A retired teacher who loves West Texas, its flora and fauna, and its people, Linda's stories paint pictures of life, love, and learning set against the raw landscape of ranches and rural communities in Texas and the Midwest. She is a member of RWA, her local chapter of HOTRWA, NTRWA and Texas Mountain Trail Writers.

Linda writes contemporary western romances, time travel romances and futuristic romances.

Visit Linda at these locations.

http://www.lindalaroqueauthor.blogspot.com
www.lindalaroque.com
https://www.facebook.com/linda.laroque
http://www.goodreads.com/author/show/649259.Linda_LaRoque
Linda's Amazon Page